Deadly Consignment

to Warwick

best wishes

Edward Hackford 4/4/17

Edward Hackford

Acorn Independent Press

ISBN 978-1-908318-442

Published by
Acorn Independent Press
www.acornindependentpress.com

Printed and bound by CPI Group (UK) Ltd, Croydon, CR0 4YY

About the Author

Edward Hackford was born in Boston, Lincolnshire and studied Science and Theology at Cambridge. He has worked extensively as an election observer in emerging democracies such as Moldova and Kosovo, and has witnessed, first-hand, the effects of economic and political change on every day people, and particularly the aspirational youth. It is this insight he shares with the reader in Deadly Consignment.

Formerly Chief Executive of St Albans District Council, now retired, Edward has been Chair of the Trestle Theatre Company, Secretary-General of the European Consortium of Local Government Chief Executives' Associations, a non-exec Director of an Enterprise Agency, and a Trustee of St Albans Cathedral, alongside his international election monitoring work. His hobbies are chess, bridge and squash. Deadly Consignment is his first full length novel.

MAPS

SERBIA
Belgrade
MONTE-
NEGRO
MITROVICE
'Fish' Road
KOSOVO
PRISTINA
'Duck' Road
PRIZPEN
ALBANIA
KUKËS
DRAGAS
Mountains
SKOPJE
FYRO
MACEDONIA
Road

UKRAINE
EDINET
BALTI
MOLDOVA
CHISINAU
ROMANIA
MIHAILOVCA
CIMISLIA
UKRAINE
BLACK SEA
Road

Contents

To Jill,
Jonathan, Christopher and Elizabeth.

PART 1

THE BODY

Chapter 1

Leicester - January 2004

Saturday 10th January 2004 was a crisp frosty morning in Leicester. The winter sunshine gleamed on the lightly frozen grass verges. It was the sort of morning that lifted the spirits. Peter Clayton was driving the short distance from his home for his 10:30 a.m. meeting with Michael Burton, the managing director of Polymer Plastics Limited, at his office on the Troon industrial estate on the outskirts of the city.

The meeting was scheduled for a Saturday because it was not strictly business. Michael and Peter were members of the same squash club. Both were enthusiastic amateurs. Peter was on the club committee and had responsibility for organising the end-of-season club tournaments. In particular he was charged with the task of finding a sponsor for that event. Michael, a self-made businessman, heading up a successful, even though modest, plastic-injection-moulding operation, had offered his firm's sponsorship. Their planned rendez-vous was to sort out the details.

Peter's day job was as a senior in the local District Council planning department. He parked his lease car, a black VW Golf GTI, in the visitor's slot in the factory car-park, empty save for a metallic blue BMW saloon with Michael's distinctive personal number plate, and alongside it, a dark blue Mercedes.

True to his conscientious nature, Peter was on time for his meeting. Shortly before 10:30 am he locked his car and walked across the empty tarmac towards the bland 1960s single-storey red brick office block that fronted the factory premises. From here all manner of plastic products from dustbins to fascia boards emerged with regular monotony to supply an insatiable market demand for products that had replaced metal and had contributed to the demise of Britain's steel industries.

The double glass doors into the reception area were already unlocked. Peter made his way past the front desk, with its printed notice telling whoever might be interested that the office was closed. The cleaners had done a good job. The close-carpeted foyer was well hoovered, the waste bin empty and the desk surfaces neat and tidy. The Managing Director's office was just off to the right. Peter presumed that was where Michael would be waiting for him. "Hallo!" he shouted to announce his arrival.

He approached the Managing Director's office door, and gave a courtesy knock. Through the half glazed door he was surprised to see there appeared to be no-one in the office. The door stood slightly ajar. The desk computer terminal was live, brightly coloured fish floating lugubriously across the screen. A black leather upholstered swivel chair was lying on its side, and a small gun-metal wastepaper bin had been overturned. More disturbingly, two feet in brown casual shoes were protruding from behind the desk.

Peter's curiosity and anxiety mounted. He nervously eased open the door and advanced to peer over the desk. As he did so, he inadvertently nudged the computer mouse, at which the aquatic scene on the screen gave way to something equally colourful but startlingly different – an image of a naked woman, kneeling on all fours with a young man energetically pumping himself into her. Peter had time for no more than a cursory glance. Instead he was transfixed by the spectacle on the floor beyond the desk.

Michael Burton was prostrate on his stomach, his head turned to one side, his eyes wide open and bulging unblinkingly. A metal wire was attached to each wrist, one sheathed in black plastic and the other in red. These two wires gathered themselves together into a grey heavy-duty electrical flex, similar to those used for wiring up electric ovens. At the end of the flex was a plug fitting into a socket in the wall. Both plug and socket were badly charred. More importantly, the body was lifeless.

Five minutes earlier, Peter's composure and demeanour had been calm and tranquil. Now his pulse was racing. A faint sweat had broken out across his body and beads of perspiration stood on his forehead. Michael Burton's squash playing days were over. Still less was he in a position to talk about sponsorship. Peter's brain struggled to comprehend the sickening scene in front of him.

Peter was used to thinking things through, - that's what planners did, in a measured and considered manner, with time to evaluate all the facts and ensure that decisions were robust and well-founded.

But he was singularly ill-equipped to deal with the unprecedented; still less with death. An avalanche of emotions pounded through him; he was distraught, he felt nauseous, his hands were trembling uncontrollably, he was muttering inanely to himself. With some dismay he realised, despite the countless images of death he'd observed dispassionately over the years on TV and in the cinema, this was the first real dead body he had ever seen. He was not prepared.

His initial reaction was to run outside and shout for help, but even in his panic-stricken state he knew that this would be pretty useless. The industrial estate was almost deserted on a Saturday morning and the nearest houses were nearly half a mile away. Running for help was a waste of time. He must dial 999.

The desk phone gave a continuous burring tone – damn, no outside line, but he could resort to his mobile phone. He snatched it from his anorak pocket and dialled the emergency services, moving, as he did so, out of the office into the factory foyer to put some distance between himself and the distressing vista in the office. Within a short time he was rehearsing the morning's drama to a measured calm voice at the other end of the line.

"Stay where you are, sir. Don't touch anything. We'll be with you in five minutes."

With this reassurance ringing in his ear, Peter elected to leave the foyer of the building and wait quietly in his car till the police and emergency services arrived. His emotions were beginning to settle, though his hands still had a residual tremble. What he really needed was a cup of tea to calm himself.

It was then that the morning took another twist, leaving Peter doubting his own sanity. Moving out into the fresh air again, he stared in astonishment at a now vacant parking area. There was no sign of his car, nor that of Michael Burton's, nor the Mercedes. It was hardly fifteen minutes since he had parked there and during that brief time the three vehicles had been spirited away. As he tried to digest this further complication, his mobile phone vibrated in his pocket. Reading the digital number print-out, he was pleased it was Jenny, his wife, calling him. His relief was short-lived. Before he could get a word in, she launched into a minor tirade.

"You clot! I thought you were going to your meeting in your car, so why's it still parked in our drive? You know I haven't got a key to it. So I can't get my car out of the garage to take Jonathan to football. Why didn't you think about that before you left? You're so stupid! Anyway, thankfully Mr Selhurst was outside washing his car next door and has agreed to take us. We should just be able to get there in time if we leave now. But I thought you should know I'm not a happy bunny!"

Peter could not believe what he was hearing. How could his car be back at home? He was utterly bewildered. He attempted a response, but Jenny was saying she had to dash and would catch up later, and he might well expect a delayed lunch in view of the hassle he had caused her. He mustered a despairing goodbye and left his wife to cope with the domestic demands while he tried to make some sense of the events cascading around him that fateful morning.

Standing alone in the milky sunshine of the now deserted car-park, with the body of Michael Burton lying prone and lifeless in an office barely twenty yards from him, Peter was more disorientated than he had been in years. In one hand he carried a slim briefcase holding the squash club sponsorship papers. In his other hand he was still clutching his mobile phone, which triggered his recollection that when he had switched on the phone to call the police, it had alerted him to a message waiting in the memory. He called the answer service and listened.

"You have one message received at 7:21 p.m. on Friday, 9th January. To listen to the message press one."

Peter did as he was bidden.

"Message for Mr Clayton. This is Mr Burton's PA speaking. He's asked me to tell you he has a last-minute chance to spend a few days in Rome and has to catch the early flight from Stansted tomorrow morning, so regrets he will be unable to keep his appointment with you. He's really sorry but expects your discussion can be picked up when he gets back. Hope you get this message in time." It was a woman's voice, unknown to Peter, but he had no reason to doubt its authenticity.

"To listen to your message again, press one. To save the message, press two. To delete the message, press three."

Peter's brain was becoming numb trying to digest yet more conflicting and confusing information. He pressed one to absorb carefully what had been said, then saved the message for future reference. If his mobile hadn't been switched off overnight, he would have picked up the message earlier. Instead of finding himself in this dreadful situation, he would have been watching Jonathan racing around a soccer pitch. The normality of his Saturday morning had exploded around him, all because his phone had been switched off a few hours.

Time to reflect further was curtailed by the strident arrival of two police cars and an ambulance swinging into the car-park, blue lights flashing and sirens sounding. The emptiness was suddenly transformed. Vehicle doors sprung open. Uniformed officers and paramedics advanced purposefully towards him. There was a sense of assurance in their bearing, their firm focus, their transparent competence, and their calm urgency. Peter felt a measure of relief that at last he was no longer alone, and could begin to share with others the drama he had been trying to come to terms with on his own.

"Mr Clayton? I'm Detective Sergeant Crabtree and this is Detective Constable O'Malley. Could you show us where we need to go? We'll bring the paramedics with us in the hope they may be able to do something."

Peter led the posse of five people into the foyer and showed them the office where he had discovered the body. He hung back in the entrance having no great desire to revisit the distressing scene that had greeted him there barely half an hour ago.

"Mr Clayton," said Crabtree from within the room, "Would you mind stepping inside a moment to confirm what you found here?"

With some reluctance he entered the office for the second time. The policemen and the para-medics were standing around looking at him quizzically. In addition to their presence, Peter was amazed to observe there were other significant differences in the scene in front of him. For one thing the computer screen was dead and appeared to have been shut down. The leather office chair was now standing upright in its normal position. The wastepaper bin was back in its usual place. The electric leads and plug had disappeared and, unbelievably, there was no sign of Michael Burton's body. In short, the office appeared exactly as it would do so on a normal Saturday morning.

"Not sure what's going on here, Mr Clayton," said D.S. Crabtree impatiently. "All looks pretty normal to us. No sign of any breaking and entering. No sign of any violence – and certainly no sign of a dead body!"

"Rather begs a few questions, don't you think? Like, how did you manage to gain access to locked commercial premises at a weekend? And how did you get here without any means of personal transport? And, more to the point, why did you call out the emergency services on what appears to be a wild goose chase? If there is a crime here, it's more like wasting police time!"

To add to his misery, Peter had not yet told the police about the phone message he had received cancelling his appointment that morning. It occurred to him that this would make his presence at PPL offices at that time seem even more suspicious.

It was all too apparent he was in no position to give any sort of rational explanation to the police about the events of the last hour or so.

Whether Michael Burton was alive or dead, or whether he was on holiday for a few days in Rome, was becoming less pressing for Peter than proving his own sanity and protecting himself and his family from being swallowed up by the events of this cataclysmic morning. He had a young family to look after, a mortgage to pay, a professional job to hold down and a reputation with friends and relatives which were all at risk if he didn't get a grip and begin to make some sense out of all this. Out of adversity his resolve began to crystallise.

"Sergeant, I realise from where you stand, all this looks unbelievably bizarre. But I'm not loosing my marbles. What I would like to do is make a statement and then sign it to be as accurate a record as I can give you of the sequence of this morning's events. I am not prone to fantasizing and I've no reason at all to have dreamed up the trauma of discovering the dead body of my squash colleague. Is it better to make the statement here or at the police station? Something very odd has been going on. The only clue I can give you to try to convince you of the truth of what I've told you is the fact that the office doors here were unlocked when I arrived. I don't have a key and the building alarm must have been disarmed. It didn't sound off when I entered. Despite what you might think, clearly I am not the only person to have visited these premises since the place was cleaned and locked up last night."

"We'll need a statement in any case, so I'm quite happy to do as you suggest. The ambulance and paramedics can stand down, and we'll take you with us to the station in our car as you appear to have no transport of your own here. First we have to make sure these premises are secure."

A few quick radio calls established where to find the factory caretaker. One of the police cars remained until he arrived to check over and re-secure the offices, while the detectives drove a still very bemused Peter Clayton to the police station.

Elsewhere in Leicester, Jenny Clayton was giving appropriate support and encouragement to her son, Jonathan, as his side struggled one-nil down at halftime. Whether their goal had been off-side, Mummy had no idea – she had no clue what that meant anyway, but Jonathan and his fellow team-mates needed much consoling about this perceived injustice. The fathers present seemed more boisterous in complaining to the referee, and were not much impressed with Jenny's sentiment that it was taking part that mattered!

She called Peter on his mobile to check how and when he was going to get home, and to reassure him that Jonathan had arrived in time for the match. The father of one of his friends had offered them a lift home after the match, so hopefully the normal Saturday pattern of events in the Clayton household could be picked up from then.

The mobile vibrated in his pocket as the police car cruised to the station, carefully observing the statutory speed limits.

"Jenny here – just trying to touch base to see when we might see each other again! Where are you? When and how are you getting home? Sorry to say Jonathan's team are losing one-nil at half time."

"Well, actually, it's a long and complicated story. No need to worry, but at the present moment I'm in a police car intending to make a statement at the police station about the saga of events I've been through this morning. I hope that won't take more than an hour or so and I should be back home for lunch about one o'clock."

"But I thought you were due to meet up with your squash friend to talk about sponsorship or something? What went wrong?

Are you hurt? Have you done anything stupid? What on earth's going on?" The irritation that had been apparent in her voice during the previous call had now given way to palpable anxiety and concern.

"I'll explain all that later", he said. "It's too complicated to tell you over the phone. In any case we're just arriving at the police station and I need to give them my full attention for the next half-hour. Don't worry, I'm in no trouble - it's with Michael Burton that the trouble lies. That's what I've got to try to help the police with. Must go now – tell Jonathan to get stuck in. One goal is not too difficult to get back. Take care. Bye."

They pulled up at the police station, and he followed the policemen into the building.

"Well now, Mr Clayton," said Crabtree, once they were in the interview room, "Perhaps you'd like to start at the beginning and try to convince us that we've not been chasing shadows all morning!"

The solid permanence of the police station, and an over-strong cup of tea, gave Peter a much needed confidence boost as he set out to try to rehearse in fine detail how his Saturday morning had been turned upside down and inside out to some very sceptical policemen.

Chapter 2

Kosovo - 1998

It wasn't the brutal beating meted out to his father by the Serb soldiers. Nor was it the shame of the terrifying rape of his precious sister by the same men. No, what decided the issue for Habib Peci was the calculated, clinical reprisal exacted on the innocent Serb family some weeks later by his own kith and kin. That was the final straw. "Proportionate revenge" they called it – an eye for an eye.

What future was there in such a community of hate? There must be a better place to be. He was still young, barely sixteen, but that fateful summer of 1998 crystallised his resolve. However long it took, he would use his wits, his time, his energy and he would find a way out.

Mitrovice in Kosovo was never high on the list of "must visit" tourist destinations. It straddled a murky river, which separated the Kosovar Albanians from the Serbs. The linking bridge was reminiscent of Checkpoint Charlie in the former divided Berlin. At each end there were sandbagged sentry points manned by French soldiers, part of the NATO's KFOR (the Kosovo Forces Of Reconciliation) peacekeeping force. Armoured cars in battle colours guarded both entry points. Patrols kept watch night and day with rifles at the ready. Barbed wire bristled everywhere.

Serbs who ventured southwards across the bridge without KFOR protection risked their lives. Equally, the Kosovar Albanians who tried to revisit their lost homes on the north side were in similar peril.

This became the fragile truce line between the two factions, established after the NATO bombardment ended the war between Slobodan Milosevic's Serbian Army and the Kosovo Liberation Army, the KLA. Only by virtue of the huge concentrations of KFOR troops deployed across the country could the unstable "peace" be maintained.

Not surprisingly, Kosovo's economy was in a parlous state. Mitrovice's large chemical factory was derelict. Residual dumps of chemicals leached unrestrained into the subsoil and thence to the river, contributing to the town's reputation of being one of the most polluted in Europe. The roads were strewn with axle-wrecking potholes. The electricity supply was spasmodic, heating unpredictable, and tap water unsafe to drink. Buildings devastated by bombing and neglect remained ugly and unusable.

It was no surprise that Habib Peci was keen to get away from this bleak, unremitting environment to try to find some other haven where life could offer more to an intelligent, ambitious young man. He had seen too much. The atrocities committed by both sides during the war were still raw in everyone's memory. The mutual hatred between both factions was endemic and barely veiled.

Habib's family were caught up in all this like pawns in a game of chess. In 1998 at the height of the troubles, he lived with his father, Agim, and mother, Aferdita, in a large apartment block on the north side of the river in Mitrovice. He was fifteen years old, still at school and doing well. His eighteen-year-old sister, Shyret, also lived at home. She had left school and spent her time helping her mother while trying to find a job, a difficult prospect in such a run-down community. There was an older brother, Mustafa, aged twenty-one. Along with many of his contemporaries, he was away from home most of the time serving with the unofficial Kosovo Liberation Army.

Despite their ethnic identity as Kosovar Albanians, the Peci family had lived on the north side of the river since the days of Marshal Tito's Regime. They felt reasonably integrated and had tried hard to live peaceably with their predominantly Serbian neighbours. But the troubles had made things increasingly difficult. There was great pressure on them to leave and move into one of the Albanian communities on the south side. Daily, they heard of atrocities in other parts of the country. They knew that whole villages of their compatriots were on the move in bleak weather conditions, trying to cross the mountains into Albania proper to escape the depredations of the Serbian Army. Grim pictures of this pathos were being beamed across the world's television channels.

Then came an appalling setback for the Kosovo Liberation Army on 5th March 1998. The Serbian Army, allegedly 5,000 strong, surrounded the KLA Commander, Adem Jashari, at his home in Drenica village about 25 miles west of Mitrovice. He refused to surrender. The Serbian response was brutally efficient. His homestead was pounded mercilessly by their tanks and machine guns. Along with Adem Jashari, all seventeen members of his extended family, including babies and grandparents were killed. Their graves now rested on a windswept hillside nearby, guarded daily by KLA soldiers, a shrine to the cause of an independent Kosovo.

The KLA was knocked onto the back foot while the belligerence of the Serbian soldiers towards the unwanted "Albanians" in their midst grew by the hour. Kosovar Albanian families living in "Serb areas" began to be more and more fearful, but the Peci family bravely decided to hang on. It was a fateful decision.

On a warm Friday evening in mid May of that year, while Mr and Mrs Peci and their two children were watching television, they heard heavy boots pounding up the stairwell towards their apartment followed by loud thumpings on their front door. As they shot up from their seats in alarm, Agim went to the door in trepidation to see what was happening. He was confronted by seven Serbian soldiers in battle fatigues, inebriated, unshaven, and each brandishing a Kalashnikov rifle. They smelt of sweat, dirt and alcohol, and they were in aggressive mode.

"Now, Mr Peci, why the fuck do you still choose to live in Serb territory? We think you would be much better off living among your own rabble south of the river, or better still, in Albania. What about it?"

The family huddled together petrified, not knowing how to react. The soldiers were not there for reasoned debate.

"We're thinking about it," replied Agim rather weakly.

"Thinking! Thinking!" came the ferocious response, "We'll give you something to concentrate your fucking thinking. Your pretty little daughter can come with us till you've decided!"

Shyret clung to her mother desperately in the corner of the room. Habib cowered behind the sofa. Her father tried to plead with them. His daughter was still young, a virgin, she was a good girl, had never done any harm to anyone, could he give them money instead?

"Sure, sure!" said the leader, "How much you've got?"

Agim went to the small safe deposit box hidden under the sofa. Banks were not functioning in Mitrovice so this was where he kept his meagre savings. He offered the contents to the soldiers in the hope of persuading them to leave the family in peace and to protect his daughter.

When the soldiers had counted the money and pocketed it, they scoffed back at him with disdain. "So this is all you think the little whore's worth!! What a bloody awful father! Can't let her stay behind with such an ungrateful parent, can we boys?"

They advanced into the room and manhandled the girl out of her mother's craddling arms. Both were sobbing hysterically. Agim's cool snapped. He raced at the soldiers and began thumping and kicking them for all he was worth. But he was no match for them. They rained blows down on him with the butts of their rifles, on his head, his arms, his groin, his back. He slumped downwards to the floor. There they finished the job off by kicking him till he was unconscious, blood pouring from wounds on his head and from his broken mouth.

They wrenched Shyret away and frog-marched her out of the apartment. Habib was helpless and speechless, crying plaintively alone behind the sofa. Aferdita, still hysterical but more focussed, was forced to choose between trying to rescue her daughter or tending her wounded husband. The choice was made for her. The soldiers slammed the door behind them and raced off down the stairs with the girl. Aferdita rushed to the kitchen to get towels and warm water and gently laid her husband's head on a pillow on the floor while she bathed his wounds and tried to staunch the flow of blood. Habib came round to help. Gradually his father regained consciousness. He was in acute pain all over his body, but thankfully he was still breathing. Now faced with the supremely critical task of helping her husband, his wife's composure had returned. She turned to her fifteen-year-old son.

"Habib, we must get news to Mustafa and tell him to come home quickly to help us. Run across the bridge. Tell our friends there what has happened. Ask them to send someone to the KLA headquarters in town and ask them to radio the army team that Mustafa works with. He's not far away. Ask them to send a nurse back with you to help me here. I'll look after Dad. He'll be OK, but we need help quick. Off you go."

It was a mile run to their friend's house in the warm evening air as the sun was setting over the western edge of the valley. The Albanian bush telegraph was activated immediately. A nurse was with Habib within ten minutes and, by that time, a message over the radio telephone from the KLA HQ in the town had reached Mustafa. The gravity of the events that had occurred at his home meant that he was given priority use of one their Toyota pick-up trucks. He covered the twenty miles of dirt tracks and potholed roads at speed and was in his parents' apartment barely one hour after the evening's assaults. His mother recounted the saga while the nurse ministered to her husband's needs. Mustafa listened with concentrated anger and dismay. His father had massive bruising all over his arms and back. The left side of his face was blackening. His eye was so swollen it was closed. He had lost two teeth and his mouth was bleeding internally. He had a large gash on his head, which throbbed painfully. There was a constant singing noise in his ears. His chest hurt and his right leg was numb from the thigh down. The only consolation was that he was conscious and alive.

They had no idea of Shyret's whereabouts. But they were filled with foreboding and feared the worst.

The soldiers, meanwhile, had forced the daughter into their army truck and driven up into the hills behind Mitrovice. While elsewhere, not far away, desperate radio messages were being sent out to contact Mustafa, they parked their vehicle in a deserted clearing, obviously well known to them, and pushed the girl to the ground in front of the truck. The air was still warm and the sun was setting in streaky reds and orange reflecting off the clouds. In other circumstances it would have been a balmy evening to be out in the hills.

"Now you little whore, time to make a proper woman of you! OK? You've two choices – either you cooperate and enjoy it, or you don't? Which way is it to be?"

Shyret's response was to spit at them.

"OK darling, if that's how you want it, suits us!"

One soldier grabbed her arms above her head. Two others held her legs firmly. She tried to struggle and kick but they were too powerful for her. They removed her skirt and underskirt, opened her cardigan and blouse and, without more ceremony, ripped off her underwear. She lay there on the ground pinioned by their arms still wearing her Muslim headscarf and socks and shoes, but with the rest of her body exposed to their gaze.

"We need a good look at what she has to offer, don't we boys? Put the truck lights on!"

The men holding her legs forced them wider apart. They gathered round her prostrate body with the truck lights spotlighting her most private parts, cheering and jeering with cans of beer in their hands. One of them started to make her drink some beer from a can. When she attempted to spit it out, they forced her mouth open and kept pouring until she choked on it.

"About time you Muslims got a taste for beer!" More jeers and raucous laughter.

"Daddy says you're still a virgin! Isn't that nice? We love a virgin! Time for a little christening before you enjoy losing it!"

One the soldiers poured beer between her legs, and then one after another, each of the soldiers took her, the rest cheering each one on till he finished. She had tried to resist ferociously when the first man began, only to receive a rifle butt across the top of head, which left her dazed and only partly aware of what was then happening. Not satisfied with the degradation already imposed, the soldiers then rounded off their evening's entertainment by urinating over her while she lay slumped on the ground in distress and shock, her groin bruised and painful, and bleeding.

"OK, darling, time to go home and tell Daddy and Mummy what a lovely time you've had being fucked by real men! Let's get going!"

They lifted her into the truck and threw the remnants of her clothes in with her. She covered herself as best she could by wrapping her blouse and cardigan around her and pulling on her skirt. They bounced back into Mitrovice and stopped up at the foot of the stairs leading up to her apartment. She was heaved out and left in a heap on the steps. The soldiers' truck drove off into the dark night.

Shyret knew where she was and struggled, on hands and knees, to climb the four flights of stairs till at last she reached their door. She fell against it sobbing with despair and knocked feverishly to be let in. Mustafa opened the door and took her in his arms. They laid her on her bed. Their distress at seeing her condition was tempered with relief that at least she was alive and had come back home. Her mother helped her into a warm bath and did what she could to help her wash away the physical degradation of what had happened, but there was little that could be done about the long-term psychological damage, to say nothing of the opprobrium that attached to Muslim girls who lost their virginity before marriage.

After a fitful night's sleep, helped somewhat by the sleeping pills and painkillers that the nurse had administered to both father and daughter, the next morning Mustafa heard the grim details of what had happened to his precious sister at the hands of those animals. Coupled with what he had seen and heard from his father and the rest of the family, Mustafa's anger focussed rapidly into a steady resolve and determination to exact revenge for what had been done to his family.

Vengeance, they say, is a dish best served cold – clinically conceived and executed. That would have to wait. The immediate issue was to get the family out of this Serbian area into an Albanian enclave. No time could be lost. They were lucky that they had friends south of the river with whom they could stay on a temporary basis. They gathered their belongings together and, in two journeys, using Mustafa's truck, they vacated their apartment that day. The bulky furniture they had to leave behind till later.

Surrounded by friends and their caring hospitality, the whole family felt able to recoup at last. Soon they would find another apartment, probably vacated by one of the many Albanian families who had elected to leave Kosovo completely and go to Albania. It did not take long. Within five days they had somewhere, not as large as the apartment they had left, but adequate enough, at least until the troubles were over. Mustafa took the truck back to the north side with two sturdy friends to fetch their remaining furniture.

It was only six days since they had left. But it was too late. The front door of their apartment was hanging off its hinges, the furniture had disappeared, the fixtures had been vandalised and the bath and living room used as a latrine. The walls were covered in anti-Albanian graffiti. The family home of more than twenty years had been desecrated beyond redemption. Mustafa was in no doubt this was the work of the Serbs in the neighbourhood. It cried out even more loudly for vengeance. His resolve was fixed. It would take time, but not too long. It would be premeditated and clinical.

It would be no less proportionate. But this time it would be the Serbs who suffered. It would be their time to shed tears. And they would be bitter.

Chapter 3

Moldova - 1999

Like Kosovo, Moldova is not a major tourist destination. Few people even know where it is. Landlocked, with Ukraine to the north, east and south, and Romania on its long western border, it lies a few miles north of the Black Sea. In Soviet times, Moldavia, as it was then called, enjoyed modest prosperity. The collective farms, the bedrock of its economy, were spread everywhere across the rolling countryside, and provided enough, and more, for the nutritional needs of its four and a half million inhabitants. The Moldavian vineyards produced adequate quantities of agreeable wine, which flowed easily into the wider market and thirsty throats of the Soviet Bloc countries. Electricity had reached most villages, though, once away from the main centres of population, water still had to be drawn from communal village wells. Schools functioned and a major concrete highway was being built to link north and south.

But by western standards things were still backward, and slipping further behind, as the economies outside the Soviet Union gathered materialistic momentum. So when Perestroika under Gorbachev allowed Moldova and the other Soviet Republics to achieve national independence in 1991, there was huge relief and excited anticipation that the new freedom would herald a massive surge in economic wellbeing. The glamorous images of western lifestyles propagated by the television channels would now be accessible. Capitalism would replace communism and with one leap they would be free – at least that was the theory, and that fuelled the popular expectation.

The reality was different. The collective farms fell apart. The cattle and livestock were divided among families, each now responsible for their own "property", while the abandoned communal farm buildings fell into disrepair, an inescapable eyesore on the edge of each village community, and a daily monument to the failure of the new "capitalism". The external market for Moldovan wines dried up and with it the influx of much-needed foreign currency. The road-building programme stuttered to a halt, schools and village community centres could no longer afford maintenance budgets, the imported electricity supplies became even less reliable, fuel became more costly and scarce, and when the individual cow belonging to a particular family died, there was no longer the collective security of the old system to fall back on. Within less than a decade Moldova had replaced Albania as being the poorest country in Europe.

Leaving Chisinau, the capital of Moldova, there was a wide concrete highway, potholed and in need of urgent repair, which led south to the large town of Cimislia, 50 kilometres or so from the capital. From there a road, more accurately a cart track, lead eastwards to the village of Mihailovca. The five miles between the two were best negotiated in a four-wheel drive vehicle, and preferably not attempted at all in times of snow and frost. But for Moldovans outside the few cities and large towns, this was the norm.

In Mihailovca pride of place was given to the new Orthodox Christian church, bearing testimony that despite desperate poverty, resources could still be found for things of enduring significance. Not far away, the village community hall was in a more parlous state with broken windows, no functioning heating system and threadbare lightbulbs hanging unceremoniously from the flaking ceiling.

As in most villages, there was no commercial activity of any sort except the labour-intensive demands of the surrounding fields, and the daily task of leading out the family cow into the highways and byways to find fodder, usually the responsibility of a grandmother or the youngest family member when out of school. Along the main roads there were vehicle-repair sheds for tending the regular breakdowns of the few cars and trucks whose owners could afford the price of fuel, but the most reliable transport was the four-wheeled, rubber tyred, v-shaped ox-carts that trundled along at tortoise speed behind their uncomplaining mules.

Vladimir and Inga Snegur had lived in Mihailovca for many years. Vladimir had been head stockman at the collective farm, but that role had long since disappeared and all he had now was his patch of field and garden to keep the family fed. Inga, his wife, still taught in the village school and was glad to have such a fulfilling and continuous responsibility in a community.

Their two children, Pavel and Nina, were born four years apart, the boy in 1978 and the girl in 1982. As was the norm in Eastern Europe, they were doted on by their parents and grandparents. Any spare money that the family ever had was spent on clothes for the children and their welfare. In Moldovan villages the children were a stark contrast to the adults – happy, smiling, mischievous, energetic, well dressed, while the adults were morose, depressed, tired and dowdy.

In Pavel and Nina's early years, their parents were fully employed; father on the farm and mother in the schools. Income was steady, if not spectacular, and their position in the village hierarchy accorded the family respect and social acceptance. Then came independence, just as Pavel was moving into his teens and wondering where to go for further education, and Nina would soon have to move to secondary school in nearby Cimislia. Life became progressively harder. Money became more and more scarce. Vladimir's job folded as the collective farm closed down. He joined the ranks of those who now exchanged skills and labour rather than money to obtain services. Their only consolation was Inga's continued vital role in the village school.

By various means - not what he knew but who he knew – his father succeeded in obtaining a place for Pavel at the Chisinau Children's Hospital to train as a male nurse. He moved to the capital in 1997 to stay with a distant relative in their basic four-square Soviet-style standard apartment: kitchen, washroom, bedroom and sitting room which converted into another bedroom at night, on the tenth floor of a monstrous concrete block of flats in the city suburb of Buiucani. The lifts worked sometimes, as and when the electricity supply was not on one of its periodic failures. The corridors and stairs were grubby, covered in graffiti, and persistently smelt of urine. The light bulbs had all gone. But inside, the apartments were decked out like little palaces, heavy wallpaper, proud dark wooden furniture handed down through generations, rich brocade curtains, elegant thick tablecloths, and mouth-watering smells emanating from the cooking stove. When the communal heating system was working, the apartment was like an oven: when not, it was time for overcoats and prayers that the supply might not be too long before being restarted.

The contrast between Chisinau and Mihailovca was staggering. High-rise buildings, wide metalled roads, supermarkets, parks, disco halls, newspapers, coffee bars, restaurants, buses, taxis, big hotels - even a few street lights in the central areas. Chisinau was modest by the standards of most capital cities, but for Pavel it was like a dream. He settled down to work in the hospital. Initially his training, so-called, was that of a dogsbody, fetching and carrying, doing the menial jobs that others seemed disinclined to do. He did not mind. He was earning money, making new friends, and enjoying a social scene that had been totally outside his experience in his home village. He was even able to send some money back to his parents from time to time, which gave him a satisfying sense of maturity and achievement.

After a few months the opportunity came to move into an apartment with a group of colleagues from the hospital, so he could be nearer the city centre. What he saved on bus fares, he spent in the bars. And he had a regular girlfriend, Tanya Voronin, three years younger than him, also in training to be children's nurse at the same hospital. As he left his teen years behind, he felt pretty good. The world didn't seem too bad a place.

Back at home his sister, Nina, was progressing through secondary school, with no great academic successes, but with a host of good friends, the ability to add and subtract, to read and write, and to speak her native Moldovan, which is Romanian to all intents and purposes, and with a reasonable competence in Russian, the compulsory second language. She also had one lesson a week in English, which was fun because it helped her and her teenage friends comprehend some of the words of the endless flow of pop songs emanating from the West. She was not to know how even a scanty knowledge of that language would stand her in good stead in the future.

The time came for her to leave school, and with it a dilemma: What to do now? Her schools results were not sufficient to secure a higher-education place. But for a popular, vivacious, sixteen-year-old girl in a village there was not much on offer in the heart of Moldova in 1999. Mihailovca had a meeting point for youngsters, best described as a glorified shed. It had a few desultory coloured lights when the electricity was functionning. There was a small Panasonic ghetto-blaster, which played cassettes or CDs at considerable volume, on the shelf beside the bottles of Coca-Cola, Mars bars, crisps, and chewing gum, the essentials to life as a village teenager, providing they had the money. Higher up on another rickety shelf, was a small-screen colour TV showing a continuous flow of snowflaked pictures, acting as an additional noise backcloth to the racket of pop songs that formed the compulsory environment for adolescent growth and development.

This was the sum total of village social life for the teenagers. Things were fractionally more animated in Cimislia, but that was a five-mile walk away along the muddy potholed road. Unsurprisingly, young people quickly tired of this modest diet, and hankered for the bright lights elsewhere. Chisinau, the capital, was the magnet, and now that Pavel was well established there and sending home such glowing reports, Nina's ambitions to join him there grew by the day.

It was not as though the absence of social life could be compensated for by securing satisfying employment and income in the villages. For a young girl there was no paid work, nothing except the prospect she would help with the household chores, look after the cow, work in the vegetable garden, and search the surrounding countryside for firewood to build up the winter stocks - in short, the same traditional tasks associated with rural life since mankind adopted an agrarian lifestyle.

With television, radio and pop songs unremittingly preaching the glamour of the world outside the village, the average youngster rapidly lost interest in the juvenile satisfactions of the rural idyll. When Nina turned seventeen, she decided she had waited long enough. Nothing was getting any better. Her frustrations were leading to frequent heated arguments at home, so it came as no great surprise to anyone when it was agreed, enthusiastically by her, but reluctantly by her parents, that she could join her brother in Chisinau to seek such fame and fortune as she could. It was, after all, only fifty miles away and she would come home as often as possible and Pavel would be there to keep an eye on her. He had lots of contacts to help her find a job and she could stay with their relatives to begin with. "No problems, surely!" she insisted to her parents.

Nina relocated to the capital with her meagre belongings in September 2000, and moved into the same apartment to sleep on the same sofa bed that Pavel had done three years before. She was surprised how homesick she felt and how, from a distance, the simple routines of village life took on a rather more attractive memory. But after all the arguments she had gone through to convince her parents she had to do it, Nina was determined to make a go of things. There was no turning back. There was nothing to go back for.

Chapter 4

Kosovo - 1998

The news of the Peci family trauma passed through the Kosovar Albanian community like wildfire. In their new apartment they were surrounded by a well of sympathy from neighbours, matched in equal measure by yet another surge in the deepening hatred and hostility towards the Serbian perpetrators of this latest horror, and the burgeoning catalogue of other atrocities against their compatriots.

Mustafa and his KLA colleagues considered their options. They were Muslim, but it was the old Jewish philosophy, not the Christian philosophy, that was dictating their plans to avenge his family's sufferings. "An eye for an eye, a tooth for a tooth." So it would be. "A blow for a blow, a bruise for a bruise, a rape for a rape". He would not rest till they had exacted similar payment in suffering from their Serbian enemies. And the sooner the better.

About a mile to the south of Mitrovice there was a Serbian enclave comprising a small Orthodox Church and cemetery. Next door was the caretaker's house. Throughout Kosovo, Serb churches had been systematically desecrated whenever they were left unattended. Despite all the animosity around them in this mainly Albanian area, the Mitrovice caretaker and his wife felt a strong sense of religious obligation to stay in their home to protect their church and the graves of their ancestors. Their social life was limited. Most of their friends had now relocated into the Serb areas north of the river. Their two children, six and eight years old, went to school there and the parents spent as much time there as they dared. But their compelling concern for preserving the sanctity of their church meant they needed to stay close by their enclave most of the daytime and every night. The conflict between their duty to look after their church and their responsibility for the safety of their children was a constant anxiety. They knew they were an easy target so long as they stayed in such a vulnerable position. What they did not know was that Mustafa had them in his sights.

It was the shortest night of the year when he made his move, just over one month after the attack on his family. There was a residual summer light in the night sky at 11 p.m. when the Toyota truck cruised quietly to a halt in the precincts of the Orthodox church. Mustafa and three KLA colleagues climbed out. They were wearing combat dress and carrying automatic rifles. Their faces were obscured in black balaclava hoods. The fifth person with them was Habib, now just turned sixteen. Mustafa had insisted he come along to witness the avenging of what had happened to their family. Habib had been reluctant but his brother was fired with the passionate belief that it was a matter of family honour to share this together. Their father was still recovering from his injuries and too ill to take on the responsibility for redress. It was a man's work, so it fell to the brothers to do their duty. Habib had to be there.

They hammered on the caretaker's door, broke open the lock and charged into the sitting room to confront the terrified couple. Their children woke screaming and rushed in to join their parents.

"Get the kids out of here!," ordered Mustafa. The mother ushered the children back to their room and tried to pacify them despite being so distraught herself. One of the men slammed the kitchen table against the door so the children could not re-enter.

While one of the KLA fighters held a rifle to the head of his wife, the husband's hands were lashed behind his back with heavy-duty packing tape, and his ankles tied together. He was made to sit on an upright chair while more binding tape was passed from his wrists, behind and under the chair to be wrapped round his ankles. His mouth was gagged, leaving his eyes and nose free. He was, by then, strapped onto the chair, immobile and unable to do anything or say anything.

The rifle that had been held against the wife's head was then transferred to her husband's. So far very few words had been spoken. Vengeance was a dish to be served ice cold.

"Undress!" was the short emphatic command. "If not, your husband loses his brains. Take your pick!"

There was no choice. Sobbing and desperate she removed her clothes and stood before them in the full glare of the kitchen light, vainly trying to cover as much of her nakedness as possible with her hands.

"Lie down!" She did as she was bidden.

The intruders tied one of her wrists to one of the table legs and one to the other. They then took a small length of nylon cord and tied it round one of her knees. She was lying on her back. They pulled the cord so her knee was bent up tightly against her tummy. The other end of the cord was wound in a loop around her neck and then fastened onto her other knee-joint pulling that leg hard up against her belly. If she tried to straighten her legs the cord tightened round her neck, but if she kept her legs up and bent her neck forward she relieved the pressure. She was trussed like a chicken. With her legs bent so far upwards, her nakedness was obscenely exposed in the kitchen light. To ease the pressure on her neck she was forced to look down at herself. The ropes around her wrists prevented any other movement.

"One month ago, less than two miles from here, our sister was raped without mercy by courtesy of a group of your animal Serb soldiers. We would like to repay the compliment – payback time we should call it! No doubt your husband would like to watch!"

Two of Mustafa's colleagues then took it in turns to rape the prostrate woman, - no eroticism – just premeditated clinical defilement in front of her desperate husband. She was a mature woman in her early forties, not unused to sexual intercourse, and she had given birth to two babies. Without too much discomfort she could accommodate the urgent thrusts of these young men as long as she relaxed, kept her head forward and her legs held high. Notwithstanding the shame and indignity, this was something she would grin and bear.

"We presume you enjoyed all that as much our sister did!" they jeered at her.

The woman was slumped on the floor sobbing uncontrollably, still trying to keep the pressure off her neck, when she felt the cold steel of a rifle muzzle being forced into her vagina. Her husband watched in despair, unable to do anything.

"Now you dirty fucking whore, we're going to give you the thrill of your life. We'll count down together till we pull the trigger so we all can savour the moment! Ten, nine, eight, seven, six, five, four, three, two, one, zero!" they chanted.

There was a click of the trigger - then nothing - except raucous laughter from the assailants.

"Just a little joke!" they mocked as the sobbing woman and her husband moaned in terror.

"Now – what else did your Serbian friends do to our family home? Well, they trashed it – so payback time again folks!"

They smashed first the little Orthodox shrine in the corner of the room, before systematically breaking everything and anything that their rifles could destroy. Next they untied the woman's wrists and rolled her onto a small rug, on which they dragged her outside. Two of them pulled the husband still lashed to the chair, to join her and another went to fetch the small children to bring them outside. The smell of petrol filled the night air as Mustafa doused the pile of smashed furniture inside before throwing in a match and watching the hungry flames begin to devour their meagre possessions and ultimately the whole house.

"One or two more things yet," said Mustafa. "Your soldiers seemed to think that women made good urinals! We must follow their good example, don't you think?"

In full view of her uncomprehending children, they each urinated over the prone woman, still tied in a foetal position but now with her hands free.

"Last little job now.Your kind considerate soldiers beat my father unconscious with their rifles, but we'd like to give you a choice.You can have the same treatment he received, or you may prefer to be treated like the 7,000 of our Muslim brothers who were massacred in cold blood at Srebenica in Bosnia last year, courtesy of your Serbian troops."

They ripped off the gag from the caretaker's mouth to hear his reply.

"You are animals! May you all rot in hell! And God grant you no mercy, you scumbags!"

The butts of their rifles cascaded onto him, crushing into his defenceless body and head. The chair toppled over and he lay unconscious in a bleeding heap beside his wife. The muzzle of a rifle was placed against his head and another countdown began. This time when the rigger was pulled, the crack of an explosion propelled a high velocity bullet right through the caretaker's skull. At least his earthly misery was over.

That of his wife and children continued, mitigated, at long last, by a small measure of relief as the Toyota truck drove off in cloud of dust and they were left to their own devices. With her free hands the mother wrestled with the knots around her knees until they finally loosened. In the garden shed at the back of the church were some of her husband's gardening clothes. She had no option but to search the pockets of his dead body for the keys to the shed. She found an old jacket and pair of overalls to cover her nakedness, and set off in the darkness to trudge, with her children, towards the bridge and the relative security among their own people on the other side. There was no more she could do for her husband, nor their church. Her children were now her only concern and she would not fail them however much her own body had been abused and defiled.

Habib had been a reluctant witness to the evening's terrible events orchestrated by his own brother. He had declined when invited to urinate on the woman and had played no direct part in the assaults, except as an observer hardly daring to watch. As he saw the caretaker's head pulverised by the bullet, he could contain his nausea no longer and vomited uncontrollably into the grass in the darkness. When young, he had been best friends with Serb children. He remembered their games together in the summer fields. He remembered how they had fished in the steams around the town. He remembered the winter ice and snow – snowballs and snowmen and sliding on the frozen lakes. He remembered happy walks in the hills, and the sweeping views back over his beloved hometown. He remembered birthday parties with cream cakes and jelly.

These were the beautiful things he had believed were the essence of growing up in such a happy place. At school he'd loved the books that told heroic tales, some true and some fictitious, but all with messages that good would triumph over evil, that freedom and happiness were there to be grasped, that reading and writing and arithmetic were important, and that the future for sensitive, intelligent young boys like him beckoned with opportunity and hope.

The atrocities he had witnessed in his own home, and now here at the caretaker's house, were not compatible with that dream. He thought he understood the concept of family honour but if its redress involved the horrors of these nights, he wanted no part of it. The hatred on both sides was ingrained, unrelenting and unforgiving. In that moment, Habib resolved there was only one course for him when he grew up. He would leave Kosovo to those whose ideology could tolerate such evil in their own midst. He would find some way to go to a new place where kindness and the simple joys of life prevailed. Kosovo, for him, had become a wretched and benighted place. The fields of his youth were now full of mines. The river was polluted and the fish had all died. There was no more music and no more dancing. He saw no future for himself in this unremitting climate of fear and bitterness, hatred and intolerance. When the right moment came, he would escape.

Chapter 5

Moldova - 2000

Making a go of things in Chisinau was, of course, far easier said than done. There were four basic ingredients to the challenge – accommodation, income, job, and social life – not necessarily in that order and, in any case, they were to a large extent interdependent.

The sofa bed in her relative's apartment provided a temporary solution to Nina's accommodation search, but the inconvenience of sleeping in the sitting room, and the distance from the city centre meant that a more permanent and more convenient arrangement would need to be found sooner or later.

Social life would hopefully develop of its own accord. Pavel and his girlfriend, Tanya, would help smooth the path for that in due course. The first priority was to secure a job and some income. But employment vacancies in Chisinau were few and far between. Those that did come up either required some sort of qualification, which Nina did not have, or were filled by the old boy's network with friends or by someone who could bribe their way in.

The only recourse open to Nina was to take short-term casual jobs until she could find something more permanent. Her brother introduced her to the cleaning superintendent at the hospital where he worked, and that led to an early morning, three-hour floor-washing stint, two mornings a week, at the princely rate of the equivalent of one US dollar a day. In addition she took on lunchtime dishwashing at a restaurant in the city centre on Tuesdays and Saturdays, again at one dollar per session. On Saturday nights she served at tables in a bar doing four hours for one dollar plus gratuities. This piecemeal ad-hoc amalgam of jobs had been assembled by the end of her second week in the capital and looked set to generate an unsteady income of over five dollars a week. For a young student in the city, this was just enough to get by on.Most importantly, it enabled her to contribute some housekeeping to her hosts, pay for the bus fares to and from the city centre, and have enough spare pocket money to go out on the town with friends without feeling too impoverished.

In another monstrous grey concrete block of apartments, not more than a hundred paces from where Nina was staying, lived Larissa Braghis with her parents and husband, Dumitru, on the seventh floor. They had been married for four months, a rapidly arranged affair, because of a serious lapse in concentration on both their parts after a drunken party with friends in March of that year. As a result, Larissa was now seven months pregnant.

She worked as receptionist in the DHL courier service main branch, just off Boulevard Stefan Cel Mare, the thoroughfare that bisects the city centre. It was a good place to work. Her colleagues were great fun. Two girls worked in the small back office doing all the paperwork and handling the international telephone and fax enquiries. They had just installed their first online computer and were already recognising the benefits of email business communication. The boss, Vladimir Voronin, was congenial, middle-aged and laid back. The fifth member of the team was a newly qualified driver who took responsibility for their van and motor-cycle deliveries. Vladimir Voronin had one daughter, Tanya and she was deeply in love with a young man who worked at her hospital, Pavel Snegur, Nina's brother.

On the morning of Monday 2nd October 2000, Larissa Braghis woke earlier than usual thinking that her period had started. By the time she had reached full consciousness she was in considerable panic.

"But I'm pregnant," she thought. "Women don't have periods when they're pregnant" . Between her legs she felt the telltale signs of gentle bleeding. She roused her sleeping husband and asked him to call her mother quickly; this was women's business.

The emergency admission to the maternity hospital was by no means straightforward. After doing what she could to staunch the flow of blood with a towel, her mother called in neighbours to help with the arduous descent down fourteen flights of stairs, with Larissa strapped onto a chair. Another neighbour's car was requisitioned for the journey. As usual, its engine battery was flat, but willing hands soon gave it the necessary momentum to get started. Behind a badly cracked windscreen, and followed by plumes of blue oil smoke from the exhaust, Larissa was finally delivered to nursing care at the hospital two hours after her distressing discovery.

The doctor's examination diagnosed immediate need for complete bed-rest, and close nursing attention for the foreseeable future, or she might lose her baby or have to undergo an emergency Caesarian operation. Larissa Braghis was unlikely to be back in the DHL office again for some time.

When he received the call from her husband, Vladimir Voronin was very sympathetic. "Or course it would be difficult for the office to manage without her, but her health and welfare were more important. Tell her to keep smiling, not to worry about anything else except making sure that the baby was born bonny and well. Give her our love and best wishes," he said.

Two minutes later he was on the phone again to the florists, and within half an hour a bouquet and get-well card were on their way to the hospital in the DHL van, expressing the good wishes of all her DHL colleagues.

Over dinner that evening, Vladimir recounted the events of the day. In the sympathetic hearing of his wife and daughter, he expressed his anxiety about Larissa and her unborn baby, and touched on the problems the office would face without a receptionist. It was crucial to get someone in quickly who could converse easily in Russian and Moldovan, someone he could trust fully when everyone else was otherwise occupied, someone who could start very soon, and someone whose personality would match the easy-going ambience of the DHL office image.

"I think I know someone who could do it," said Tanya.

So it was that the sister of Tanya's boyfriend, Nina Snegur, found herself sitting in the DHL office at nine o'clock the next morning, being interviewed by Mr Voronin. One hour later, she had phoned a restaurant from that office and told them they would be short-handed in the dishwashing department that lunchtime. And a call to Pavel meant he was left with the task of informing the cleaning superintendent at his hospital that her casual employment there was ceasing forthwith. By midday, when the girls in the office were ready to take her with them for a cigarette, a sandwich and coffee in the next door cafe, Nina was already familiar with her seat at the front desk, had learned the basics of being a receptionist, and was enjoying the prospect of congenial hours of work and a regular wage of seven dollars a week plus a bonus of five to ten dollars at the end of each month depending on the flow of business.

She had been in the city for less than a month and things were looking as bright as she had dared hope. The remaining quest for more permanent living accommodation found its solution two weeks later. She moved in to a shared apartment in the older part of the city near the University with three girls, whom she had met in the growing circle of friends she was making through the discos and coffee bars that her work colleagues and Pavel had introduced her to. And there was an added bonus – a boyfriend, Ion, who worked with her brother and who was more than ready to widen her social life. In less than eight weeks the letters home were glowing with enthusiasm and her parents could be reassured she had made the right decision. As the year 2000 drew to a close, Nina felt very good about the way things were going.

Regrettably her euphoria would be short-lived.

Chapter 6

Leicester – January 2004

Clifton Comprehensive School in Bristol was no exception in having its fair share of good and bad teachers. Mr Jones was head of geography – "Spike Jones" as he was dubbed by the pupils. He was one of the goodies. Well, that was the opinion of the kids and that was most important. He enthused about his subject. With Spike Jones in front of the class geography was fun. So when Peter Clayton's O-level results came out in 1985, it was no surprise he had a top grade in geography, alongside the other eight subjects he had passed. Calculations and measurement had also always come easy to him so his choice of sixth-form subjects settled on Geography, Maths and Physics. His A, B and D grades at A-level secured his place to study at Aberystwyth University, and, inspired by Mr Jones's charismatic teaching, geography was the natural choice as his main subject. A moderate 2:2 Hons degree then provided the foundation for his postgraduate Town Planning Diploma at Cardiff.

After a brief flirtation with a private consultancy firm specialising in speculative property development planning applications, he gravitated easily to the more secure and strategic environment of the local Planning Authority. His progression to Assistant Director level at Charnwood District Council in Leicestershire had been steady and merited. He looked well set to continue that career path, perhaps not spectacularly, but to greater heights. He and his family felt comfortable and secure in a middle England sort of way.

He had met Jenny at university where she was training to be a nursery assistant. After their marriage she had no difficulty in securing jobs wherever they lived with the added benefit that nursery assistant hours were linked to school terms so she was always free when their boys were on holiday.

Regrettably, the events of that Saturday morning, 10th January 2004, were now threatening to explode irreversibly all over the carefully constructed suburban security of the Clayton's lifestyle. As Peter took pen to paper in the soulless surrounds of the police station, he knew he was fighting hard to preserve everything that held their life together. Either option arising from the morning's events was unpalatable. Either he had been hallucinating, or he was caught up unwittingly in a grotesque death. If the former, he feared for his long-term mental health and that was distressing enough. If the latter, as he was the key witness, where would it lead? How far would he become embroiled, given that he was the one who had stumbled on the body before it had been secreted away? Ruthless people might adopt ruthless means to cover their tracks.

The police statement was crucial to setting things down while they were still fresh in his mind. His natural propensity for figures and facts and precision spurred him on in the hope that the police might then begin to take him more seriously.

> Leicestershire Constabulary
> Statement by Peter Colville Clayton, dob 12 July 1968.
> Married. Two children.
> Residing at 55, Chantry Gardens, Leicester.
> Date 10th January 2004
> Time 11:55 a.m.
> Present D/S Crabtree; D/C O'Malley.
> This statement is made voluntarily and without duress.
> Signed Peter Clayton

and thereafter followed a succinct, precise, unemotive catalogue of the dramatic events of the last ninety minutes of Peter's life, the key components being:-

> 10:15am Left home driving my own black Golf GTI for appointment to meet Michael Burton at his office.
> 10:28am Arrived and parked in Polymer Plastics Limited factory carpark and entered unlocked office door. Noted two cars in carpark, one Burton's BMW and the other a Mercedes.
> 10:30am Discovered body of Michael Burton on the floor of his office, apparently electrocuted, desk-chair and waste-bin overturned and computer live.

10:32am Phoned emergency services. (Police switchboard confirm call received at 10:32:21. Concluded at 10:43:12.)
10:45am Discovered carpark was empty. All three cars, mine and Michael Burton's, and the Mercedes had disappeared.
10:46am Received phonecall from wife, saying my car now parked back in our drive at home.
10:48am Listened to answer-phone message cancelling the morning's appointment with Mr Burton.
10:50am Police and emergency services arrive on scene.
10:55am No sign of body in the office. Everything seemingly back to normal. Chair and waste-bin upright. Computer shut down. No sign of any electrical wires.
11:25am Leave PPL premises in police car after police had ensured arrangements were in hand to secure building. Ambulance and paramedics stood down.
11:35am Phone call from wife while en route to police station.
11:40am Arrive police station
11:55am Begin this statement.

After carefully checking the content, Peter signed again at the foot of the document, noting the time as 12:22 pm., followed by countersignatures from the two policemen present.

Studying the timing sequence there were two critical periods. The first was that between when Peter left his car in the car-park and then returned to find it had disappeared from there, only to be informed by his wife that it was back at his home by 10:45a.m. The distance between the two locations was just over two miles. The time elapsed between him last seeing his car in the carpark and his wife seeing it at home was fifteen minutes. Although improbable, it was quite possible for the car to have been driven between the two places in that time if someone was very organised and discreet.

The other critical period was between Peter first discovering the body and his second visit to the office with the police by which time the body had disappeared. These were timed at 10:32 a.m. and 10:55 a.m., a period of twenty three minutes. Again this would have been sufficient time, indeed patently had been, for an efficient removal of the body and setting back the office to normal, if someone was swift and purposeful.

Peter was relieved not only to have got things into print in some detail, but also to reassure himself that the sequence of events was technically feasible. Even the sceptical detectives agreed on that.

There remained, however, any number of inconsistencies, not to say hardly credible elements to the morning saga. The police, though still less than convinced, were nevertheless disposed to try to help Peter where they could. In particular they were prepared to use their good offices to get to the bottom of the phone message he had received cancelling his appointment with Michael Burton.

They contacted Stansted Airport and established that RyanAir flight number FR 3004 had left on time at 7:00 a.m. that morning for Rome Ciampino airport, where it had touched down at 9:30 a.m. English time (10:30 a.m. Italian time). More importantly the passenger list included a Mr Michael Burton, apparently travelling alone, though that could not be known for sure. He would have had to produce a personal identity document, usually a passport, before being allowed to board the flight. According to their records, RyanAir had him booked to return on flight FR3007 due into Stansted at 16:30 hours the following Saturday. They had no idea where or how he might be contacted in Rome or where he may have headed after leaving the small Ciampino airport situated some fifteen kilometres to the south of the city.

RyanAir was not geared up to dealing with direct approaches from the public, as the vast bulk of their business was conducted over the Internet, so it was especially helpful of the police to dig out this corroborative information. But for Peter it only confounded things further. He knew he had definitely seen Michael's body lying in the office in Leicester some two hours earlier, but it now appeared that Mr Burton, or at least someone answering his description and using his identity documents, was in Rome at that time. The jigsaw did not fit together, and Peter seemed the only one holding both pieces in his hand. Apart from his testimony, no one else had any reason to believe that Michael Burton had met an untimely death. And not surprisingly no one else was going to be enthusiastic about pursuing his rather far-fetched story simply to put Peter's own mind at rest.

One option was to go home quietly, get on with life until next Saturday and wait patiently to see whether Michael Burton emerged from the Arrivals Hall at Stansted airport off the RyanAir flight from Rome. It occurred to him that anyone going to Stansted airport would usually travel by car, because train and coach links from Leicester there are not easy. If the real Michael Burton had caught that flight, more than likely he would have used his car, with its distinctive number plate. Would the police be in a position to establish whether that car was parked in the long-stay park at Stansted? As a further gesture of help, D.C. O'Malley agreed to contact the airport police to see what they could discover.

In between the odd highjack alerts every six months or so, Stansted police had a very boring routine so it was not an unwelcome request to try to locate Mr Burton's blue BMW with its personalised registration number. It was not too difficult either, because although the longstay carparks are vast, the flight times dictate where cars should be parked. That morning cars were being ushered into Carpark J.

It was now nearing 1:00 p.m. and Peter was increasingly conscious he should be making tracks for home. Jenny would be waiting anxiously to hear what had been happening and any delay would only add to her stress. There was really no need for him to stay at the police station any longer. A copy of his statement had been formally filed under a reference number LC/St-PB/10/01/04. He had his own copy in his pocket. D.C. O'Malley undertook to phone him at home with any more information that came to light from Stansted.

With some relief and trepidation he accepted a lift home from another officer and was just stepping across the threshold of his front door when the phone started ringing. Jenny answered it and, discovering it was the police station, anxiously passed it over to Peter.

"O'Malley here. Stansted police done a good job. Bloody 'mazing how quick they can do these things. Anyway, not sure you'll be pleased to know but they've located Mr Burton's car in the long-stay park at the airport where they would have expected to find it if anyone wanted to catch the early-morning Rome flight. Doesn't seem to add up with your story, sir, but let us know if you think of anything else. We'll just hold things on file for the moment – nothing really for us to follow up, is there? Hope the weekend goes a bit better for you. Bye for now."

Jenny hovered near the phone, her earlier irritation now completely given way to anxiety. Her eyes betrayed her impatience to hear what had been going on. Lunch was going to be a perfunctory affair. The children had been shepherded into the sitting room to watch a cartoon. Peter, now able to relax a little, looked sallow and drained. The latest phone call from O'Malley had only served to complicate matters. He needed a cup of tea, time to think and time to recoup. But rehearsing everything to a sympathetic wife was going to be helpful therapy. Whether two heads would be better than one in making sense of it all remained to be seen. Little did he anticipate that during his rehearsal of events, his wife would fix onto minutiae which might confirm the veracity of her husband's morning trauma.

Chapter 7

Kosovo - 1998-2003

When Saul of Tarsus set out from Jerusalem on his journey to Damascus in the first century AD, his intent was to wreak havoc among the embryonic group of Jesus supporters living there. Somewhere along the barren desert road, he was stopped in his tracks by a blinding light, which left him temporarily sightless. What actually transpired is open to conjecture, but the consequences are irrefutable. From being an energetic persecutor of this new Christian heresy, he was converted into its most ardent advocate. More than most, he was the driving force that transformed Christianity from a small Jewish sect into a global religion. This was the defining moment in the life of St. Paul. The rest of his life could be described as "the postscript".

Most people experience defining moments in their lives. The events of August 1998 in Habib Peci's life were one of those defining moments. At the tender age of sixteen, he may not have been able to articulate it, but the traumas he had witnessed had affected him deeply. His affection for the place of his birth and childhood had been destroyed at a stroke. The scales had fallen from his eyes. He now saw the fragility of the things around him, the things he had once held so dear, and had seemed to him, when a child, so secure and abiding. His elder brother had become someone to be feared, rather than held in awe. His family home had crumbled. His parents and sister were broken people. He was living in temporary accommodation and what the future might hold was no more than a blur. The response of most of his classmates to the atrocities they had witnessed was to stoke up their hatred and animosity and enlist in the Kosovo Liberation Army at the earliest opportunity. Habib had a different ambition.

Ideas and aspirations are not difficult to dream up – achieving them, turning them into reality, is the hard bit. Habib had decided what he wanted to do. He knew from films, television and books there was a world out there that offered much more than the wretched prospects around him in Kosovo. That's where he wanted to be. The dilemma was how to get there.

Habib was a pupil at the Ismail Qemajli school in the centre of Mitrovice. He was one of the brightest pupils of his year and had already acquired a basic knowledge of the English language. If he were to leave Kosovo, the language he needed most would be English. Eastern Europe and the Balkans offered no great prospects. Western Europe would be the place to head for. Many Kosovar Albanians had relocated to Germany as *Gastarbeiten* – ("guest workers") – on temporary work permits and were regularly sending money back to their families to offset the stultifying unemployment problems in Kosovo. But Habib's English was better than his German, and he felt instinctively that the UK, and perhaps ultimately the USA, were where his dreams of a better life could come to fruition.

Language was one thing, but the most important ingredient in achieving his goal was money. By their meagre family standards, he would need lots of it. Habib had heard of the clandestine opportunities for getting out of Kosovo. His family and friends talked in hushed tones from time to time of acquaintances who had quietly slipped away and were now domiciled in far-flung countries, illegally perhaps, but able to send money back home, and content that they had remunerative work, however menial, and that they were away from the conflicts and reprisals in their home villages.

The networks to facilitate this were complex. There were two types of operation: the traffickers dealing in drugs, prostitutes, weapons and children, and the smugglers who dealt in goods and illegal immigrants. Both were orchestrated by swarthy, humourless men in black leather jackets, meeting late at night in smoke-filled bars, scattered along the immigrants' trails across Europe. The major lubricant for the operation was money. People talked of $5,000 US or more having to change hands to secure a passage, and even then much had to be taken on trust. There were stories of people being left stranded halfway to nowhere, people being apprehended and returned ignominiously, people dying on cross-sea voyages, people getting sick, people being incarcerated – and not one of them ever seeing their money again. There was no redress when dealing with this twilight world. But the pressure to leave Kosovo's troubles, and the attractions of the West were more than enough incentive for a steady stream of hopeful, desperate people to take the risk.

Young though he was, Habib had identified the two key essentials to achieving his goal – a good grasp of English, and a piggy bank of at least $5,000. There was also a third element – that was discretion. He would guard his ambition jealously, even from his own family. He was still in the last years of school and he would use those to concentrate on improving his English. Out of school, he would seek any odd jobs he could get hold of to build up his savings. He knew it would take time – a long time – but he was in no hurry. He could not contemplate such a dramatic move until he was at least a few years older. Meantime he would plan, and study, and earn, and try to keep his secret.

At an international level, events were unfolding rapidly. The experiences of the Peci family in Mitrovice were being replicated all over Kosovo and the wider world was becoming increasingly distraught at the ethnic-cleansing policies being so remorselessly pursued by the Serbian Army under Milosevic. Sanctions and diplomacy were having negligible impact. Hoards of desperate refugees were being herded out of their home villages into the mountains towards Albania to escape the atrocities. Television screens throughout the West captured the suffering and distress of thousands of families on the move, their plight made worse by the rapidly deteriorating weather as the winter months approached. Their fragile polythene sheets were no match for the freezing sleet and slanting rain from unremitting grey skies. Their tractors and carts became bogged down in the mud and slush. And where were they to go? Albania was their only hope, but it was one of the poorest countries in Europe and patently had no capacity to absorb this tide of refugees, which in numbers equalled a quarter of the total population of Albania.

Final ultimatums had been ignored, and the NATO bombing of the Serbian forces began in May of 1999. After a few weeks of defiance, Milosevic succumbed and was deposed, and Kosovo became a Protectorate under the United Nations as part of the wider Federal Republic of Yugoslavia. The United Nations Mission in Kosovo (UNMIK) was created and moved in to administer the territory. Security was provided by the KFOR troops, multinational brigades from Belgium, Denmark, Greece, Italy, Jordan, Luxembourg, Morocco, Russia, the UEA, Britain, the USA, France and more. And with the improved security in came the international relief agencies, almost like vultures on a corpse, UNICEF, WHO, UNHCR, USAID, Council of Europe, Save the Children, OSCE, World Vision, Caritas France, the Danish Refugee Council, the Italian Consortium of Solidarity, the Red Cross - the list went on. As Kosovo struggled to rediscover a more peaceable way of life and reabsorb returning refugees back into their communities, it found itself teeming with international soldiers and non-governmental organisations, NGOs – the acronym for modern relief and aid agencies, the "do-gooders" of the twenty-first century. A fragile peace was restored. Serb enclaves in Kosovo were guarded twenty-four hours a day with barbed wire and armoured cars, and in the Serbian areas, Kosovar Albanian enclaves were similarly protected. Schools could again use the Albanian language for teaching, which Milosevic had outlawed. The region began to approach something more like normality despite still looking like a war zone, with military vehicles and soldiers everywhere.

Habib may not have understood the strategic political, social and economic objectives of the NATO bombing, but the outcome of this international intervention led directly to unforeseen beneficial spin-offs for him personally. It's an ill wind, they say, that has no merits.

For one thing, the arrival of the troops and the aid agencies brought with them a huge demand for interpreters from Albanian into English and vice versa. Habib was sitting in the front line and more than ready to help, albeit with his limited vocabulary. The contact with "the foreigners" was itself a significant spur for developing his language skills and he soon became much in demand. And "the foreigners" brought with them spending money such as Kosovo had not seen for many years. Habib was rewarded for his translation services, modestly by Western standards, but handsomely by his. His piggy bank began to fill at a rate he had never envisaged.

The other unexpected spin-off was that the soldiers of the KFOR peacekeeping forces were expected to keep their vehicles clean and smart. Unfortunately the roads and tracks throughout Kosovo, particularly after the rains, made that a never-ending chore.

Kosovo's entrepreneurial response was the burgeoning of roadside "carwash" facilities across the country. All they needed was a hard-standing, a hosepipe, some brushes and rags, and an eager band of young men. A large army truck could be washed clean in fifteen minutes, and this earned an easy five to ten dollars. The soldiers were more than happy to forego this chore in return for such a modest outlay from their generous pay-packets. At the end of a good day, always better after rain, the happy band of young men could hope to share out among themselves $100 or more. Habib was quick to avail himself of this additional income stream. In the light evenings after school, and at weekends he would spend as much time as he could helping at the vehicle-wash. And his presence there was always welcomed by both fellow-washers and the soldiers because he could speak some English, which added to the occasion as stories from both sides were exchanged.

And as he became better known to the troops, inevitably as among all young soldiers posted abroad away from their homes, the conversation turned to girls – more particularly – who's available, and where, and when? Kosovar Albanian families were, in the main, Muslim, and sex was kept at low profile in their communities. Muslim girls were not so accessible as in more liberal communities. Television and films were censored to ensure nothing untoward was broadcast. Fraternising with the peacekeepers beyond friendly exchanges in shops or cafes was frowned upon.

There were, nonetheless, a sprinkling of young ladies not averse to the company of virile young soldiers whose pockets more than matched their appetite for the feminine touch. Habib was now nearing eighteen years old and well aware of the girls who had gone through school with him who might welcome a clandestine encounter. So, unbeknown to his parents, he tapped into another remunerative strand of employ by arranging meetings between local girls and soldiers in a smoke-filled coffee-bar just a short walk from the fortified bridge separating the Serb and Albanian communities in Mitrovice. Again his translation skills were much in demand to lubricate these initial encounters, until, in due course, the couples in question slid away to less public locations, where touch, rather than talk, was going to be all that was needed.

By the time Habib had left school his time was almost fully occupied in these various pursuits. His family were glad that he was so busy and proud that his ability to speak English was giving him so many opportunities. He was able to give his family some money each week, which they so appreciated. His piggy bank was filling at a satisfying rate, so much so that when he reached the age of eighteen he had gone to Pristina, the Kosovo capital about thirty miles south, to open a personal savings account at the bank there.

Because he was so well known to the NGOs and soldiers in and around Mitrovice, it was no surprise that his services were called upon in 2001 when the preparations were being made for the democratic elections for a Kosovo Assembly. These were to be supervised by an international team under the auspices of the Organisation for Security and Cooperation in Europe, the OSCE. Each polling station needed an interpreter, as did so many of the officials drafted into Kosovo to set up the infrastructure for the November election. In the months leading up to it, there were many calls on his language skills, and on the days immediately surrounding the election he was fully employed earning $40 a day, which was more than most of his compatriots could earn in a month. The fact that a peaceful and transparent election could be successfully conducted in Kosovo was good news for the community at large. For Habib it meant his bank account swelled even more.

August 2003 was hot and summery. It was five years since Habib had witnessed the family atrocities at first hand. He was now twenty-one. The country's fragile truce was holding. The troops and NGO activity had become part of the fabric of their daily lives. But prospects of training for a career and long-term employment were still a pipe dream for most young people in Mitrovice. Economic activity was spasmodic and almost always directly linked to initiatives of the KFOR troops and the development agencies. These were, no doubt, laying the foundation for future stability and growth, but an intelligent ambitious young man like Habib could not afford to waste the best years of his life while Kosovo got its act together. He had no reason to falter from his fixed resolve. He now had a thorough working command of English and his Pristina bank savings had topped the $5,000 target. The time had come to make his move.

It was not difficult to arrange a meeting with someone, who knew someone, who in turn had contacts with someone, who could facilitate a clandestine transit to the West. Secrecy was paramount.

His family still knew nothing of his plans. They were aware of his savings account but had no idea how large it was or what he intended to do with it.

He met Osman Ibrahimi late one afternoon in the coffee shop near the bridge. Osman was wearing the uniform of his trade – black jeans, black shoes, black leather jacket and a black moustache. He had spent seven years working in Germany sending money home and had now returned to join his wife and two children back in Kosovo. He was fluent in German and had a smattering of English, but more particularly he had established links across Europe with illegal-immigrant networks. He was now using that intelligence to earn his living in Kosovo. Outside the coffee bar it was a warm, sunny August afternoon. Inside the atmosphere was dense with smoke and the odour of thick black coffee. The shop awning and the high concrete buildings across the pedestrianised street combined to frustrate any of the sun's rays from reaching inside, contributing to the furtive ambience of their hushed conversation.

"Yes, it was possible to arrange things," explained Osman. "Yes, it would cost money. $500 up front and the rest in instalments at each stage. Timing was crucial. Getting into Albania was the first step. That had to be over the mountains. They were impassible in winter. You have to be across no later than the end of October. You need to travel light but nights could be very cold, so warm hard-wearing clothes are essential."

"Yes, there were contacts and safe houses at various locations en route. Yes, there was an established Albanian community in the UK. They had ambivalent feelings about Kosovar Albanians, but money would smooth those emotions. It was sensible to have an identity card with you, but keep it hidden. You won't need a passport. There are only three borders to negotiate – into Albania, into Italy, and into the UK. Each one would be crossed by bypassing the official customs posts."

"The first $500 instalment will get you into Albania and onto the trail. You will need another $1,250 to cross Albania and then by boat into Italy. The journey up through Italy and France would be another $,1000. The cross-channel bit into the UK would be a final $2,000. You also need pocket money to survive for however long the journey takes."

Whatever question Habib asked, there was a calm measured response from Osman. He knew his trade well. There was a ruthless logic and precision in his demeanour, which brooked no argument. In the event of any difficulty, Habib would be on his own. He carried all the risk. And at any suggestion of a betrayal of the networks, the culprit would find himself with concrete feet at the bottom of well, no questions asked and no appeal. Habib was dealing with men with disciplined focus. They had the competence and resources to deliver what he sought, but they would show little mercy if things went pear-shaped.

"So when could I go?" asked Habib.

"The latest you can cross the mountains is the end of October. Can you be ready by then?"

"No problem."

"What about the money? I do nothing till you pay me".

"I'll let you have $250 this week and $250 the day we leave from Mitrovice. Is that OK?"

"We'll meet here in one week's time. You give me the money then – and I mean $500 – then we're in business. If not, forget it!"

"Right, I'll fix that. Will you be able to tell me then when I leave and what I do?"

"You'll get all you need for each stage at each stage. The less you know the better, for everyone's sake. If you keep paying your instalments, things will be explained when you need to know – but not until then. In the meantime, you say nothing to no one. Whatever story you tell your family and friends is up to you, but any reference to me or our organisation, the deal is dead, and you've said goodbye to your money. Is that understood?"

Habib did understand. He felt a surge of adrenalin as he realised his long-held ambition was about to take shape. He had two months to get organised. He could not conceive where things would lead, but his course was now set.

Chapter 8

Moldova - 2001

By the standards of most children brought up in the villages and rural parts of Moldova, at the age of seventeen, Nina's sexual knowledge and experiences were pretty normal. Her first memory was when as a group of ten-year-olds, the girls had agreed to take off their knickers to show the boys "theirs" if the boys would show "theirs". This ritual lesson in basic anatomy, replicated amongst most young children across the ages, was quickly followed by a resumption of the more important matters of climbing trees, chasing butterflies, playing hide and seek and fishing.

The second memorable moment was at the age of thirteen when she was out swimming in the local river with two girl friends and a boy, a year older. Relaxing on the bank afterwards, the girls dared her to "touch the boy's thing". Nina was uncertain. She knew it was something her parents would not be told about. As the boy undid his trousers she became aware of the first male erection she had ever seen. The other two girls proceeded to demonstrate what was expected of her, and to retain her street credibility she really had no option but to follow suit. In the end it was no big deal.

The third stage of her voyage of awakening was the groping phase. On dark evenings in secluded nooks and crannies around the village, pubescent youngsters locked themselves in embraces while impatient hands wormed their way inside underwear to caress the soft white flesh of inner thighs and nubile breasts. Clumsy, furtive and inexpert though it all was, Nina felt the first flickerings of pleasure and marvelled how even at her age a girl could have such a hold over the opposite sex. It felt strangely satisfying to be so desired.

Her latest experience was in the year before she left home, when boyfriends were becoming more demanding endeavouring to press their prowess between her legs. On two occasions she felt the bulbous head push a few centimetres inside her secret crevasse. She was surprised how easily it went in and despite its size, how cosy it felt. But far more importantly the overriding fear of pregnancy meant the intruding member had to be ejected immediately. Whatever the boy may have hoped for, his partial advance was abruptly and unceremoniously terminated, and that was the end of the evening's embraces.

When Nina arrived in Chisinau, her experiences were not unusual for a girl of her age from the provinces, but to all intents and purposes she was still a virgin. That was in some contrast to Chisinau girls of a similar age. It explained why her new boyfriend, Ion, was so discomforted when his advances met with a degree of reluctance and surprise. She had just turned eighteen. Nina had no compelling objection on religious or ethical grounds. It was just that her upbringing had instilled in her a feeling that she had to be sure about the guy before she allowed him to go too far. But the glittering life she was enjoying in her new-found freedom was already melting her traditional attitudes. It was all too obvious that sexual freedom was the norm amongst the young people with whom she worked and played. Her boyfriend was good-looking, kind and not too pushy. He had a good job, danced well, and was popular amongst her friends. Their passionate embraces after the clubs and coffee bars had closed convinced her how much he loved her and her reluctant resistance finally succumbed to his urgings a month or so after they had started going out together.

He seemed very sure of himself and, being a nurse, had persuaded Nina that coitus interruptus was a perfectly reliable method of birth control. Nina enjoyed their couplings but always felt a little diminished and unfulfilled when he withdraw at the critical moment.

December 2000 was a time of great adventure and excitement. It was only sixteen weeks since she had left home, uncertain and unsure what the future would hold. Now she had agreeable employment, a modest income, a convenient apartment, a vibrant social life, and a loving boyfriend.

The festive season was approaching. Modest decorations were going up in the streets. Parties were becoming more frequent and the New Year celebrations in Chisinau were going to be altogether different from anything Nina had experienced in Mihailovca.

The Eastern Orthodox Church celebrates Christmas on 7th January. It had been some time since Nina had last seen her family, mainly because there had been neither opportunity nor money for a return journey in those first hectic months. But Christmas was the time to be home. That was the occasion when she would take presents and share with her parents the exciting details of her new-found lifestyle. The more intimate aspects of her friendship with Ion she would omit, but she was sure they would be happy that things had turned out so well. Sooner or later they would want to meet him and they would like him. For the present they could rest assured that Nina was in good heart and in good form.

It so happened that Christmas Day was when her next period was due. It did not come. The pleasure of being at home, and meeting her old school friends who all seemed strangely dull and old-fashioned these days, meant that initially she could not give much thought to this little problem. Anyway, perhaps all the excitement had momentarily upset her hormones. It would no doubt come in a few days.

It didn't.

The New Year had started on such a high - now it had a dark shadow of anxiety hanging over it. The weeks stretched into February and still nothing showed. Chisinau had a good range of pharmacy shops and pregnancy-testing kits were one of the most popular sale lines. It was on St Valentine's Day 2001 rather ironically, that Nina Snegur used one of these kits and discovered, as she feared, that coitus interruptus had failed, probably after the mid-December engagement party for one of Pavel's friends. She was two months pregnant.

The stigma of pregnancy out of wedlock was probably less acutely felt in former Soviet Bloc countries than in the Western world. For some time abortion had been an alternative but acceptable form of contraception. Even so, for a young single girl in a new environment, being pregnant at eighteen was a crushing blow. Nina sobbed herself to sleep that night while she considered her options.

For the moment only she knew, and at least for a few days that secret was going to be closely guarded. Her work colleagues presumed her pallid complexion and subdued temperament was because of the time of the month, or she might be having a hard time with her boyfriend. Girls in their teens were prone to unpredictable swings of emotion: best not to interfere unless asked to do so.

In the cool light of day there were really only two alternatives; to have the baby or to have an abortion. Both options presented difficulties. If she were to have the baby, would her boyfriend be happy about it? Would he be prepared to set up home together, as a married couple or otherwise? If he was not interested, it would probably mean going back home to her parents, the premature end of her stay in Chisinau, and a return to the provincial lifestyle that she now almost despised. And with a young baby to look after, how would her marriage prospects be affected? More worryingly, what sort of man would want to take on someone else's infant?

On the other hand an abortion still loomed as a fearsome experience. What would it feel like to lose a baby deliberately? Who would do it? Where could it be done? How much would it cost? The practicalities were daunting. But the clock was ticking. If abortion was to be the answer, some quick decisions would be necessary. The starting point for trying to sort out her emotions and to think what best to do must be a frank confidential discussion with her boyfriend to see what he thought about it all. He was older than she and a nurse, so he probably understood these things better than her anyway.

It was a much more subdued couple that sat at the scratched formica coffee table in their usual cafe the following evening. They had chosen a secluded corner and met well in advance of the time their friends usually came in. Nina had told him the news. Ion was chain-smoking. His body language was not comforting. He avoided her eyes. Instead he focussed on the stub ends in the cracked saucer on the table between them. He leaned back in his chair, fidgeted, and looked at the ceiling, anything to avoid the pleading, desperate looks that burned towards him from Nina. Surely he could say something to help her. Tears welled around her eyes.

"What should we do? What's for the best?" she pleaded.

"How do you know it's mine?" came the response she had never dreamed of hearing.

There are times when what is not said conveys more than what is said. Did he really think she had been going with other boys? His response clearly told her he thought she had. Did he not understand she loved him? His response seemed to imply that was of no great concern to him. Was he not prepared to accept some responsibility for her condition? His response suggested he was preparing to wash his hands of the problem. As she stared towards him in disbelief, she knew the disintegration of their friendship had already begun. The well of her despair deepened. For two months she had danced and partied and drunk and made love with this man, and now at a stroke he had revealed their friendship had no depth at all. There was no need for further debate.

"For God's sake, do you really, really think that this is someone else's baby? Do you really think I've been two-timing you? Do you really think I'm a slag? You're an utter sod! I hate you. Get out of my life, you bastard!"

She threw the dregs from her plastic coffee cup at him and stormed out, striving to hold back her tears and sobs till she was sufficiently distant to avoid him seeing her dignity collapse.

Nina Snegur was pregnant and she was going to have to face the consequences on her own. The choices had now narrowed to going home to have the baby or have an abortion. There was of course a third more dreadful option, that of ending her life. But Nina knew that however hard things were to be, she would not be overcome. Her next step must be to find out more about what an abortion would involve. No need for final decisions yet, but the more facts at her disposal, the more informed would be her choice. There was a brutal logic to her predicament, and it was best to face up to it rather than pretend otherwise. Realism rather than idealism would be the yardstick by which she would now have to live.

Chapter 9

Kosovo – October 2003

Ready – get set – go!!

Habib had spent five years "getting ready". He had needed a working command of English and a stack of dollars in the bank. That was done. He now had two months to "get set", before the "go".

Getting set meant preparing himself physically and mentally for the cross-Europe trek. According to Osman, allowing for transport connections and possible delays en route, it would take about two months to reach the UK. He would have to travel light – a lightweight rucksack to carry changes of underclothes and socks, some extra shirts, wash bag, small towel, kitchen roll, a spare pair of trainers, another pair of jeans, a torch and a knife. While travelling he would wear dark jeans, robust waterproof shoes, a warm shirt, and jumper under his black leather jacket. He needed to be compact and inconspicuous.

As arranged, Osman was at the cafe a week later. A sealed envelope with the $500 was handed over. Osman pocketed it without opening it. If the money wasn't correct, Habib would get no further than the outskirts of Mitrovice, but he knew it would be. The departure date was set: Friday, 24th October 2003. Osman had a copy of the booklet issued to polling station election supervisors in November 2001. From this he had copied maps of the KFOR routes across Kosovo, each coded with the names of animals for easy reference. The road from Mitrovice to Pristina was the "Fish" road, and then it was the "Duck" route, all the way to Prizren and beyond to the Albanian border control point at Morini. This was the route Habib would take. He knew the road to Pristina well and had been to Prizren twice before to attend a funeral and a wedding of distant relatives, but the road beyond that was unknown to him. They would meet again the day before he left. Osman would then give him final instructions to reach his first safe house inside Albania.

How he took care of his money was up to him, but Osman made it clear he would have to pay his way with ready cash at each phase of the journey. Habib decided to take large denominations of dollar bills – 40 one-hundred-dollar bills and another 500 dollars in small denominations, including a clutch of single dollar bills to take care of tips on the way. The hundred-dollar bills would be sealed in two polythene envelopes, twenty in each, spread flat and secreted under the insoles inside each shoe. The rest he would wear in a money belt round his waste inside his shirt. If the worst came to the worst and he was mugged, he hoped that the assailants would think the money belt was all he had and be glad to relieve him of that, without realising he had other money hidden in his shoes. It was all he could do. He had to carry ready cash and the risks were considerable. But he was fit, intelligent and streetwise. He was confident he would cope.

Through September and the first two weeks of October he earned as much extra money as he could. He went into Pristina to buy what he needed at the local street markets, including two dozen packets of cigarettes and a selection of CDs (illegal copies of pop music, recent film releases and some porn from the road-side traders, which cost no more than one or two dollars each). All these he intended to use as "sweeteners" along the way whenever circumstances demanded it. His bank would have the rest of his money ready in dollars for him to pick up in the third week of October.

Telling his family was the hard bit. Kosovar Albanian families were closely knit. The Peci family had gone through traumatic times together. Their lives had at last begun to settle into a tolerable routine. They didn't see much of the eldest son, Mustafa. He was away most of the time with the KLA as a sort of reservist ready to unleash commensurate reprisals whenever any Serb aggression against the Muslim community was reported. Shyret, their daughter, had become reclusive since her terrifying ordeal and seldom ventured out, except to work a few hours each week as a receptionist at the optometrist's shop near the river bridge. Agim had not worked since his savage beating, and was still in poor health. Aferdita's time was devoted to the household chores and a part-time cleaning job in the United Nations Mission in Kosovo local headquarters.

Habib, in contrast, brought vigour and vitality into the household, and his contributions to the family budget made all the difference. When they learned of his plans, there was despair and tears. His mother flung her arms around him and begged him not to go. His father sat wearily in the chair nonplussed and ambivalent. His sister was hysterical.

Habib was not surprised at their reaction, but it was still hard to maintain his resolve. This family was his life. And he was theirs. However constrained their circumstances, without Habib's exuberance, his stories from the soldiers, and his comings and goings, the future loomed bleak for those he was leaving behind. There was little Habib could say to reassure them. He didn't know what the future might hold. He didn't know if he would be able to send money back home. He didn't know when he might see them again. Illegal travel one way was difficult enough, but he hadn't a clue what might be involved in trying to come back to visit.

He did his best. He promised his mother he would come back, maybe in a year or so. He would get a job and he would send money home. They would be proud of him. He would make the best use of his skills and intelligence. There would be many opportunities there, which he could never hope to have here. They didn't have to worry – many young people went away to University or to other jobs at his age. This was a chance he had to take. It would be best for all of them in the long run.

And what should they to say to their friends and neighbours? Just tell them "Habib's gone abroad to work. Speaks good English, you know – bright boy, lots of contacts with the NGO staff from Western Europe – they need someone who knows Kosovo to help in their offices out there. Oh, yes, he'll come back home to see us regularly. Might meet a nice girl out there, you never know, do you? A good thing that youngsters get out to see the world rather than hanging around at home, don't you think?"

Late summer in Kosovo is an agreeable time of the year. The sun is still warm but not stiflingly hot, and lower in the sky, it highlights the rich autumnal browns and greens on the rolling hills around Mitrovice. There is a mellowness and tranquillity in October before the harshness of the winter months sets in. If ever Kosovo is to attract tourists again, this is the time to come. But for Habib it was the time to go.

Osman was at his usual coffee-stained table in the corner of the café at the appointed time on the day before D-day. This was his final briefing. Habib had taken a pen and paper and listened intently. First he was given a copy of the map of Kosovo taken from the election supervisor's manual. Contained in a small flimsy polythene A4 envelope were copies of a map of the Kosovo town of Dragas and the mountain area between there and Kukes, the town in Albania on the other side of the border. Most importantly there were two addresses, one in Dragas and one in Kukes. These were the key locations he had to reach to lock into the next stage of his journey. Once he had made contact, he must destroy the addresses. The people he met there would be working under false identities. Under no circumstances should these be revealed to anyone else, least of all to any officials. Osman also gave him a slip of paper with a contact address in London, near Finsbury Park Station. Habib secreted it with his money. Hard to get his mind around that at present. Getting out of Kosovo was the immediate challenge. He needed to be ready to leave from outside the cafe at 9:00 a.m. next morning, and there could be no fond farewells, no family, no friends present.

That evening the family had a subdued meal together. Mustafa came home for it, and a few close relatives and two of his friends. In all, less than a dozen people – these were the only ones who knew he was leaving, and except for his immediate family, most of them had only a vague idea that he was going off to Europe to work as a translator, but knew not where or how. In the circumstances it was better not to ask too many questions.

Habib did not sleep well. His mind was racing with apprehension and excitement. He was up at daybreak and made a final check of his rucksack and its contents. His mother packed him some food and a plastic bottle of water. The large-denomination dollar bills were hidden in his shoes. The money belt was round his waist. It was a crisp morning so his sweater and jacket did not feel too cumbersome. The family exchanged final hugs and kisses in the confines of their own home. The tears flowed again and not even Habib could staunch his emotion as he too sobbed his farewells. And then he was off, his rucksack slung over one shoulder – a final wave at the corner of the street before he turned for the ten-minute walk along the broken pavements to the rendez-vous.

The cafe was already open. A number of unshaven individuals were seated inside drinking thick black coffee and filling the fresh morning air with plumes of acrid tobacco smoke. Osman was outside talking to a taxi driver. In Kosovo there are broadly four types of vehicles on the roads. There are the military vehicles in full battle camouflage colours; then there are the NGO and Aid Agency vehicles, hundreds of them, almost invariably large 4x4s, disparagingly called "urban-assault vehicles" -Toyota Landcruisers, Mitsubishi Shoguns, Nissan Patrols, and the ubiquitous Landrovers, all aggressively labelled with their agency logos; then there are a smattering of prestige cars, the Mercedes, the BMWs, the Audis, with smoked-glass windows driven by Kosovar Albanians whose income stream is doubtless related to the twilight world of organised crime; finally there are the "old bangers", driven by the rank and file, old Opels,VWs whatever, held together with chewing gum and chicken wire and driven on a wing and a prayer. Few, if any, would pass a M.O.T. test, but these are the vehicles that keep Kosovo's life moving. The taxi outside the cafe was one of these.

Osman introduced Habib to the driver. He would take him to Dragas. The distance was about 120 kilometres and the journey should take two to three hours depending on road-blocks between military sectors. Mitrovice was in the French sector, Pristina the British sector, and Dragas the German. The driver opened the boot of the car and put the rucksack inside. Habib made sure it was locked. There had been a number of instances where belongings in unlocked boots had been stolen while cars had been waiting at traffic lights.

Osman had settled the journey payment with the driver so that they could leave as soon as Habib wished. They shook hands. Habib felt a sense of foreboding. Osman had become a sort of lifeline for achieving his ambitions. Now that last thread was being severed. From here on he was on his own.

The beaten-up taxi swung out onto the potholed roads in the centre of Mitrovice and joined the main "Fish" trunk road south towards Pristina. Habib sat in the front passenger seat making conversation with the driver, but giving as little away as possible. The UNMIK forces kept the main roads in good condition, so progress was speedy as the flat landscape of central Kosovo unfurled on either side of the road. Everywhere, totally uncoordinated from a town-and-country-planning viewpoint, new homes were springing up in the fields, traditional Kosovo style, made out of breeze blocks, three stories high with steep sloping roofs to allow the winter snow to slide off easily. Most were unfinished, their owners waiting for more money to be transferred from relatives working overseas. The "peace" had given a new confidence for rebuilding to start, but the scars of the deep-seated divisions were still evident along the roadside as every few miles the taxi took him past the fortified enclaves of Serb homes and Orthodox churches, each protected by razor wire, six-wheeled armoured cars and soldiers on twenty-four-hour alert.

They passed through the outskirts of Pristina around ten o'clock and turned south-westwards, still following the "Duck" highway. It was a beautiful morning. The sun, shining from behind, bathed the stunning mountains ahead of them in the glorious colours of the early morning. Beyond that impressive skyline lay Albania. A queue of traffic loomed up. They slowed to a crawl. A large truck had lost a wheel and turned on its side, blocking half the carriageway. Its load of timber and cement sacks were strewn over the road. The traffic was inching past slowly, helped as always by the KFOR soldiers who were dealing with the accident. A large army mobile crane was in the process of righting the truck and the British KFOR soldiers were clearing the road with an efficiency that Kosovo would otherwise find hard to match. It was symptomatic that the basic infrastructure of the country was underpinned by the peacekeeping forces. They had to ensure roads and communications were kept open, so they, rather than the local garage breakdown services, were the ones who dealt with the road accident. Kosovo's economy was still artificially buttressed in so many ways.

After passing through the village of Shtime, the British sector gave way to the German sector, which extended up to the border. A routine road checkpoint marked the sector boundary. Another slow-moving line of traffic eased its way through, the soldiers giving perfunctory nods when satisfied there was nothing suspicious in transit. Every so often a vehicle was drawn aside and given rather more intensive attention. Although guns were held at the ready, everything was done in good humour. There was an air of goodwill all round. Most Kosovar people were glad of the calming role of the KFOR forces. It was only those involved in more dubious activity that showed any resentment. Habib felt a measure of anxiety as they approached the white and red striped barrier across the road. He had his story ready. "Going to visit a relative in Dragas who was ill. Coming back on Sunday. Yes, he had his identity card." No problem – the barrier rose upwards and he was waved through with a smile and wished a happy day. Habib's spirits rose a little. Only a small hurdle, but so far so good.

Another 30 kilometres to Prizren – Osman had given him a copy of the town map taken from the election supervisor's manual. The "Duck" route passed through the town centre alongside the river. It was almost midday and much hotter as he heard the muezzin's call to prayer for Friday mosque. His driver seemed to know the road well and made his way through the crowded potholed streets to pick up the main road westwards. From here it was only 20 kilometres to the border control point on the main route to Kukes.

But that was not where Habib was heading. His first stop would be Dragas. They would turn off the main road to the left, seven kilometres before the Morini border crossing and head up into the mountains to Dragas, the largest town – a village really – in the southern triangle of Kosovo territory wedged in between Macedonia and Albania. The road became more treacherous. There was little or no maintenance here. Every so often there were unexpected rock-falls, with steep ravines on either side towards which the unstable verges lent precariously.

After a bumpy nerve-racking half-hour, the taxi drew up in Dragas town square. Prayers were just finishing. There were a few parked cars scattered around. The worshippers leaving the mosque were in relaxed mood in the sunshine and heading for homes or coffee shops. Black crows glided effortlessly between the higher buildings. There was little noise – just a warm contented stillness in the air. It all seemed rather unreal to Habib, who was more used to the hustle and bustle of his home-town and Pristina, the capital. He got out of the taxi and went to the boot for his rucksack.

"That'll be $20," said the driver.

"I thought Osman had paid you!" said Habib.

"Not for the bag – that's extra!" replied the driver.

"Are you serious?"

"Two choices, boy – you pay and get your bag, or you don't!"

The boot was locked. There was really no choice. Habib paid the extra fee and took unceremonious leave of the driver. He had a premonition that this might be the pattern of things to come – he'd better be philosophical and not get too uptight. He would have no natural friends from now on. He was going to have to buy whatever he needed, information, lodging, travel and food. But trust and friendship were not commodities being traded. Contracts for service would be cash-based and short-lived. He had to be under no illusion about that.

In his pocket he had the address in Dragas that Osman had given him, as well as a small map of the village. The streets were not named, but there was a faint cross and a number on the map and that was where he had to go. He had also been given a contact name – a fictitious one – and a coded question. Dragas was not very big, about a kilometre from one end of the village to the other. There was a football pitch not far from the centre and, beyond that, a small block of run-down apartments. He made his way there and climbed the stairwell, dank and dismal even in the heat of the day, and knocked tentatively on the door numbered 12. A middle-aged lady wearing a hijab and ankle-length dress opened it a few inches.

"I've come to see Mr Banjuka about some lessons in German," said Habib, perfectly reciting the lines he had been given by Osman.

The lady looked at him quizzically and then closed the door. Habib felt a small stab of panic. He checked he had the right number and that he was in the right block. There really wasn't anywhere else it could have been except here and the number on the door was as clear as could be. If things had gone wrong at this early stage, he could at least get back to Mitrovice pretty easily and hunt down Osman again. These thoughts were racing through his mind as he stood there feeling very alone when the door reopened and a kind-looking older man wearing a long off-white kaftan greeted him. "Salaam alaikum. I give German lessons. Would you like to come in?"

Habib Peci had made his first contact successfully. He felt a surge of relief and excitement.

Chapter 10

Moldova – Feburary 2001

For three months or more the excitement of embracing the adolescent subculture of Chisinau had been all absorbing. Nina had waxed eloquent to her family how much she was enjoying life and what excellent opportunities there were for her. At work she was using both her languages, Moldovan and Russian, and occasionally even her smattering of English came in handy. Her vibrant outgoing temperament matched the ambience of the DHL office and her colleagues there. Her social life was on a different planet compared to what would have been accessible to her in her home village.

Now, at a stroke, a huge cloud hung over everything, making all else seem counterfeit and ephemeral. Nina had never felt so solitary. The father of her embryonic child had turned out to be an utter shit. There was no possible help coming from his direction. She could not bear the thought of telling her parents. Her new-found friends were self-absorbed. She dare not reveal her predicament to them for fear of losing their respect and friendship. There was only one person to whom she could turn, her brother Pavel. He was a nurse and well connected in the city, having lived there for over three years. He must be able to help her.

They met in a secluded coffee bar away from the main streets. The few other customers there must have thought they were having a lover's tiff as Nina sobbed out her story in hushed tones to her bemused brother.

"What can I do? Do you know anything about abortions? Can it be done secretly? Does it cost an arm and a leg? Should we tell Mum and Dad?"

The flood of questions poured out. Pavel listened sympathetically. That in itself was a comfort to her.

Yes, he did know about these things. Her predicament was not unusual amongst young people in Chisinau. Some women offered a clandestine service in their homes for a fee. That was a risky business. There were horror stories about abortions that had gone wrong. But Pavel knew of a doctor at the hospital where he worked who did provide a professional abortion service.

"Maybe I could arrange for you to see him?" said Pavel. "You could find out whether he's prepared to do it, and how much it would cost."

"Do you think you could fix that up?" asked Nina. "I can't hang about. If it's going to be done, the quicker the better."

"OK," said Pavel. "I'll do that. We don't need to tell Mum and Dad anything – that would just complicate things. Meantime, you just try to rest and get on with your life as normally as possible."

Nina now understood why she was experiencing morning sickness, but that wasn't too debilitating, and after a shower and light breakfast and fresh air on her walk to work, she was usually able to put on a brave face and do what was necessary. Her friends knew she had broken up with her boyfriend. They assumed her deflated mood was because of that. They had all experienced love problems. Sooner or later you got over them and life took on its rosy hue again.

It was a dull Saturday morning as she somberly made her way through the wet slush on the uneven pavements for her appointment with the doctor. A raw cold wind was blowing sleet into her face. The grey Soviet-style blocks forming the bulk of the hospital complex matched her grim mood. An anonymous pair of hands emptied a bucket of slops from an upstairs window into the yard. There was a dead rat caught in a gully of rusting pipes that buried themselves into the bowels of the hospital wall. A steady stream of steam hissed its way out of a fracture in the pipework. This was the most important children's hospital in the whole of Moldova. Its exterior reeked of neglect. Maintenance of even this precious facility attracted no priority because of the parlous state of the country's economy.

Nina was oblivious to all this. She had only one focus as she sat huddled on an iron chair in a nondescript waiting room smelling of disinfectant. The walls were decorated with children's drawings. The dark brown linoleum floor was polished and spotless. The hospital may have been desperately short of drugs and modern medical equipment, but it had in plenty a phalanx of committed

Moldovan women who worked for a pittance to keep the place clean, and cared for the hospitalised children.

A well-built middle-aged rosy-cheeked lady in a blue smock self-importantly ushered Nina into the adjacent office. At the other side of the desk sat the doctor himself. He was small and cadaverous, with a pasty face that seldom saw the sunlight, and black greasy hair combed flat on his head. Two days of beard growth emphasised his sallow complexion. There were dark rings under his eyes. It was hard to comprehend that it was probably this man's skills that would determine Nina's future.

Introductions were perfunctory. Nina didn't catch his name so forever referred to him simply as "the doctor". He understood she was pregnant. He would have to do his own tests to verify that. They would cost $20. He could take samples today – she could have the results in two days' time. If pregnancy was confirmed he could perform an abortion. There would be an initial payment of $100. He would then admit her to a small ward in the hospital. The final balance of his fee was $200, which would have to be paid before the operation. If the tests confirmed she was two months pregnant, as she had said, the abortion should not be problematic. But the sooner it was done the better. Certainly within the next eight weeks.

The doctor delivered the information with cold clinical precision. For him this was not a sentimental exchange. Whatever emotional turmoil the young lady might be in was not his concern. He offered a professional service. She could take it or leave it. He was not short of work. This was the third woman he'd seen this week in the same condition and with the same request. Every year there were millions of abortions across the old Soviet Bloc. It was a way of life where contraceptive devices were scarcely available or too costly. Any moral or emotional baggage around the procedure had long since been outmoded by pragmatism.

The consultation lasted barely fifteen minutes. Nina listened to every word with desperate attention. Confirmation as to whether or not she was pregnant was of prime importance. Nina's next step was crystal clear. She would give a urine sample today. She didn't have the $20 test fee on her, but would leave her wristwatch as security if he would accept that till she came back in two days. He declined her offer, but agreed to do the tests knowing that, like all the others, she would find the money somehow to hear the results. The lady in the blue smock supervised the sample provision, labelled it and confirmed when she should come back.

The same bleak weather greeted Nina as she took her leave down the cracked concrete steps at the hospital entrance. She wrapped her scarf round her face and hunched herself up against the unkind elements. Two days to think and plan. But no final commitment yet. She would tell Pavel all about it tonight. She felt slightly more relaxed for the first time since discovering she was pregnant. She also sensed an easing in her depression as she could now focus on a possible way forward.

Pavel took the call from his sister on his mobile at lunchtime. As on all Saturday evenings, he and his girlfriend expected to be out that evening, enjoying life in the coffee bars and discos. But he agreed to meet Nina later in the afternoon when he had done some shopping.

Nina had five hours to kill. She had no great desire to meet up with friends until she had talked through things with her brother. She mooched along the main boulevard, in and out of the few shops selling clothes and goods she couldn't afford. It served to fill in time and to keep warm. But mostly she sat alone in coffee bars smoking and churning over things in her mind. When Pavel eventually arrived, Nina was more composed than she had expected to be.

"I'm waiting for the test results, but I've no doubt they will be positive. I've got to find $20 to pay for them. Then he wants $300 to perform an abortion. I would need to have it within the next two months. Didn't like him much, but he seems to know what he's talking about. Very matter of fact about it all. I guess he's done hundreds.

"So at least I now know what the choice is. I'm not going to any back-street butcher. Either I cough up $300, or I have the baby and go back home to live with Mum and Dad. Once they get used to it, I'm sure Mum will be delighted to have a baby around. It's happened before and I guess I'd get by. But compared with life here, it will be like going back to prison. I'm not sure I could stand that. The baby would be OK, but I'd go mad.

"But where the hell do I find $300 in a few weeks? It'd take me nearly a year to earn that amount. I suppose I could borrow it, but everyone seems to think the guys that lend money just rip you off. Until I can get hold of that sort of money, I don't have any choice, and I might as well start packing up to go back home."

"Well," said Pavel, "I don't have any spare money. Nor do my friends. But there are some blokes around, and women too, who seem to be loaded. I could make enquiries and see if anyone's got any ideas how you could lay your hands on a loan that could be repaid slowly – say at $2 a week for three years. Sounds a long time, but I guess you should be able to find other ways of earning extra money so you could pay it off quicker."

Nina drew hard on her cigarette. Her emotions were boiling over. "Fuck it, fuck it, fuck it! Why the hell am I in this mess? How do these other guys have so much cash around? I'd like to shove Ion's balls down his throat. So bloody confident he wouldn't come inside me! Now he just pisses off – leaves me in the shit and presumably is shagging around somewhere else to his heart's content! What in God's name can I do?"

"One step at a time, little sis," said Pavel, trying to soothe her down. "We might be able to raise the money. We've got a few days to try to sort something out. Why don't you come with us tonight? It'll be good to get out and about. No harm in having a few drinks and a laugh and we'll keep our ears and eyes open to see if anyone has contacts that could help. No worries about bumping into Ion. He'll run a mile if he sees you. Go back and get ready. Forget about this lot for tonight and have a good time. Meet us at seven o'clock inside the Hard Rock coffee bar. That OK?"

"You're a hero, Pavel. Don't know what I'd do without you. I really do need a good laugh and some company. I guess when you think about it, I can't get pregnant twice at the same time, can I?"

For the first time in their last two meetings they laughed out loud, together, at what she had said. Maybe tonight would be a turning point.

Nina still had her enviable figure. Two months of pregnancy had not yet affected her waistline. She paid a quick visit to a hairdresser on the way back to her flat. Black was the "in" colour. She showered and slipped into her best black slightly flared linen trousers. Her black top clung snugly round her nubile breasts, leaving a tantalising inch of bare midriff between it and the top of her trousers. She made up her face with an enthusiasm she had lost over the last few days. A silver chain crucifix round her neck and a low-slung big buckled belt round her waist complemented her high-heeled black-patent leather shoes. She was ready to go out on the town. It was not her nature to be down in the dumps. She threw her long black coat over her shoulders and went out into Chisinau's freezing evening air. Tonight she would prove to herself that she was not going to give in.

Pavel and Tanya took good care of her. Tanya knew that Nina's friendship with Ion had exploded unceremoniously. Nina wasn't sure whether she knew about the rest but that was no hindrance as they met up with their friends first in the coffee bars and then in the disco clubs. The music was loud, the laser lights garish, and the atmosphere thick with smoke, noise and sweat. And the alcohol flowed.

Nina plunged into it with reactive enthusiasm and the ambience quickly anaesthetised her deep-seated worries. She danced with abandon, she clung closely to the young men who wrapped themselves around her, she drank whatever was offered, and she laughed. And at the end of the evening, inebriated, hot and carefree, knowing her last escort was expecting the full works, she had no inhibitions in letting him take her. For the first time she could enjoy herself without the frustration of a withdrawal at the climactic moment. "You can't get pregnant twice at the same time" kept ringing happily through her mind as his arms clung tightly round her. She hardly remembered his name, but what did that matter? She had had a good time. Tomorrow she might have a sore head, who cared?

They were round the back of the disco hall, standing in a darkened doorway. It was a chilly evening but she had kept her long coat around her, her trousers and pants pushed down, somewhat inelegantly, below her knees to facilitate their coupling. It was so much more easy for men. A quick zip was all they had to do.

"You were great, Nina," said her companion as he nuzzled into her neck, "Really great!"

"Thanks. You were great too," said Nina as she regained her composure and adjusted her lower garments into respectable mode.

The alcohol had dulled her brain cells so it took a while for what he had said to sink in. She had no recollection of ever meeting him before this evening, nor being introduced. But he was well turned-out, very sure of himself, a good dancer, probably ten years older than she, and not short of money. He was only the second person in her life she made love to properly. She had no regrets, but what had he said?

"How the hell do you know my name?" she asked quizzically.

"I've a good friend who knows your brother. We were at the bar together earlier. Your brother seemed to think you had need of some money, so I thought I ought to get to know you. Maybe I could help?"

"Well you certainly got to know me!" exclaimed Nina. The excitement and distractions of Saturday night in Chisinau were now rapidly dissipating into more sober conversation.

"If you're interested in what I have to offer, meet me tomorrow afternoon at 3:00 p.m. with a clear head in the front lobby of Hotel Dukro, near the Government buildings. They are some leather sofas just to the left inside the main entrance. I'll be there with a friend. You can bring your brother if you like, but you may prefer to discuss things privately. That's up to you. Do you know where it is?"

Nina knew the hotel. Her office frequently delivered packages there for visiting business people. Nothing ventured, nothing gained. Nothing to lose as far as she could see. She agreed to be there to hear what he had to say. They wandered back to the front of the disco hall. It was 2:00 a.m. and most people were wending their way homewards. Nina declined her new lover's offer of a lift home. It would have been nice, but probably a bit risky at such an early stage. Pavel and Tanya had waited for her. The three of them walked – taxis cost money – to their respective homes in a happy mood through the darkened streets of the raw-cold sleeping city.

They talked at length about the evening and Nina was teased about the young men she had danced with, not least the one she had spent some time with round the back. But some premonition held Nina back from revealing all that had been said. For the present her visit to the Hotel Dukro tomorrow would be her own closely guarded secret. If her head would stop spinning, she would sleep soundly tonight.

PART 2

EXIT STRATEGY

Chapter 11

Leicester – January 2004

In western cultures the institution of marriage has taken a bit of a beating in recent years. Commitments "for good or ill, for richer or poorer, in sickness and in health, till death us do part" are no longer in vogue. In the United Kingdom over half of the new partnerships between men and women are outside the formal bonding of marriage in either a civil or a religious format. In conformity with the spirit of the age, a commitment to anything or anyone longer than is personally convenient to the individual is deemed unnecessary. Trust should be the bonding glue that holds relationships intact – no need for any overlay of religious ceremony or statutory documents. They diminish, so it is said, rather than enhance the liaison.

Of course the world of commerce and business is rather more prudent. The panoply of the legal profession depends on the absolute prerequisite that commitments need to be bound by written contract duly signed and transparent. No sentimental reliance here solely on trust. Hard experience has shown that trust is fine when the going is good, but when things turn sour, a formal contractual basis for relationships and business is hugely important in working to resolve difficulties.

The Clayton's marriage, now of twelve years' standing, had been pretty good all round. Apart from childhood ailments, occasional misunderstandings and the odd mishaps with cars or in the house, nothing of major consequence had disturbed the steady and happy ambience of their family life. That is, until now.

As Peter sank wearily into the kitchen chair in front of his beans on toast, Jenny was not at all sure whether her husband was in some sort of trouble with the police. If so, that would be potentially devastating for his job prospects, their marriage, and ultimately the children's future. Or he might be suffering from some sort of mental breakdown, which would also have distressing repercussions on the measured security and prospects for the family. Peter meanwhile was trying to come to terms with a morning of confusion, distress and bewilderment. He needed a sympathetic listening ear while he tried to sort things out in his own mind.

In such moments of crisis the age-long strengths of the marriage bond come in to play. Jenny and Peter both knew that they would support each other. Whatever else might be invading the gentle normality of their lives, be it mental or physical, they would tackle it together. That said, there were many questions to address.

Peter, with both hands gripped round a sustaining cup of tea, bent forward over the kitchen table to help focus his thoughts, and began his story. He showed Jenny the statement he had prepared at the police station and while he finished off an apple, two chocolate biscuits, and drank a second cup of tea, she read through the written document intently.

Peter amplified the text here and there. Jenny inwardly digested the saga of events. However bizarre and incredible things might seem, she was prepared to believe Peter was not hallucinating. Out there something serious was going on, but which, so far, the police had no reason to pursue. Jenny's protective instincts were mobilised to try to identify where and how her husband's story could be validated by some objective criteria. Peter was still in a mild state of shock, trying desperately to reconcile two apparently irreconcilable scenarios: one the vivid, ghastly sight of Michael's body when he first saw it, and the other, the complete and utter normality of the same office so soon afterwards.

The most recent piece of confusing information concerned Michael Burton's company car. Peter was adamant it had been in the firm car-park when he arrived there at 10:30 a.m. that morning. Jenny had no reason to doubt his word on that. But the Stansted Airport police were now saying that at 1:00 p.m. on the same day it was parked in the long-stay park there. The obvious question was whether it was realistically feasible to get from Leicester to Stansted in that slot of time. A rapid search of the family road atlas soon verified that a drive along the A47 to join the A1 near Stamford, then southwards on the dual carriageway to the Alconbury junction to turn onto the M11 would bring you to Stansted easily within two hours. Yes, it was perfectly possible if someone were sufficiently organised and determined.

The rather more baffling question mark lay on the movements of Peter's car that morning. Again, he was unequivocal. He had driven himself to the factory premises in his own car. How else could he have got there? What happened then and how it came to be back in their own drive he could give no explanation.

"Do you still have the keys?" asked Jenny. It was an obvious question, but one that had, so far, not occurred to Peter in view of all the other dramatic stimuli that had been invading his mind that morning.

"Yes, I'm sure I do. They should be in my anorak pocket. I put them there after I locked the car when I left it in the car-park. I remember checking I'd locked it properly because it was such an open and isolated area."

Jenny got up and fetched his coat from the hall cupboard. Peter felt in the pockets. He found his mobile phone in the pocket where he expected to find his keys, but there was a singular absence of keys. Belatedly it dawned on them both that if Peter did not have the keys and the car had been driven back to their house somehow, there was a significant likelihood that the keys were still in the car and probably had been all morning while Jenny was furiously trying to make alternative arrangements for transport to the football match.

With some apprehension they went outside to look. The car was unlocked. The keys were there in the ignition. They were undoubtedly Peter's keys; it was his own key ring carrying an image of St Christopher bearing the infant on his shoulders. The discovery was both a relief and yet a further puzzle. But Jenny was determined to get to the bottom of how this could be. She did not believe in miracles or magic. There must be some way of explaining how this had all happened.

There was, of course, another scenario, albeit difficult to contemplate, that Peter may have had a black-out or memory lapse. He could have left the keys in the car himself, and travelled to the plastics factory by taxi or some other means. To confirm his account, it was crucial to establish that the car had actually been driven that morning, and had not stood unused in their driveway since last night. First they had to try to work out what might or could have happened to the car keys.

Painstakingly they went over the details again together – when he had arrived at the factory, Peter locked his car, and put the keys in his pocket, yes, probably in the same pocket as his mobile phone. Yes, he did take the phone out of his pocket while he was in the office where he had discovered the body. Yes, he was in a panic and could well have dragged out the keys at the same time. Yes, he did walk into the foyer while preoccupied and talking to the police on the mobile. Yes, the call did last about ten minutes while he tried to explain everything. No, he didn't go back into the office. Yes, he did dictate to the police on the phone his full name and address. Yes, he was agitated and probably speaking in loud tones, so if anyone was in the vicinity they could have overheard him. No, he hadn't thought about the keys again till Jenny had prompted him a few minutes earlier.

However improbable, there was the possibility that Peter had inadvertently dropped his keys while making the emergency call. A person hiding in the office could then have picked them up while Peter was in the foyer and used them to drive his car back to the address they had heard him dictate slowly over the phone to the police.

Why this should have been done was still a mystery, but a sinister interpretation was beginning to emerge. Peter's presence at the plastics factory that morning, for someone at least, was probably a grave embarrassment. The return of his car to his home would have removed that part of the evidence of his visit. Dreadful though it was to contemplate, the elimination of Peter himself, in a manner similar to the elimination of Michael Burton, would have removed the other evidence of his presence there. The speedy arrival of the police cars and ambulance might just have saved his life.

The AA breakdown services spend much of their time answering routine calls from stranded motorists whose problems are more often than not of their own making - poor car maintenance, worn tyres, run-down batteries, broken windscreen wipers, empty petrol tanks. The Leicestershire AA control room were therefore agreeably surprised to receive a phone call that afternoon from one of their members, a Mr Peter Clayton, enquiring if there was any way to verify if a vehicle had been used within the last few hours. Mr Clayton explained that his car had been parked overnight outside his house in the drive. It was still there, but he wished to establish whether it had been moved and driven a few miles some three hours earlier.

"Well, Mr Clayton, it shouldn't be difficult," came the confident response. "If your car has been out all night and not been moved since, the engine oils will be at today's very cold temperature. In that case the temperature gauge on your dashboard will be at its lowest. The engine oil will be cold, and very viscous. If you examine the oil on the dip-stick it will feel warm and runny, if the car's been used. I hope that's some help. Glad to be of service. May I just ask while you're on the phone whether you've taken up our latest cut-price insurance offer for valued members?"

Peter thanked him for his help – no, he didn't need extra insurance cover. What he did need to do was to get out to the car quickly to test the engine-oil temperature. First turn on the ignition without starting the engine and see if the temperature needle moved. Not much, but there was definitely a slight elevation above the zero mark. Now the bonnet – yes, a residual warmth from the engine. Now the dipstick – very oily and dripping freely off the end onto a piece of kitchen tissue. And there was no doubt that the oil felt warmer than the water in their cold tap.

It had not taken long. It had been pretty basic physics after all, but it was sufficient to satisfy both Peter and Jenny that the Golf had been used that morning. At the very least that confirmed for Peter another small but vital piece of the jigsaw of his version of the morning's events.

Although the wider significance was by no means clear, Peter was beginning to feel calmer in himself as he became increasingly aware that he was probably the only witness to something fatally serious in Leicester that morning. But now that he and Jenny were no longer anxious about the state of his mental health, how could he convince anyone else, the police in particular, that something was amiss?

The children's cartoon had finished. They had eaten their chocolate-spread sandwiches and ice cream lollies and were besieging the kitchen making further reflection and analysis on the day's events somewhat tricky.

"We're going over to see Simon and Freddy at Auntie Margaret's for tea. Why don't you go upstairs to your room and watch Stars Wars again?" The DVD player was a convenient de facto baby-sitter. Peter and Jenny still had other issues to pursue while things were fresh in their minds. The most obvious was to try to understand how Peter could be so convinced that the body in the office was that of his squash colleague while apparently RyanAir were flying Michael Burton to Rome at the same time.

"We could try his PA to see if she can throw any light on what's transpired. How long had she known Michael was going to Rome? When did he book his flights? Does she know where he is staying? Is there any way he can be contacted? A few answers to those questions might give us some clues. How do you contact him when you try to fix up a game of squash?" asked Jenny.

"By ringing him at home or on his mobile. Of course, why didn't I think of that before?" No need to involve his PA at this stage. The squash club members were issued with a club booklet at the beginning of each season with contact numbers for everyone so they can arrange their games. With some degree of apprehension Peter phoned his home number. He and Michael were not in the same league so did not often play each other. This was probably the first time he had phoned him at home for some months.

"Hello, Shirley Burton speaking."

"Oh hello, I was trying to get in touch with Michael about squash. I wonder if he's around?"

"You don't seem very up to date, I'm afraid. Michael moved out of here three months ago. As far as I know he's living in a flat above some shops somewhere. I don't think he's on the phone there, but he has a mobile. I can't help you much more. What he's doing with himself these days is his own business!"

"Oh I'm so sorry to have troubled you. I do have his mobile number so I'll try him on that. I apologise if I've caused any distress. Goodbye."

Michael Burton might have been doing well in his business life and he was pretty proficient on the squash court, but it was apparent that his domestic life had gone sour, and that quite recently. It was also clear his wife was in no position to give any help in deciphering today's events. But at least there was the possibility of contacting him on his mobile – that was of course assuming Peter had been mistaken in thinking the body he had seen was indeed Michael's. If it wasn't, that opened up another can of worms, but first things first. He dialled his mobile.

"This is the telephone answering service for the mobile phone assigned to Polymer Plastics. At the beep please record your message. If you wish to record a further message press 1..."

Peter hung up. They seemed to have reached a dead-end in trying to make phone contact. What else could they do? It would still be useful to talk to Michael's PA, but there was no particular urgency in that. It might alarm her unnecessarily if he contacted her at the weekend, and, in any case, it would probably be better to wait till Monday, when she might notice anything unusual in the course of her working day.

They still needed to find some objective corroboration of what Peter had witnessed on his first visit to the Michael Burton's office that fateful morning. He and Jenny had mulled over that aspect from various angles. The partially open door, the live computer, the overturned chair, the wastebin on its side, the lethal wires, the charred plug, and the grotesque sight of Michael's prone body with those lifeless staring eyes, and then, barely twenty minutes later, all was normal. There must be some clue in there somewhere to corroborate the terrifying sight that had greeted Peter's arrival on such a mundane mission.

"How charred was the plug?" asked Jenny, "Can you picture it?"

"More than vividly. I winced when I thought of the huge charge of electricity that must have surged through his body. The charring at the plug was testimony to that. I assumed the plug must have been loaded with a heavy-duty fuse to cause such burning before it fused."

"If the plug was so burned, wouldn't the wall socket also show some signs of charring as well?" asked Jenny.

"I'm sure it would, but when I went back into the office, I was so transfixed at not seeing the body and everything else being set back to normal, I never thought to look at the wall socket. I wonder if that could be the vital clue that might make the police take what I have told them more seriously? Perhaps I should ring them again and see what they say? Why not? O'Malley did say I should get in touch if I thought of anything else they ought to know."

Police stations are of course manned on shift patterns. Detective Sergeant Crabtree and D.C. O'Malley went off shift at 2:00pm. "Sorry, sir, - they should be back on the early shift on Monday morning if you want to speak to one of them, or can anyone else help?" asked the duty officer.

It seemed that they were going to have to bide their time till Monday morning at least. In the meantime, it grieved Peter to think that if Michael Burton had indeed met with a violent death, the perpetrators were gaining more and more time to obliterate their tracks.

"I don't think we can do much more today, Jenny. I just want to sink back with a whisky and chill out for the rest of the day. Are you OK to take the children off to Margaret's on your own?"

The children were duly summoned and coated up, not without some shrill complaints that they were being dragged away from a "very exciting bit" in Star Wars. Peter went out ahead of them to move his car so Jenny could get hers out of the garage for the first time that day. He opened the doors, gave Jenny a peck on the cheek and helped pile the two boys into the back safety seats.

"Aren't you coming with us, Daddy?" asked Robert, the younger of the two.

"No," said Peter, "I'm feeling tired and want to watch the football results on the telly."

He began closing the rear door of the car when Robert continued "Daddy, who was that funny man who brought your car home this morning?"

Chapter 12

Kosovo – October 2003

In the book *Surprised by Joy* by C. S. Lewis, the author makes the point that real joy is spontaneous and unexpected. It is also elusive and ephemeral. The mere process of reflecting on it, examining it, and analysing it automatically evaporates the emotion. Joy exists like an electron. It is there, but disappears the moment the focus falls on it. The actual act of seeking it changes its nature, and it is gone.

It was such an emotion, spontaneous and unexpected, that Habib felt as he was welcomed into the home of Mr and Mrs Banjuka, though it was doubtful whether this was their real name. He was shown into a spacious, sparsely furnished living room. The afternoon sun was streaming in through the west-facing windows. Beyond he could see the mountains majestically silhouetted against the burnished sky. Mr Banjuka invited him to take off his jacket and seat himself on one of the two enormous heavily brocaded sofas in the room, their garish designs clashed with the equally strident colours and patterns on the rugs strewn across the floor. But this was Kosovo's style and Habib felt comfortably at home. Both his hosts were barefoot and in conformity with their custom Habib had also taken off his shoes and left them at the threshold.

Mr Banjuka arranged himself on the other sofa with one leg curled contentedly under him. He was wearing a long faded white kaftan and the traditional Albanian qeleshe, a white cap, on his head. While his wife proffered a glass of cold fanta orange and a large slice of lemon cake, topped with a sticky sugar coating, Mr Banjuka welcomed their guest, praying that many blessings be upon him.

Habib had not expected such kindness and hospitality. He felt an emotional surge of relief, a sense of elation and release from anxiety. His experience with the taxidriver and Osman's dire warnings had prepared him to expect the worst. The chances were that the key contacts along his route would be unsavoury and unsympathetic, the sort of people normally best kept at a distance. But here in this simple home, Mrs Banjuka was treating him like his mother would, and her husband was a model of benign hospitality.

"All travellers are welcome here," said Mr Banjuka. "We wish you Allah's protection in the name of His Prophet, Mohammed, blessings be on his name. You must take your ease now. You have a long and arduous road to travel. The way will sometimes be hard, but your faith in the merciful Allah will keep you from falling.

"After you have finished your refreshment, you should rest on a bed. This evening we will take food together, and then my son will show you the way into the mountains. They are the eternal hills and you will take strength and comfort from them if you respect their dignity and the power of their Creator. When you follow the way of goodness and prayer, the tracks will lead you to peace and prosperity."

After Habib had eaten a second slice of cake, Mrs Banjuka showed him into a small room with a narrow bed. Mr Banjuka went to the front door, picked up Habib's shoes and brought them to him.

"Remember, my son, when travelling upon unknown paths among unknown people, never leave your possessions unattended."

Habib's heart missed a beat. For five years he had worked all the hours he could to earn a pile of money. The bulk of that was now secreted in the soles of his shoes. And he had idly left them at the door without so much as a thought. Never again must he be so careless.

As soon as the door to his room closed, he tied the shoes to his rucksack and then placed that on the bed as a pillow. It was just after 3:00 p.m. Mr Banjuka had told him to get as much rest as possible. He had a long night ahead when sleep was not likely to be on his agenda. He lay back on his makeshift pillow and relaxed as well as he could. It was only a few hours since he had left home, but already he was mentally, even if not physically, far away. He felt secure here, and lay wondering what was next in store. His eyes closed and it was with a start he was woken by gentle tapping on the door.

"Peace be with you! We would like you to take food with us, Mr Peci."

It was already seven o'clock and a delicious smell of lamb stew greeted him as he joined his hosts at their table. He was famished. Except for the slices of cake, he had not eaten since breakfast. He had not forgotten about the food his mother had packed for him, bread, tomatoes, bananas and biscuits, but that he would save for when he really needed it.

Mr Banjuka thanked Allah for their food and, as they ate, explained what the next steps were to be. His son would arrive shortly with a companion and would drive Habib up into the mountains in a four-wheel-drive truck. This would take him to the border crossing point. They would get there just after dark. The crossing was at the highest point of the pass through the mountains. From there the track descended westwards for about ten kilometres before joining the Prizren-Kukes main road. After that he would have another five kilometres walk to his next scheduled rendez-vous in the town of Kukes. Osman had already given him the address and contact code.

"They are expecting you to arrive in the morning." Mr Banjuka told him. "You will be walking downhill most of the time, so it will not be too tiring. But the track is stony and uneven. You will have to tread warily in the dark. Your ankles will ache. The walking will take about four hours, but you are young and strong and Allah will protect you.

"You rest when you feel tired. If you hear any trucks or people, you must stop and hide until it is safe to go on. Use your torch only when essential. Make no noise. Keep drinking water and eat if you are hungry.

"You must arrive in Kukes in the daylight. So you walk in the dark till you reach the main road. Then you stay hidden there till the sun is well up. As soon as the road is clear, start walking the last five kilometres. That will take only an hour or so. Plan to be in Kukes by about nine o'clock and go straight to the safe house."

Habib took it in. He ate heartily. At nine o'clock the noise of a vehicle outside signalled the arrival of his escort and transport. He thanked his hosts profusely and offered them gifts of cigarettes and a DVD. But they neither smoked, nor had any facility for playing a DVD. So instead he offered them a ten dollar note. They accepted it gladly and told him it would be placed in a tin box under their bed where they were gathering money to finance their planned trip to Mecca, their life's ambition and duty to visit the holiest of the holy shrines of Islam.

It was a treacherous drive up into the mountains. His escort's Mitsubishi Shogun was travelling without headlights. They were barely able to get out of second gear. The vehicle bounced from rut to rut, boulder to boulder. The wheels spun and skidded on the loose gravel. The dark mountain sides sloped sheer and forbiddingly upwards on one side of the truck, and, on the other, they plunged away into the black vastnesses of the valleys below. Habib clung to the handgrip above his head with one hand and held firmly onto the seat in front with the other. He kept his body relaxed so he swayed in sympathy with the unpredictable lurches and bumps. The 4x4 ground its way yard by yard up the steep ascent.

After twenty minutes of unremitting bouncing, the Mitsubishi took a right turn off the track into a clearing, which had evidently once been a marble quarrying site, probably in the days of a united Yugoslavia under President Tito, now abandoned. In the half-light of the truck's sidelights, the old quarry workings were still visible, all in a state of irremedial decay. Here and there were huge lumps of rough-hewn marble forlornly waiting for aborted transport to destinations across Europe. They parked the truck carefully behind the derelict buildings well obscured from the track they had just left. The sidelights and engine were turned off, windows opened, and cigarettes lit up. They waited in the quiet of the cooling, sleeping mountain. The sky was clear, the stars vivid in the heavens and the moon just beginning to rise. Only the noises from distant birds in the forest broke the pervading silence.

"OK, we wait here," explained his escort. "The border crossing has two guards. They close and lock the barrier at dark. Then they come down the mountain for the night. No trucks can get through till the next shift goes up to open the crossing point next morning at daybreak. But it's no problem to walk through by the customs huts. Sometimes the barrier is left unlocked. That's when the guards have been bribed so a truck can go through unnoticed at the dead of night. Tonight it will be locked. No traffic will come through till tomorrow."

After time to smoke two cigarettes the sound of a vehicle engine and lights announced that the border guards were on their way down. They ground past the abandoned quarry in second gear without a glance, intent only on reaching their homes in Dragas as soon as possible. When the last vestiges of their vehicle's noise and lights had disappeared the Mitsubishi gently eased out from the security of the derelict buildings and began the final two miles of tortuous ascent.

It was no less hairy than the first stage. They passed a small hamlet, the village of Orchusa, where, a year earlier, the inhabitants had strongly objected to the opening of this border crossing, because Albanians were allegedly crossing illegally into Kosovo, and threatening their own local market profits. A dog yapped in the night, and there was a glimmer of light in a few windows, but otherwise there was no sign of life. Another arduous fifteen minutes of driving ensued until they reached a clearing on a small plateau where the customs post was situated. The rusty red-and-white-striped metal barrier marked the end of the road for the truck. The crossing point was deserted.

Habib jumped down, much relieved that that part of the journey was over. He fished out two packets of cigarettes from the rucksack, gave them to his escorts, thanked them and bid them farewell. The truck did a three-point turn in the clearing and set off for its cautious descent. Habib watched it disappear from his life. When he could no longer see its rear lights, he hitched his rucksack onto both shoulders to distribute the weight evenly. He then slipped round the border barrier, which posed no deterrent to pedestrians, and set off on the track beyond to begin his descent down the western side of the mountain. It was much colder at this altitude. He was glad of his jumper and leather jacket. In a few weeks the winter weather would set in and this pass would become snowbound. It was eerily quiet. The moon was shining wispily through the high-blown clouds. The trees stood dark and sombre, towering above him on both sides of the track. There was barely a breath of wind.

He carried his torch in his hand, using it as sparingly as possible. Once his eyes had adjusted to it, the faint moonlight was sufficient to pick out his path. The track was wide enough for vehicles, so not difficult to follow. The only real problem was avoiding twisting his ankle in the ruts and potholes. He made steady progress. He had had a rest in the afternoon, a good evening meal and it was still only 11 p.m. He felt fit and it was mainly downhill. His spirits were high, but it would be a long walk.

He had gone no further than a mile or so when he heard the intermittent barking of dogs. He pressed on cautiously and began to discern the outline of more houses towards the side of the road. He had been told this would be the Albanian village of Orgjoshte.

It suddenly dawned on him that he was actually now walking in Albania, the first time in his life he had been outside his native Kosovo. It was an odd feeling, because it felt no different, yet he was now an illegal immigrant in a foreign country, a status that would prevail for he knew not how long.

He trod quietly past the dormant village and after 45 minutes following the valley downwards he came to the T-junction where he knew he had to turn northwards, to his right, to head to where the track would, in due course, intersect with the main road. So far, so good. Time for a short rest, a drink of water and a chance to take off his shoes to give his feet a breather. He checked the polythene envelopes inside the insoles to ensure his precious dollar bills were still intact, and not spoilt by the rigours of the walk. No problem.

The moon had sunk below the horizon again and the night seemed so much blacker. He needed to use his torch more frequently, and his progress was decidedly slower. Even so, it was still the early hours of the morning and he had plenty of time to reach his destination, even walking slowly. He stumbled a number of times and slipped backwards once, grazing his hand slightly as he broke his fall. He licked it clean and sucked the blood off, held his hand above his head for a few minutes till the bleeding stopped and carried on the descent as the track continued to follow the line of the valley downwards. He was feeling more weary now. He had walked for over two hours. He decided to take a second break – more water and one of the bananas his mother had packed for him. He thought longingly of home as he rested against the rocks on the roadside in the inky stillness around him. He gave his feet another breather and closed his eyes. There was still a gnawing anxiety that he might have taken a wrong track somewhere in the darkness, so it was not possible to relax properly. Adrenalin was still pumping through him, and he had no desire to sleep, not yet anyway.

He pressed on. It was about half an hour later that he first saw the occasional lights of vehicles in the distance. He reckoned they must be on the main road. If so, he was on the right track and nearing the intersection. His subliminal anxiety receded. With each step he could now see the distance to this critical junction steadily decreasing. The track began to level out and the junction was now barely ten minutes' walk away. It was still pitch dark and far too early to arrive in Kukes. He had to find somewhere to hide up till daybreak, as close to the road as he dared go. It would be foolhardy to use his torch. In any event the beam shone no more than a few yards and that was not much use in searching for a sheltered hideaway. He walked on slowly, peering around for shelter. At last he found what he looking for – a tumbledown hut on the outskirts of a field, probably used for farm labourers to rest in during the heat of the day. He used his torch pointing directly downwards, with his fingers over the lens to reduce its glow, and made his way along the side of the field to the hut. It smelled of musty hay and dried corn. Its decaying roof had numerous holes but there was no rain so that didn't matter to Habib. A piece of rusty old farm machinery, almost overgrown with weeds, occupied the majority of the space, but there was enough room for him to lie down on the soft surface of old hay. He was well hidden from the track. It was about 3:30 a.m. He would wait for three hours or so. By then the sun would be up and he could gauge when it was best to leave his hidey-hole and complete the final leg of his trek. The most arduous part was over. He had survived that without too much trouble. He could now rest up and hopefully relax for a few hours. He closed his eyes and dozed off.

Chapter 13

Moldova - February 2001

From the outside, the Hotel Dukro looks impressive. It stands eight storeys high. There are up to forty rooms on each floor and those overlooking the Stefan the Great Public Park have private balconies. From the higher floors there are pleasing views towards the white stone Government buildings, and the city-centre parks. The tired and battered taxis standing on the road outside the main entrance somewhat diminish the impact, and unwittingly serve as an appropriate foretaste of the dated, drab interior.

Ten years after independence, and with its economy in bad shape, Moldova still struggled to shed its Soviet heritage and attitudes. The hotels in Chisinau reflected that. The entrance foyer in Hotel Dukro was vacuous and bland. The pervading gloominess was because half the lights were not functioning, either because no-one could afford new bulbs or as a crude means of saving on electricity bills. The reception desk was mean and the staff working there were preoccupied with running the hotel rather than serving the customer. Western concepts of service had yet to take root.

When Nina arrived she was, nonetheless, glad of the foyer's warmth, happily escaping the freezing temperature outside on such a grey February afternoon. She had slept well, but the morning had been fragile. Doses of black coffee and a few cigarettes had restored her to some sort of normality. In the cool light of day she had to take stock. Unprotected sex might not create a pregnancy problem for her in her present condition, but it did bring other worries. She was glad she had had the good sense to wash herself thoroughly before going to bed and hoped that would be enough.

Then there was the anxiety of what sort of proposition this guy might make. She wanted the money desperately. She was becoming convinced that an abortion was the only realistic option, but that needed a mountain of money. How far was she prepared to go to acquire it? Would he offer to lend it to her at extortionate interest rates? Would he want her to do something criminal or fraudulent? Maybe he had an exciting job she could do? At least she hadn't committed herself to anything yet. She could always go back to discuss it with Pavel if she was in a quandary.

Her anonymous new friend was lounging on a tired sofa, which had seen better days, in an alcove some distance away from the reception desk. There was an unemptied ashtray of cigarette butts on the much-marked coffee table in front of him. He was wearing tight black jeans and an expensive black leather jacket. Around his neck, loosely draped, was a long grey woollen scarf. He had a fine head of stylish black hair, a strong handsome face, with more colour than most city-dwelling Moldovans managed in the depth of the winter months, and keen alert eyes that spoke of worldly wisdom. The only unoccupied car parked outside was a gleaming black series 3 BMW with darkened windows. Nina assumed it was his. It matched his self-assurance and composure. By comparison with this guy, Nina reluctantly conceded that the young men in her own group of friends, including Ion and Pavel, were but callow provincials.

Beside him, equally impressive, was a sophisticated young woman probably nearing thirty years old. She sat forward on the sofa, knees together, the ash from her cigarette contributing to that already in the overfull ashtray. Her hair was tinted and swept back, carefully contoured but casual. She wore a tight black designer leather skirt that showed off the mature shape of her elegant legs. They in turn were sheathed in fishnet stockings through which could be seen the tattoo of small seahorse on her right ankle. There was a thin silver chain around her other ankle. Contrasting chicly with her lower garments she wore a high-buttoned blouse in rich gold coloured brocade that complimented rather than emphasised her upper figure. Around her shoulders was a dark coat, slung nonchalantly. Her fingernails and toenails were varnished in dark translucent purple which had something of the night about it. Her face was lightly bronzed – quite out of character for Moldovan girls generally – and her lipstick matched her nail varnish.

Nina knew that her mother would have immediately labelled this woman as a tart. Such women provoked feelings of disgust and irritation mingled with an uncomfortable sense of envy that they so patently attracted the admiring glances of their menfolk, and, no doubt, much more when their wives' backs were turned. Nina felt somewhat intimidated by her, but that was soon swept away by the warmth of their greeting and the evident interest that they showed in her.

The light lunch she had eaten had steadied her morning's nausea and she was happy to accept the offer of a beer despite the time of day. She sat opposite them on the other side of the coffee table and was guiltily conscious that, somewhere buried in her psyche, she felt a measure of pride that this handsome young man had made love to her the night before. It gave her some leverage in their encounter today, which made her feel less out of depth than might otherwise have been the case.

"Your brother said you were keen to lay your hands on some money. What sort of sum are you looking for?" asked the calmly spoken man.

"I need about $300 and pretty quickly," Nina replied. There seemed no reason to be other than frank.

"That's not too much of a problem, is it? Do you want to tell us what it's for or is that a secret?"

Nina found it hard to comprehend how anyone could be so casual about what for her was nearly a year's wages. These people were clearly working within different financial parameters. But why should she tell them what it was wanted for?

"Well, I guess that's my business. I'm happy to repay the money back as quick as possible. Are you able to lend me some?"

"We don't lend money," he replied.

Her heart sank. What was this all about then?

"Let me be frank with you. We know a lot of girls of your age often need money. We also know the cost of an abortion is about $300. It doesn't take much brain-power to put two and two together to guess why you need the money. If we've got it wrong, you may as well tell us."

Nina thought hard. What was the point of being coy? She nodded her affirmation. Now what would he say?

"OK, we've got that straight. We also know you're eighteen, and we can see you are an attractive young lady. We also know you're pretty vibrant and exciting when you let your hair down, based on last night's evidence!"

Nina wasn't quite sure how to respond to all this. At least it was all complimentary and she ought not to be dismayed by that. But where was all this leading?

"So let's talk in confidence. You can walk away whenever you want – no compulsion on you whatever, but we can offer you a way to earn quick money, and there will be no need to think about paying back. All we do is take some commission on the income you generate. Would you be interested if you could make the $300 you need in less than a month? Indeed, if you worked hard, in less than a week."

Nina gulped down some beer. She was finding it hard to take it all in. The prospect of that amount of money so quickly was barely comprehensible. She was not totally naive. That sort of money only came out of crime, drugs or sex. She was not going to get into crime and drugs were off limits. That left only sex. Ironically, it was sex that had got her into this mess. Could she really contemplate using it to get her out of it? She would keep her thoughts to herself for the moment, and continue to play the innocent.

"How can anyone make that sort of money legally?" she asked rhetorically.

Her companions smiled. "Depends what you mean by legal. But we're not suggesting you do anything to get you into trouble with the police."

"So what?" asked Nina rather belligerently.

"Let's not beat about the bush. You are a very desirable young lady. There are a lot of men out there, and indeed some women, who like to make love to beautiful young girls. And they pay well for the privilege. We could help you set things up and provide security for you. You would do only as much or as little as you want, and when.

"To be frank, we need someone quick. One of our girls has gone down with a bad attack of gastric flu. Another fell over on the ice two days ago and has broken her ankle. So we are two girls short just as were expecting a big surge in business. A week today we have the Parliamentary Elections. On Wednesday about two hundred foreign election observers are due to check into our hotels to monitor the election process. They will be around for a week or so. Some of them will be looking forward to a few days away from their wives and enjoying a fling with a Moldovan girl. We don't want to let them down, especially as they pay so well. We would like you to help us, and at the same time make the money you need to sort out your little problem. So that's it in a nutshell. How does it grab you?"

Nina was reeling inside, but struggled hard not to show it. "Keep calm, Nina. Pretend it's no big deal. Ask a few more questions. Keep them talking while you try to get your head around this," she mused inwardly to herself. She knew about the election, but politics didn't interest her much and she had no idea about the potential influx of international observers.

"Whatever happened last night, I'm not a whore, you know. I've certainly never done anything like this before. How do you know I'd be able to do that sort of thing? Don't you need lots of experience - which I haven't got?"

"Lack of experience isn't a problem. In fact it's an asset! Many men prefer that. And take my word for it, you will have no difficulty in providing what they want. When they meet you, they'll be eating out of your hand."

Nina had not known what to expect when she had agreed to their talk. Now a huge new unknown world was opening up for her, but one which would devastate her parents if ever they came to know she was involved in it. Her brother too would be less than sympathetic, and she could be ostracised by her Chisinau friends if they were to find out. The crucial question was whether she could do this secretly without telling anyone. Perhaps she could earn the necessary money in a few weeks, pay off the doctor, get the abortion, and then be back to normal life again without anyone being any the wiser. Her mind was a whirl of thoughts and emotion, but it was best to give nothing away at this stage and see what else they had to say.

"So what does that mean exactly? Eating out of my hand? How much do people pay for making love like this? How long does it take? How often do you do it? There's lots of questions I need answers to before I could consider such an idea. Money's not everything, you know, and I could probably get it some other way," she said rather haughtily, trying to keep some initiative in the conversation.

"Well maybe you could. That's up to you. We can answer all your questions, but there's no point in wasting more of our time if you're not up for it. We need someone quick. There are others out there we can approach, but you're our preferred choice because we think you've got what it needs and could do it OK. Do we fuck off now or do you want to hear more?"

Nina knew in her bones that finding the money elsewhere would be a nightmare. Why not hear them out so she could get a fuller picture? There was a quiver of realisation in her that, in spite of her dismay at the prospect, in the absence of any other alternative, she might be persuaded that a short-term stint could be the answer.

"Why don't you tell me more about what it would involve? Can't really decide 'till I know what's it like, can I?"

"Fine. Let's get down to more serious business. We know your name. Time you knew ours. I'm Stefan. This is Zvetlana. I provide security and organise things. Zvetlana and a few other girls do the business. We'll answer your questions, but we'd better make it clear from the start that we don't take kindly to anyone who breaks the rules. I'm sure you understand that. We can make things pretty difficult for those that do. Usually families are not at all thrilled to hear the things their darling daughter has been up to. So we start from a basis of confidentiality and trust. OK? Any questions on that?"

Nina was surprised and alarmed as the velvet glove became momentarily transparent to reveal the iron fist inside. But she knew this clandestine world was no children's party and in any event would not expect to play other than by the rules if she did decide to join in.

"I guess I've got lots of questions," she said, "and I still need lots of answers. This is all outside my experience, you know. I'm going to have to think hard about it all before I can make any decisions. You want someone in the next few days, so we had better keep talking."

"That sounds good sense. I'll leave you with Zvetlana for an hour or so. She can tell you all you need to know. I'll be back about four thirty."

With that Stefan left. He walked with unashamed assurance through the foyer. She noticed that the receptionists accorded him a deferential nod and smile. He was clearly well known in these parts. It was unclear whether the acquaintance was based on fear or respect.

"I think we need to talk woman to woman," said Zvetlana as she stubbed out the remains of her cigarette. "I've been in this business for ten years. There's not much I don't know about it. So where do we start?

"We work the hotels in Chisinau. Simple stuff. We wait to see a light in someone's room when they've come back to the hotel after a night out. Twenty minutes later, when they've had time for a pee, taken off their tie and shoes and settled on their bed for a read or to watch telly, we phone their room direct. If they say they're interested we go to their room. The hotel receptionists turn a blind eye to us because we keep them sweet with backhanders. Then it's fifteen to twenty minutes with the client. He pays and we go back to the car where Stefan waits for us outside in the carpark. He's always there in case there's any trouble, but that seldom happens. We keep in touch by mobile phone. We give him a retainer - $10 for each client we see. On a good night we expect five or six jobs. We like to have at least two girls working each hotel. How much we charge depends on what the client wants. But you could earn your $300 in less than two weeks even by servicing only one guy a night."

Nina was riveted. She had vague ideas of what went on in this twilight world, but here was this elegant woman rehearsing it all to her in matter-of-fact detail, just as though she were describing the workings of the DHL office.

"Sorry to be so naive, but how much do they pay for making love?"

Zvetlana smiled. "Making love is not the way we describe it – better call it having sex. No kissing and cuddling involved. Just get on with the job and leave at the first opportunity, making sure you've got all your stuff and the money. The cost depends on what they want. There's a simple tariff – hand-job $20, blow-job $30, straight sex $40 and up the arse $50."

"Well the first three are probably OK," said Nina, suddenly feeling embarrassed and self-conscious, "but I'm not going anywhere near the last" .

"No problem, you set the limits – they take it or leave it. If they get stroppy, just walk away or call Stefan. He'll be at the door of the room within minutes with a key from reception so he can get in.

"Let me give you a few other quick tips. You need to take care what you wear. Trousers are no good. They take too much time to get off and on again. So wear a skirt or dress, preferably one that unbuttons down the front. Makes things easier and quicker. Remember, men prefer black or red underwear, and never wear tights. They are a real turn-off. Suspender belts always go down well. Always insist they use a rubber. Take a supply with you in your handbag. Some guys offer to pay more to do it without a rubber, but my advice is never let them. You don't know where they've been before. You also need a tube of moisturising cream – it helps with hand-jobs and any fun in your arse. Keep your mobile close by and switched on with Stefan's number printed in so all you do to call him is press one button. But that's only a precaution. I doubt if I use it more than twice a year.

"Most men are really nice. They treat you well. They appreciate what you do for them and pay up without a murmur. When you arrive they are often more nervous than you are. But once alone with you they soon become over-excited. Even taking things slowly, they will be raring to go and it's unlikely to be more than ten minutes or so before they shoot their load. Then all they want to do is to roll over, fart, smoke a fag, and recoup their energy for a few minutes. That's the time you make your exit. Dress quickly. Grab the money and leave before they've decided they're keen for another go. It's really quite simple. Believe me. There's no easier way to earn money around here. What do you think?"

Nina was struggling to absorb it all. A few months ago she would have run a mile from such an idea in disgust and dismay. Now the seductive logic of the proposition was gradually beginning to take shape in her mind as the quickest, simplest and least disruptive way out her difficulties. The options were no less stark: have the baby and go back home to a primitive lifestyle she could hardly bear to think about, or have an abortion. The only constraint on the latter course, apart from any moral considerations, was finding the money. And here was a solution to that dilemma. If all she was hearing was true and if it worked out well, within a month or so her life could be back on track again. Perhaps she'd be somewhat wiser and chastened, but otherwise things would be as before. That was an enviable prospect.

"So if I did agree to do this to help you out, when would I start?"

"As soon as you like – but certainly we would like you to start not later than Wednesday for the reasons Stefan explained. I guess you need time to think about it. Why not sleep on it tonight? We'll meet again tomorrow in your lunch-break. You just tell me what you want to do then and we'll fix the details. Stefan's just driven up outside, so I'd better be off. See you tomorrow in the Zoe coffee bar about one o'clock. OK?"

They stood up. A perfunctory kiss on the cheeks, a brief handshake and Nina was on her own as the afternoon light faded outside. She sat down again and tried to gather her thoughts. It had been a mind-blowing two hours. Nina Snegur had a tough decision to make. And this time it was one she had to make on her own. A brisk walk home through the chill evening air would probably crystallise the key issues, but in essence, could she or could she not live with the prospect of becoming a whore, even if only for a few weeks? Or did she want a baby at the age of eighteen? The options were clear. She had all the information she needed. It was just the decision that was difficult. A sleepless night was more than likely.

Chapter 14

Albania - October 2003

Albania is a spectacular country, the interior is an intoxicating mixture of snow-capped mountains, precipitous valleys, fresh water lakes, torrents and rivers, while the flat coastal belt borders the Adriatic with a Mediterranean climate and tourist possibilities that could rival the Italian Riviera.

Unfortunately the political, social, cultural and geographic isolation of Albania under the crushing Marxist regime of Enver Hoxha for forty years left Albania's economy and lifestyle locked in a time warp. It also meant that Albania's beauty and potential was a closed book to the rest of the world, except, that is, for the few engineers, first from Russia and then China, who had been given political clearance after the post-war years to come to the country to try to develop its industries. By the 1970s they had all gone home, and, more to the point, had taken their technological skills home with them. The industrial enterprises and factories they had pioneered across Albania, albeit with no regard for the pollution and environmental damage they caused, sank into disrepair and decay. Albania emerged unenviably as the poorest, most backward country in Europe. Even the Kosovar Albanians regarded themselves as a cut above their neighbours.

None of this was of much concern to Habib Peci as he woke with a start at the sound of a tractor noisily chugging its way up the track he had walked along during the night. He moved stealthily to find a crack between the decaying planks of wood that made up the hut he had slept in, so he could see what was happening outside while keeping himself totally hidden. Still as a mouse, but with heart beating fast, he watched the tractor meander toilsomely upwards until it was well out of sight. He relaxed.

Wide awake now, it was time to take stock. His digital watch told him it was shortly after half past six. It was light but the sun had not yet risen over the mountains. The hut lay in shadow on the western slopes. The night had been cold. Habib had not been too conscious of that while negotiating his descent, but now he felt chilled and his legs ached. He guessed it would take another one and a half hours to reach his rendez-vous point in Kukes. He had been told to be there about nine o'clock. Plenty of time therefore to breakfast on his mother's tomatoes and some bread.

Obsessively he checked his shoes again, even though they had been securely laced on his feet all night. All OK. That was a relief. Weather was still kind. It looked like it would be another fine day once the early mist in the valleys had cleared. He rinsed out his mouth and drank some more water, taking care to leave a few mouthfuls in his water bottle just in case he had any difficulty in getting fresh water in Kukes. He hitched his rucksack onto his shoulders, checked carefully that no-one was around, and set off along the field edge to rejoin the track.

It was 7:00 a.m. and good to be walking again. He followed the route of a disused railway track and after ten minutes he had reached the main road. Although he felt conspicuous, the advice from Osman about what to wear meant that he looked much like any other young Albanian trudging along. The country's parlous economy meant that for many people walking was a necessity – indeed, the only way of getting from village to town. The build-up of early-morning traffic signalled that the main border crossing at Morina on the Kukes-Prizren road must already be open, but Habib was already on the Albanian side. That hurdle was now behind him.

He walked alongside the main road, following it into the centre of the town, feeling the warmth of the sun on his back as it crept over the mountains behind, burning off the early mists. He felt in good spirits. Kukes was a bustling place. The morning market stalls were laden with fruit and vegetables, and the cafes lining the main street were steaming out a mouth-watering aroma of traditional thick black coffee. Most of the local male population seemed content to relax in the fresh morning air, drinking coffee, reading newspapers, and sorting out the world's troubles at the cafe tables. Meanwhile the female population were equally absorbed in bargaining at the market stalls and fetching and carrying their household supplies. Young people were not much in evidence at that hour, but the scene was not at all unfamiliar to Habib. It reminded him of his home town of Mitrovice. As he mused on that, he realised it was only yesterday that he had left home. It had been a momentous twenty-four hours, and now he was an illegal immigrant.

His Albanian, although in the Kosovo dialect, stood him in good stead and after two brief enquiries he found himself standing outside the rendez-vous cafe address that Osman had given him.

"I've come to see Mr Banjuka," he told the unshaven, morose-looking waiter clearing one of the tables, a stained cigarette hanging loosely from his mouth. It had been explained by Osman that each of the contacts he would meet was to be called "Mr Banjuka", at least for the purposes of moving along the immigrant trail into and through Albania.

The waiter looked at him quizzically. "No Mr Banjuka here," he said.

Habib persisted and showed him the scrap of paper with the address of the cafe on it and Mr Banjuka's name. The waiter went inside. Habib heard muttering behind the beaded doorway that separated the kitchen and cafe counter. Another man appeared, pale-faced, moustachioed, about twenty-five years old, wearing the endemic black jeans, shirt and shoes.

"You want Mr Banjuka? He's not here. He went to Tirana two days ago. Should have come back last night, but his car's broken down."

"When's he going to get back?"

"Your guess's as good as mine – maybe today, maybe tomorrow. Depends how long it takes to fix the car."

Habib's heart sank. He presumed the young man knew why he was there, because he knew Mr Banjuka's name. Even so, in the absence of his named contact, there was no way Habib was going to enter into further discussions with anyone else about his present plight.

"OK, I'll call back later," he said as casually as he could muster.

It was bad news Mr Banjuka wasn't there, but it was good news he had found the right place and at least they knew whom he wanted. No panic, time for a cup of coffee. He walked back to the main street and was on the brink of ordering when it dawned on him that he had no local currency. He had to find a money-changer.

The economies of the so-called emerging democracies are continuously greedy for foreign currency, particularly US dollars. It was not difficult to find a small, seedy office just off the beaten track where currencies could be exchanged with minimum fuss and virtually no documentation. Habib located the relevant exchange bureau in Kukes without any trouble; his dilemma was how much money to change. He didn't know how long he would be in Albania, but it would certainly be longer than a few days. He decided to change two twenty-dollar bills and one ten. That gave him a fistful of Albanian money which should stand him in good stead for the immediate future until he knew what else to expect. He returned to the town centre, ordered his coffee and a cake, and watched the daily life of a foreign country playing itself out in front of him for the first time in his life.

He made the coffee last as long as possible. Then he meandered into the market and bought some apples and bread. Idling time away was not difficult for people not used to full-time employment. Two middle-aged men were squatting on the pavement crouched over a battered chess board deeply concentrated on the struggle for supremacy between the white and black pieces. A small group of observers were giving unsolicited but appreciated advice from time to time. Like most East Europeans, Habib was familiar with chess and could see, despite the down-at-heel setting and the cloud of cigarette smoke hanging malevolently in the air around the board, that this was not a novice game. Black had played the Dragon Variation of the Sicilian Defence and was bearing down hard with his fianchettoed bishop on white's queenside, while white's pieces were pressing forward in a kingside attack. It was absorbing stuff and the minutes ticked by unnoticed.

At midday he returned to the rendez-vous cafe enquiring again after Mr Banjuka. Still not there. The smell of lunchtime food from the cafes along the street whetted his appetite. He ordered some rice and grilled chicken legs, washed down with a Coke.

Another sit in the shade under a tree with his rucksack propped behind his back while the clock over a shop selling spectacles moved languidly forward. If it were not for the gnawing anxiety about whether his contact would turn up, he could have easily slipped into a pleasant post-prandial snooze. His mind kept turning over what he might do if Mr Banjuka failed to arrive. He really had no plan B, except perhaps to retrace his steps home, but that he could not contemplate. His mind was a blank when it came to other realistic options about what to do next.

The sun was moving lower in the western sky, signalling the end of another warm tranquil autumn day, when he trudged back to the rendez-vous for the third time. If he had no success this time he would have to start searching for a small hotel for the night. It was an empty prospect because he was uncertain how long he might have to kick his heels in this place.

The sight of a dusty and rather dented Opel saloon outside the cafe and the immediate appearance of a well-built middle-aged man, with sweat rings on his shirt around his armpits, whom he had not seen before, quickly dissolved his disconsolate mood.

"Ah, here you are! Been expecting you. Had a bit of trouble with the motor. Sorry 'bout that. Now we've got to sort out getting you to Tirana as quick as possible – too close to the border here and too conspicuous. Everyone knows everyone in this place. The sooner you're away the better for all of us."

Habib had had no opportunity to inquire whether this was the Mr Banjuka he was seeking. But from what he said, it was transparent he must be.

"What time is it? Just after four o'clock! That's too late to get you to Tirana today. But we better move you on to Peshkopi and you can stay the night there. About four hours from here."

He pressed a few buttons on his mobile phone, and had a hurried conversation.

"OK – I've fixed transport. You leave in fifteen minutes. First we need to talk privately about one or two things."

Habib wondered what this might be – he had had a stultifying day as far as mental activity was concerned, the chess match excepted, and now all his focus was on the next phase of the journey, due to start in a matter of minutes.

"OK, my son, you know all this costs money. I need two hundred dollars to pay the driver. Then I tell you where you'll stay tonight in Peshkopi – nice place, no trouble. Tomorrow you take a bus from there to Tirana – that'll take five or six hours, and I'll give you the address in Tirana where you go. Is that OK? You got the money?"

Habib was shaken back to the real world. This was commercial transaction not a humanitarian mission. His feelings were totally irrelevant. He asked to go to the toilet. In the limited privacy of the cubicle with its malodorous hole in the ground, he removed a shoe and carefully extracted $200 from under the insole. After secreting the rest of his worldly wealth back into the shoe, he returned to his anonymous contact, now seated at a table in a dark recess in the interior of the cafe, drawing deeply on a cigarette and holding a cup of steaming black coffee in his other hand. He proffered the money. It took no time to count –two $100 bills.

"Very good! Maybe a cup of coffee before you leave?" Habib was happy to accept.

"How's Kosovo then? At least that murderer Milosevic is in gaol."

Habib told him things weren't too bad now the UN soldiers were around, but he really had no great enthusiasm for reflecting much on what he had left behind. The rather contrived exchange of pleasantries came to a natural end when another bruised and battered car drew up. The driver and "Mr Banjuka" exchanged warm greetings and wished each other peace and prosperity.

"This is your driver. He will take you to Peshkopi."

A slip of paper was passed to Habib. On it was written an address of a lodging house in Peshkopi and, more importantly, the name and address of his next key contact in Tirana, the capital. However agreeable a place was Kukes, it had been frustrating to be stalled there for a few hours. He pocketed the slip of paper carefully and bid farewell, now committing himself to the care and custody of yet another instant companion. He remembered the mistake he had made on his first taxi-ride – still only yesterday. This time he was careful to keep his rucksack close by him on the car seat, not in the boot.

When the Russians, and latterly the Chinese, had been so heavily engaged in helping Albania's "great leap forward" as a beacon of the Marxist economy to the Western world, the connecting roads between the main towns had been improved and surfaced with tarmac. These served primarily to facilitate the movement of the ugly heavy trucks that underpinned developments across the country designed to transform Albania's antiquated peasant culture into an industrial economy. But private ownership of cars was banned. Even in Tirana it was all horse-drawn traffic until the end of the 1980s, the only cars being the large black Russian saloons that ferried government ministers about. The roads throughout the country then were deserted except for horse-carts and the lumbering trucks.

Two decades later Albania was unrecognisable. Roads were now congested with private and commercial traffic, all moving at frantic pace with little regard for road safety. The Highway Code was not high on the agenda for most Albanians. Although most of the pioneering industrial plants had closed down and were now in terminal decay, the external aid programmes had generated another surge in infrastructure development. Huge trucks still clattered along the road network, but now they were fancy western models, not the ugly Soviet variety.

For Habib the immediate consequence of this massive social and economic shift was that the road surfaces on which they now travelled had been mercilessly hammered and broken up by the colossal increase in traffic. In the absence of any regular maintenance, foundations were subsiding everywhere and the ride resembled that of a roller-coaster. Potholes and rock falls from the valley sides appeared at random. Each were negotiated at speed - it all added up to another hair-raising journey, with Habib clinging tightly to handgrips and the dashboard. Things became even more hazardous as darkness fell. They continued to hurtle along the winding road at breakneck speed, often dazzled by the unforgiving headlights of oncoming traffic, charging at them like a jousting knight. Even more unnerving were the vehicles careering along without any lights at all. But at least he was moving, and the bones of a twenty-one-year-old were still sufficiently supple to ride this out.

Just before ten o'clock the scattered lights of Peshkopi town appeared spread prettily across the valley to their left. The driver turned towards them, crossed a long cantilevered bridge over a glistening expanse of water backing up from a dam on the Drini Zi river and dropped down into the main street of the principal town for the Dibra Prefecture, famous for its healing spa waters. They drove to the eastern outskirts and pulled up outside a dimly lit lodging house. Habib confirmed that this was where he was supposed to be. He shook hands and made to leave the car. He couldn't. The door was locked. In the dark he fumbled around for a handle to no avail. He looked for help to the driver, who had now leaned back comfortably in his seat and was lighting a cigarette.

"Taxi fare first!" he said.

"But I paid the man in Kukes. He said that was for getting me here."

"Well he was wrong, my friend – you pay him for what he gave you! You pay me for what I do for you– simple really. Seems fair, don't you think?"

Habib had to think quickly. "OK – how much?"

"$50 to get you here and $25 for me to get back to Kukes. Usually I charge higher rates for night driving, but I'm letting you have a cheap rate, cos' you seem a nice young chap. That's good of me don't you think?"

Habib tried to bargain. At least he was where he wanted to be, and it was unlikely this guy would want to keep waiting too long, so he might be prepared to compromise.

"Will you take $50? I haven't got much money left and I need some to pay this place tonight and to get to Tirana tomorrow."

Above all Habib didn't want to have to search in his shoes for the money. If he could keep the sum sufficiently small he could use the cash in his money belt. The windows of the car were steaming up and the atmosphere was tense.

"OK. $50 – I can't stop here all night arguing."

Habib asked him to put the interior light on. As discreetly as possible, he felt inside his belt and produced five ten-dollar bills. Licking his fingers and still holding his lighted cigarette, the driver checked them meticulously, then went round to the passenger door and opened it from outside. Rather too late Habib took note of the fact that his interior door handle had been removed. Another costly lesson he had had to learn. Next time he would negotiate a price in advance.

The driver, now beaming, let out his clutch noisily and surged off with a cheery wave. Habib pushed the lighted bell button beside the door of the lodging house. It was opened by a kindly old lady wearing a black hijab. Yes, she did have a room for the night. It would cost 1,500 Albanian lek - equivalent to about $10,- and breakfast was included - payment in advance. She took his money politely and asked him to sign in and write down his home address and passport number. Habib thought quickly. He gave the address of the Kukes cafe and manufactured a fictitious number as his passport. The lady seemed unconcerned as long as something was written down. She escorted him up two flights of the dingy staircase and gave him a key to room ten. It had a bed, a rug on the floor, a chair, a table on which stood a small jar of faded artificial flowers looking somewhat pathetic, and two threadbare patterned curtains partially obscuring the light from the street-lamp filtering into the room through the grubby window. The lady had shown him a toilet closet and washroom halfway down the corridor.

Habib locked the door. He slung the rucksack on the bed beside the wall. He was tempted to keep his shoes on, but decided he could tie them to the rucksack and sleep against it. He took off his jacket, checked the window was securely fastened, jammed the chair up against the door handle and at long last enjoyed the luxury of lying flat, and quiet, and still, and warm on a bed. It seemed a long time since he had done that. Things weren't going too badly. He was learning as he went along but his dollars were being used up quicker than expected. He began adding up how much so far, but before reaching a final total he was sound asleep.

The loudspeaker call to prayer of the muezzin woke him at daybreak. He had slept like a stone for six or seven hours. The room was chilled. First he checked his rucksack and shoes - no problem - then he opened the curtains, and lay back on his bed to watch the sunrise glinting over the hills beyond the town. After half an hour he could hear sounds downstairs. He took his washbag to the bathroom, making sure his room was securely locked. No need to bother with shaving, so after a perfunctory wash and toilet stop, he gathered up his jacket and rucksack and went downstairs.

The old lady was sitting demurely on her own at one of the four square tables in a sort of dining room. There was a welcome aroma of fresh coffee in the air. On one of the tables was a chipped plate depicting a rather incongruous pattern of an olde worlde English rose garden. On it was a slab of butter and a dollop of red jam. Beside it was another plate with two rather grey slices of bread.

"You like omelette?" asked the lady. Habib nodded, and a few minutes later he was tucking into a breakfast considerably more appetising than he had expected. The old lady maintained a polite distance, hovering near the kitchen.

"More coffee?" she asked. Habib was pleased to accept. More importantly he was pleased that this was probably someone he could trust.

"I need to get to Tirana," he said. "What's the best way?"

"No problem, we have many small buses going each day from Peshkopi. You just walk to Cultural Centre and then you take the road to the place where all the buses and taxis stop. You pay the driver and he'll take you to Tirana."

He finished his meal and asked if he could refill his water bottle. After a last visit to the toilet, he hitched his rucksack back onto his shoulders. The lady gratefully accepted the two-dollar tip he offered, bowing slightly with hands together. She wished him peace, prosperity and a safe journey, and pointed the direction he needed to go. "May Allah protect you," she said.

There was a line of minibuses to choose from. He moved along it asking which were bound for Tirana and what was the cost. It was clear that prices were pretty much the same, so he chose the one that was already half full in the hope it would soon be leaving. He paid his fare and settled into a window seat, his rucksack firmly stowed beneath his legs. It was just after eight o'clock and the early-morning sun was giving way to ponderous clouds. The weather seemed to be breaking. He was not too concerned. He had slept well, he had eaten well, he had survived the hair-raising drives and was on the road again to his next crucial goal, Albania's capital city.

The journey from Peshkopi follows a tortuous route out of the mountains until it reaches the coastal plains. The road clings to the sides of the deep valleys and gorges carved out of the landscape by the rivers over the centuries. After an hour's driving it passes through the sombre mining town of Bulqiza, once vibrant with a bustling economy and over 6,000 men working the coal mine there. The enormous Soviet-style concrete apartment blocks still stand incongruously on the gentle mountain side, disfiguring its natural beauty like a scar across the face. Now, fewer than 600 people dig for coal. The rest of the community languish round the town centre like flotsam passing the time as best they may. Their clothes and demeanour betray their poverty and hopelessness. It is a scenario repeated across the world in Britain, the USA, Russia, wherever the industrial revolution has come and gone - the bosses have found an escape but the workers are left to decay with their families alongside the abandoned mines, which had once been the life-blood of their community. There is nothing to do, nowhere to go, and no money to buy anything. They cling like leeches to passing trade as buses and trucks and cars disgorge a steady stream of people looking for food or drink en route to somewhere else that does not reek of such cloying despair.

Habib's minibus made brief stops here and there to take on and let off passengers en route, but in Bulqiza, there was a longer stop to allow everyone time to stretch their legs and buy refreshments. Habib decided to stay put. He had a good seat by the window. His rucksack was secure where it was under his legs. He took a swig from his water bottle and ate one of the apples he had bought in the market yesterday. It had started to rain, which added to the disconsolate ambience of the town. Sheltering under plastic sheets as makeshift umbrellas, street hawkers were tapping on the bus windows exhorting him to buy from the basket of goodies they carried. Habib sat tight.

After fifteen minutes they were moving again, the road continuing to hug the river valley with periodic vistas of magnificent ravines and torrents. The rain had set in steadily now and thick grey cloud shrouded the tops of the mountains. The volume of traffic was increasing and the minibus ploughed through showers of dirty spray thrown up by the wheels of trucks, oblivious to all except their own destinations. The next stop was Burrel, a more congenial place despite the inclement weather. The people here seemed less threatening. There was a busy market and all manner of shops selling furniture and clothes and electrical goods and building supplies. Habib decided he ought to take this opportunity to relieve himself. He hoisted his rucksack onto his back and wandered out into the rain. He bought a fold-up umbrella from a stall for 300 lek. It would come in handy he was sure. He returned to the minibus as soon as possible to try to retain his seat. Too late! A large lady in a voluminous dress had deposited herself on it. On her lap were three huge bags of shopping and under her feet two live chickens with their legs tied together. Habib squeezed into the seat beside her and stowed his rucksack adjacent to the chickens. It was going to be less comfortable from now on.

The minibus drove on through the unremitting weather. Habib's eyes began to close and his head fell back against the seat as the endless miles unwound themselves under the wheels. The motion was soporific and he dozed intermittently, sometimes waking with a start to find his head resting against the ample bosom of his seat companion. She seemed not to mind, and in the fug inside the minibus, he sensed a gentle motherliness emanating from her, which was strangely comforting.

They came to a road junction near a dried-up river-bed and a dilapidated bridge. The minibus negotiated the bridge, jolted over a few potholes and then moved out onto a straighter, flatter section of road. They had reached the coastal plateau. The twisting and turning abated and the road condition improved, and with that, the speed of the vehicle. The rain still slashed down hard across the windscreen and the landscape became altogether more drab and dismal.

Habib checked his watch. It was just after one o'clock. He was beginning to feel hungry when the minibus conveniently drew into a wide flat car-parking area outside a long double-storey restaurant. He did not know it, but the driver had a private remunerative arrangement with the owner to ensure passengers always had a half hour break here at mealtimes. Taking great care to keep his money belt out of sight, and with his rucksack firmly on his shoulders, Habib joined the other passengers at a table round a communal plate of grilled steaks and chops, fried potatoes and salad. It was a feast. Some were drinking beer with it but Habib stuck to his Coca-Cola. The bill came to 500 lek each. Not knowing quite where or when his next meal might be, Habib was happy to pay that.

They were at the junction where the road forked west for Durres on the Adriatic coast or east to Tirana. The minibus set off on the last leg of the journey through the sprawling outskirts of the city. The turn round in Albania's prosperity in the last two years had seen a proliferation of building, mostly unplanned and ad hoc, financed by monies sent back to the country from family relatives working abroad, as well the international aid that was pouring in now Albania seemed to be embracing the principles of transparent democracy in both its political and commercial activity. As the buildings proliferated so did the traffic, even more so. The minibus speed had now been reduced to about 10 mph by both the rain and the traffic congestion. It was a tedious hour until at last they pulled into a parking area near the city centre, teaming with people and taxis and minibuses, despite the inclement conditions. The passengers unpeeled themselves from their seats for the last time and Habib stood surveying the chaotic scene around from the shelter of his umbrella wondering where to go next.

He had the address on the slip of paper in his pocket. He stepped carefully across the waterlogged potholes of the bus park and showed the address to a taxi driver.

"How much to take me here?" he asked. The taxi driver couldn't read so he had to say it out loud to him.

"500 lek," came the reply.

"Too much," said Habib chancing his arm at bargaining again, and made to move off to another taxi.

"OK, I do it for 300 lek."

Habib climbed in, keeping a tight hold on his rucksack and checking first that there was a working door handle. Ten minutes later they drew up outside a nondescript block of apartments somewhere south of the Lana river. As was the case all over Tirana, at the instigation of the city's go-ahead Mayor, Edi Rama, the depressing communist-style concrete facade of the building had been painted in strident colours, yellow, blue and green alternating from stairwell to stairwell. Even on a gloomy wet late-October afternoon, the livid colours gave a lift to the spirits. At least something was being done to move Albania away from its dour past.

Habib paid off the driver, glanced again at the slip of paper, and headed for stairwell D. The usual stench of communal neglect greeted him as he entered, a mixture of dried urine, cooked cabbage and dank mould growth. He climbed to the fourth floor and knocked on the door of flat number 416.

"My name is Habib Peci. I have been told to meet Mr Banjuka here," he said.

The tall pale-faced young man who had opened the door quickly pulled him into the room without a word and locked the door. Habib could feel his pulse racing. If this were a trap, he could be overwhelmed easily, and could lose all he had. He knew no-one. He had no idea where he was, and nobody else knew where he was. A cold shiver of fear and apprehension passed down his spine. He braced himself for the worst.

They walked down a short dark corridor and entered a sitting room. The furnishings were sparse. The rain was beating hard against the large cracked window. A dirty net curtain strung across it provided some privacy from the block of flats at the same level immediately on the opposite side of the street. It all seemed very bleak. On the sofa sat another man, well built, probably about forty years old, wearing a singlet that was long overdue for a wash. His muscular hairy arms were tattooed, and a half smoked cigarette drooped from his lips underneath a fine black moustache that curled down at the corners of his mouth.

"Welcome to Tirana!" he boomed. "Glad you got here – wondered if we would ever see you! Expected you yesterday. I'm Toci. This is Rahmani. Make yourself at home!"

Hardly home, thought Habib. But thankful and much relieved that his fears of being robbed and beaten to pulp had not been realised, he took the extended hand of welcome and shook it warmly.

"Salaam alaikum." He had arrived in Tirana.

Chapter 15

Moldova - February 2001

Different cultures and different times have seen a wide repertoire of aids to decision-making. In classical Greece, a pilgrimage to Delphi to consult the Oracle was the best bet, but as the advice was usually given in the form of a riddle, the way forward was never very transparent. In primitive Africa, the witch-doctor was the guardian of wisdom. By shaking a motley handful of old bones and seeing how they assorted themselves, he would endeavour to appraise supplicants of what supposed fate lay in store for them. In biblical times, the warlords consulted the prophets. The sycophants told them what they wanted to hear. The less subservient told "the truth" and often lost their heads in consequence because it wasn't what their lord and master wanted to hear. In more recent times, those who believed in the spirit-world would consult a clairvoyant and the Ouija board, while religious folk resorted to fervent prayer to find answers to anguished dilemmas, often relying on random verses from a holy book to guide their way forward.

Nina did not know about the Oracle at Delphi, and there were no witch-doctors in Chisinau. She had no access to Old Testament prophets, did not believe in spirits and was not religious, so none of these options were available to help her decide what she should do. The stark reality was that this was a decision she was going to have to make on her own. There was no-one she was prepared to discuss it with. Only a handful of people knew she was pregnant – the doctor, but he was anonymous and totally confidential; Ion, her ex-boyfriend, who was certainly going to keep his mouth shut for fear of having to accept responsibility for her condition; and Pavel, her brother, who would keep her secret with her. But none of them knew of the Hotel Dukro proposal about how to raise the money she needed. That was, and would be, her own personal, closely guarded secret.

She arrived back at her shared flat after a chilly walk home, still churning everything over in her mind. Her flatmates, totally oblivious to her soul-searching discussions that afternoon, were keen to go out for Sunday evening's frolics before the burden of the week's work engulfed them. Nina made her excuses – headache, time of month, whatever – and was left alone to reflect on what response she would make to Zvetlana when they met up again tomorrow. It was a choice between the lesser of two evils. One moment she felt inclined to follow her natural instincts to have the baby and the pleasure that could bring. Then the downside crowded in. She was sure she wouldn't be able to cope. But earning the money for the abortion meant becoming a whore for a few weeks. Was that something she could live with for the rest of her life?

Still vexed and unsure, she was making her second cup of coffee when her mobile rang.

"Ah, hello Nina? Vladimir Voronin here – from the DHL office. Sorry to disturb you on a Sunday evening. Expect you're out enjoying yourself somewhere, so won't keep you long. Remember Larissa – not sure if you ever met her, but she was doing your job at the office before you came on board. You probably know she had a bonny baby boy just before Christmas and is now fully fit again. Lives at home with Mum and Dad so they are looking after the little one in the daytime.

"She called me this weekend to say she's OK to come back to work now. Puts us in a difficult position. I'm sure you understand. You know how it is with contracts of employment – hers is sort-of permanent whereas yours is temporary. It would be nice to have you both, but we really haven't enough room in the office, and frankly our profits can't stand us taking on extra staff at this stage. I suggested she starts back next week so it would give you a week or so to find something else. You've been great and we've really enjoyed having you with us. Rest assured, you'll be our first choice if anyone else goes off. We'll keep in touch.

"Actually I've got a friend who runs a small travel agency. I think he may be looking for someone to help in a few weeks. I'll put in a good word for you. He's likely to offer about the same as we do - $7 a week, so that should be OK for you. Take care of yourself. I thought you would like to know as early as possible, before the rest of the staff know what's to happen. See you tomorrow. Bye for now."

And that was that. The kettle had boiled. Mechanically, slightly dumbstruck, she poured the hot water onto the instant coffee powder, and stared blankly at the bleak impoverished kitchen cupboards. She would be unemployed within a week, groping around again for any odd job that might come up. Little or no money to spare, and still faced with the enormity of the choice of finding $300 or having a baby. Yet out there was the chance of so much easy money. All she had to do was say "yes" when she saw Zvetlana tomorrow.

The call from Mr Voronin had suddenly put a new and urgent perspective on things. It was a hard world. Even nice guys like him had to leave her to her own devices when push came to shove. Wasn't she too young to be encumbered with a baby as a single parent? What could she give to such a helpless mite? The few months away from her home village had opened her eyes to wider horizons. There was no going back. Abortion was no big deal for most women. Why should she be so squeamish about it? The chance to earn the money she needed was being offered to her on a plate, money she could never dream of anywhere else. Prostitution, they said, was the world's oldest and most widespread profession. Why should she feel so guilty about it? In any case, it would only be for a few weeks. No-one else would know, and then she could pick up the pieces of her life again. "To hell with the lot of them!" she said to herself. "I'll tell Zvetlana I'll do it!"

She was in bed when her friends returned. Her mind was clear. The tortuous dilemma had crystallised into a calm and focussed resolve. It was her secret, and hers alone. She sank into a deep sleep, more relaxed than she had thought possible.

At the office next morning there was much expression of regret that she would be leaving them at the end of the week. Nina took it in her stride. They all promised to help her find something else. She would be an asset to any office. Something was bound to turn up. Nina was going to miss them too, she knew that, but that was the least of her worries. In the cool light of the morning, the firm resolve which had given her such undisturbed sleep, was rather less robust as she watched the people of Chisinau hurrying past the steamed-up office windows, huddled down in their coats and scarves against the cold. Today, things seemed rather less clear-cut than they had last night. She watched the clock as it painstakingly clicked away the time till her crucial rendez-vous.

She made her excuses not to join the others for their regular Monday lunch together when there was usually a post-mortem of the weekend's adventures. Zvetlana was waiting for her, smoking, lazy and confident in a quiet corner of the coffee bar. Compared with her poise and self-assurance, the rest of the clientele seemed immature and brash. It was hard not to be impressed. A beaming smile, a warm handshake and a kiss greeted her. Nina ordered an espresso and sausage sandwich.

"Don't worry about that, I'll pay," said Zvetlana. "So how are you today? Had any further thoughts about what we talked about yesterday?"

Nina was not prepared to admit she had thought of nothing else since then, but the warmth and poise of her companion was melting away the "cool light of day, cold feet" feeling of the morning. The resolve of last night was resurrecting itself. The logic had been straightforward then. Now it was reforming itself in the presence of Zvetlana. Nina hardly knew her, but it was difficult not to be impressed by her. She seemed so totally at ease and in charge of both herself and all else around. Worldly wisdom it might be, but not many of Nina's other companions could match her. They all had a plethora of personal insecurities, clothes problems, money worries, health anxieties of one sort or another most of the time. Zvetlana stood out in complete contrast to all that. It was not unnatural to want to emulate her. If the profession she had adopted paid such dividends both in terms of money and strength of personality, it was very tempting to follow her path.

"Yes, I have thought about it all," replied Nina. "I think I'd like to give it a try, maybe for one or two nights to see how I get on. If it doesn't work out and I'm a total failure, I can just give up, I suppose?"

"Have no fear – you'll be OK. You'll knock them out with your figure! Talk to me whenever you want. I'll give you more tips as you go along. I guess everyone is anxious first time but there's really no need to be. It's dead easy. You'll see. So where do we go from here? Can you remember all the things I said yesterday about what to wear and so on?"

Nina said she did – indeed, every syllable was imprinted in her mind.

"Right, would you be OK to start tomorrow night? Stefan and I could pick you up at nine o'clock in the evening outside this coffee bar. Depends how busy things are, but we may not get you back home till the early hours. Is that OK? Are you still keeping your job going? You may be a little tired next day. Friday and Saturday nights are usually the busiest – but you can always have a lie-in then the next morning."

Nina nodded her agreement. She would be hanging on to her job for the time being. No need to tell Zvetlana it was coming to a premature end. She finished her modest lunch. She had announced her decision. The die was now cast, though she could of course not turn up tomorrow if she had second thoughts. On the Sunday Zvetlana had told her what was needed. She had a day or so to get herself ready. There really wasn't any more to be said. They stood up and left the coffee bar. Zvetlana gave her a peck on both cheeks.

"You're going to make a lot of men very happy. Makes me envious! See you tomorrow!"

Nina watched her stride off down the main street, self-assured as ever, her long dark coat swaying from side to side, and admiring glances of men of all ages following her every step. Her half-hour lunch-break was up. She must get back to the office – but not for much longer. A new life was dawning, and nine-to-five office hours would soon be history as far as Nina Snegur was concerned.

Only then did she suddenly remember she had not yet had confirmation of the hospital tests. They had said they would be ready in two days. That was today. She swore at herself for forgetting. There was always a vague hope the test might prove negative. In which case none of this torment and worry would be necessary. Her lunch-break was up. No time now to go up to the hospital, but she could phone Pavel on her mobile as she walked back to the office. Perhaps he could try to get the results for her? He said he would try.

He returned her call later in the afternoon. They had the results, but they wouldn't give them to a third party without written authority, nor until the $20 fee had been paid. She would have to go there herself - they were open this evening till eight o'clock. That was no problem. Nina would get there, clutching her last straw of hope that the pregnancy testing kit she had used had got things wrong and that her absence of periods was an hormonal upset rather than anything else. But in her heart she knew it was a forlorn hope.

She scrounged a few dollars from each of her friends and together with a little she had saved from her earnings she had just enough to pay her dues at the hospital. She sat again on the iron chair in the soulless, overheated waiting room impatient to hear the verdict. It still smelt of disinfectant. The head of a nurse appeared at the small glass window that served as a reception hatch. First the money, then a slip of paper with an illegible signature, presumably that of the doctor, underneath two printed boxes, one marked positive, the other negative.

There was a solitary tick against the box marked positive. So that was it. No reprieve. She trudged back to her flat through the dark streets in sombre mood. She knew what she had to do.

PART 3

PROGRESS

Chapter 16

Leicester - January 2004

Robert's insouciant query provoked a startling, and totally unexpected response from his parents.

Peter and Jenny Clayton were not particularly religious, but deep-seated echoes from past Sunday School experiences resonated through their consciousness as they stopped short in their tracks at their son's question. "Out of the mouth of babes and sucklings …"

Jenny did not start the car. Peter did not close the door. The visit to Auntie Margaret was clearly going to be delayed for a few moments at least while the weakest member of the family reluctantly reconciled himself to face cross-examination about his dramatic revelation.

"What did you say?" demanded a disbelieving Peter. "Did you see a man bring Daddy's car back this morning? Can you remember what he looked like? Where were you when you saw him? Was he on his own?..." The questions cascaded over the poor little lad who felt he must have said or done something reprehensible. As tears welled up in his eyes, Jenny decided to take a rather more sympathetic approach to the interrogation.

"Robert, was it a nice man that brought Daddy's car back? Was he big and strong or tiddly?"

"I don't think he was very nice – he was like the man in the films who jumps about and kicks people and swings a big sword round in the air."

Jonathan was listening intently to his brother's inarticulate efforts, and, as the elder brother, took on the masterful job of elucidating the rather feeble descriptive attempts of his younger sibling.

"He means Bruce Lee who does all the Kung Fu stuff!"

"When he left Daddy's car did he walk down the road?" asked Mummy.

"No, he got into another big blue car waiting for him and it drove away."

"Were you in your bedroom?"

"Yes, I was watching Mr Selhurst wash his car. Then Mrs Selhurst came out and told him his coffee was getting cold, and then the man brought Daddy's car back."

Mr and Mrs Selhurst were the sort of neighbours that families with young children dream of. Mr Selhurst had retired two years earlier from his job as a senior clerk in the local Inland Revenue office. Out of his retirement lump sum he had paid off their mortgage and bought a new Vauxhall Astra.

He had taken up golf and was also secretary of the local Rotary Club. In his youth he had collected toy soldiers. It was the Clayton's good fortune that not only were Mr and Mrs Selhurst willing and available to be babysitters from time to time, but when they did come round, Mr Selhurst always delighted the boys' hearts by bringing with him the treasured toy soldiers.

Saturday morning was the time for cleaning and polishing his new car. It was the wife's task to make mid-morning coffee for her car valet husband at about 10:30 a.m.

So it was that as the Bruce Lee look-alike was delivering Peter Clayton's car back into his drive at about 10:40 a.m. that morning, next-door Mr Selhurst, fortuitously or otherwise, was indoors imbibing his caffeine to boost him for the final assault on polishing the Astra, which in turn left little Robert as the only witness to the comings and goings in Chantry Gardens at the critical moment.

The cross-examination had lasted barely three minutes, but during that brief exchange Peter and Jenny had the corroboration they needed that someone else had been driving their Golf that morning, that he was a youngish athletic man of oriental appearance, that he had an accomplice, and that they left in large blue car, which more than likely was Michael Burton's BMW. If they were right in their previous analysis, this car then set off from Leicester to be parked a couple of hours later in a long-stay carpark at Stansted Airport.

A convincing pattern of events was clearly emerging, but the problem persisted that there was still no evident crime which would demand more serious police involvement – no body, no car theft, no break-in, no damage, no violence, nothing except the uncorroborated testimony of what Peter had seen – and then not seen – in Michael Burton's factory offices.

"Robert, you've been a good boy to remember all that. Thank you very much. You go off with Mummy now to Auntie Margaret and have a play with Simon and Freddy. Daddy will stay at home and have a rest. Take care!"

Seatbelts fastened, a final rather more fulsome kiss of au revoir mingled with relief for Jenny and they were off. Peter switched on the TV to catch up with the Saturday afternoon football results, not least to see how Leicester City's efforts to avoid relegation were faring, poured himself a small measure of whisky, and put his feet up on the pouffe in front of the fire. At last he had time to reflect and take stock. Nothing more could be done to try to get to the bottom of things till Monday, and then they would see what further chats with the police and Burton's PA would throw up.

The TV news was just moving on to the weather forecast when the doorbell rang. Not too late –about 6:00 p.m. but still a dark chilly winter's evening and not a time for unexpected visitors. Probably some collectors for Christian Aid or the Salvation Army.

"Good evening sir. Mr Peter Clayton?" asked the smartly suited, stockily built middle-aged man at the door. Having established Peter's identity, he proffered his own identity card confirming he was Detective Sergeant Blundy, who had taken over the shift at the police station from the earlier Dectective Sergeant that day. He had been made aware of the events of the morning. He thought Mr Clayton would be interested to know that a body had been found, and his presence would be appreciated to confirm this was the same body he had reported seeing. They would prefer to deal with the identification immediately so they could lose no further time in starting a major police investigation.

Peter's relaxation had been short-lived, but this was good news. Hopefully this would remove the burden weighing heavy on his shoulders and allow the police to begin formal enquiries into an unexplained death. First, a quick call on the phone to tell Jenny what was happening. He would be back in an hour or so, probably before she and the boys got home. Any hold-ups and he would ring her again. Jenny too heaved a sigh of relief. At least the police were now taking things seriously. It had been an upsetting day for the family, but any future involvement for them would surely now be as unwitting witnesses to a rather nasty episode. Jenny did not know Michael Burton personally so she had no particular emotional baggage about his death. Their contented suburban lifestyle had been given a jolt, but not one that need have any adverse long-term consequences. With a good nightcap, they should sleep more easily in their beds tonight.

Peter exchanged his slippers for a pair of robust outdoor shoes, put on a warm sweater and his anorak, slipped his mobile phone into his pocket, set the house alarm, left a few indoor lights on, locked the front door behind him, and accompanied the policeman to the waiting car.

In his early teens Peter had been besotted with prestige cars. He took Autocar magazine each week. On birthdays and at Christmas he'd always asked for books on the latest Jaguars, Mercedes, Aston Martins, Lambourghinis, BMWs, Maseratis, and the rarer handmade models such the British TVR and the Swiss Montiverdi. His interest in cars persisted into his adult years and although he could not afford the really top models, his Golf GTI was a good compromise, fast and stylish whilst accommodating the needs of a growing family. It was second nature therefore for him to note that the police car was an E class Mercedes, although not the latest model.

Detective sergeant Blundy seated himself beside Peter in the back seat. The driver sped off, apparently heading for the mortuary. Peter had some apprehension about this, but at least it wouldn't be anything like the shock of his first sight of the body. He did not actually know the whereabouts of the mortuary, so had no idea how long this identification would take.

As the early-evening orange streetlights whisked past along the Leicester ring road, Peter observed that speed limits were of no particular consequence when a police car was in hurry. The policeman beside him was remarkably mute, for a policeman that is, and in an effort to relieve the mild tension he was feeling, Peter essayed to engage him in conversation, without much success. No, he didn't follow football. No, he didn't live locally. No, he wasn't married. No, he hadn't been in the Leicester Force very long. No, he didn't know that Mr Burton and Mr Clayton played squash in the same club.

It was hard going and Peter decided to give up the unequal struggle to be sociable, and let his attention focus on other things, like the driver who was wearing gloves and staring unblinkingly ahead without ever endeavouring to participate in their laboured conversation. Peter's gaze fell on the dashboard with its array of Mercedes lights, always understated, but speaking of quality and power. It was then his slightly soporific consciousness registered something odd. Didn't official police cars have walky-talky radios fitted as standard equipment?

With disturbing tardiness, his brain began to ratchet into gear – the police usually have up-to-date cars. This vehicle was the old E class, which meant it must be at least five years old. Police cars would normally have a radio. This one didn't. When not on emergency calls, police are not expected to break speed limits. This one was apparently oblivious to them. Policemen are not usually monosyllabic. These gentlemen were more than economical with conversation.

Peter was rapidly coming to the conclusion that things were not all they should be. Indeed, though he hardly dared admit it to himself, the dreadful reality was dawning that this was probably a bogus policeman and a bogus police vehicle. His palms began to sweat and for the second time that day his heart was thumping with anxiety. The next half hour would confirm it or otherwise, but for the present, it looked remarkably likely that Peter Clayton had been kidnapped.

Chapter 17

Albania - November 2003

In the hierarchy of human needs, food and shelter rank at the top. Job satisfaction and leisure pursuits languish towards the bottom of the list. Somewhere in between come security, health, education, and social interaction.

Habib did not require a sociologist's evaluation of his predicament to identify his priorities. Now he had arrived in Tirana, first and foremost he needed a roof over his head. For food he had money enough to buy what he needed, but keeping that secure was an equally pressing anxiety. He did not know what was to happen next. Would he stay at this place or somewhere else? He knew he had to reach Italy and at some stage that would involve a clandestine sea trip across the Adriatic. But he had no idea when, where, or how. As he stood in the down-at-heel sitting room of apartment 416 in the tired block of ill-maintained dwellings in the disconsolate suburbs of Albania's capital on that rain-swept Sunday afternoon, Habib's thoughts were racing through these uncertainties.

His single reassurance in the midst of all this strangeness was that Toci had been expecting his arrival and had given him a warm welcome. Hopefully the answers to the questions buzzing around in his head would emerge over the next hour or so. In the meantime he'd best be patient as his host extended his welcome by offering a steaming cup of hot sugared tea, and a seat on the threadbare sofa to watch the live football match flickering across the TV screen that dominated the room. Lazio versus Palermo – a needle match in the Italian league – followed avidly by Albanians, and not to be missed, regardless of whether an illegal immigrant had just walked into the flat.

The match finished in a draw, affording a measure of satisfaction to the Albanians, whose intrinsic sympathy and support lay with the Sicilian team, the underdogs. Another five minutes of vociferous match analysis by the armchair experts, before at long last some of Habib's queries began to be addressed.

First a cross-examination about where he'd come from, who he was and where he expected to be going. No need for any dissimulation as Habib explained all that. Then onto the more urgent matters as far as Habib was concerned. The next boat that could take him from Albania to mainland Italy was scheduled to go across overnight in four weeks time. It would leave from a beach in a cove on the Albanian Riviera near Corfu. More details of where and when nearer the time. He would have to stay in Tirana till then. There was a bed he could use in flat 416 – to be more precise, a mattress on the floor in the second bedroom, alongside two others occupied by two young Albanians from a village near Shkoder in the north, who were also hoping to get out on the same boat. He would pay 500 lek a night for the accommodation, provide his own food and do his own washing. There was a communal bathroom, and he could use the kitchen and sitting room to watch TV.

The best news was that Toci had a friend who could give him some temporary employment during his enforced stay in Tirana. The surge in building work across the country as the economy picked up had spawned a proliferation of small-scale brick-making enterprises. In particular Toci's friend had the use of a patch of derelict ground just off the main road to the airport and had set up his business there. The resources were basic – a makeshift shed of corrugated iron, a water-tap, a small two-stroke cement mixer, a few spades and tools, and a dozen or so iron moulds for the making the breeze blocks. Business was brisk and labour intensive. Habib could help out there and earn some pocket money – 500 lek a day, plus 2 lek for every brick he made. He should be able to make about 250 bricks a day. He would also have to help with stacking and loading bricks and unloading deliveries of sand and cement.

But before all that Habib had to settle his major account. The "fee" for getting him across to Italy from Tirana was $1,250. Of that he had to pay $500 up front to Toci now and the rest to the boat captain on the night of their departure. It all seemed well organised. The prospect of temporary work was a bonus. That should pay his living expenses while in Tirana without biting further into his dollar savings. A short visit to the bathroom enabled him to extract the required $500 from his insole discreetly. Toci counted it carefully. All correct.

"That's fine. We're going to get along famously!" he said. "Tomorrow I'll take you out to the work site – we leave at 7:00 a.m. Best get some sleep now."

It was only about 8:00 p.m. but Habib had had a long tiring day. He was only too glad to retire to the bedroom and slump down on his mattress. He was careful to keep his rucksack behind his head as a sort of pillow and his shoes firmly tied onto his feet. The rain still beat against the grubby windows and the murky street lamp shed an ethereal residual light into the room. Hanging on one of the walls was a faded print of a nondescript Austrian Alpine scene replicated on chocolate boxes and jigsaws around the world. Apart from that and the three mattresses on the floor, the room was bare - no furniture, no cupboards, no chairs, no table, no carpet. But it was more than adequate shelter from the elements and for four weeks' duration. Habib would not be daunted by these Spartan conditions. He was sound asleep when his other two bedroom companions dossed down for the night on the mattresses alongside him.

The knocking on the door woke him up. It was dark. He had no idea what time it was. "Time to go to work," said a voice. His companions did not stir, but Habib grabbed his rucksack and slid quietly out of the room. A single dusty bulb hanging from a bare wire lit up the hall. Toci was further along the corridor, dressed, smoking and waiting for him. A quick toilet visit and sluice of water over his face in the bathroom – no time and no need for a shave – and they were on their way down the dingy stairwell for the ten-minute walk to the minibus park near the Dinamp Stadium. The rain had stopped, but water stood everywhere in dirty brown pools and puddles in the roads and on the footpaths. The first lesson in countries like Albania where highway maintenance is an optional extra – never walk in puddles! They may be a few inches deep, but they may disguise a pothole two feet deep. Habib had learned this lesson well in Kosovo from bitter soaking experience.

It was grey and overcast as the loaded minibus, fuggy with smoke, cheap aftershave and miscellaneous body odours, ferried them through the crowded early-morning streets towards Druga Durrestit, the airport road. They had stopped at one of the street vendor stalls near the bus-park to pick up a greasy sandwich. Habib happily sank his teeth into it. That would serve as his breakfast. He still had a bottle of water with him if no other beverage was available at his work place.

The bus dropped them off just beyond an industrial estate where a number of recently built warehouses and factories were already opening up for the day's business, another indicator that economic activity in Albania was on the up. A few minutes walk along the roadside and they arrived at the site.

They were greeted by an elderly man. He had a tough weatherbeaten complexion and a whispy greying moustache. His shoulders were stooped forward. His gnarled and calloused hands betrayed years of heavy manual work. On his head he wore the jaunty qeleshe. His checked shirt and trousers were bespattered with dust and dried cement. His fingernails were likewise ingrained. He was on his own.

Toci introduced Habib to him. His other helpers had left for various reasons. He had a big order for bricks. His rheumatism and other aches and pains meant he could no longer do the heavy work. He needed a strong young man to help him. He grasped Habib's hand in an iron handshake, bid farewell to Toci, and took him to the workshop to show him the ropes. Habib was carrying all his worldly wealth with him – the clothes he was wearing, the contents of his rucksack, and the precious dollars in his shoes.

He stowed the rucksack in a corner of the shed and set to work at the old man's instructions. The cement mixer whirred into life – noisy and smelly. He shovelled in the appropriate quantities of sand, shingle and cement, then added the water and after a few minutes, the grey concrete sludge was ready for pouring into the moulds, enough for a dozen breeze blocks with each mixer load. They needed time to set, and during that time he prepared the next load for the mixer. If the proportions were exactly right, the setting time was quick, and within half an hour the bricks could be taken out of the moulds and left to harden off in the air while the next batch were prepared.

Habib took to the job easily and even enjoyed it. From time to time small pick-up trucks arrived. Some came to take a delivery of bricks which he helped to load. Others would arrive with sacks of replenishment sand and cement. The old man supervised operations with genial firmness while Habib supplied the hard labour. At the end of the day the old man carefully counted the brick quota and delved into his back pocket to peel off Habib's day's wages from a wodge of crumpled notes. He bid farewell, waited at the roadside for a return minibus, and retraced his route back to the city. He felt tired but pretty good.

There were two immediate snags he would need to address. The work was filthy and his clothes and shoes were already coated in cement dust and dirt. He had to find some old work clothes quickly. That he would do in the street markets. But the bigger problem was how he was to keep secure and safe the small fortune he still had secreted in his shoes. He really could not avoid removing his shoes at night and he needed different footwear for the job.

He was still wearing his money belt containing the lek he had exchanged while in Peskopi. Passengers in the minibus directed him to the market nearest to the bus terminus. It was still in full swing, catching the customers returning to the city after a day's work. After some light-hearted banter and haggling over price, he acquired a cheap shirt, a pair of blue jeans, and a synthetic pair of trainers that should stand him in good stead for a month of brick-making.

He returned to flat 416 with a takeaway meal to spend a convivial evening with his companions watching an indifferent medley of TV shows. He was careful to take his clothes – in particular his shoes – into the shower with him before retiring. The water was lukewarm, there was no soap – something else he must get – and the only towel he had was small and threadbare. But things could be worse. Tomorrow he would tackle the problem of where and how to keep his money safe. As he lay in bed turning this problem over in his head, his thoughts inevitably wandered back to home. It was not yet four days since he had left, but so much had happened that he wanted to share with his parents. He knew they would be anxious to hear from him. Another task for tomorrow – how to get a message home? In spite of himself, a surge of homesickness welled over him. He buried his head in the mattress to hide his tears. The enormity of the unknown ahead of him momentarily overwhelmed him. He fell asleep feeling lonely and scared. The gremlins of despair are always more active in the midnight hours.

Next morning he woke with renewed spirit. The grey weather

over the weekend was giving way to a crisper clearer morning. Once he reached the work-site he decided to ask the advice of the old man about what to do with his valuables, without saying what they were or how much.

"No problem," said the old man. "Always think of somewhere no-one would ever look. Come with me."

He took him round behind the workshop. Among a tangle of weeds, there were discarded parts of old machinery, a pile of used cement bags, assorted pieces of old timber, and numerous broken breeze blocks of all shapes and sizes. In short, a tip of neglected rubbish. The old man moved some of the planks of wood and prised up a broken slab from the ground. He took a shovel and dug a small hole underneath where the slab had lain.

"There – stuff what you need in there in a polythene bag. Put the soil back, then the slab of concrete where it came from and then rearrange the old planks over it. No-one will find that place in a hundred years."

The old man then left him to it and returned to the workshop. Habib had a dilemma. How far could he trust the old man? He seemed kind and honest enough, but how could he be sure? He would run a test. He took $100 out of his shoe, wrapped it in an old polythene bag and buried it as instructed.

The next day it was still there, undisturbed. He waited two more days to be doubly sure and then decided to bury the rest of his batch of dollars, but these he sunk deeper in the ground, covered them with a layer of earth and then left the $100 note nearer the top before closing off the hideaway again under the slab and the pile of timber. Next on his agenda was to make contact with home.

His telephone call was from a communal telephone booth in the city centre – it cost 1,000 lek, and he was able to speak only to his aunt, because his family had no phone in their apartment. It was easier talking to his aunt but the five-minute call seemed to end before he had hardly started.

"Tell Mum and Dad I'm fine. Journey's gone well so far. No problems. Staying in Tirana for a month before getting a boat to Italy. OK for money – in fact, I've got a temporary job here and a decent place to live. No regrets. Can't wait to move on. I'll keep in touch. Tell them not to worry. Miss everyone. Give them all my love." The call was over before he realised he had heard almost nothing about how was the family and everyone else at the Mitrovice end. Ah well, next time he would get that in first.

The countdown of days passed agreeably enough. He got on famously with the old man and they worked harmoniously together. He slipped into a daily routine of early rising, breakfast on the hoof, a fuggy bus-ride, a hard day's work – unless it was raining too heavily, when work was replaced by nostalgic exchanges between the two of them in the shelter of their workshop – takeaway evening meal, television, light banter and chatter with Toci and his companions, clothes-washing and then bed. It was an acceptable routine, tempting almost to believe in it. But two incidents drove home to Habib the fragility of the arrangements.

On the third week of his stay the three companions had just bedded down for the night, when Toci knocked on the door and asked one of his Shkoder companions to come out to the sitting room. The door closed behind him. In a short time there was the sound of raised angry voices. Then the thumping began. Then the moaning and cursing. Then more thumping. Then dragging sounds and doors opening and closing quietly. Then quiet. Then the sound of someone returning, and the TV coming back on.

Habib lay on his mattress petrified in the darkened bedroom. What would happen next? Half an hour passed. Nothing. Just the background noise of the TV. He could hear the breathing of his other companions on the far mattress.

"What's going on?" he whispered.

"Big problem" said the faint voice from the other side of the room. "My friend told me about it yesterday. He couldn't pay the money they wanted. They said he would have to leave. He argued with them. Told them if they didn't give him time to get the money, he would go to the police. Stupid cunt! What did he expect? These guys don't take prisoners. If you cross them, you're dead meat, my friend. End of story!"

On one level what he had heard had resurrected all Habib's anxieties, but at another he felt a massive sense of relief. He had paid his dues. No reason for him to fall foul of the route masters. It was unlikely they would see their third companion again. Best to lie back and get some sleep. Tomorrow was another day.

The other more upsetting event occurred at the end of his last week. He arrived at the workshop on the Thursday at the usual time to find the old man in a state of some distress sitting disconsolately on a pile of cement bags, smoking, his head in his hands. The cause of his distress quickly became apparent. The doors of the workshop had been forced during the night and the cement mixer and brick moulds had disappeared. Nothing else was missing but Habib was filled with panic at the thought that his secret hiding place might have been discovered. He raced to the back of the shed and frantically shifted the timber pile. He wrenched up the concrete slab and dug furiously with his bare hands. Relief. Everything was intact. But perhaps now was the time to repossess his treasure and resecrete it his shoes in anticipation that within a few days he should be moving on.

Although Habib had lost nothing, the old man had lost the ingredients of his livelihood. They talked about what could be done. The old man was philosophical. He could probably get some more moulds and another mixer fairly easily. It would cost money, but then he would start making money again once he had them. Life always had its ups and downs. No need to get too worked up. He would get over it, but it was still a bit of a blow. First thing to do – "Tell Toci. He will know how to help," he said.

Habib registered that there would be no further work for that day at least, so offered to retrace his journey to the city as soon as he could and let Toci know what had happened.

It was just after ten o'clock in the morning when he finally reached the apartment. He trudged upstairs and used his own key to open the front door. There were noises coming from his bedroom. Sounded like a bit of a party, men's and women's voices, giggling and laughing. He looked in the sitting room. No-one there. He moved towards his bedroom. The door was ajar. No need to go in to see what was happening. The three mattresses had been pushed together in the middle of the room. Cavorting on them were two young women and a rather skinny pale-skinned young man. The women were kneeling astride their companion facing each other, one over his face and the other over his groin. They all seemed to be a having a good time. They were all totally naked. The buttocks of the young lady with her back to him were tattooed with two English words, one on each cheek -"Fuck" and "Me". In the corner of the room his friend Toci was videoing the energetic proceedings with a zoom lens. Habib had seen pornographic movies back in

Kosovo. What he had never seen before was the moment of their creation. He was at a loss as to what to say or do. He retreated embarrassed and self-conscious. Toci came to the rescue.

"Habib, my God! What in hell's name are you doing back at this hour? You're supposed to be at work! What the fuck's going on?"

Habib averted his eyes from the tableau on the mattresses and explained what had happened. Toci listened intently to all he had to say. The old man was his uncle of whom he was very fond.

"Sod it, sod it," he said. "OK you lot, get dressed. We'll finish this some other time. I've got some urgent calls to make and a few scores to settle."

There was menace in his tone. He had fingers in many pies and Habib was glad to be considered a friend rather than an enemy of this man. He thought chillingly of what had happened to his bedroom companion two weeks ago. He had better make himself scarce till the end of the normal working day, and then come home at his usual time and see what had transpired. He whiled away the rest of the day mooching round the city.

That evening Toci reported back. His networks across the twilight world of Tirana had identified the culprits. They would not be doing anything like that again for a long time. Sadly they had met with a little accident, which had left them with broken arms and broken legs. He was happy to say that his uncle was now back in business and there would be the usual day's work for Habib tomorrow. Now time to watch the television. Habib deemed it prudent to enquire no more.

Two days later, on Saturday morning, the 29th of November, Toci announced that tomorrow they would be moving. The next and vital stage of their trek was about to begin. They needed to make sure everything was ready for an early start on the Sunday morning. The journey south would take about seven hours.

"Get a good night's sleep tonight because you will be travelling all day by minicab and all night by boat on Sunday. You'll have to pay $750 to the boat captain before you can board. Better make sure you have that ready. Take a good supply of food and drink. Don't forget your torch. Be prepared to get wet and it will be cold. This is not a tourist trip."

Habib absorbed all the advice. That afternoon he made a last call to his aunt in Mitrovice to let his family know he was on the move again. He did not know when he would be able to contact them next, but they shouldn't worry. He could take care of himself. Everything was going according to plan. He wished Allah's peace and blessings on all his loved ones at home.

He checked through his rucksack and stowed away fruit and biscuits and a bottle of water for the journey. He discarded the work clothes, which had stood him in good stead at the brick works for a month but were now too filthy to be of any more use to him. He settled his board and lodging costs with Toci. Secretly he counted out $750 dollars and stowed it separately from the rest of his money under the insole of his left shoe. He would wear his warmest shirt and jumper under his leather jacket. He had bought a thin plastic cycling cape from the market. That was rolled up and tied to the top of the rucksack. He hoped it would be adequate to shelter him from the elements. On his head he would wear his baseball cap. All set to go, he and his remaining Shkoder companion settled down for their last night in apartment 416.

It had not been easy to sleep – too much to think about, too much apprehension, too much adrenalin flowing. He was glad when Toci summoned them for the off as dawn was breaking. Habib thanked him for all the help he had been and gave him five packets of cigarettes from his stock of goodies. Toci was undoubtedly a hard man, but he had been a good friend to Habib. He was visibly touched by the gift and flung his arms around him to wish a safe journey. There were few people on the streets at this hour on Sunday morning as the now familiar battered taxi pulled away into the traffic. They were on their way. It was good to have a companion. They had lived and slept beside each other for four weeks, had experiences in common and were embarked on the same venture. And two always felt safer than one! It really was time to formally introduce themselves to each other.

"My name's Habib by the way."

"Mine's Bledar." They shook hands and bid each other the best of luck, as Tirana ebbed away behind them. They were going to need it.

Chapter 18

Moldova - February 2001

Tuesday, the 20th of February 2001, dawned crisp and sunny for a change. The light frost on the Chisinau rooftops reflected the slanting red beams of the early-morning sun, lending a pleasing beauty to the elegant old buildings. There was just a hint of spring in the air, but people knew that this was just an illusion. There could yet be another month of snow and ice before Moldova's winter finally gave way to blossom on the trees and flights of returning birdlife. For most, it was just another day of humdrum work. In their heavy dark overcoats they walked in battalions to their respective sites of employment, heads down, fur-capped, hands deep in pockets. Despite the lift in the weather, the communal air of grim determination was maintained. Moldova was a place where living was primarily about surviving. The young people may find escape into music and booze and drugs, whatever, in the dark evenings, but the daylight brought reality back into focus. There was not much fun on the city streets from dawn to dusk, and even the young were sallow-faced and heavy-eyed at that time.

Nina was not paying much attention to either the frost or the early-morning sun or the droves of people intent on their own business. She had other more absorbing matters on her mind. There were things to do, and they had to be done without giving away what she was up to.

During the night she had turned over everything in her mind time and time again. She had told Zvetlana she would do it and the results of the hospital tests had confirmed her resolve. It was now time to think about practicalities. First there was the question of what to wear. Zvetlana had been very helpful. No problem with black underwear and hold-up stockings. She had all those. She never wore tights on evenings out anyway. She also had a short floral dress in soft cotton that buttoned down the front. That should be OK. Her coat was long, dark, and slim-waisted with an imitation fur collar. That was elegant and warm. Should be ideal. What about footwear? This was the time of year when she preferred her calf-length black leather boots. They complimented her coat and looked fine. But were they too cumbersome for pulling on and off quickly? They had long zips down each side. They should be OK.

What else? She already had tubes of hand-cream and tissues and a mobile phone. Zvetlana had mentioned rubbers. That was tricky. Nina had never used any, still less bought any. But they were available these days in chemists. Just a question of having the brazenness to go in and buy some. That would have to be done discreetly. Not sure what her friends would say if they saw her buying contraceptives. She could always say she was just being prepared for any irresistible overtures from new boyfriends. In the event she was able to slip off on her own during her lunch-break and acquire the necessary. In the outlying villages and towns it wouldn't have been so easy. They were not cheap, but hopefully they would more than pay for themselves. The one positive advantage of her new trade was that it was always cash on the nail, no long waits for people to pay their dues. If all went well, she would earn the cost of the rubbers several times over before the day was out. It seemed unreal, but that was the truth of it.

It was hard to pin down her feelings. Apprehension, guilt, excitement, nervousness, curiosity and dread all wheeled around in her as the clock inexorably ticked on towards the defining moment. The evening meal with her flatmates was something she would have preferred to avoid, but keeping up normal appearances was best, so, despite adrenalin reducing her appetite to almost nothing, she gossiped and joked with them as though this were any routine night. The little, rather more challenging, problem was how she was going to explain leaving their conviviality mid-evening and not getting back till very late. Best to keep things simple.

"'Fraid I'm going out and leaving you lot tonight. I've got a little assignation. Not sure what will come of it, but he seems a very nice guy and you never know, do you? Don't wait up for me! It could be a long exciting night – at least, I hope so!"

"Oh, who's a dark horse then?" they all crowed. "No wonder you weren't hungry! Come on tell us who he is – we can keep a secret, don't you know!"

"You must be joking! You lot! It would be round the city before I'd got my pants down if I told you. You'll just have to guess, but I'm not telling. My little secret and that's that!"

Half an hour later, bathed, oiled, face made up, hair combed out luxuriously in tresses over her collar, swinging her compact handbag with its essential contents and dressed in her leather boots and long coat, she made her dramatic exit to loud ribald comments from her admiring flatmates. It was 8:30 p.m. – plenty of time for the walk into the city centre, as always the only problem was the absence of street lighting and the profusion of unguarded potholes that littered the pathways. Of all nights, this was when she needed to be most careful. Her preparations had been meticulous. She wanted to look her most sophisticated. It was one way of dealing with the butterflies in her stomach. Her parents had always told her that it was the butterflies that stimulated you to do your best in exams. She hoped they were right. Tonight was uncharted territory for her. She had faced no greater test of her capabilities. If ever she needed to perform well, this was it.

Outside the Zoe coffee bar, she attracted many admiring looks from passers-by and not a few invitations for a drink. They were easily, even contemptuously, dismissed. The ten-minutes wait made her wish she had set out a little later. It was icy and the wind, though light, was penetrating. Under her coat she had minimum protection against the cold. It was a relief when Stefan and Zvetlana drew up spot on time. The interior of the car was snug and warm. Gentle sentimental music was wafting from the CD player. It was an atmosphere of calm and relaxation. Nina unbuttoned her coat and sank down into the rich comforting leather of the back seat. The warmth of the car soaked out the chill from her body as Stefan negotiated the city streets. In five minutes they arrived in the darkened park opposite the Hotel Dukro, now looking drab and forbidding in the absence of any exterior floodlighting.

Stefan manoeuvred so the car was parked facing the building, but partially obscured by the leafless trees. From there they had a reasonably uninterrupted view of the full front of the hotel. The lighted bedroom windows, usually with curtains drawn, made it obvious which rooms were occupied and which were not. In Stefan's presence, Zvetlana had been less chatty. The engine was switched off, cigarettes lit up, and the side window opened an inch or so to let out the smoke. At last the silence was broken.

"So here we are," said Stefan. "Are you all set?"

Nina's enthusiasm was ebbing by the minute. They sat there in the dark. He had switched off the music, and it was deathly quiet now, except for the occasional taxi that cruised to and from the hotel, picking up or depositing passengers, all muffled up against the cold. It was rather like watching a film. Everything seemed distant and detached. Nina couldn't help feeling they were like bank robbers in hiding waiting for the right moment to strike. Even so, she wasn't going to betray her anxieties to Stefan.

"I'm fine. What happens now?" she replied with false self-assurance.

"We just wait to see the next light go on in someone's room. That usually means they've just come back and are planning to go to bed. They've always had a few drinks and are feeling mellow. More important, this is when they're feeling lonely, and if they're used to a woman in bed with them at night, wife or whoever, this is the moment they are most vulnerable to propositions. We give them ten minutes or so and then ring their room. On average about one out of five say 'yes'. Then we move quickly before they have a chance for second thoughts.

"Have you got everything I suggested?" asked Zvetlana.

Nina affirmed she had.

"OK, a few last tips. Keep smiling. Plenty of oohs and aahs. They like to think you're enjoying it. Tell them how manly they are. They all like to be complemented on their prowess, though most are pathetic, especially when they've had a skinful of booze. They respond to compliments like little kids. And when you've finished tell them how great they were. That's usually good enough to earn an extra $10 bonus. You may as well milk them for all you can get out of them."

Stefan laughed coarsely.

"Don't listen to him. He's just crude. You know what I mean. I'm talking about money – just you keep control, enjoy yourself if you can, but never forget it's a business transaction and what you want is the most money for the least effort on your part. No place for sentimentality. I tell you, it's like shelling peas. You'll see.

"Have you got your mobile? We need to put Stefan's number in the memory. Keep it switched on all the time and close at hand. I seldom use it, but it's a nice safeguard. Stefan will sort any problems in no time if you call him. I can assure you they won't trouble you again when he's finished with them."

It was nearing 9:30 p.m. when the first new light appeared in a bedroom. Stefan used a pencil torch to look at a brown folder on his lap. Nina could see from the back seat it was a sketch of the hotel front. In the rectangle of each window on the plan there was a seven figure number. The light had appeared on the fifth floor, three rooms in from the left end. Stefan's finger located the exact room on the plan. Then he pressed into his mobile phone the number in that rectangle, stored it and waited.

Another light appeared, this time on the third floor, and the same procedure was repeated. Five minutes later there was a third new light. A third number was entered into the memory. Nina was intrigued. There was a military precision about how Stefan was organising things. When sufficient time had elapsed after the first light had come on, Stefan recalled the room number from the memory and pressed "call". He passed the phone to Zvetlana. Nina could just hear the faint ring tones, while her eyes were glued to the room window above them on the fifth floor in which the phone would be ringing.

"Hallo, ja, was ist?" came the response.

Zvetlana started in Russian.

"No understand. You speak English? German? No speak Moldovan. Sorry," came the response.

Whoever it was didn't understand either Russian or Moldovan. He sounded German, but that was no use to Zvetlana. Simple English it would have to be.

"Good evening, sir. You want nice girl. You like good time I think."

There was a long pause, then a cautious "Sorry, my English not good. You say me what you want."

"I think you good man. Maybe you like sex girl tonight? Moldovan girls very beautiful. I come to your room. Yes?"

Another long pause. "How much?"

"Cheap price. Maybe $40 – different things –different price. Promise good time."

Heavy breathing and another pause. Zvetlana continued "I think you happy I come – I see you five minutes. OK."

Another short pause and the line went dead.

"OK," said Zvetlana, "He's on the hook. Didn't say yes, but didn't say no. He'll be in a quandary, not knowing whether we're coming or not, but when he gets the knock on the door and sees you, he'll want you. Sounds as though he's from West Europe - German or Dutch or Scandinavian. They're usually good guys and generous. Should be an excellent start for you. Do you want to take him or shall I? We need to move quick though."

This was it. Now or never. If she was going through with it, no point in prevaricating. She needed the money. She was all set. For Nina the next half hour was going to be pivotal. This was why she was here. She couldn't turn back now.

"OK, I'll go. What do I do?"

"Right," said Stefan, "he's in room 505. Walk straight into the lobby. Take the lift to the fifth floor. Walk to your right. His door is towards the end of the corridor on the left. Knock gently on the door. If he doesn't answer, knock again a little more loudly. If still no answer, try a third time with a big knock. If he doesn't answer, leave and come back here as quick as you can. If he does let you in, you play it by ear and it's up to you. But don't overstay – you ought to be back here in less than an hour or he's getting more than his money's worth. Room 505 – don't forget. Best of luck."

Nina opened the car door and felt the chill night air engulf her. As she wrapped her coat around her, Zvetlana opened the window with a last piece of advice.

"By the way, there's a ladies' room near reception in the foyer. You can use that to clean and tidy up a bit afterwards if you need to. Forget about the reception staff. They know what it's all about and will turn a blind eye. And don't worry. It'll all be fine. You see."

First there was the fifty-metre walk across the dark park, then a short climb up some steps, across the road in front of the hotel, through the double swing doors, and across the foyer to the lift. Nina felt as though she were sleep-walking. This was surely someone else, not her. It was all happening outside of her. Six months ago she was in a different world living as a naive, slightly rebellious teenager in a rural village in the heart of Moldova. Now pregnant, sophisticated and alone in the capital city she was shamelessly espousing the life of a whore. Such a seismic shift was difficult to get her mind round. All she could do was detach herself and pretend the treadmill that was taking her forward was none of her doing.

The lift lurched to a stop. The doors opened onto a grubby threadbare green carpet running along a poorly lit corridor. Turn right, he had said. A few trance-like steps and there was the anonymous brown door on her left marked 505. She could still turn back. She didn't need to knock, but the mechanical dreamlike momentum within her somehow lifted her hand to tap on the woodwork. There was sound of movement in the room. She could still run off – but now she couldn't – the door had opened.

There he was, tall, well built, wearing a silk dressing gown and beckoning her inside. The door closed quickly and silently behind her.

Gerd Mueller was born in 1960 in Winnigen, a small West German village by the river Moselle, a few miles upstream from the historic city of Koblenz. His father had inherited the family vineyards on the south-facing slopes of the river from his grandfather who had been killed in the war on the godforsaken Eastern Front, as the Russian forces swept back the retreating Nazi army across Belarus in 1944.

In the 1960s West Germany's great economic revival was moving into full throttle. The European consumer markets were opening up and German technology, business acumen, and financial muscle meant they were better placed than anyone to cash in. Their burgeoning wine trade had not yet had to face the fierce competition that would eventually come from South Africa, Australia and California, and the Mueller family were able to ride the crest of the wave. They had the vineyards. German wines were in great demand. They had modernised their production techniques. They marketed aggressively, and their families prospered.

Inevitably Gerd was drawn into the family trade. He studied horticulture at university, specialising in viticulture. On graduating he travelled widely absorbing what the competition was doing and contributed his experience and academic knowledge to furthering the family fortunes. His reputation reached the corridors of power in Brussels and by his late thirties he had been appointed by the EU as a special advisor on economic development programmes to assist the recovery of the wine industry in emerging democracies whose economies had fallen apart after the collapse of the Soviet Union.

So it was that Gerd Mueller found himself in Moldova in early 2001, based in the capital for a week to study the problems of marketing their excellent wines in competitive western markets. His task was to devise a strategy for the regeneration of their once admired wine industry.

Some ten years earlier, he had married a longstanding school friend, Anna, and they had produced two energetic sons. As soon as the boys were at school fulltime, his wife had gone back to work as a research assistant for an eminent politician, and become progressively more and more absorbed by her job, working unsocial hours with many late evenings. The bulk of the domestic chores gradually shifted towards Gerd as he frequently worked from home and could be more flexible. Anna had decided their family was large enough, and her fatigue at the end of each working day was such that the physical side of their relationship slowly withered. They were both devoted to their boys. They had settled in the lovely suburban village of Waldesch, just south of Koblenz where their home lacked none of the modern amenities. They were respected and popular members of the thriving village community, not least because of Gerd's excellent connections in the wine trade. To all external appearances, they were a balanced, prosperous family with everything going for them, a lovely home, good professional jobs, plenty of money and a wide range of friends and colleagues.

Only one thing was lacking. Anna seemed unconcerned about it, but for Gerd it was a constant gnawing ache that demeaned his manhood.

He had arrived in Chisinau on a Moldovan Airlines flight direct from Frankfurt the previous day. Tuesday had been spent meeting officials and visiting some run-down vineyards a few miles outside the city to gauge the size of his task. That evening he had been wined and dined at a local restaurant where he had ample opportunity to sample the local wines. They were very agreeable, the only problem being they were not being produced in anything like sufficient quantity to be able to market them seriously in the West. The challenge was to raise production levels dramatically without sacrificing quality, and then orchestrate a professional marketing campaign. Once tasted, the wines would sell themselves. He arrived back in his room 505 at the Hotel Dukro at 9:30 p.m. feeling mellow and replete. The phone rang just as he was about to get into bed. The offer in broken English took him off his guard and penetrated his defences before he could rationalise his response. When the knock on the door came and he saw the young lady standing there so desirable and available, the overwhelming lack of female intimacy in his life obliterated any residual hesitation. The bedroom door closed on the outside world. No-one else would share this compelling moment.

He knew nothing of her world; she knew nothing of his. Two total strangers, unable to communicate except in stilted syllables of a language foreign to both, driven by ageless procreative forces, stood facing each other in a characterless bedroom – a desk table the length of the wall down the right side, a utilitarian single bed against the other, brown plywood headboards at either end, a well-used armchair near the curtained window, an antiquated TV, a thick garish Moldovan rug on the floor, a bedside table and lamp and his expensive suitcase stowed in front of the built-in wardrobe.

"*Schon, sehr schon*," he said.

"No understand, small English - please," she replied.

"You very beautiful," he replied.

He took both her hands in his and kissed them gently one by one. Nina's contact with reality was slipping even further away. She had never been so graciously admired before. He reached to the top buttons of her coat and slid it off, folding it carefully before laying it on the chair. She tossed her hair so the tresses fell naturally over the nape of her neck, as he enfolded her in his arms. He was the biggest man she had ever embraced, and still residually bronzed, unlike Moldovan men. She felt like a fragile nymph against his muscular body. The hardness of his desire pressed through the thin membrane of clothes separating them.

After what seemed longer but was probably only a few moments, he moved to the buttons of her dress until the shoulders fell away and the dress slipped to the floor. Still wearing her boots, she stood before him gauchely, but relieved not to be embarrassed by either her figure or her lacy underwear. He took a step back and admired her again. "*Schon, schon – du bist sehr schon*" – it sounded the same as before.

He folded her in his arms again and she could feel him fumbling with her bra hook without success. She reached behind and undid it for him, pulled her arms forward and let it tumble down to join the dress on the floor. He cupped her nubile breasts in his hands and gently nestled his face in them, and then without warning hoisted her in his arms like a rag doll and laid her softly on the incommodious bed. He moved to the foot of the bed, raised each of her legs in turn, and unzipped her boots one by one, easing them off and standing them neatly by the chair. As he took off his dressing gown Nina found herself feeling foolishly shy and embarrassed to look at him, not least because his excitement was so evident. He squeezed onto the inadequate bed beside her, slid one arm round her neck, the other between her thighs, and started gently caressing her. Nina had made love before, but almost always in cramped uncomfortable locations, usually with only the minimum amount of clothing removed, and with minimum preliminaries. This was a new sensuous experience, which served only to reinforce her light-headedness. Her remaining clothing cover was now irrelevant and she reached down to remove the last barrier to his caresses.

The touch of his fingers around and inside her moist crevasse caused shivers of desire within her she had never experienced before. She bent her legs and opened herself wider to him in automatic response. Her head was giddy with pleasure and she willed him to do more and more.

He seemed to be fumbling with something on the bedside table. When she opened her eyes momentarily to see what he was doing, he had opened a condom packet and was clumsily trying to roll it onto his erection with one hand.

Nina remembered Zvetlana's advice and realised with a jolt of dismay the mistakes she was making. She had left her handbag with her rubbers and mobile phone in it on the table the other side of the room, too far to reach without disrupting proceedings. She had not meant to do that. Fortunately her lover was remedying the condom problem by using his own. She also remembered this was supposed to be a business transaction, but she had not mentioned money. For her the sheer sensual pleasure of their coupling was so overwhelming, the prime reason she was there had been temporarily forgotten.

His fumbling complete, he moved across her. She didn't know whether she should open or close her eyes, but his entry into her was slow, measured and deep. He breathed an intense sigh of relief. Nina was conscious only of his size within her, so different from her past boyfriend. She was anxious whether she would be able to cope, but as he began to move inside her, everything responded in harmony. Her thoughts and feelings became solely focussed on the core of her being. Too soon, too quickly she felt his final thrusts and knew that his desire had been satisfied. He tried to keep the dead weight of his body off her and showered her forehead with gentle kisses.

"Danke schon, danke schon, sehr gut, sehr gut, danke schon," he whispered into her left ear.

After a few residual thrusts and precious moments of calm, gentle embrace, he manoeuvred himself beside her again and slumped back on the pillow. His penis, now becoming limp but still sheathed, looked less aggressive and more vulnerable. Nina had an overpowering urge to curl up beside him and cuddle him. Her body was still aglow, vibrant with sensations that she wanted to preserve as long as possible. Then a total surprise. As she nestled against him, she became conscious of tears rolling quietly down his cheeks. Her maternal instincts were even more stimulated.

"Sorry, sorry – not be sad. This good time. You good man. Thank you. Make very happy love," she attempted to cheer him up, remembering belatedly Zvetlana's exhortation that she should always compliment her lover's prowess and performance, though she could not have been more genuine in her remarks to him.

"Sorry," he responded. "You very lovely. Me very happy. Thank you. Thank you. I sad my wife we not make love strong now. I forget love so good. You very good to me. Thank you."

Nina tried to comprehend what he was saying. They both had very limited vocabulary, but with a few basic words and, more especially, in their actions they were establishing some sort of communication with each other. There was no doubt they had both enjoyed their love-making. It seemed he had a problem with his wife, but Nina couldn't fathom what that might be.

She would have liked to stay the rest of the night there, but as their conversation became more focussed and serious, so reluctantly she recollected her more pressing goals. She placed a gentle kiss on his cheek and prised herself from the bed. Her bra and pants were retrieved quickly. She stepped back into her dress pulling it up onto her shoulders. The boots went on easily and she picked up her coat and handbag ready to go. This was the tricky bit. Would he offer or would she have to ask for the money?

Her lover still lay prostrate on the bed but he had pulled across a blanket to hide his nakedness. He opened the draw in the bedside cabinet and without a word handed $50 to her.

"No, no - too much – price is $40, this too big," she said to him.

"All good, you keep money, me very happy. Maybe you come again tomorrow, please? You give me phone number please?"

Nina was nonplussed. It seemed he wanted her tomorrow again. Would that mean another $50? He gave her a pen and a piece of hotel notepaper and beckoned her to write down her phone number. Nina could see no reason not to, so she gave it to him.

"Very good. Thank you. My name is Gerd. What name you?"

Nina told him her first name. He put out his hand and she took it to shake their goodbye. She threw her coat over her shoulders, eased the door open quietly and left. Once in the corridor reality came surging back. She checked her watch. It was nearly 10:30 p.m. She had been with him for about forty minutes, perhaps the most memorable minutes of her life. She felt a lightness in her step in stark contrast to when she had walked the same corridor such a short while earlier. Even the lift seemed to work more smoothly. She almost ran across the foyer and through the park to join Stefan and Zvetlana again.

She jumped into the back seat. Stefan was alone.

"Where's Zvetlana?" asked Nina, suddenly slightly anxious that the one she trusted most was absent.

"She's on a job. Went a while ago. She'll be back soon. How did it go? No problems, I guess?" he asked.

"Fine," she said, reckoning the least said the better. No need to tell him she had given the German her phone number, nor that he wanted to see her again. That was her little secret.

"Got off to a good start then. No problem with the fee?"

Nina said that was all okay, but didn't tell him how much. Then she remembered the obligation to pay something to Stefan for orchestrating everything and providing back-up security. She valued all that and proffered him the $10 per client fee Zvetlana had told her about.

"What's this then? It's $50 a night, you know!"

Nina was mortified. He really couldn't mean that. "But I thought Zvetlana had said it was $10 each time. Have I got it wrong?" she asked plaintively.

"Too right, my darling! $10 per client on the understanding you do at least five jobs a night – after that it's all yours, but minimum cover is not less than $50. Hope that's a bit clearer now."

Nina fought to grasp all this. She wished Zvetlana were here. Had she been led up the garden path? Five encounters a night was a daunting prospect. As far as tonight was concerned she would have nothing to show for it unless she did some more, whereas all she really wanted to do was go home, curl up in bed and reflect on the memorable experience with her German. She tried to keep her cool.

"So I need to do some more then if I'm going to be able to pay you for tonight?"

"That's up to you darling, but you owe me $50 dollars before you go home tonight. It's your decision how you earn it."

"OK. Are there any more lights on up there? I guess I need to get on with it then!" She tried to sound chirpy and unfazed. Inside she was churning uncomfortably. Could she screw herself up to do it all again, and perhaps again, and again tonight? Just take it one step at a time. Keep calm. She did a quick mental calculation. What she had earned already would pay off Stefan for tonight. Anything else would be a bonus and straight into her pocket. That was why she was here. Deep breath – let's see what's next.

And there at last was Zvetlana swinging her way back to the car through the trees, job done. It was a comfort to see her again. What story would she have to tell?

Chapter 19

Albania - November 2003

The history of mankind is littered with human folly. Perhaps the most monumental is the Great Wall of China – 3,500 miles of massive stone and concrete, snaking inexorably across mile upon mile of inhospitable mountain terrain, as high as a house and wide enough for a horse-drawn chariot to be driven along its battlements. Every half-mile or so there is a watchtower rising twenty feet above the top of the wall. The building was started by decree of Emperor Qin Shi Huang at the end of the third century B.C. Its purpose was to protect the northern perimeter of his empire and keep out marauding barbarians from the untamed Mongolian vastnesses beyond. It took fifteen years to build at astronomical cost in terms of materials, suffering and human lives.

But it didn't work! By the time it was finished it was in the wrong place, as the empire's borders were changing all the time, and in any event the indigenous would-be invaders quickly identified ways and means of breaching the defences at the dead of night when the watchtower guards, bored out of their minds at their godforsaken outposts, lapsed into alcoholic or opium induced stupor. Now it remains as a marvellous tourist attraction boosting China's burgeoning tourist economy, with the reputation of being the only man-made structure on earth visible from outer space.

As Habib and Bledar relaxed in the back of their taxi accelerating away from Tirana along the deserted Sunday morning road in the grey dawn, China's ancient folly was not something they had the slightest interest in, but in a few hours' time, although they did not know it, they themselves would be making use of one of the residual elements of Albania's comparable monumental folly.

When Hoxha broke off relations with Russia and left the Warsaw Pact in 1968, Albanians were greatly in fear of another "Czechoslovakia", expecting that their country would be invaded by Russia to re-impose Soviet allegiance. The Albanian leader's decreed response was to build the notorious "bunkers" throughout the country. They were supposed to provide a village by village defence system. There were two types. The smaller family-sized version was about ten feet in diameter, six feet high, with walls of reinforced concrete 12 inches thick, and a mushroom-shaped domed roof of similar thickness. Each had a low narrow access door and slit apertures on each wall to take a rifle. Each was built to the same specification.

The larger version was to accommodate big artillery guns, usually built into the side of hills, much higher and more spacious, and fortified all round with reinforced concrete.

Every village, every town, every city was required to build a proliferation of these at every strategic point. The propaganda was unequivocal. The continuation of Albanian life and culture depended on these bunkers. In these the people of Albania would be able to see off the aggressors when they came. And so the bunkers were built – thousands upon thousands, on the hillsides, on the beaches, on the roadsides, in fields, in the towns, in the villages, everywhere – and not one of them was ever used in earnest. Today they still remain, scattered throughout the country, an ugly enigmatic eyesore to paranoia and dictatorial folly. Some are used as chicken houses, some as store sheds, and some on the beaches are painted in exotic colours to serve as play houses for youngsters.

As the early-morning miles sped away, Habib and Bledar were unaware that one of these larger-style bunkers would serve as the assembly point for the group of illegal immigrants due to embark on the boat that would take them across the Adriatic Sea that night. It was tailor-made for that purpose. It was sunk into the cliffside, overlooking the sea, but carefully disguised both from the land and seaward sides. It was soundproof, weatherproof and remote, and provided close access to the sandy cove that would be used by the boat to take on its clandestine passengers.

The bunker's original purpose was to defend the cove, an ideal secret landing point for an invading army. Now it was equally ideal for taking off illegal immigrants. It was two miles from the nearest village. It had high cliffs on each side and a steep precipitous path down a rocky gully to the beach. A rough track from the village allowed vehicles to reach the bunker and that now sufficed for access to the top of the cliffs. The bunker had no peacetime purpose whatever, except perhaps for furtive encounters of courting couples or under-age drinking binges. It had the residual dank, neglected smell of old concrete, dried urine, and musty mould. But for assembling in secret a group of two dozen disparate individuals arriving that evening from all parts of Albania prior to a speedy embarkation and departure by boat from the cove, the bunker was ideal. Comrade Hoxha deserved a measure of retrospective appreciation for his foresight!

Habib and Bledar knew the name of the place they were heading for, Dhermi, but they had to rely on their driver to get them there. It was a long journey - first the good road, flat and fast towards Durres, then a turn southwards, parallel to the sea, to pick up the main highway across the Albanian flatlands between the mountains and the sea passing through Kavaje, Lushnje, Fier, and finally reaching Vlora on the coast. The drive was tedious and uneventful, but that was no bad thing in view of their incipient apprehension about what was in store. Conversation was desultory and the two backseat passengers dozed spasmodically while the driver charged at the road ahead as though desperately late for a crucial appointment. His chain-smoking shrouded the inside of the car in a permanent haze.

Just offshore from Vlora is a small island called Sazan. Over the last century its territorial sovereignty has oscillated between Albania and Italy. Since 1947 it has been Albanian, but an Italian radar tracking station is still permitted to operate there, its main function being to pre-empt illegal smuggling of goods or people in boats from the southern Albanian shores across to Italy. Unfortunately for Italy, but happily for the people traffickers, a high range of mountains south of Vlora reaches down to the sea and impedes the radar signals in the vicinity of Dhermi. The coastline there not only provides a number of secluded sandy coves, but is also protected from radar surveillance. In short, with the added bonus of the redundant artillery bunker as a staging post, this was an ideal spot for getting illegal immigrants away from Albania.

It took the taxi about four hours to reach Vlora. They pulled into a roadside truckstop for a perfunctory lunch and petrol refill. The weather was grey and chill but there was no wind. Having lived all his life inland, Habib was not aware what a blessing that would be for their overnight sea-crossing in a small boat. The driver was anxious to keep going. It would take another two hours to reach the assembly point. The road was going to get worse and more mountainous and he wanted to get there before dark.

They enjoyed the westerly vista over the bay towards Sazan island for the next half an hour and then hit the mountain range. The road ascended alongside the valley cut through by the river and after a steep, bumpy, hairpin climb they were rewarded in the late afternoon with majestic views, albeit grey and murky, southwards across the Albanian Riviera with the Greek Ionian islands in the distance, dominated by the celebrated tourist magnet of Corfu. Then more hazardous hairpins until they caught sight of Dhermi village nestling in a saddle of the mountains overlooking the sea. About a mile before the village the driver slowed and turned right off the make-shift road onto a track reaching across the fields towards the cliff edge. It was not really for ordinary cars, but bore evidence of recent use by other vehicles, probably 4x4s. The taxi slithered from rut to rut and eventually reached a turning point where the driver made it clear that this was as far as he was going.

The place was deserted. It was dusk. There were no lights to be seen. The late November air was damp and cold. Gulls were circling and screeching overhead as they swooped round the cliff edge. They seemed to be voicing resentment at competition for their space. The sea stretched ominously grey and forbidding out to the west till it merged indistinguishably with the leaden darkening sky. For Habib it was an environment that was foreign and foreboding.

"Are you leaving us here?" he asked.

"I've got my orders – deliver you two to the cliff top, and show you the path down to the bunker. You wait there till someone comes for you. I've got to get the hell out of here quick before anyone notices my car and starts asking questions."

The two young men grabbed their rucksacks and made sure they'd left nothing behind in the car. Habib fished out two packets of cigarettes and gave them to the driver together with one of the illegal porno DVDs he had brought from Kosovo. For good measure he also gave him 1000 lek note as a tip, mainly out of relief that for once they were not being ripped off by a taxi driver.

They stood silently together and watched the taxi disappear slowly whence it had come. The piercing sound of the gulls was their only company as they turned and trudged towards the little track that began winding its way down the slope. There was just enough light to see where they were putting their feet, but the rocks were slippery and the descent required patient negotiation. Habib was thankful he was wearing a robust pair of shoes. They spoke little and then only in whispers. Without expressing as much, they were both quietly glad that they were not doing this on their own. They could see and hear the gentle waves caressing the beach below them. Habib had never before seen the sea for real. From films and TV he had rather expected it would be blue and foam-flecked and inviting, not grey and flat and sombre.

After five minutes the track levelled out and turned back towards the cliff face. Standing gaunt and menacing, the bunker loomed into view, its main entrance pointing out to sea. It was then they heard the voices, faint and furtive. Someone else was there. Habib and Bledar stopped dead in their tracks. They both sensed how vulnerable they were. If this were a trap, they could be rolled over easily, robbed of all they had and left hopeless and helpless. But what else could they do? There was no option but to go forward. Having come so far, they had to believe things would unravel in their favour.

They made a cautious approach to the bunker in the gloomy twilight. To be too quiet might startle the people inside and they may then react adversely. Equally, if they shouted ahead, that might provoke fear that the bunker's occupants had been discovered by the security forces, and lead to an equally adverse response. In the end they did what came naturally. They walked stealthily forward, side by side, and didn't speak. They were fit young men and ready for action with fists clenched. The only sound they made was their feet on the rubble of the track heading towards the bunker.

The voices from inside became more distinct until they had reached about ten yards from the entrance, when abruptly everything went eerily quiet. They stopped and listened. Suddenly a fierce beam of light from a powerful source danced over them. They could see nothing as it momentarily blinded them, but they could hear well enough the voice that screamed at them through the light and dark.

"Stop where you are. Don't move a muscle or you won't see your mother again. Stretch your arms high above your heads. Now kneel down."

The light source and the voice and feet advanced towards them, but still dazzled by the beam trained on them, they could make out little of what lay beyond.

The voice spoke again. "Listen carefully, I don't want to have to repeat myself. We know who we're expecting. A loaded rifle is pointing at both your heads. If you don't fit the bill, God help you. So let's know who you are. Where've you come from? What's the names of the contacts that brought you here?"

Habib and Bledar had nothing to hide. They could only rehearse the truth. If that didn't suffice, there was nothing else they could do. They had no escape. To climb back up the cliff would expose them as sitting targets in the glare of the light beam. The only other course was a headlong descent to the bay but that would leave them trapped by sea and cliffs. Resigned to their fate, they answered as required.

"OK so far, but tell me, Mr Habib Peci," continued the voice. "What was the name of the man who gave you German lessons in Dragash?"

In his answers Habib had rehearsed only the details of his time crossing Albania. He had not mentioned the Kosovo part of his journey. He was surprised, but also reassured that this disembodied voice on a bleak cliff face in the middle of nowhere was evidently aware of the trail of contacts from where he had started. He had no difficulty in remembering the name of Mr Banjuka and his wife who had been so kind to him on the first day of his travels. Bledar was posed a similar testing question. They both gave the right answers.

"OK, that's fine. Welcome - get off your knees and come inside."

The light beam was extinguished. There were four men standing in front of them. Each was dressed in the familiar garb – black woollen bobble hats pulled over their ears, a black handkerchief across the lower part of their faces, black leather jacket, black polo neck shirts, black jeans and boots, and more to the point, two of them had rifles slung casually across their arms.

Inside the bunker there was already a group of a dozen or so other people. Most were men but there were a few women too. They were all muffled in warm clothes and each had a suitcase or a rucksack similar to Habib's. Some were standing, others were sitting on the remains of broken wooden crates. Most were smoking. Apart from the pervasive bunker smells, there was nothing else of note. The only light was from two guttering candles perched on a cleft in the rock-face that formed the rear of the bunker. It was a lonely, disconsolate assembly. Conversation was minimal and a feeling of bewildered apprehension prevailed.

One of the masked men, clearly the owner of the voice and the leader, ushered them into the bunker. He explained they were waiting for more people to join them. They were expected soon. There would be a four-hour wait before they climbed down to the beach. The boat would come for them at 10 p.m. Meanwhile no-one was to leave the bunker unless they had to go outside to relieve themselves. No noise, and bearing in mind it was going to be a long night, they might like to rest up.

Habib and Bledar took themselves off to a corner, spread their waterproof capes on the insalubrious floor, and took the chance to sit down and eat and drink some of the goodies from their rucksacks. The four minders squatted at the entrance of the bunker, guns cradled in their arms, smoking and chatting intermittently in low voices. The screeching of the gulls had ceased. Above the murmured conversation, the only sound was the gentle incessant washing of the waves into the cove. It was strangely comforting and reassuring. Nothing more to do for the next few hours. Habib stretched out and dozed fitfully, mildly surprised at how relaxed and excited he felt at the prospect of the next phase of his adventure. Mitrovice seemed a long way away. He had no wish to turn back.

Despite his drowsiness, from time to time he was conscious of more people arriving and being ushered into the bunker. Everyone was a stranger and each seemed content to mind their own business. There was no false familiarity and certainly no contrived jocularity. This was serious stuff. Lifestyles, livelihoods and even lives were at stake. For most of the souls huddled together in the bunker this was the moment of reckoning. Nothing would be the same again. They were sacrificing the known for the unknown. The risk was incalculable. The past was etched vividly in their minds, but the future was a blank. This was not a time for light-heartedness, but for focus, for resolve, and for prayer to whatever god they believed in.

His dozing was abruptly curtailed.

"On your feet, you lot!" the voice shouted. "Get all your stuff together. We're going down to the beach. No lights – no talking.

It's rocky and slippery and steep. Just take your time – but you're on your own. We don't provide a rescue service."

"One last thing before we go down – the little matter of payment. You all know the rules: $750 each for the trip. Can't handle that on the beach, so you pay now as you leave. Get your money out. One at a time."

The two riflemen stood just outside the entrance, the two others inside. Habib and Bledar stood in line waiting their turn. Slowly the line advanced. One of the minders carefully counted the dollar bills, watched by the other holding a small torch so they could see what they were doing. Each payment was secured in a plastic band and slipped into a black imitation-leather briefcase. Habib had removed his shoe quietly in the darkness and taken out the secreted polythene envelope with his money in it, the $750 already counted before leaving Tirana. When he reached the entrance it was quickly checked – seven $100 bills and one fifty. Bledar followed him and they joined the growing group waiting outside with the two riflemen. There was a faint moon in the sky, its filtered light just managing to penetrate the high wispy clouds. The temperature was much cooler outside the bunker, where the warmth of two dozen bodies in a confined space had generated its own micro-climate.

Habib was reflecting that it was on such a night as this that he had walked across the mountains a month ago, but this time it was the sea that was beckoning, ceaselessly continuing its gentle caress of the beach below them. It was at that moment that a commotion started inside the bunker. The two riflemen sprang to alert and advanced to where their two colleagues were in debate with an agitated young man. Only with considerable restraint were voices being kept under control. The issue was simple. The young man was $100 short. He was sure it had been there. Now it was gone. Too bad – he was going to be left behind. He was desperate and pleaded his case, cupping his hands together in instinctive supplicatory mode, with tears coursing down his cheeks.

His pleas fell on deaf ears. "No money – no go! You know the rules!"

They gave him back his clutch of dollar bills and dismissed him to the back of the bunker where he stood whimpering to himself, painstakingly recounting his money in the light of the candles.

The remaining "customers" passed through without incident. Only the young man remained. There was a sombre, tense hush among the rest of the group now gathered outside in the dark waiting for the descent to begin. One rifleman and the leader had gone inside to "reason" with the young man. In the stillness, their hard uncompromising dialogue carried on the air to those outside.

"We don't have time to fart about. We know you've enough money on you to survive when you're across the water. Don't fuck with us! Give us the $750 and get your arse out of here with the others!"

"You don't understand what I'm saying. I did have the whole amount, and more, to use in Italy when I got there. But it's disappeared. I had it when I left Tirana. I know I did. I checked it twice. But there's only $650 left. I don't know where it's gone. I think someone must have stolen it. For God's sake, believe me."

"Well isn't that just too bad?" was the response, "Let's check how much you've got and we'll see what we can do."

The young man proffered his dollar bills again. He watched them count out $500. His hope was that that they would realise he was telling the truth and relent about how much they were to require of him. He was wrong.

"Right, we take $500 to cover our expenses. You can have $150 back to cover your expenses in getting back to where you came from. That all seems just and fair, don't you think? And one last thought. We know exactly who you are and where you and your family live. Any thoughts you might have, my friend, of divulging anything about this operation, and it will be the worse for them. I'm sure we understand each other perfectly, don't we? Now get the hell out here and don't let's see you again unless you come with the right fucking money!"

The candles were blown out and the last rites of the bunker sojourn were completed. The young man was bundled out and directed back up the cliff path with a rifle pointed towards him. He merged quickly into the blackness, as though he had never been.

It was a very subdued group of climbers that began the final descent, two minders leading the way and the two riflemen bringing up the rear. The faint light of the moon was sufficient to make out the track without the need for torches. The only other illumination was the dozen or so pin-prick glows of red stretching out along the path from those who tried to pacify their nerves with a cigarette. Those carrying suitcases rather than rucksacks on their backs were finding it tough going. Frequently both hands were needed to maintain balance and grip on the treacherous terrain. It was not long before someone lost their footing. There was a crunching, scratching, tumbling sound followed by curses and profanities. The line came to a halt. It was difficult to see what had happened ahead. Then people started moving again. A few metres further down Habib and Bledar passed one of the group sitting on the ground. He was an older man with a small dark beard, wearing a qeleshe. He was nursing his ankle and clearly in some pain. His suitcase had burst open beside him. He was trying to drag himself downwards sitting on his backside and pulling the case along behind him.

"Anything we can do?" asked Habib.

"For the sake of Allah, please, please help me!" he begged.

He was in great distress. The facts were stark. He had already paid his money for the boat trip. The earlier experience of the young man made it crystal clear he wouldn't see that again, but his fall had left him with a twisted, perhaps even broken, ankle. There was no way he could get back to civilisation without assistance but he could expect no help from the minders. That had been made explicit. The rest of the group were going to catch the boat regardless. They weren't going to turn back at this stage. The prospect of being left alone and incapacitated on the cliff-side was looming large. That filled him with dread. He had heard stories about how ruthless the people traffickers were. The removal of all identity papers from pockets, a bullet in the side of the head and a roll down the cliff into the dark unforgiving sea was the most convenient method of disposing of redundant passengers.

"Please help me get down the cliff. I'll make it worth your while when we get across. Allah will reward you in mercy, blessings be upon His Name."

"OK, we'll do what we can," said Habib.

It had always been second nature to Habib to try to help people in need. That's one of the reasons he had reacted so badly to the cruel premeditated violence he had witnessed in Mitrovice. These were the values that fed his drive to seek out a place where more civilised standards prevailed. He preferred to "bind up those in need" rather than "cast them down". Like a good Samaritan, he would not walk by on the other side.

Bledar picked up the suitcase and pressed it as tightly shut as he could and stowed it under his arm. Habib helped the man to his feet and took his weight on his shoulder with the man's arm slung round him. It was slow going. The rest of the group were steadily passing them as they each negotiated the downward slope at their own pace. There was still no sign of any boat. It was very dark but the white crests of the waves could be seen faintly in the bay below as they coursed in like streamers along the shoreline. Habib was sure that the boat would be silhouetted against the breaking surf if it were there. The fact that it hadn't arrived yet meant they could take their time. The accident had happened about halfway down so that left the final 200 foot or so to cover, and even going painstakingly slowly they arrived at the foot of the cliffs only five minutes after the last of the main group had reached there.

They set the injured man on a rock to take the pressure off his ankle. He showered them with thanks. They knew he would need help getting into the boat. That shouldn't be too much of a problem, nor disembarking. The tricky question was what he was to do when they reached Italy. But that was tomorrow's agenda. The matter of the moment was what was to happen next. It was an odd scene: A motley group of darkly clad strangers, standing incongruously on a secluded beach, clutching their meagre possessions in thin chilly moonlight, with the waves of an inky black sea quietly shushing to and fro, totally indifferent to their plight. Apart from the waves it was unutterably quiet.

The leader of the minders had advanced to the water's edge. He carried the powerful lamp that had so dazzled Habib and Bledar a few hours earlier. They could see its beam stretching out westwards across the tumbled surface of the sea. It flashed three times. Then a pause and three more flashes. Then a long pause followed by three more flashes. Then all was dark again. Those who had kept their focus out to sea would have seen one short flash of red light pierce the otherwise unremitting blackness out there. No-one spoke, but the leader rejoined the group. Everyone waited.

After about five minutes, the faintest of engine noises could be heard gradually drawing closer. Eyes peered into the distance.

Some thought they could make out the dark silhouette of a boat, but the motor noise faded. It was replaced by the sound of gentle rhythmic splashing, which merged insouciantly with the noise of the breaking waves. After a further five minutes everyone could discern the outline of the boat as two sets of oars on either side heaved it steadily with the surf towards the shore. About five yards from the water's edge it slid gently to a halt. Two of the minders had gone to meet it, and they grabbed the rope that was slung at them from the prow of the vessel. A narrow gangplank was swung out to the side and then unfolded in four sections, each about four feet long. When fully extended it reached almost to the water's edge. The sea lapped around its foot. There was a single rope handrail. In rough conditions it would have been hazardous, but on this night the elements were in a kindly mood.

The leader ran up the gangplank and greeted a big burly man on board with a bear-hug. He was carrying the briefcase. The moon was sinking towards the horizon but it still shed enough residual light to make out what was happening in the darkness. The two men, one who was presumably the captain, disappeared from view for a short time while the other crew members used their oars to keep the boat steady head-on to the shoreline as the waves ran around it. The minder on the shore kept a firm hold on the rope to keep the bows hard in.

Having completed the transaction to both sides' satisfaction, the leader came back ashore and signalled the embarkation of the passengers, now down to twenty-three, assuming the injured party could make it. Even though conditions were calm, most succumbed to wet feet as they tentatively negotiated the gangplank. There were more anxious moments as, one by one, the exodus began. Bledar and Habib hoisted the injured man to the shoreline and then, inch by inch, manoeuvred him along the gangplank. After some effort, they were at last able to heave him over the side and let him slide down onto the deck of the boat. They were the last on board. The loading operation had taken barely fifteen minutes. The rope was thrown back and while the crew members leaned backwards on their oars to keep the boat steady, the passengers were herded to the stern. Their combined weight gradually lifted the bow off the sand and the boat slipped slowly backwards as the pressure on the oars urged it away from the shore. Once the boat was fully off in deeper water, the passengers were rearranged evenly around the perimeter of the vessel. Each sat on the deck with their backs against the gunwale, their cases or rucksacks clutched beside them. The boat slewed round until its bows faced the open sea. Yard by yard, the four oarsmen eased the heavy craft across the undulating waves further from the shore. There had been no fond farewells and with barely a handwave, the four minders had trekked off up the beach and melted away into the night. They had served their purpose. Habib could not fault their efficiency, but it was a ruthless efficiency and he was glad to no longer be beholden to them. The austere Albanian coastline was fading behind. Ahead lay Italy - the land of beauty, love and music. Habib could hardly wait.

Chapter 20

Moldova - February 2001

Zvetlana bounced back into the car and flopped down into her seat, laughing and waving a fistful of Russian roubles.

"Well that was fun! Russian guy - completely pissed when I arrived. Staggering around, totally naked, with a litre bottle of vodka, three-quarters gone, whimpering he couldn't raise it. Please could I help? I did a quick strip-tease while he lay on his bed, cradling his bottle. No effect at all – then I gave him a good massage. Still nothing - so I rubbed some cream on the top of his prick and told him he'd come! He was so sozzled he couldn't tell the difference, showered me with thanks, saying he knew he was man enough! What a joke! I helped myself from his wallet – he didn't care – poor sod won't remember anything in the morning, but there's at least a $100 worth here I guess. Easy money! Wicked really!"

Nina was riveted and bemused by what she was hearing, but more focussed now on how she herself was going to fare next time. Stefan had called another two numbers, both robust negatives. The next bedroom light had come on and this time he gave the phone to Nina. She emulated Zvetlana's seductive overture. The responder replied in Russian, reasonably coherently – he would not be averse to receiving a visit. Nina told him she would be with him in a few minutes. Already she felt more confident and in control.

When he opened the bedroom door, she had no illusions other than that this would be a business encounter. He was middle-aged, short, stout round the waist, moustached, and wearing ill-fitting, out-of-date flared trousers and a badly ironed striped shirt, open at the neck; not someone she would normally have given a second of her time for. He had had a few drinks but was courteous and helped her take her coat off. Nina was more with it this time.

"Hello, happy to meet you, what can I do for you sir?" she asked, and outlined to him the tariff for her services that she had learned from Zvetlana.

Her anonymous friend indicated he was happy with that and started unbuttoning her dress. Doubtless her clothes were coming off sooner or later, so Nina was content to let him take the initiative, reacting as seductively as possible, even though rather contrived, as he removed each garment.

"Shall we leave my stockings on?" she asked, knowing that they were always the most time-consuming element when redressing. "It's more sexy, don't you think?"

Her companion agreed and moved back to admire her as she posed for him, naked but for her hold-up stockings.

"Shall I get on the bed?" asked Nina.

"I hope you don't mind, but I prefer to do it standing up from behind, if that's all right? I have trouble with my back when I lie down. It's easier if I stand."

Nina was slightly nonplussed but thought quickly how best to manage his preference.

"If I bend over and hold onto the arms of the chair, do you think that would be OK?"

Her companion thought it would. Nina made sure her handbag was within easy reach and produced a condom. She took charge of that little matter. Her gentleman friend seemed more than compliant. She unzipped his trousers, and rolled on the rubber. She turned her back towards him, stood with her legs planted a foot or so apart and leaned forward onto the arms of the chair. Surreptitiously she looked between her legs to see the rubber was still in place as he pressed into her.

His loins bounced energetically against her soft buttocks and she needed a firm grip on the chair. She remembered to make appreciative noises, and complimented him on his prowess. As he became more excited, so his gentlemanly conversation gave way to more lurid commentary. Nina had already discovered that men liked to talk dirty when having sex and took it all in her stride. She could feel him reaching his climax. He grasped her tightly round the waist as his final thrusts delivered the last offerings. She waited a few moments, and then gently withdrew herself from him. He moved backwards to his bed and slumped down.

Nina knew the drill. Dress quickly. Keep saying nice things. Then the money. She asked for $45 – normal tariff plus $5 for the use of her condom. No problem. He paid what she asked, but in roubles. That didn't matter: it was all hard currency. She threw her coat round her shoulders, bent down to give him a peck on his forehead, waved a coquettish farewell with a smile and, with a final 'You were great!' made her exit from his life.

It was less than half an hour since she had left the car. She was $45 dollars in credit for the evening so far. It was 11:30 p.m. – probably time for one more before she went home. Zvetlana had been right. If you kept in control it was like shelling peas.

Her final customer of the evening was just before midnight, another businessman, this time from the Ukraine so their conversation was again in Russian. He was younger and more personable. He had a wife he told her, whom he loved dearly so he didn't want to be unfaithful. But apparently blowjobs were OK for his delicate conscience. Nina obliged. This was not her favourite sexual pastime but she could always sense when the man was about to come and could make sure he was out of her mouth in time. The advantages were that it was quick, unencumbered, and there was no need to take off too many clothes. By 12:30 a.m. she had left her client with his clear conscience and was back in the car, another $30 to the good. She told Stefan for a first night she felt she had had enough and would like to go home. He had his $50 so he didn't mind. Business was falling off now anyway, and as soon as Zvetlana returned they delivered Nina back to her flat.

"See you tomorrow then? Meet us in the carpark opposite the hotel? We'll be there - same time. OK?" said Stefan and, without more ado, accelerated away into the darkness.

The rest of her flatmates were asleep. After a thorough shower and a welcome cup of tea, Nina gratefully crashed on to bed, her own, shortly after one o'clock. She was exhausted, too tired really to think about anything. But in her purse was $75. That would have taken ten weeks to earn working in her office. Tonight it had taken her barely four hours. Now she could see her way to the abortion. Suddenly she was in charge of the options. She could relax properly for the first time since that dreadful moment when she found she was pregnant. But it was at a cost. Weariness made it impossible to give any more thought to that at the moment. Nina Snegur had taken a quantum step forward in life skills. The unanswered question was where that would lead. For the moment however she didn't care. She slept like a baby.

Wednesday morning dawned grey, overcast and dry. Chisinau was back to its normal raw, cold February self, making it even more difficult to crawl out from under the warm bedclothes to face another day. When she did finally emerge there was much teasing from her flatmates, mainly coarse and suggestive, not least because she had come back so late, and that on a weekday. Nina kept her secret, laughed at their inquisition, and determined to get on with the day as though nothing had happened. That took some doing. Each time her thoughts wondered back to last night, she could hardly believe it had been her. But the very tangible wad of money in her purse was proof enough. The continuing difficulty now was going to be how to preserve her secrets.

Fortunately things in the DHL office were normal and there was no need for any dissembling. In any event, she had only three more days before her employment there ceased, and it was her colleagues who were at pains to be nice to her and encourage her. Nina had decided the best way to keep up appearances was to find some other work, albeit part-time. She wouldn't be able to cope with early-morning cleaning at the hospital so that was a non-starter, but lunch-time bar work might be OK and that would provide a convincing cover for her having money in her pocket.

But more importantly, she needed to get in touch with the doctor at the hospital. It was only a few days since she had had her consultation with him, though it seemed like a lifetime, so much had happened since then. She phoned Pavel on his mobile in her lunch-break to ask if he could fix something for Saturday morning.

"Hi sis," he answered. "So what's the result of the hospital tests?"

Nina suddenly realised Pavel hadn't yet heard. He knew she had been hoping for better news but was not surprised when she told him the tests had been positive. He would try to fix her up with an appointment to see the doctor, but how was she going to get the money? She hated lying to her brother. He had been a huge support all along, but she could not bear to tell him the truth. She quickly attenuated their conversation, rather weakly saying she had met someone who was able to lend her what she needed. She would explain more when they next saw each other. Had to dash now to get back to work.

She had just reached the office when her mobile rang again. Probably Pavel with a quick reply, but when she looked at the digital read-out on the phone she didn't recognise the number.

"Hallo, Nina Snegur here", she answered trying to think who this could be.

"Hallo, here is Gerd. Remember? Last night. I say I phone you, yes? You OK?"

Nina stopped in her tracks and instinctively turned away from the office door to take the call, desperate lest her office colleagues should hear any of this conversation.

"Yes, yes - Nina here. I very good," she responded, not knowing quite what to say even in Moldovan, let alone in broken English.

"We meet again tonight, yes? Please, very much I want you. OK?"

Nina was panicking. How should she respond? She really would like to see him again. He was impressive, handsome and sensitive. But she was supposed to be doing "business" again tonight with Zvetlana and Stefan. Her German friend probably knew that, but their communication problems made it impossible to enter into any meaningful dialogue with him about how to meet, where, when or whatever. Nina had to think quickly.

"OK, I come your room – maybe ten o'clock. Stay small time," she said.

"Very good. I am happy. I think you remember room number 505 – you are very beautiful girl." The conversation ended as abruptly as it had started.

In spite of all the emotions coursing through her, Nina had trouble keeping awake that afternoon and resolved to try to get some sleep before she went out again that night. But she would also have to find time for some food, and do some washing and be all set to meet up with Stefan by mid-evening. Suddenly her life felt very crowded, and not a little complicated by the continual pretence she had to keep up with all her friends and acquaintances. It was going to be hard, the sole consolation being that it would only be for a few weeks.

Escaping from the flat again that evening predictably provoked even more ribaldry. "Wearing the same outfit again, eh? He must fancy you in that short skirt! Well, it does make it easier, doesn't it? Hope you haven't bothered to put any knickers on! Don't want to slow things down, do you? Can we come and meet him?" It was all in good fun and Nina let it bounce off her. If only they knew! Outside the Hotel Dukro in the dark on a cold evening, things were altogether less jocular. The large influx of international election observers had now arrived. Tonight they would be finding their bearings and travel weary, so business would probably not be too brisk, but from tomorrow onwards there should be big earnings. Zvetlana and Nina could expect to be busy. Stefan hoped they were in good heart. It might be a tiring few days ahead.

True maturity, they say, grows out of learning to cope with conflict, pain, grief and suffering. Nina's only physical suffering at the moment was her early-morning feelings of nausea, but that wasn't too much of a problem. If she had any grief to cope with it, it was probably around the prospect of aborting a foetus, but there were so many other considerations flying around, any grieving about this was still psychologically buried deeply within her. She was not in any physical pain. But Nina was beset with a basketful of dilemmas, conflicts of loyalty, and deceptions, not least from her parents and brother, the ones who loved her most. Trying to pick her way through all these would tax anyone, not least a young, inexperienced girl, alone in a big city.

And now there was to be an added complication. She had already embarked on a Jekyll-and-Hyde life in respect of her friends, following a normal routine twenty hours of each day, but the other four hours living in a totally different twilight world about which she was determined the other world would know nothing. Now she was about to complicate things further by another deception. Her German friend wanted to see her. She wanted to see him again but she was not going to betray her plans for that assignation to the only two people, Stefan and Zvetlana, who frequented her few hours in the twilight world. That was going to be another layer of deception.

Pregnancy, an impending abortion, prostitution, and deceptions here, there and everywhere, had precipitated Nina into a cauldron of emotion that was fast contributing to her maturation. It was sink or swim. Nina had no intention of drowning. One step at a time – she would get there in the end, though if pressed, she wasn't too precise about where that would be, but it was basically about surviving. That she could understand.

The influx of election observers that day had filled every spare room in most of Chisinau's major hotels. There were far more bedrooms with lights on tonight than the previous evening. Whether this augured well for business was yet to be seen. The first few calls Stefan made had met initially with non-comprehension and then rapid embarrassed sign-offs, as though the very phone call itself was in some way contaminating. Even so, on the seventh call there was a positive response. Nina elected to take it. It was another Russian speaker, probably well used to the call-girl system in Moldovan hotels and not so averse to receiving an invitation. Nina's experience the previous evening held her in good stead. It was a routine straight sex request. No complications, a middle-aged man who was quickly satisfied and seemed more than happy to sink back onto his bed for his night's sleep without more ado enabling Nina to leave in less than half an hour, $40 dollars to the good.

Nina checked the time. It was nearly ten o'clock. Instead of returning to the car she took the lift to floor five and stepped out into the lobby at that level. She pressed Stefan's number into her mobile.

"Hallo, Stefan here," he answered, "Are you in trouble? I'll be there in two minutes. Hang on!"

Nina was quick to reassure him. "No. No. Don't worry. I'm fine. Look, I've just finished that job. No problem, but as I was leaving I bumped into the guy I saw last night. He asked if I would come again, so I'm going straight back there. He's easy, and has good money. I'll be back when I've finished there. OK?"

A few moments later Nina was inside room 505 again, enfolded in an embrace that spelt volumes about the German's long-term deprivation of female warmth and softness. Their lovemaking was frantic, their desire mutually fervent. There were no tears this time as they stretched contentedly against each other's bodies on the confines of the perfunctory bed after the first urgent thrusts of their lust had been satisfied. Conversation was necessarily monosyllabic.

"I like you very much. Very lovely woman. You make love very good," he said as he gently caressed her dishevelled hair, which spread haphazardly over the pillow. Nina felt more than content and basked in his flattery, closing her eyes to drink deeply of these rare sensuous moments. She knew she could stay with him for up to an hour without causing complications with her colleagues. Barely twenty minutes had elapsed since she had arrived in his room, so no need to hurry away yet. His hands glided all over her and, against all the rules of being a good whore, she kissed him with open mouth in response to his caresses, and in appreciative reciprocation her hand went down to begin to massage him again.

He took her for the second time, more slowly and more deliberately, both of them savouring the moments. There was no need for talk. They each knew they were articulating their thoughts and feelings without words. Their bodies were suffused with soft, emancipated affection. But the clock was ticking. Nina at last had to make a move. Her companion was all but asleep in her arms. She squeezed away and dressed speedily.

"I think it good we meet again?" said Gerd smiling contentedly at her as he lay prostrate on his bed. He reached to the bedside drawer and proffered another $50. Nina wanted to try to explain to him she really enjoyed their time together and didn't do it for the money, but her limited vocabulary prohibited that, and in any event there was still Stefan's account to settle. The money was essential for that. There was one other thing she was unable to articulate, even to herself: that her affection for him was stronger than she dared admit.

"Much work this week – maybe I see you Saturday, Sunday. Better afternoon I think?" she replied.

"I go back Germany Sunday morning. Saturday good. We meet have lunch I think – you come, one o'clock. Hotel reception. Take taxi – you know somewhere we eat. OK?"

Nina signalled her agreement to all that. Saturday was clearly going to be a busy day. She still hoped to see the doctor that morning and she knew Stefan and Zvetlana were counting on her to help with the "business", which was likely to be very brisk that evening.

When she returned to the car, she couldn't face any more couplings that evening. She made excuses that she had a headache and felt slightly sick. Stefan shrugged his shoulders. That was her problem not his as long as she paid him her dues. She gave him the fifty dollars, which left her with a net gain on the evening of $40. That was good enough. She was already over a third of the way to her target figure after only two nights. No need to go mad. Two or three jobs per night would get her there quick enough. It was only 11:00 p.m. Zvetlana was still busy. She elected to walk home. Fresh air would do her good she said. More to the point, she would be in bed at a more civilised time, would get less ragging from her mates and hopefully would catch up on some much needed sleep. She told him she'd be there as usual tomorrow. He stressed that it would be busy. She'd better not let him down. She wouldn't.

Pavel phoned her in the office next day. The appointment with the doctor was made – early Saturday, and she needed to bring $100 in cash as initial deposit. During her lunch-break she revisited the two bars where she had had casual work before. They were glad of the offer of more help, especially now the city had such an influx of foreigners. When could she start? They really needed her now, but Sunday would be OK. Three hours each day for the following week, and then as they needed her. $1 each session. Nina didn't care about the money; she was now working in a different income bracket. This job would just serve as a cover. Only last week, she would have happily welcomed this rate of pay: now it seemed derisory. Guiltily she mused to herself why Moldovan girls were so content to work for such low wages when there was such an easy alternative. Little did she realise that many weren't, and it was they who were feeding the human trafficking trails across Europe.

The next two days were busy, both night and day. Her evening activity had quickly settled into a routine even at this early stage. The foreign visitors had been courteous and generous. Language was no handicap, and Nina's good looks and expertise were a real bonus to mainly middle-aged men indulging in a furtive secret fling without fear of wives, families, or colleagues getting to know of it. The net gain for Nina from the Thursday and Friday nights was another $135, the only real problem being the effort of getting up early on the Saturday morning for the doctor's appointment after the exertions of the previous evening.

It was another bleak, clinical consultation. The doctor took the $100 and gave her a scribbled receipt. She should come back in ten days for the operation. She would be in hospital for two days. She could tell her friends whatever she wished, but afterwards she would need at least a week or so to convalesce. It wasn't just the clinical side – that was fairly straightforward at this early stage of pregnancy, but psychologically she would feel pretty low for a while, as well as being very tired for a few days after the anaesthetic. Her admission was set for Tuesday, 6th March, in the evening. Don't eat anything from 8:00 p.m. onwards. The operation would be first thing next day. Was that all clear? Did she have any questions?

There was a plethora of anxious queries wheeling round in her head, but at the crucial moment none of these could be coherently formulated. Instead she told him that was all OK. She would be there at the appointed time.

"You will need some sort of transport to take you home afterwards. It's better if you have a friend with you to make sure you're all right. Can you fix that up?" Nina assured him she could.

"One last thing, Miss Snegur – you won't forget to bring with you the balance of the fee, $200, will you? We won't be proceeding without it, and I'm afraid you will have to forfeit the deposit if that happens. I'm sure you understand. We do have so many expenses to cover."

It was hard not to feel desolate as she left the dreary confines of the hospital precincts. The weather matched her mood. There was nevertheless a small gleam of happiness overarching all that. At one o'clock she would be in the hotel foyer again to meet up with her German friend. He would revive her spirits and she would gladly give herself to his every wish. She had only two hours to wait.

PART 4

SPIRALLING RISKS

Chapter 21

Leicester - January 2003

In Georgia the river Aragvi collects the melt waters from the snows in the Caucasian mountains. Further south it meets up with rain waters off the mountains of northern Turkey flowing eastwards in the river Mtkvari. In the dramatic valleys where the two rivers converge nestles the ancient capital of the kings of Georgia, Mtskheta. Tradition ascribes the founding of the city to a descendant of the biblical Noah, and the majestic Mount Ararat is not far distant.

In the heart of Mtskheta is Svetitskhoveli Cathedral dating from 1010 AD. Within its hallowed walls stands a tall pedestal richly decorated with coloured frescos, under which allegedly lies buried the robe of Christ. From here, Christianity spread across Georgia and despite the country's economic difficulties following independence from the Soviet Union, the Orthodox Church has continued a vital part of their culture for the fiercely independent Georgians.

On the wall of the Cathedral, behind the pedestal shrine is another fresco dating from the sixteenth century about two metres in diameter depicting the signs of the Zodiac. It symbolises the happy conjunction of old astrological myths and the teachings of the Church. The mural reflects the belief that no man is his own master.

In the twenty-first century things are no different. Events on one side of the world have direct and indirect repercussions on the other side. A taxi held up in traffic in Tokyo results in a missed flight, which means a contractual payment fails to be made by a deadline, which means a company fails to secure crucial new business, which means fifty men lose their jobs in the north of England, which leads to family stress and a heart attack, which leaves a family fatherless, and so it continues. The waft of a butterfly's wing on one side of the globe, it is said, can cause a cyclone on the other.

As Peter Clayton considered his options on a chilly January evening from the back seat of the speeding Mercedes on the Leicester ring road, he was not particularly philosophising on the broad sweep of history, nor had he any awareness of the message of the Zodiac fresco in Mtskheta Cathedral. If he had, he would have quickly registered considerable empathy with the belief that man was not master of his own fate. Fewer than ten hours previously, his life had been following its satisfying unspectacular suburban pattern for a Saturday morning. That had now all been blown apart. But the events that had conspired to bring him to this pass were beyond his cognisance. Unknown to him, they had been activated many thousands of miles away, a year or more before.

Plastic injection moulding had become a major international industry in the last half-century. Leicester had its fair share of such small commercial units and Michael Burton had been the head of one of these. He attended Wyggeston Grammar School and after good O level results went into the sixth form to study science and mathematics. Chemistry was his best subject – organic chemistry in particular. He was also sporty and played for the school at cricket and football, so it was no surprise he became keen on squash later in life. He enjoyed a steady supply of girlfriends and dived deep into the vibrant social life that a city like Leicester offered. He was not the world's most ardent student, so when his A-level results emerged rather modestly graded, he elected to leave school and joined the laboratory staff of a local plastics factory.

His outgoing temperament, his easy manner and his affability, together with his scientific bent, equipped him well to progress. He moved from the laboratory to sales and marketing, then to production, a short time in accounts, and finally into senior management. He married a local girl, Shirley, with whom he had two children, and in his late thirties took on the top job of managing director on a good salary package.

Although his career advancement had been enviable, the challenges facing the plastics industry were growing by the day because of the increased competition from overseas suppliers, where labour costs were so much lower than in the UK. His task as M.D. to produce a good-quality product at a competitive price was a daily headache. One of the biggest single expenses was the cost of manufacturing the injection moulds. Every order for a new plastic product required the manufacture of a unique metal mould to very fine tolerances. Once this had been properly engineered, the plastic product itself could be reproduced by the thousand at relatively low cost. The demise of engineering in the UK meant it was becoming increasingly difficult to locate firms who could build moulds in quick time to tight specifications at low cost. Not surprisingly, firms such as Polymer Plastics Limited had to look abroad, not least to China, to find suppliers who could manufacture these moulds more competitively.

The English National Opera company's modern but short-lived production, Nixon in China, was based around President Nixon's visit to Peking in 1972 which supposedly marked a seminal moment in opening up the country's leadership to the western world and international commerce. China was still to endure the desperate times of the Cultural Revolution and the Tiananmen Square massacre in 1989, but with the assimilation of Hong Kong into the economy in 1997, the next decade saw a colossal surge in the freeing up of the country's institutions. The sixteenth Annual Congress of the Chinese Communist Party meeting in Beijing in November 2002 formally passed the epoch-making resolution that joint projects with capitalist companies were acceptable. Inward investment galloped ahead, the Chinese market being seen as the biggest potential for growth in the world.

The Chinese have a strong engineering tradition and for non-complex manufacturing products could offer both skill and low labour costs. They had the facility to make plastic injection moulds and to make them at competitive cost compared to Western Europe. In particular, in Chengdu in Sichuan Province in central China, Suchou Engineering were specialists in manufacturing such moulds, but marketing their competence and capacity on a global basis was not one of their fortes.

Hardly surprisingly, Michael Burton was unaware of this vital piece of business intelligence as he moaned to colleagues at the hotel bar just before Christmas 2002 about the cost of manufactured products in Europe on the occasion of Leicester's annual Chamber of Commerce dinner and dance. Present by invitation at the evening's festivity was a representative from the government's "Business Link" office. Michael's private views about the value of the service rendered by government advisors to businessmen working in the real world were unprintable, but could probably be summed up in the aphorism – "Those that can, do. Those that can't, advise!" But on this occasion he was prepared to be more attentive when the business link adviser showed some genuine interest in his tale of woe. He suggested Michael might attend a small seminar in London to be run by Trade Partners UK – an offshoot of the government's Department for International Development – the main object being a networking opportunity for UK business people to meet counterparts from the Far East with a view to identifying projects of mutual benefit.

So it was, on a chilly January day in 2003, almost exactly a year to the day before Peter Clayton would find himself contemplating his options in the back of the Mercedes, that Michael Burton was on the early bird train from Leicester to London, heading for the office of the British Consultants' Bureau off Victoria Street where the seminar would be held - a typically British affair, no glitz, a modest functional room, pour your own coffee, some bland digestive biscuits, a slightly dated overhead projector, Powerpoint (if anyone knew how to set it up), polite introductions, an exchange of business cards, three ten-minute presentations about business opportunities in the Pacific Rim, questions, and a light stand-up buffet lunch of lifeless sandwiches during which the networking was supposed to happen.

Most major embassies were represented, Japan, South Korea, China, the Philippines, Malaysia, Singapore. Bonhomie on such occasions is somewhat contrived and it is always difficult to make the best use of the event.

Michael had escaped the clutches of a middle-aged lady from the Thai Embassy who was trying to discover contacts in Leicester for clothing imports, and moved on to tackle a rather sickly looking dessert while discussing potential for enhancing the tourist offer in Japan with a diminutive and poorly spoken visitor from the Japanese Tourist Bureau. At last he reached the coffee stage, where at least one hand could be free most of the time to shake hands or fish a handkerchief out of the pocket when needed. It would not be too long before he could make his exit. It had been an interesting event to the extent that it had confirmed for him that these well-intentioned government initiatives were mainly about image rather than substance.

Also taking coffee was Mr Ding Quan of the Chinese Embassy. At the exchange of business cards, with remarkable directness, Mr Quan began asking Michael about the business and its profitability. With nothing to lose, Michael regaled him with his worries about the high cost of engineering in Europe and the difficulty of obtaining good-quality manufactured goods at costs that maintained profit margins. Within a few minutes Michael had forgotten his coffee as it cooled in his hand. Mr Quan apparently believed that there were companies in China who could produce plastic product moulds at very competitive prices. If Mr Quan's assertion was true, this could give Michael's company a huge competitive edge over his rivals. Of course there were issues of quality control, engineering precision, delivery time, transport and installation, but Mr Quan was firmly of the opinion that none of these were a problem. He would get back to Mr Burton within two days with the names of one or two engineering companies in China. His company could contact them direct. They would be able to answer more detailed questions and hopefully talk more specifically about costs so Mr Burton could calculate the true potential for a "made in China" label on his factory moulding machines.

Michael had stayed longer than he'd expected to and only just made it to St Pancras station in time to sink into his reserved seat on the train back to Leicester. He settled down with the Evening Standard feeling a positive glow of satisfaction that, after all, his journey might have been useful, and, dare he hope, could well lead to a major advance for the company's profitability. No need to get too excited though – there was always the possibility he may never hear from Mr Quan again. He dozed off feeling more relaxed than usual as the warm inter-city train hurried him northwards through the bleak hibernating winter landscape while the day gradually gave up its struggle to keep darkness at bay. Perhaps he should re-evaluate his views about Business Link advisers after all.

Judy Makepeace could not catch his name properly, but two days after Michael had been down to London there was foreign-sounding gentleman on the line wanting to speak to Mr Mitchal Bwarthon. She thought he said he was Mr Khan. Did Mr Burton want to take the call? Michael was deeply involved in a meeting with his Head of Personnel – he didn't like the new title "Human Resources Director", too impersonal he thought – about a case of alleged sexual harassment. One of the girls in accounts had complained that a sales rep was continually making suggestive remarks to her.

"Mr who?" said Michael irascibly.

"Mr Kwon or Khan I think. Said he met you in London. Had some information to give you."

"Oh, yes – yes, put him through. I don't think it will take long."

"Mr Quan here. Hello I want Mr Bwarthon. Hello, yes – we talk at the meeting, you remember? Yes I say I give you good contact with engineering company in China. I give you two. One - Chou Ling Foundry in Xiang. Another one - Suchou Engineering in Chengdu. Both very good – you telephone or fax or maybe email. I speak to them yesterday. They say they can supply you what you want."

Michael thanked him profusely for getting back to him so quickly. Painstakingly he took down the dictated contact email addresses and phone numbers. Mr Quan advised him their English language skills over the phone might be limited. Better if Mr Burton could make initial contact through an interpreter able to converse in Mandarin Chinese. Again many thanks to Mr Quan – no harm in trying. Could be an interesting time ahead, but doing business in Chinese was not the easiest of prospects.

"Judy, I need someone who can speak Chinese – I guess we could just ask at the local Chinese take-away if they can put us in touch with an interpreter? Or, maybe we could try the Yellow Pages directory? What do you think?"

"Leave it to me, Michael. I'll get onto it and get back to you when I have something."

Michael and the Personnel Director resumed their mournful task, a lose-lose one if ever there was one. They would set up a formal investigatory hearing and ask the salesman to come in with a friend or his union representative and start the process. Michael lamented how much of his time and energy was spent on non-productive tasks such as this. Small wonder the company found it difficult to keep in profit. Regulations, bureaucracy and red tape dominated their lives. Everything was about process, with less and less time for productivity initiatives.

At least Mr Quan had focussed his enthusiasm on a new avenue to explore which could have a direct bearing on productivity and profit. That was the sort of thing that motivated Michael and he would give it prime attention – just as soon, that is, as he had identified a way of communicating his needs and hopes to two far-flung corners of China.

Yongqing Jabo came from the inner Mongolian autonomous region of Northern China. She was a bright girl, did well at the local school, went on to further education and then to University where she specialised in English studies. There she met her future husband, Chen Jianxiong, the son of a successful restaurant owner who also had interests in Hong Kong. After graduating in 1998, they first set up home in Hong Kong so he could manage his father's businesses there, until asked to move to England to help develop their burgeoning Chinese Takeaway business. The Midlands was a major growth point and Leicester, as one of the more agreeable and prosperous places to live, was where they settled. Chen devoted himself to the restaurant trade while Yongqing was much in demand coaching Chinese on a private tuition basis and attached to De Montford University.

Judy Makepeace's enquiries homed in on Yongqing as exactly the language expert that Michael Burton needed. She was fluent in Chinese. She had lived in the UK for a few years and had both a good theoretical and practical command of English and was well versed in commercial matters by virtue of her husband's work. Her fees were not modest - £50 per hour to the commercial sector - but it was a price worth paying as far as Michael was concerned. He welcomed her into his office later that week.

He agreed the terms of their business relationship. She would assist him in the office whenever he needed to talk to China directly by phone. In addition she would translate any faxes or emails Chinese to English, and English to Chinese by return mail, because speed of response was crucial to him. There was likely to be a flurry of activity to begin with but thereafter things might blossom or they might fold up, so there was no guarantee of long-term work, but while it lasted he would make sure she was well rewarded if she worked closely with him and above all did so in commercial confidence.

"Are you happy to start now? No time like the present!" he asked. She confirmed she was more than happy to do so.

Within a few minutes a phone was ringing somewhere deep in China's heartland not far from the magnificent Terracota Army unearthed on the outskirts of Xiang. It rang and rang. Michael's enthusiasm began to falter. Could this really work? Seemed such an extraordinarily long shot. He must be stupid to think he could fathom the intricacies of Chinese commercial practise at such distance and with such miniscule knowledge of what it was like out there. Yonqing put the phone down and respectfully pointed out that it should not be a surprise that there was no reply. Although it was four o'clock in the afternoon in Leicester, it was actually midnight in Xiang at that precise moment!

"How stupid of me!" said Michael. "Could you come back tomorrow morning and we'll try again then. Would 8:00 a.m. be OK for you? Then it will about four o'clock there won't it? Shall we try that?"

The next morning he carefully recapitulated with Jongqing the gist of his enquiry. He wanted to know in principle whether the Chinese factory could manufacture plastic injection moulds to his firm's specifications: What materials did they work in? What quality controls did they have? What sort of timeframe did they work on? What delivery methods would they use? How would they cost the contract? He would want an exchange of written confirmations by email or fax, which he would then study, after being translated by Jongqing. If there seemed the possibility of doing business he would arrange to go out to meet them at their factory, to see their operation at first hand and to look at the quality of their products.

The first phone call was to the Xiang factory. Again there was no reply. The phone rang on plaintively in the distance and Michael tried to conjure up in his mind what sort of environment surrounded that solitary ringing tone. He really had no idea. It all felt strangely unreal. His expectations began to flag – probably he would be better employed sorting out the accounts clerk's harassment claims.

But Mr Quan had supplied him with two contacts. No harm in trying the second. Jongqing rang the second number. Michael listened on the speaker phone.

"cho-la-hung-tu-no" came the answer– at least that's as much sense as Michael could make of it. Jongqing quickly launched into a speedy measured response. As the conversation proceeded for five then eight, nine, ten minutes, it became marvellously clear that Polymer Plastics Limited of Leicester, England, had established contact with Suchou Engineering in Chengdu, Central China some 6,000 miles away.

Good marketing may have not been their forte, but the opening up of China's commercial activity to global opportunity and the decisions of the sixteenth Communist Party Congress had now spawned the first embryonic breakthrough for Suchou Engineering into the export market. For Michael Burton this was the first tentative step into a year of dramatic travel, challenge and ultimately tragedy. If he had been a contemplative man, he too, like Peter Clayton, would have reflected how on such thin threads of unexpected and unplanned fortune each of their lives hung. He could hit a squash ball where he wanted it go, but in the greater scheme of things, Michael Burton was not master of his own fate.

For the moment, however, things were definitely on the up. Within a few months he had established a contractual arrangement for most of his plastic injection moulds to be manufactured in China, at a quarter of the cost he could source them from European suppliers. His largest order was due to be delivered by sea container to his Leicester factory towards the end of the year. Michael Burton's firm now had a real edge in undercutting competitors. Things boded well for future profitability. He was a happy man. Even the firm's personnel problems seemed less onerous.

Chapter 22

Italy- November 2003

The distance between Albania and Italy at the closest point across the Strait of Otranto, which separates the Adriatic and Ionian seas, is almost exactly fifty miles. In good weather a high-speed launch can cover that in less than three hours. But high-speed launches are noisy and not designed for large groups of people. A ferry from Corfu to Brindisi, following a similar but longer route, chugs across at about ten knots and would hope to take no more than seven hours. But that is highly visible and equally noisy. Neither is well suited for clandestine trips of illegal immigrants.

The small boat on which Habib and Bledar found themselves looked like a coastal fishing boat that had seen better days. It was wooden, clinker-built, and smelt of stale fish. Its few pieces of ironwork were well and truly rusted. The ropes were frayed and discoloured. The small wheelhouse towards the front of the vessel was open at the back and could provide only a modicum of protection from the elements for, at most, four people. The deck sloped steeply upwards towards the bows. The stern was low and flat and in the middle was what appeared to be a covered hold, presumably where fish catches were stowed while out at sea. If the weather turned sour, there was precious little shelter for the passengers. Habib and Bledar had taken the precaution of putting on their waterproofs. They huddled under them as though in a mini tent, sitting with their backs against the side of the boat.

The boat rocked fore and aft as the oarsmen manoeuvred it over the undulating swell further and further from the shore. The coastline was by now barely visible. Albania was slowly fading out of Habib's life, at least for the foreseeable future. At his school in Mitrovice, he had studied maps of Europe, such as they had there, and tried to visualise his route to the UK. He had taken particular note of this phase of his projected journey. He knew how much sea they had to cross and it didn't require a degree in mathematics to realise that at the rate they were moving, not even walking pace, it would take all day to reach Italy. No surprise therefore, after ten minutes rowing, when they had reached about a half a mile out to sea, the captain pressed a small button in the wheelhouse and the engine in the bilges spluttered into life. It was quickly throttled back to a quiet tick-over, and the boat's speed moved up a gear.

The captain was slipping away as discreetly as he could. With no lights on board the vessel, he had judged that they were sufficiently distant from the shore that the gentle throb of the engine would not now betray their position. Minute by minute, travelling at this faster speed of about five knots, they were gradually moving further out of earshot. Habib was again doing some calculations. He had never been out at sea before and the adventure was stimulating his thinking. At this rate the boat would make about ten miles every two hours. That would take ten hours to get across – fine, except that meant they would arrive offshore just after dawn in broad daylight. Habib guessed that that was the last thing they would want to do. Still, the crew ought to know what they were doing. Judging from the smoothness of the operation so far, they had evidently done it many times before. He would just have to sit back and let things unfold as they would.

The journey settled into a steady rhythm. Pinpoints of red glow began to appear around the boat as cigarettes were relit to relieve the tedium. Like Habib, few of his companions had been on the open sea before. It was a surprise to them how much the boat's bucking and tossing increased as it moved further from the mainland and hit the heavier swell in the Strait. Inevitably the incessant motion began to take its toll. Seasickness is a strange, unfair phenomenon. Quite arbitrarily it affects some and not others. Fitness has nothing to do with it. The older man with the injured ankle was crouched beside Habib. He seemed blissfully at ease with everything while Habib began to feel increasingly queasy. After half an hour, he could feel the bile rising in his throat. Two or three others were already retching over the side. The smell of their vomit was the last straw for Habib. He too lurched to the side of the boat to deliver up to the Mediterranean the remnants of the little snack he had enjoyed with Bledar while sitting in the bunker a few hours earlier. He slumped back to the deck, feeling somewhat better and took a swig of water from his bottle to cleanse his mouth. They had been sailing for less than an hour. The prospects of hours more of this perpetual unpredictable motion filled him with dismay. He huddled down under his waterproof, took in gulps of fresh air and tried to fall asleep. This was going to be more of an endurance test than he had expected. Bledar meanwhile seemed totally unaffected, and somewhat amused that Habib's constitution couldn't cope.

There was still little wind but the moon had set. It was pitch black. Their boat still showed no lights. From time to time the steaming lights of other shipping appeared at a distance; a green light on the starboard side indicated a small vessel heading northwards – a red light on the port side was a boat heading out of the Adriatic to the wider Mediterranean. Additional white lights somewhere on a masthead indicated the larger vessels. Each time the captain saw one he throttled back and steered a course that took them well clear.

It was about an hour into their voyage when Habib's mental calculations proved correct. Two of the crew went astern and uncovered a twin 60 horse-power Johnson outboard engine. They unclamped it, lowered it over the stern into the water, and fixed it securely on rear brackets. The starter button was pressed and a huge surge of raw power gripped the small craft. The boat's inboard engine could no longer be heard as the twin screws of the Johnson bit into the sea. The bows of the boat lifted and suddenly they were moving at a great rate of knots crashing from one wave crest to another. The captain was no longer concerned about noise. Presumably he was sufficiently far out into open sea that that was not now a problem. His immediate and over-riding objective was covering the sea miles as rapidly as possible. Habib could feel and hear the boat's timbers creaking under the strain as they were subjected to this unaccustomed power and speed. The motion of the boat changed dramatically. The twin screws held the vessel tight onto the water at the stern while the bows buccaneered forward with lashings of spray cascading over the deck from time to time. Those who had been feeling seasick quickly became more preoccupied with keeping dry and keeping warm. It was a chill night and the air was now rocketing past them at over 20 mph. Sitting on the deck had become much more of a hazard. Every so often the boat would lurch upwards and then crash down into the trough of the next wave. That was a bruising experience for passengers still sitting on the deck. One by one they began to stand up and let their legs take the strain, while keeping a tight grip on the boat's handrail. The relaxing gentle cruise had now become a roller-coaster ride. Sleep was out of the question. Hang on. Try to keep dry. Don't complain.

Going back to his mental arithmetic, Habib worked out that at this rate, they should take barely two hours to come within sight of the Italian mainland. They would be offshore well before daybreak, probably in the early hours of the morning. Some of the car journeys he had endured were hair-raising enough, but this was altogether different. He was still wearing his baseball cap, which protected his head, to some degree, from the spray that was splashing all over him. His waterproof cape deflected most of that onto the deck, which was awash and increasingly slippery. His cold and numb hands gripped the rail . He wondered how the other passengers were faring. Some had no waterproof cover. They were getting drenched. He did not envy them. He had slung his rucksack on his back and under his cape that was keeping reasonably dry, but those with suitcases could see them becoming soaked as they lay on the deck with water sluicing around them. The next two hours were going to be very long. Nothing to do except grin and bear it.

Habib and his companions did not know how lucky they were. Some six weeks later, on the night of the 9th January2004, the same boat that they were on was to attempt a similar crossing, but in vile weather. It was carrying thirty-five passengers including the crew, far more than it should, even in calm weather. It was bitterly cold. The wind was roaring from the north-east so in the lee of the Albanian shore the sea was not too turbulent. But ten miles offshore things were totally different. Waves were crashing right over the boat. Everyone was saturated and freezing cold. The boat was being tossed about like a cork, and taking on water in buckets. The screws of the outboard engines were frequently out of the water as the boat plunged down yet another huge trough in the sea before rearing up on the crest of the next tortuous wave.

The boat became waterlogged. It could hardly make headway because it was so low in the water. Everyone was standing knee deep in the water on the deck. The wind chill factor began to take its toll as it ripped through their soaking clothes. One after another, the passengers began to succumb to hypothermia. The crew were helpless and, in any case, intent only on saving their own skins. They huddled together in the wheelhouse to escape the brunt of the elements. The passengers were left to their own devices. The captain decided to turn back but that only made things worse. They were now fighting into the teeth of the wind. In desperation the passengers decided to take matters into their own hands. One or two had mobile phones and they sent out mayday distress calls to try to get help. The messages were picked up by the coastguards. High-speed rescue launches and helicopters were scrambled. It was like trying to find the proverbial needle in a haystack. But the rescue services knew the illegal smuggling routes and were able to calculate where the distressed vessel might be. Unfortunately they were too late. Of the thirty-five on board, only eleven survived. The desperate risk of seeking a new life had finished for most in a cold watery grave.

It was as well Habib and his fellow travellers had no foreknowledge of this. It would have compounded their discomfort. It was hard enough anyway. When he was leaving Tirana, Toci had warned him he might not get much sleep that night. It was only now that Habib was taking full cognisance of what he meant.

It is a truism that nothing lasts for ever. Sadly that means all good things come to an end, usually too soon. By the same token, awful experiences come to a stop sooner or later. The voyage fitted into the latter category. It had to be endured. Just try not think about it too much. Minute by minute they were getting closer to when it would end. It was a bonus for Habib that he was young and fit and resilient. Bledar seemed to be coping OK as well. But the older man with the bad ankle was in more trouble. He really couldn't stand, so chose instead to sit on his dilapidated suitcase. He did have a waterproof coat of sorts, so he was able to keep reasonably dry, while the suitcase acted as a cushion for his posterior against the buffeting of the boat as it leapfrogged forward. But he was bounced about continuously and his ankle was troubling him greatly.

The passengers reacted with undisguised relief when at long last the captain throttled down the powerful Johnson engines and let the boat settle back to its more leisurely pace propelled by the small inboard motor. Habib judged the time was about one o'clock in the morning. They had been going flat out for around two hours. He peered forwards to see if he could make out the Italian mainland in the darkness ahead. He could not, but what he did see were two or three periodic points of white light in the far distance spread some way apart. These were not vessels. They were static, and flashed at different frequencies – lighthouses marking the key headlands and rock outcrops on the coast. Italy was close. The discomforts of the voyage gave way, thankfully, to feelings of anticipation and excitement. The boat was probably about five miles offshore. With luck they would be stepping on to terra firma within an hour or so. A murmur of more animated chatter welled around the boat.

"We've been lucky so far," said their injured companion. "Keep your fingers crossed our luck will still hold. May Allah preserve us. The next hour is the most critical."

Habib was puzzled. "Why's that?" he asked.

"Patrol boats. The Italians aren't too keen on hordes of immigrants flocking in from Albania and elsewhere. They know this is the closest part of their coastline to Albania and they try to prevent illegal landings by patrolling up and down here most nights. If they locate us, things could turn nasty. You've noticed that the crew haven't stowed away the big engines. That's so they can quickly re-engage them if a patrol boat comes along. They try to out-race them back to the open sea. The Italians don't mind if we get chased away. But our "friendly" crew do have a rather unpleasant way of making sure they get a head start."

"What's that?" enquired Habib, intrigued that this part of the journey could in any way be more fretful than the last couple of hours. Their colleague lowered his voice.

"They throw one of us overboard! Simple as that! They don't care what happens to any of us. They've got their money already. The patrol boat has searchlights. The crew wait till the beam is on their boat, then they pitch someone into the sea, regardless of whether they can swim. The patrol boat has no option but to go to the rescue of the hysterical soul in the water. By the time they've hauled them on board, this boat has put the best part of a mile or so of open sea between them. That's usually enough to make it into non-territorial waters before being overtaken. Very clever really, but you need to be pretty ruthless to do that sort of thing."

"Then what happens?" asked Habib.

"Good question! It's up to the captain. You hear lots of stories. Some boats go further up the coast. The passengers are bundled ashore anywhere and left to their own devices. Lost and disorientated, that usually means they are picked up pretty quickly by local police, and that's the end of their quest for freedom. But there are other grim tales of some crews throwing all their illegal passengers into the sea. No-one knows if that's true. But as far as we are concerned the quicker we're ashore the better. The next hour is the most risky time."

Habib felt a shaft of cold dread pass through him. He had survived the seasickness, the wet, the cold, and the discomfort. He had not been double-crossed by either those on the shore or the crew of the boat. Yet everything now hung on the thin thread of chance – would they be intercepted by a patrol boat? That was something over which they had no control. In total darkness, their little craft was inching its way towards the coast with the inboard engine throttled back as quietly as possible. The captain's eyes and those of his crew were peering out anxiously across the waves through all points of the compass. A hush had again fallen on the passengers. They too were worried, having reached so far, that things might go pear-shaped at the last moment. The minutes ticked away. The lights on the shore became progressively more distinct as the lighthouses continued indefatiguably to flash their signals to seafarers. The dark outline of the southern finger of the Italian landmass gradually emerged on the western horizon. Still no sign that anyone had detected their cautious approach. There was a cruel logic – the nearer the shore they were, the more difficulty they would have in evading capture if a patrol did arrive. They were safer further out to sea, but to disembark meant they had to go in, and going in meant they were standing into danger, as the sailors would describe it.

They had crept quietly forwards for nearly three-quarters of an hour when suddenly a new flash of light appeared ahead of them. Three bursts of a beam. Then three more. Then a long pause followed by three more. The captain picked up a battery powered red lantern normally secured on the port side of the boat. He gave a long single flash, and readjusted the line of his approach to head towards the flashes they had seen. They could now hear the waves breaking on the beach and against the cliffs. The boat's engine quietly died. The four crew members shipped the long oars back into their rowlocks and began the backbreaking rhythm of rowing the boat forward gently and quietly on the swell towards a cove which gradually formed itself out the darkness ahead of them.

It had been about four hours since they had experienced similar sensations as they drifted away from the Albanian shoreline. A tight anxious silence dominated the passengers and crew. The creaking of the oars and their regular paddling of the water were the only sounds, and that was more than disguised by the noise of the incessant surging of the waves on the beach. If a patrol boat came round the headland now they would be trapped in the bay. Habib's emotions were urging the boat on as fast as possible, but their speed was dictated by the strength of the four oarsmen. They knew what they were doing. It was a case of "more haste, less speed". Faster rowing would make more noise, be more exhausting and less effective. The boat was making steady headway and their rhythm was resonant with that.

There was a short sharp low-voiced command from the captain. "Everyone get to the stern, quick, move."

The passengers gathered their respective belongings. Habib took off his waterproof cape, rolled it up and attached it to his rucksack. He was ready to go, hands free and keen. With the weight of bodies at the back, the bows were now high out of the water as the boat glided to a soft landfall on the beach. The rope was thrown ashore and only then did they discern two or three people standing there in the darkness. The gangplank was unshipped and assembled out board. When extended it finished about a yard from the edge of the beach. More wet feet in prospect, but that was the least of their concerns.

"OK, everybody off. Mind how you go. Don't hang about. We need to get out of here too bloody quick."

The passengers needed no second bidding. One by one they felt their way down, one foot in the waves and then a short leap to the pebble shore. Habib and Bledar were last off so they could help their injured companion. This time the crew helped as well. It was clearly in their own interests to get this guy off speedily so they could be away fast. It was another tricky manoeuvre, but at least it was downhill. At the foot of the gangplank they could not avoid getting all their feet wet and the final effort finished with Habib and Bledar falling over in a heap on the beach. But they had made it. Already the boat was moving off. They were not sad to see it leave. A new lesson Habib had learned was that he wasn't cut out to be a sailor. As they plodded their way up the beach away from the water's edge, they were surprised to hear the boat's large Johnson engines roar into life. The captain was certainly in a hurry. Now they no longer had any illegals aboard, being caught by a patrol wasn't so critical. What mattered was getting out to sea in the shortest time possible, notwithstanding noisy engines. The fact that it might draw attention to a local beach surveillance patrol was clearly of no concern to the captain and his crew.

In the darkness, Habib followed the group led by the new guides who had met them on the shore. He and Bledar did their best to help their injured companion keep up. He hopped and limped and leaned heavily on Habib's shoulder. He winced with pain each time he accidentally stumbled onto the damaged foot, but he was determined to stay with the rest. Now they had a steep hill to climb, again in the dark, but, surprisingly, it was easier going up hill than down, because they were facing the slope rather than walking with their backs to it and could use their hands more naturally to assist in their balance. Even so, it was slow going. Many were feeling very fatigued after the trauma of the crossing and were not as fit as Habib and Bledar. The only sound was of concentrated heavy breathing, punctuated periodically with the odd curse when someone lost their foothold or accidentally grabbed a thorn bush to steady themselves.

The track eventually led them to an open space at the top of the cliff, which looked like a car-parking area used, no doubt, in the tourist season as a marvellous viewing point. There was no view to be seen that evening. The only sign of life was two white Iveco vans standing side by side somewhat incongruously in the deserted car park. They were a very welcome sight. With the minimum of fuss the rear doors were opened and the exhausted travellers climbed in, a dozen or so in each. There were perfunctory bench seats along each side of the vans, but no windows. The doors closed, the engines started and the vehicles moved off.

So this was Italy. Habib wanted to shout with relief. Instead he settled himself down on the seat with his rucksack stowed underneath. His feet were still damp from his unwelcome paddling in the sea. He was anxious lest the seawater had penetrated the polythene envelope in his insole where he still kept the precious dollars that would have to see him through the next two thousand miles of journey over land. Checking that would have to wait. This was the time to sit back and relax as the vans gathered speed and hurtled forwards into the night. Suddenly he felt unutterably sleepy. His eyes closed. The motion of the vehicle was soporific. No fear of seasickness here. Things were going OK. Tomorrow would be another day. But that could wait till then.

Chapter 23

Moldova - March 2001

To dress over-smartly for a lunch in Chisinau on a Saturday would be unusual, so Nina elected to wear casual clothes, trendy black jeans, her leather boots, a black silk top, her warm long coat, and an imitation fur Cossack-type hat. She also took with her a small pocket dictionary she'd borrowed, Moldovan - English. By the time she had washed and changed and walked into the Hotel Dukro foyer just before one o'clock, her mood had considerably improved since leaving the hospital. This was fun. Something she had never done before. Gerd was waiting. He greeted her formally with a light kiss on each cheek, took her arm politely and led her out to a waiting taxi.

"You tell taxi where we eat, please," he said.

Nina hadn't thought about that but decided a chat with the taxi-driver might identify some good suggestions. Then with the help of the now precious dictionary she ascertained that Gerd thought a typical Moldovan eating-house would be fine. The trouble was there was little that was very authentic and unique to Moldova. Eating out was not on the agenda of most ordinary folk. In the towns and villages restaurants serving meals to the public were few and far between because no-one had any money to go out to eat. Chisinau however did have a reasonable selection of restaurants offering West and East European menus. They decided to head for a Ukrainian.

Nina was relieved there was no-one there she recognised. Gerd chose a bottle of red Moldovan wine and they smiled and laughed their way through the meal with much recourse to the dictionary. Painstakingly Nina learned about his family and in mispronounced monosyllables slowly unfolded to him something of hers. She had not enjoyed such a relaxed and happy meal for a long time. It was a real tonic, and, suffused with the wine, she was in a generous mood of abandon when the taxi delivered them back to the hotel in mid-afternoon. Their lovemaking was carefree and unashamed. There was no time pressure and after each intimate adventure they could sink back into each other's arms and snooze contentedly.

Gerd had given her his contact addresses in Koblenz, his telephone number at work and his private email address. All that Nina could give him were the DHL office details. She tried to explain that she was leaving that job as of today, but she hoped her friends there would be able to pass through any messages from him. He had her mobile phone number as well. She also gave him her flat address but postal delivery services were suspect and anything that might be in any way valuable was often "lost in the post" en route. They would try to keep in touch. Gerd assured her he would certainly contact her whenever he came back to Chisinau. His project was likely to bring him there two or three more times at least.

"I think it good you come to Germany. Many things you want to see. I show you my country. Think it possible you come?" he asked.

Six months ago the world beyond her home village of Mihailovca was a million miles away. Now new horizons were opening up faster than she could believe. Her move to Chisinau had been dramatic and expanded her experience irreversibly, but the prospect of visiting beyond the bounds of Moldova or its adjacent countries was still a dream.

"I think that very nice. Maybe I try? Big journey. Much money. We talk next time you come Chisinau." She gave him another huge embrace, fastening her lips onto his as though her life depended on it.

Dusk was falling and Nina knew that in a few hours she had to be back again to join Zvetlana and Stefan for the Saturday night demands. She dressed. They kissed their farewell and Nina took her reluctant leave, but now walking with a zing in her step. She felt could face the night's challenge with a new expectation that there were other exciting opportunities ahead that might soon come within her grasp. Having a baby would destroy all that potential. A few more nights' work was the only way to keep open these more ambitious options. Her clients tonight she would gratefully oblige, just as long as they coughed up the dollars. Nina could sense, even after so short a time, she was already becoming a little blase about it all.

There were four more encounters that evening. In her recollection they were already blurring into each other. Three were foreigners - French, Belgian and Dutch, and one from the Ukraine, all reasonably easily satisfied, although two had pressed her to stay the night. Their money was good and Nina was able to secrete away a further $95 after her evening's exertions. It had been a long, full day and she was mightily relieved to sink at last into her own bed. Tomorrow she would lie in, and chill out, and maybe dream of the Moldovan Airways flight leaving Chisinau airport that morning with her adoring German winging his way back home. What would he tell his wife? Would she even care? When could Nina hope to see him again? Was it really possible she could go to Germany to meet him there? These were all delicious thoughts, which she could mull over happily in her own mind while the rest of her friends wrestled with the more mundane distractions of the Chisinau adolescent scene.

As she wandered unkempt round the kitchen next morning in her dressing gown making herself a coffee, the clock was edging towards midday when suddenly she remembered.

"Oh shit, shit, shit – I promised to be at the bar helping out today starting in twenty minutes! Sod it, I've got to get my skates on!"

There was no doubt whatsoever that she had to do this to maintain her cover for having money in her pocket. It was a partial defence against awkward questions. Coffee gulped down, a high-speed wash and brush of the hair, quick dress into casual gear and a race into town to the bar. At least she could now afford to flag down a taxi and arrived only a few minutes late. The three hours serving at the bar and washing glasses dragged along and all she could think of was crashing back onto her bed for recuperative slumber before the evening's work at the Hotel demanded her body and soul again.

Slowly the week wound its way forward in its new pattern. No longer needing an early start to the day, there was the luxury of a lazy lie-in each morning till it was time to go out to work in the bar; she spent the afternoons catching up on washing and shopping and sitting around in coffee bars talking to those of her friends who had no full-time jobs. Then out for the mid-evening rendez-vous with Stefan and Zvetlana, always against a barrage of innuendo from her flatmates who were becoming progressively more suspicious –

"Oh, Nina, not again - every night! You must be wearing him out! Doesn't he have to get up next day? Maybe he's so rich, he doesn't need to work! Or, maybe you're up to something else? Aren't you going to tell us your little secret?"

Nina was certainly not. The evenings usually threw up 3 or 4 jobs and that was adequate to pay her dues to Stefan and still take home at least $50 for herself. There had been one or two difficult episodes but so far no need to call on Stefan's intervention. That is, at least, until the Friday evening.

Most of the foreign observers had returned whence they came, and post-election life in Chisinau was reverting to its mundane normality. The call Nina took that evening was from a Rumanian politician who had stayed on after helping with monitoring the election the previous weekend. No problem with language. Moldovan and Rumanian were interchangeable. He was younger, more intense than most of her other clients. More to the point, he was determined he was the one who would decide the extent of the services he required of her. After the usual preliminaries, his intentions became very clear.

"Let's get things straight. I pay the bill. You provide the service. I don't like wearing a rubber but I do like it up the arse. And that's what I want. What could be more simple?"

Nina politely at first, and then more forcefully, made him understand this was not on the menu.

"Sorry, that's not my scene. But I can go back to my colleagues and see if they would like to help. Shall I do that?"

"Well, well my little darling, I don't think that will be necessary, do you, when you're already here and can provide everything I need?" With that he opened a drawer and produced a small, sharp kitchen knife, which he pointed towards her. Feeling suddenly very scared and vulnerable, Nina backed away. She made sure she was moving closer to her handbag.

"Now, you little whore, perhaps this will help change your mind? I'm quite happy to pay. That's what you're here for, isn't it? You wouldn't want to go away with some unsightly lacerations on your lovely body would you? They do tend to happen accidentally, you know, if people aren't cooperative."

"Well, OK, but I shall need some cream," she responded, trying to play for time. "Otherwise it's very tight and painful."

"That's more like it! What a sensible girl you are! Sure we need some cream – want to make it fun, don't we?"

Clutching her dress as some sort of ineffectual protection in front of her nakedness, she turned and fumbled in her handbag, ostensibly to locate some cream. Surreptitiously she pressed the call button on her mobile buried in the bottom of the bag. The phone rang immediately in Stefan's car. He read the print-out digital display - it was Nina calling. The arrangement was that if she didn't speak, he knew she needed help. He pressed the receive button. There was no response.

Stefan was over six feet tall, and a fitness fanatic. He covered the ground from the car to the hotel in seconds. The reception staff were well primed. They gave him the key he demanded to room 313 without demur. The lift would be slow, so he sprinted up the three flights of stairs. One knock on the door and he was letting himself into the room barely two minutes after receiving Nina's call.

Things had moved on since then. Despite her stalling tactics, her young Rumanian client was intent on pressing his demands. Still holding the knife as a threat, he had forced her to kneel by the bed, pushing her forward across it with his free hand. Nina was tearful. This was the first time anyone had forced themselves on her. None of her previous encounters had stretched beyond what she was prepared to do. What this young man was demanding had always been a background fear. Now it was real. She didn't like it and didn't want it – whatever he was prepared to pay.

When the door burst open, the tableau presenting itself to Stefan bordered on the farcical - Nina, in a praying posture naked against the bed, and the young man standing over her a knife in one hand and also naked.

"What the hell are you doing here?" screamed the Rumanian, half turning towards Stefan and still brandishing the knife. "Who the hell are you? This is a private room! Get out!"

Stefan stayed very calm. "No need to get excited sir. I'm just one of the hotel staff, making sure everything's all right, sir. I hope one of our young ladies is not causing you any problems?"

"Since you ask, if she's on your payroll - yes, she is. She is giving me a lot of trouble. Doesn't seem very happy to do her job."

"Sorry about that sir," said Stefan. "I presume you have the money OK? Is that a problem?"

The Rumanian made it abundantly clear he had the necessary and that he was prepared to pay for his money's worth. Nina still crouched across the bed like a frightened animal, clutching a small blanket over herself.

"Well," said Stefan, "man to man, if you've got the money, seems to me you ought to get what you want, sir. Let's just count it to make sure, shall we?"

Nina could hardly believe what she was hearing. She sobbed quietly to herself, burying her head into the bed covers. But to her customer, what Stefan had said was what he wanted to hear.

Stefan moved forward as the young man turned away momentarily to locate his wallet, putting down the knife so he could pull out the notes. Unfortunately for him, he was not in time to see the upward jerk of Stefan's leg, but a split second afterwards he did feel the excruciating pain in his groin as Stefan's knee crashed mercilessly into his crotch. He crumpled to the floor clutching himself, tears welling in his eyes. Again he felt, but did not see the clenched fist that quickly followed, thumping down ferociously into the back of his neck, and then the heavy boot that kicked into his midriff, crunching against his hands locked round his genitals. It was now someone else's time to sob. Stefan threw a blanket over him disdainfully and helped himself to the rest of the money in the man's wallet.

"OK, Nina, dress quick. We'll be on our way just as soon as you're ready."

She needed no second bidding.

"Now, you little slug," said Stefan, addressing the prone figure under the blanket on the floor. "One move from you before we've gone, and your prick'll be down your throat. Do I make myself clear?" He gave the blanket another hard kick somewhere in the vicinity of the man's head. There was a feeble affirmative reply from underneath as Stefan ushered Nina out and slammed the door shut behind them.

He stopped briefly in the corridor and divided the sheaf of notes in his hand between the two of them.

"This is my little bonus when I have to help things along," he explained, "How are you? Are you OK?"

Nina had been distressed but now was feeling mightily relieved and grateful. In the end she had suffered nothing adverse. She was more than appreciative of Stefan's timely intervention and had no reservations about him pocketing the money. She had done nothing to earn it anyway! Tonight though she had had enough. She paid Stefan the usual $50 protection fee more readily than ever, and took her leave.

"Oh, who's an early bird then? Nina home before midnight! What's going on?" her flatmates crowed as she walked in. "Couldn't he keep it up tonight then? Bet he's sowing his oats somewhere else, don't you?" Nina smiled at their teasing. It was all meant in good heart, though tinged perhaps with a little jealousy.

"Time of the month," she responded. "Not his fault. He's very understanding."

She slept fitfully that night involuntarily rehearsing over and over again the trauma of her last encounter. She consoled herself that things always loomed ominously worse in the midnight hours. Stefan had done his job. That was all that mattered and she was even more sure now she could rely on him. Anyway she had already earned enough money for her abortion. Every extra dollar from now on was for her own personal benefit, and she could stop whenever she wanted.

More importantly, it was now only four days before her hospital admission. What she ought to be focusing on was how to camouflage being out of circulation for a few days next week. What was she going to say to friends and colleagues?

Chapter 24

Italy - December 2003

Eligio Lubicello had just celebrated his fortieth birthday the night he sat smoking a cigarette behind the steering wheel of one of the two Iveco transit vans on the deserted cliff top at the heel of Italy in late November 2003. He was to be the lead vehicle. He knew where he had to go and what he had to do. There were risks, but he had performed this clandestine operation a few times before. No trouble – and the money was good. The Neapolitan Mafia depended on him, not just because he was a reliable driver, but because he supplied them with an essential commodity – a safe house for illegals in the Tuscan hills outside Naples. The house was, in effect, courtesy of his grandfather, Francisco. Were he still alive, it would have broken his heart that his grandson was using his inheritance so.

Francisco had believed in old-fashioned values. He had inherited his father's farm in the hills near Avellino, and under his industrious husbandry the business grew. The farmstead was extended to provide separate accommodation for his parents and he and his family lived in a spacious newly built farmhouse across the sun-drenched courtyard. On each side they built large barns to house the oil and wine presses. Nearby were the stables for their horses and open barns for their carts and machinery. Underground they dug out a cave to store the barrels of olive oil and casks of maturing wine. Chicken huts, pigsties and goat pens made up the rest of the complex. The family's own vineyards and olive groves, manicured and neat, stretched in regimented lines across the dry stony ground of the surrounding hills as far as the eye could see.

Francisco cared nothing for politics but he could not avoid the calamitous consequences of the rise of Nazism in the 1930s and the fateful alliance of his beloved country to the German war machine. As the Second World War spread its merciless grip across Europe, Francisco was drafted into the Army. He died in a bomb blast on the beaches at Anzio in 1944, his body blown to smithereens, leaving a distraught wife and six young children to try to keep the family business together. Their only son, Antonino, was barely fifteen years old and on his shoulders fell the brunt of the task. The bloom of Italian manhood had fallen on the battlefields. They would not be returning home. Survival was now down to the women, the old people and the children.

Antonino did his best, but he was out of his depth. There was too much to do on his own and, in any case, he didn't have his father's expertise or fortitude. By the time he married in 1955, the farm was in decay and the fields neglected. Oil and wine production had fallen year by year and was barely providing a living for the family. Eligio, their only son and last of their four children, was born in 1963, too young to recognise his father's increasing addiction to alcohol or to understand his mother's despairing endeavours to keep family and home together. The children survived as best they could. Surrounded by buildings in terminal decay, a mother preoccupied with household chores and always tired, a father usually absent, inebriated or in bed, and with no spare money for other than necessities, there was little option but to live off their wits. The easy temptations and opportunities provided by nearby Naples were a magnet too strong to resist. First the daughters and then Eligio drifted into the Neopolitan subculture of drugs, protection rackets, prostitution and petty crime.

By the time their father's liver eventually succumbed to the inevitable, Eligio's sisters had already drifted far away from home, and after their father's will had finally cleared through its legal formalities, Eligio found himself the sole heir of the estate, its buildings, farmhouses, barns, and hectares of neglected vineyards and olive groves. His mother, now the sole permanent occupant, old and worn beyond her years, was given lifelong rights to stay. Eligio's residence there was spasmodic, depending on whether his ephemeral lodgings with his underworld colleagues in Naples broke down or not. The fields he had inherited had been rented out to more industrious neighbours and, apart from collecting the dues, he showed little or no interest in the farm. Weeds grew unchecked at random throughout the courtyard. When the wind blew, more tiles crashed to the ground. A few solitary chickens roamed at large in the barns and outbuildings. His mother looked after them, and the dogs and the four remaining goats. In summer the farmstead baked in the unremitting sunshine. In winter it was a desolate place to be.

It was not long before Eligio's colleagues tuned into his newly acquired proprietorial wealth, albeit more a liability than an asset. And equally it was not long before the Mafia controllers of the illegal immigrant trails across Italy, the Napoli Connection, recognised that Eligio's inheritance would make an ideal staging post for their trade in human traffic – off the beaten track, never visited by outsiders, masses of buildings to absorb temporary tenants well away from inquisitive neighbours or officials, and only half an hour's drive from the city. The deal was struck. For Eligio it was an unexpected bonus. His mother was easily convinced this was a charitable venture, helping people who were temporarily homeless, and she was happily content to see some extra life and movement in the place.

Through the dark November night, this was where Eligio was headed with his latest cargo of illegals, now fitfully slumbering against each other in the back of the van. The roads were good and traffic light, but no need to attract attention by being over speedy. A steady 100 kilometres an hour would get them there by daybreak. In two hours they would reach Bari - there, a short toilet stop in a secluded lay-by and then on to Avellino two and a half hours later, autostrada all the way.

Habib was glad of the journey break. He was anxious to check his shoes to make sure the polythene envelopes had protected his dollar hoard from the soaking in seawater as they disembarked from the boat. It was dark by the roadside, so no-one could see his surreptitious shoe removal and examination of the insoles. All OK. That was a relief. The technique to safeguard his precious financial lifeline was proving effective. He took a swig from his water bottle and totted up in his head how much he had used so far – \$500 to Osman in Mitrovice when he set out, \$200 to the man in Kukes, \$500 to Toci in Tirana, and \$750 to the boat captain. Then there were the incidentals for clothes in Tirana and payments for taxis and buses – in all he had dispensed about \$2,000 so far – that left him with around \$3,000 to complete the rest of the journey. He hoped it would be enough. Just had to wait and see.

After fifteen minutes or so the two disparate groups of illegals climbed back into the vans for the final leg of the night's journey. Bledar and Habib stayed close together. They were a buttress for each other. Habib was grateful for that as he curled up as comfortably as the spartan seating would allow and dozed away the motorway miles. He was in deep sleep when he sensed the motion of the vehicle change. No longer the smooth, speedy autostrada, but now a more bumpy road that required cautious navigation. A final steep turn and then they stopped. The doors were flung open. Gestures and shouts made it clear they had arrived. Habib checked his watch. 7:00 a.m. The faint dawn light allowed them to take in their surroundings. They were in a courtyard surrounded by old buildings. One or two looked habitable. Two dogs were barking but keeping their distance. One of the drivers shouted harshly at them. They quietened quickly. There were some broken-down tractors and other machines in the open barns. Now the dogs had stopped yapping, only the sound of a cockerel and chickens broke the silence. There were no lights, and no sight nor sound of other traffic.

One of the drivers addressed the group. To Habib, and to most of them, what he said was incomprehensible. The man with the injured ankle came to their rescue. He could speak some Italian. He would translate.

"They want us to make sure we've got all our stuff out of the vans. Then we go to the big house over there." He pointed to a large farmhouse on the north side. They shuffled across and into a large room lit by two meagre paraffin lamps. A massive table stood in the middle. There were a few chairs, not enough for everyone. Habib reflected that, in its prime, this would have been an impressive dining room. Now it was tired, musty and dank. There was no heating, that was for sure. The vans had driven off. Their companion painstakingly translated what was being said.

"OK – we're here. Lots of rooms upstairs where you can bed down and rest. No-one leaves without our permission. There's washrooms and water, cold - not hot. Make yourselves at home. You stay today. We'll bring you food and drink. You just keep quiet and lay low. At nine o' clock some coffee and bread will arrive. But before that we need $200 from each of you for the van ride and your stay here.

"One last thing. We're a long way from anywhere. If anyone tries to push off on their own, we have guards on duty all the time. They don't like people who break our rules. We have contacts all around and you won't get far before we catch you. Then you'll discover how expendable you are. We have to protect our interests. Is that clear? OK – we collect the money now, then you can go and rest."

Bledar and Habib settled their debts and climbed the stairs with the rest. They elected to go to the top attic rooms. There were some dusty old beds, coated in cobwebs. Rather than commandeer one of these, they elected to install themselves in a corner of the room and sat on the floor. Nothing to do except try to keep warm and wait. It was an eerie place, but things could be worse. The weather had cleared in the night and when dawn finally broke, in spite of the neglect and decay, the sun lent a degree of warmth and charm to the surroundings. The chickens were clucking contentedly outside and it was reminiscent of his childhood at home. The jugs of hot black coffee duly arrived, complemented with some newly baked bread. It wasn't a feast but it was hugely welcome. The spirits of the motley group of immigrants noticeably improved. There was much animated chatter. They had surmounted one of their biggest hurdles. Now they could relax for a few hours. Habib had no idea what would come next, but this was clearly a staging post. He assumed a large group like this were a liability. All the organisers wanted was the money, and the sooner they got rid of any incriminating evidence, like people, the better.

Most of the group were still exhausted after their night's exertions, and settled down to try to catch up with sleep. Habib and Bledar were more interested in where they were. They reckoned a cautious exploration in the courtyard sunshine would do no harm. The warmth and freshness of the early morning revived their enthusiasm. There was a quiet beauty in the gentle countryside stretching away on every side even at this time of year. Habib reflected it was only a few weeks since he had left home. Already he had packed in so much. There had been much stress and anxiety, but it was an adventure he relished. He was just keen to keep going.

A large black Fiat saloon swept into the courtyard. Habib and Bledar backed away towards the house as three men slammed the car doors and marched determinedly in their direction, leaving the chauffeur with the vehicle. Much gesticulation and shouting indicated another dining room meeting was being called. Sleepy, slightly disorientated bodies appeared from various rooms upstairs. The services of their Italian-speaking fellow-traveller were again demanded.

"Listen hard and make no mistakes in what you have to do. Twelve of you will stay in Italy – half go to Naples, the rest to Milan. We move you tonight. One van will be here at ten o'clock. First we go to Naples – one hour. We leave six of you there. Then there's a long journey to Milan. Takes seven hours – maybe more. We drop the others at a safe house there. You must pay the driver money now. Naples $200 – Milan $500 each person."

It took half an hour for the relevant people to locate their payments and settle the demands. After what had happened to the guy in the bunker in Albania, there was no prevarication. No one was prepared to challenge what was being asked. Pay up and shut up, even though what was effectively a 40 kilometre taxi journey to Naples was going to net $1,200 and the one to Milan $3,000. Not a bad return for a night's work thought Habib as he listened and watched.

"OK, you lot can disappear upstairs now while we deal with the rest."

There were eleven left, including Habib and Bledar. It occurred to Habib that despite his companionship with Bledar, he had not so far established where he hoped to be going.

"Five of you are going to Germany and the rest to Belgium. You all travel in the same van to Genoa. There you split up. The van leaves tonight at midnight. Be ready. You'll drive all night. Then you stay in a safe house there till you get more instructions. All clear? Right - $500 each now to pay for your ride. Then you'd better lie low for the rest of the day. Any funny business and you'll regret you ever came to Italy."

But for the mellow late autumn sunshine it would have been a tedious day. Habib and Bledar sat outside in the courtyard and exchanged stories, relaxing in the tranquillity of the Italian countryside, feeling good. Their paths would diverge at Genoa. Habib had now learned Bledar was hoping to get into Germany. At midday another van drew up. The small greasy-haired driver produced two cartons of bottles of water and a dozen lukewarm pizzas, distributed in halves on receipt of $5 from each. The old lady brought across another load of piping hot black coffee. Things are not at all bad thought Habib as he dozed contentedly, trying to catch up on some sleep.

There was no lack of eagerness when the first batch climbed back into the van at ten o'clock that evening and disappeared into the black Italian night. They had been together barely two days but during that time the group had shared the same stresses and anxieties. Habib felt an unexpected sense of abandonment as they left, recognising it was a gentle foretaste of being left to his own devices sooner or later in a totally foreign environment. No need to dwell on that. Time now to check all his belongings. Rucksack OK. Some bottled water and food if needed. Shoes warm and dry and money secured. A sweater to sit on in the van. It was going to be a long night again and the seats were not designed for comfort.

Their transport arrived on the dot. Another large white transit van with no windows. The same bench seats as before – probably the same van that brought them here. Habib decided to make a mental note of the number plate this time. Then they were off along the track to join up with the autostrada. Within twenty minutes, they had negotiated the toll barrier and were cruising steadily northwards. Habib reflected how smoothly and speedily the Italian side of the operation had gone so far. In a few hours they would be ready for the strike into France. He slumped down into his seat as best he could and willed the night hours away, surrounded by ten others, all of whose futures hung on the flimsy thread of the reliability of this van and the trust they had placed in the driver. It was best not to think too hard about that. This was their only option. There was no going back and no other way forward. Just keep your fingers crossed and pray to whichever god you believed in that things would be OK.

Chapter 25

Moldova - March 2001

"Pavel," said Nina on her mobile. "I need to see you – when can we meet?"

"Can you make eleven o'clock this morning at the coffee bar near your DHL office?"

"Fine, see you then, bye."

Early-morning nausea, a fretful night, and the worry of what cover story to dream up for her imminent stay in hospital – it was not surprising Nina felt somewhat jaded as she clasped her hands round the warm bowl of the coffee cup and rehearsed to her brother the news that the abortion was now scheduled for three days time.

"Well – that's good to hear, but how the hell did you raise the money?"

"Long story really –one of the guys I danced with last Saturday night - said he could help. Met him in the week – he seemed loaded and gave me a loan. I can pay him back at $5 a week he said – so I jumped at the chance." Nina hoped she sounded convincing, but she hated lying to Pavel.

"Sounds pretty dicey to me," said Pavel. "What's in it for him? I bet he thinks he'll be entitled to a free shag whenever he wants it!"

"Well if he did, he didn't say anything like that – he seemed like a nice guy. But that's not what I want to talk about. I've got to stay in the hospital for two nights and I need to explain that to my flatmates without giving the game away. I'm going to tell them I'm off home to see Mum and Dad for a few days. What I plan to do is stay two nights in the hospital and then get a bus straight home for a few days there till I'm fit again. But I thought you should know so you can corroborate my story. Is that OK, do you think?"

"Sounds fine to me. Mum and Dad will be really pleased to see you again, but what will you tell them?"

"Oh, I'll say I've just had a bad bout of flu' and felt run down, and what with my boyfriend trouble, I thought a bit of home comfort would put me right again. No doubt they'll try and persuade me to stay, but there's no chance of that.

"There's one other thing – the doctor says someone has to meet me from the hospital when I leave on Thursday morning. Do you think you could meet me with a taxi and take me to the bus station? I can get a bus to Cimislia and then cadge a lift home from there. The only trouble is I'm not sure how strong I'll feel. The doctor says I shall need a week or so to convalesce. I just wonder how I'll cope with the journey on my own. Perhaps I should get a taxi all the way? What do you think?"

Pavel whistled under his breath. "That'll cost ten times more than the bus! How can you afford it?"

"Well, I knew I might need a bit extra so I've borrowed another $50." Nina hoped she sounded convincing.

"If that's the case, I've a better idea," said Pavel. "There's a young doctor at my hospital who uses his brother's car regularly to smuggle Moldovan brandy and drinks across the border into Ukraine. He takes a track through the hills near Basarabeasca where there's no border post. So he knows our home area well. I could ask him if he could take you. He would be reliable and you could pay him the taxi fare. What do you think? Shall I ask him?"

Nina thought that sounded an excellent scheme. To travel with a doctor in her convalescent condition would be an unexpected bonus. She went back to work that evening in buoyant mood. This would be the last weekend of offering herself up to the steady demand for sexual services from the residents at Hotel Dukro. She had already earned enough to pay the gynaecologist's fees. The weekend's earnings would be her own personal nest egg. The moral issues were no longer relevant. Might as well be hung for a sheep as for a lamb. With the end in sight, before she finished, she would try to maximise her number of clients. She was not disappointed. Nor were the seven customers who enjoyed their brief time with her, and contributed a further $155 into Nina's secret treasure hoard.

At half past midnight on the Sunday evening she took her leave of Stefan and Zvetlana. Apart from Pavel, they were the only ones who knew she was to have an abortion that week. They also knew that meant she would be unavailable for "work" for the next week or so. They had enjoyed working with her, wished her well and hoped she would come back soon. It was strange how a camaraderie of friendship grows up in any profession, generated out of the shared vicissitudes of the job, whatever it is.

Pavel phoned on the Monday morning. It was a bright spring day. Nina was having a lie-in, mulling over the anxieties of tomorrow. It was entirely rational to have the abortion, but that meant a cuddly innocent baby would never see the light of day, and her parents would be deprived of a grandchild which she knew would have so gladdened their cramped, colourless lives. But it was her life that mattered. She was determined not to let emotion undermine her resolve. She had to be tough.

"Hi, sis, I've spoken to the guy I talked about. He's called Dr Viktor Sturza – nice chap, about thirty years old. His mother works as a senior nurse here with me in the hospital. He's a trainee paediatrician. Earns a pittance – about $30 a month, barely more than I do. So he makes a bit on the side taking booze into the Ukraine –pays his brother for the petrol and use of his car. Says he's happy to meet you on Thursday and take you home. Reckons he wants about $10 plus the cost of the diesel. Is that OK?"

"That sounds fine. I'm really, really relieved about that. Thanks so much for fixing it. Will you be there? I'll be leaving about nine o'clock."

"Right, I'll be there to introduce him. Make sure he meets Mum and Dad - they'll be impressed. Their daughter friendly with a handsome young doctor. That'll be something to tell the neighbours!"

Tuesday came quickly and, by then, her flatmates had been told the cover story. Nina was taking time off to visit her parents back home. Unusually she was leaving in the late afternoon, but she explained that away by saying a friend was going to Cimislia at that time, so she was sharing a lift with him – she expected to be back in ten days or so.

"Better give us the address of your boyfriend then!" they teased. "Don't want to him to forget what to do, do we? We'll keep him happy while you're away!"

Their good humour was an antidote to her inner turmoil. She embraced them all with genuine affection and, carrying the essentials for ten days away in a small battered suitcase, she took a taxi, ostensibly for the rendez-vous with someone who was to take her home. Instead, ten minutes later, the taxi dropped her outside the hospital gate.

It was a lonely, dismal walk to the entrance despite the late-afternoon sunshine valiantly trying to chase away the last remnants of winter's grip. Piles of melting snow, now filthy and unlovely, hugged the shaded north-facing walls of the gaunt hospital buildings. As always, the sun would win in the end, spring would come, the flowers would bloom, vegetables would burgeon in her father's garden, and in spite of themselves, everyone would feel a renewed sense of uplift and hope. For the moment, however, Nina's mood matched that of the dark, dirty heaps of ugly snow.

Inside the hospital the heating was at full blast as usual, the brown linoleum-floored corridors were scrubbed clean, the air was thick with antiseptic and the furniture and fittings were sparse and worn out. Nothing had changed. A buxom middle-aged lady wearing a faded green smock, with hair encased in a tightly bound white scarf, registered her arrival.

"Now dear, first we need your $200 please. Then we can get on with things, can't we?"

Nina paid over the necessary in exchange for a scrap of scribbled paper. A thin pale-faced nurse then led her down the dimly lit corridor to a cheerless room accommodating four iron beds, four metal bedside cupboards painted dark green, a single bare light bulb suspended from the ceiling and not much else. Two beds were already occupied. Lying on top of the thick brown blankets were two women, both considerably older than Nina, drawing deeply on cigarettes, propelling wreathes of bluish smoke, swirling towards the bulb.

Nina put a brave face on it all, smiled at her companions, greeted them and began unpacking her things into her bedside cupboard.

"Stupid to do that, love," said the woman nearest to her. "Best leave things in your case and keep it locked, or you'll find everything walks! When you've been in as many times as we have, you'll soon learn. Reckon this is your first visit, is it?"

"Well, yes," replied Nina falteringly. "Are we all here for the same thing?"

"Why else do you think we're fucking here, darling? These days all the punters want is to get it up without a rubber – it pays better, but then every few months we find we've another bun in the oven. So it's back in here, and pay the doctor to get it sorted. Better to let the silly sods have it up the arse – can't get took then, can you? - and it pays better. You'll soon learn, deary." She took another self-assured suck on her cigarette, exhaling the smoke through her lips in a long slow deliberate trail, lending unspoken emphasis to the fact that no-one knew more about "the game" than she did.

Nina was at a loss how to respond. Both women were long past their youth. They were wearing hospital dressing gowns, much used and much stained despite the evidence of endless washes. Both had dyed hair, back-combed and lifeless. Their facial features were ravaged, their hands coarse, fingernails garishly painted. and the lower part of their legs, stretching out below the gown, pock-marked, thin and veiny. Nina drew the obvious conclusion. Here was the result of a lifetime of whoring. It was not an endearing prospect. Deep within her, she resolved she would never let herself end up like this. Whatever she had done or might do in the future, personal dignity and family life were things she would always cherish. Meantime she would endure, rather than enjoy, the soulless humour and earthy company of her ward mates. They did at least share the same condition.

She slept fitfully. The ward nurse woke them at 6:00 a.m. No breakfast. A shower and then into a wrap-around white smock, thin and threadbare, to cover her nakedness. Nina was first on the list. Her companions wished her luck. Despite their dissolute coarseness, they conveyed a warmth of friendship towards her, evoked perhaps by a sense of their own lost youthfulness and defeated lives. She walked in flip-flops to the operating theatre. In the adjacent room she lay on a trolley. A nurse rubbed a strong smelling fluid on her arm. She felt the small prick of a needle. Start counting. She reached seven.

Then there was only a surreal dream. A horse was running across the hills. Her parents were chasing it. Trees kept falling down to block their path. Children joined the chase. A big black hole loomed ahead of them. There was inky water at the bottom. Tentacles leapt out of it. Nina had to save her parents, but the tentacles wound round her legs. Her parents were going to fall in the hole. Her arms stretched out desperately, her legs wouldn't move. Her parents were drowning. A deep well of anguish and impotence swallowed her, her screams of despair went unheeded – and then someone was gently mouthing her name, "Miss Snegur, wake up. Time to wake up now. Miss Snegur, wake up."

But she didn't want to wake – how could she live without her parents? Didn't the voice understand they had just fallen into an abyss?

"Miss Snegur, wake up. It's all over. Time to wake up."

She would tell them. She would open her eyes and tell them of the tragedy. Then they would understand and let her sleep. Then she saw a nurse with a white scarf round her head. She had seen her before. Long, long ago wasn't it? In the hospital, the hospital where she went not to have a baby. She remembered now – perhaps that was why the tentacles had taken her parents. But the nurse was being kind and speaking gently. She felt very tired; the horse had stopped running; the black hole had gone. Instead there was a single light hanging from the ceiling and a kind lady with a cigarette in her mouth standing beside the nurse, stroking her hair. She was saying nice words.

"Come on my lovely, it's all over now. You were very brave. You're going to be all right. What about a nice cup of tea?"

It took half an hour before Nina could focus her mind properly. The cup of tea helped. She was in no pain, but her limbs were heavy and languid. She also felt unutterably sleepy. Once the nurse was sure she had adequately recovered, she was left on her own with one of the other women sitting on the adjacent bed watching over her, chain-smoking as always.

"Ludmila's being done now," she said. "Then it's my turn. You get used to it in time. How you're feeling? Took a long time to wake up. Nice dreams or bad ones? You never know at this lark. You'll be OK. The doctor's very good. Still, he ought to be, the price he charges. Best sleep now. You'll feel better in the morning. But take it easy. No more shagging for a few days at least!"

Nina was having difficulty taking all this in. The last thing on her mind was the prospect of any more sex. She closed her eyes and drifted into a half-conscious doze. It was over now. The deed had been done. Tears welled around her eyes. No baby to care for. No grandchild for Mum. Was there a God? Was this a mortal sin? Would she ever feel strong again? Half-baked thoughts washed in and out of her mind, sometimes dreamlike, sometimes wakeful. Her companions came and went and came again. Then there was the strident sound of another nurse pushing a squeaky trolley.

"Time to eat! Wake up pet. Got to build your strength up. Here you are – a nice hot bowl of soup. That'll do you good. Let's sit you up a bit, shall we? There you are. Things aren't so bad after all, are they? Get this down you and you'll soon feel better."

The soup did help. Nina had drowsed through most of the morning. Her companions continued to fumigate the small room with their cigarettes, chatting away about this, that and the other, as though they had had no more than a tooth out. A nurse came in and suggested Nina should walk to the washroom and freshen up. Her legs still felt like lumps of wood, but she was in no pain. More disconcerting was the perfunctory nappy she appeared to be wearing. The nurse explained it was only a precaution. She would be well advised to wear it for a few days until things had settled down. The washroom visit was more of an exertion than she expected. She was relieved to reach her bed again. She lay down and sank into another deep sleep.

A meal of salad, bread and sliced meat followed by a sort of yoghurt arrived in the early evening. Nina was relieved to discover she had recovered some appetite, and was feeling less feeble. Her companions continued to try to jolly her along with their non-stop chatter. It was a comfort to have their reassuring presence. They provided a measure of normality in the midst of everything.

Another deep sleep was rudely broken the next morning at the unearthly hour of 6:00 a.m., the nurse bustling in with a meagre breakfast of bread and tomatoes, making it abundantly clear to the three patients that this was discharge day. Nina's companions expressed in over-ripe language what they thought about being woken so early. One by one they used the bathroom, dressed and packed their bags. Still feeling frail, Nina was ready and waiting in the foyer at nine o'clock when Pavel walked in with Dr Sturza. They shook hands.

"You look pretty shattered," said Pavel. "Are you really OK to go all that way home now?"

"I'll be all right. I'll relax back in the car seat. I'm sure Dr Sturza will drive steadily. Then when I get home I can rest as long as I want. Mum'll take care of me. Best place to be really."

"Better call me Viktor," said Dr Sturza. "Don't worry. I'll get you home safely. It won't take more than two hours. I'll take it carefully."

A few hugs and kisses from her brother, some goodies from him to take home to Mum and Dad, her case on the back seat, and they were off – first past the dreary grey tenement blocks that ring Chisinau massively on every approach, and then on to join up with the wide metalled, but poorly maintained, highway running south westwards towards Cimislia.

"How nice it is to get out into the countryside again," said Nina. Her spirits lifted as she watched the rolling hills advancing towards them, still bare and brown after the harsh winter frosts but already beginning to respond to the gentle warmth of the early spring sunshine. Beyond them lay the distant backcloth of the higher mountains still snow-capped. Things may be primitive in the villages but it felt good to be going back to her roots. Her parents would be delighted to have her home again, and she was looking forward to being able to give them a gift of $100 from her earnings, though they were not to know from whence it had come. She would tell them she had saved the money out of her earnings at DHL. In the villages that was a small fortune.

"How about getting some fresh fish to take home?" asked Viktor as they passed by a lake still partly frozen. Alongside the road, on a rickety makeshift stall, three red-faced housewives, buttoned up in layers of jumpers and overcoats against the brisk morning air, were holding up huge fish just caught from the lake that morning, so fresh their bodies were still flexing, desperate to be restored to their natural environment.

"Great idea," said Nina. "I'll get some money out".

"No problem," said Viktor. "They sell them for next to nothing. I can get four for less than a dollar. How many do you want?"

Nina thought four would be ample, and while Viktor went off to do the good humoured bargaining, she reached over to her case on the back seat. Before going into the hospital she had made a small slit in the suitcase lining and secreted under the lining the bulk of the savings she had made while in Chisinau, sealing the slit with sticky tape. Even after paying the hospital fees, and buying some new clothes, she was still almost $250 in profit. Her parents' gift would come out of that and the rest would be her financial cushion for when she returned to Chisinau and looked for a more regular, even though so much less well-paid, job.

She was surprised the case was unlocked, but she then remembered the early morning wake-up in the hospital and hasty dash to the washroom. After repacking her wash-kit she must have forgotten to lock the case. It was then she noticed the sticky tape had been torn off and was hanging limply aside. The money had gone. Desperately she pushed her fingers deeper inside, searching vainly for the precious nest egg. There was nothing left. In her purse she had only small change.

Viktor returned, proudly heaving the fish into the boot of the car. To his dismay Nina was sobbing hysterically. "What's the matter?" he asked wondering if she was in pain or suddenly overwhelmingly homesick. Through her sobs Nina poured out her tale of woe.

"My money's all gone! It must have been stolen from my case in the hospital. What am I to do? I've nothing left hardly – not even enough to pay you. Oh, God, just when I thought everything was going to be all right, now it's all gone wrong again. I'm so unhappy. What can I do?" Her tears ran down as she sobbed uncontrollably, head buried into her handkerchief.

"Never mind," said Viktor. "Money's not everything. Your parents will be glad to see you. You'll have all your village friends to catch up with, all your stories to tell, and theirs to tell you. Don't worry about paying me. Maybe next time." He reached over and stroked her hair to try to console her, then put an arm around her while she leaned into his shoulder and drank deeply of his sympathy. The wayside fishwives were much intrigued as they watched with great interest through the car windows what appeared to them to be a lovers' tiff.

It was some time since Nina had experienced such unaffected sympathy. It was so comforting. Yes, things needed to be kept in perspective. Easy come, easy go – as they say. A few weeks before she could not have contemplated having so much money. Now it had gone, but she was no worse off than she had been that short time ago. She had made many new friends and her life experiences had immeasurably advanced. The pregnancy had been sorted out. She was in good health and now she had met a young doctor whose care and consideration, to say nothing of his good looks and intelligence, were kindling new emotions in her.

"You're right. I'll be fine. Just a bit of a shock to think those whores in the hospital may have not been so kind after all. Worse things could happen. I really appreciate your understanding, but

I'm so embarrassed I can't pay you for this journey. I'll make sure I'll do so when I get back to Chisinau and get some more money."

She dabbed her eyes, and smiled at him. Viktor let out the clutch and waved their farewell to the curious onlookers, now with much to chew over as they waited for new fish supplies from their menfolk out on the lake.

The main road took them to Cimislia but from there the last five kilometres was a dirt track, muddy and potholed in winter, bone-hard and dusty in the summer. Horse-drawn carts outnumbered mechanical vehicles. The villages still depended on communal wells for water, and their electricity supply was spasmodic, but this was her home and here were her roots.

Nina's emotions were in turmoil as they drew into Mihailovca. Viktor negotiated the last bumpy track to her parents' walled home. It was mid-morning. The sun shone weakly. The air was still. Remnants of snow huddled in shaded nooks and crannies. Dogs barked intermittently. Chickens scratched for titbits proprietorially in the muddy streets. Groups of men, looking as worn out as their clothes, stood around passing the time of day deep in mirthless talk, while, inside their homes the womenfolk busied themselves with the chores of washing, cooking, cleaning, mending and feeding that gave them, at least, a continued sense of role and purpose. The contrast with life in Chisinau could not have been more marked.

"Nina, Nina, how lovely to see! Welcome home! My, what smart clothes! But goodness me, you're so pale. Looks as though you're in need of some good fresh air and home cooking. We'll soon put that right, won't we?"

There were tears and hugs and more hugs. It felt good to be home.

"This is Dr Sturza – a friend of Pavel's at the hospital. He's given me a lift here. Really kind of him. And look what we've brought – fresh fish from the lake!"

"Oh, that's lovely. Thank you very much. Very pleased to meet you Dr Sturza. Very kind of you to bring Nina home. Would you like to come in for a bite to eat?"

The smell of wood smoke filled the kitchen, mingled with delicious odours emanating from the broth of vegetables already bubbling merrily over the fire. First the vodka, then the chatter. "No, Dr Sturza, didn't smoke – must be the only person in Moldova who didn't! Yes, he did look after children, but medical equipment and drugs were very scarce. Loved his job, not much money in it though. Enjoyed meeting Nina. Glad to be of help. Maybe they could meet up again when she gets back to Chisinau?"

Nina's parents soaked all this up, relishing that such a nice young man seemed so kindly affected towards their daughter. After the wholesome convivial lunch, they pressed onto him a basket of fresh vegetables and then he was off to retrace his tracks back to the capital, leaving Nina to come to terms again with the simple lifestyle back at home. Mother fussed over her. All agreed that rest, fresh air and good home cooking would soon restore her vigour and spirit. Little did they know, nor would they, why Nina was feeling so fragile.

The days passed happily. Two things happened. Her health did improve rapidly and, equally quickly, she got bored. The diet was monotonous. No meat, except on special occasions. Nothing to do in the village. No television. Most of the adult men seemed to have no work. Their conversation was parochial. They were going nowhere and their body language exhaled a miasma of defeat. And no-one had any money, although once or twice a few well-heeled young men would arrive in a posh car and strut their stuff, but the villagers were very wary of them. The rumour was they dealt in drugs or illicit smuggling over the border. Some even said they took young girls away to do bad things. They were not welcome visitors despite the money in their pockets.

As Nina's fitness improved, so did her sense of frustration with so little to do. She was really glad to be with her parents again, but felt guilty about how much she yearned to get back to Chisinau. Fortunately, she had always said she would stay for only a short while, so before two weeks were up she was already making plans for her return. This time it would be by horse and cart for the hour's trek into Cimislia, and then a battered bus journey back to the capital.

"Do come back soon, won't you? It's been lovely having you with us again. Give our love to Pavel. Tell him it's time he came to see us again. Take him some of Dad's fresh leeks and parsnips. Take care of yourself. We do miss you. God bless."

More hugs and tears and Nina trundled off on the cart, waving happily to her acquaintances in the village as they came out to bid her farewell. It began to rain and she was wet and bedraggled by the time she was able to install herself in a window seat of the bus. The journey was grey and dispiriting. Through the steamed up windows the countryside looked bleak. Then the miserable suburbs of the capital loomed into focus and with them the realisation that the security and warmth and comfort of home were now to be forfeited for a city life, starting again with no money, no job and uncertain prospects. The long walk from the bus station in the late afternoon gloom did nothing to raise her spirits as she made her way back to her friends' flat. At least they would cheer her up. But tomorrow she had to get her act together. First and foremost she had to find work. Without money Chisinau was not much fun.

Chapter 26

Leicester - January 2004

On the back seat of the Mercedes, that Saturday evening, Peter Clayton's adrenalin was pumping hard. He was in little doubt he was in dangerous situation. He had seen the grotesque methods used on Michael Burton. By now he was convinced Michael's death was murder rather suicide. Suicide victims are not in the habit of disposing of their own bodies. He himself seemed to be in the hands of kidnappers, and it was unlikely they were heading for an enjoyable social evening together. All the evidence pointed towards Peter having been an unexpected witness of Michael's violent demise; a witness whom it was more convenient to eliminate.

By any standards, Peter was in a stressful situation. The broad choices open to him were to find a way to escape - not easy when a vehicle was bowling along a dual carriageway at speed, or to try to tackle his captors and subdue them - again not easy when facing two people whose approach to combat was unlikely to accord with Queensbury Boxing rules.

There were, however, a few things in his favour. First the abductors did not yet realise Peter had sussed out that all was not as it should be. Second, Peter was thirty-six years old and a regular squash player, and as such a good deal taller, fitter, and more athletic than the portly middle-aged gentleman sitting next to him. Thirdly, he knew the geography of the area, and as the miles ticked away, he was well aware they were heading for the M1/M69 motorway junction, which confirmed to him it was most unlikely they were on the way to a mortuary. Fourthly, he was well clad, unrestricted in his movements, and had a mobile phone in his pocket.

His mind was becoming very focussed. For the present he could do no more than sit tight. But he could use his eyes, conversation having proved somewhat abortive. The Mercedes they were travelling in was a black or midnight-blue saloon. The interior was grey leather upholstery. It was an E class, probably the 320 six-cylinder model, about seven years old. The driver was about thirty years old with jet black hair and sallow complexion. He was of small build with a wiry frame. He could well be the Bruce Lee look-alike that his son, Robert, had seen earlier. The man sitting beside him on the back-seat was probably in his early fifties, with a noticeable beer belly. He spoke with a north London intonation but nondescript accent.

There are times when fate can deal a rotten hand. Other times the gods can intervene serendipitously. Peter had not had much luck so far that day, but events ahead of him were unfolding rather more to his benefit.

The driver approached junction 21 of the M1 from the Leicester Ring Road. Instead of taking the north or south slip road, he headed straight across onto the M69 towards Coventry. Unforeseen but unluckily for him, the Ministry of Transport had chosen this weekend to commission major improvements to the central reservation on this stretch of carriageway. Traffic funnelled down tardily to one lane, with the two faster lanes coned off by the usual profusion of red and white marker cones stretching ahead for some miles. Being a Saturday early evening and with Leicester City having no home match that day, traffic was moderate. Head to tail, it proceeded along at a stately 30 mph with little the Mercedes driver could do about it.

Whether it was caused by debris from the roadworks or an over-worn tyre was difficult to say, but after two miles of this procession the car began to sway from side to side. The driver was evidently having trouble with the steering, which ought normally to have been effortless.

"We got puncture," he announced in a curt heavily accented explanation to his colleague.

"Can you hold it or do we have to change the wheel?" asked the agitated back-seat passenger beside Peter.

"I can hold it, but I think tyre burn up. Better we stop and change it."

"Shit! OK – put your hazard flashers on and pull into the centre when you can, inside the cones."

This was a difficult manoeuvre achieved by slowing down to walking pace and then turning sharply to the right to finish up parked in the area reserved for motorway workmen, but of whom there was no trace as far as the eye could see.

Strong arc lights illuminated the scene as the driver and his portly colleague assessed the problem. Southbound traffic streamed past them steadily in the restricted lane, while northbound traffic on the opposite carriageway pounded past at high speed in three lanes towards Leicester. Accompanied with some unsavoury swearing and cursing, the car was jacked up, and the spare wheel extracted from the boot. The wheel bolts had been fitted by power tools and needed even more oaths and exertions to free them up. Meanwhile Peter was obediently situated on the back seat, having been firmly told to stay where he was.

When cones appear on motorways, they are usually accompanied by an array of other signs and wonders. Huge metallic discs demand reduced speed, followed by mandatory new speed limits enforced by strident notices declaring that everything is being monitored by police cameras. Even if the traffic is not already static, there is no chance of speedy progress again until the dreaded cones peter out and the unrestricted lanes reappear so throttles can be opened up again. The other rather odd notice in such situations is the one that requires drivers to stay with their vehicle in case of breakdown. The logic seems to be that when the vehicle stops, so will the tail of traffic behind it, which in turn will alert the breakdown gang who will come racing to the rescue.

On the M69, the manoeuvre executed by Peter's abductors had averted a tailback. What they were hoping was that they would thus avoid the attention of any would-be rescuers, as they worked furiously to remove the filthy front nearside wheel and replace it. Amidst the constant noise, the spray, the fumes and kaleidoscope of lights from traffic surging by, it was a matter of relief, even delight, when Peter, still sitting quietly in the car, saw reflected in the rear-view mirror a tell-tale array of flashing amber lights making its steady way towards them in the line of traffic. At first he hoped it was the police but their lights would have been blue. As the aggressive sequence of revolving flashes drew closer, the vehicle on which they were assembled revealed itself to be a robust pick-up truck, painted white and red, topped with a small hoist and loaded with towing equipment. The Speedy Recovery Services breakdown vehicle had arrived and proceeded to draw up just ahead of the Mercedes inside the coned off lanes, its flashing illuminations adding even more visibility to the scene, much to the chagrin of Peter's fellow-travellers, but much to his satisfaction.

This was Peter's chance to get out of the car in the knowledge that his abductors would be hard-pressed to make a scene in front of the two beefy tattooed individuals who had climbed out of their truck to see what was going on.

"Now, mate, what the fuck are you doing here? Not allowed you know! What's going on?"

"Sorry about that – just a small puncture," said the portly man trying to placate the new arrivals. "Thought we would fix it ourselves. We'll get it done as quick as possible. No need to wait around for help. Minimum disruption, you know. Just about finished now – we'll be away in a couple of minutes."

While the Bruce Lee look-alike wrestled with tightening the wheel nuts, Peter joined the group of four as they stood around the front nearside wheel, still suspended on the jack.

"Looks as though you're pretty well finished. We can bugger off and leave you to it. But you'd better get your skates on, or the bobbies will be along to sort you out," said the truck driver. He and his chum started back to their vehicle.

Peter seized his chance. He picked up the discarded punctured tyre and offered to put into the well of the boot, to which the portly gentleman readily agreed, not least so as to avoid having to handle such a messy, wet and bulky object himself. After closing the boot, Peter made as if to get back into the car on the far side. The arc lights were throwing deep dark shadows on the offside of both vehicles. Peter opened the rear door of the Mercedes and slammed it shut again, but instead of getting in, he ducked into the shadows and crawled quickly towards the pick-up just as its engine was being started. His abductors were still preoccupied in lowering the jack and making sure the wheel nuts were properly secure. Peter levered himself over the side of the truck and, using the shadows, was able to sink down among the heap of tools, cones and towing gear. He pulled a dirty piece of tarpaulin across his body and lay stone still as the breakdown vehicle eased its way back into the traffic and began to leave the Mercedes behind. He knew it would be only moments before his absence would be discovered and no doubt there would be a rapid pursuit. The important advantage was that so long as the truck stayed in the single cordoned-off lane, there was no way they could be caught and overtaken. The only question was how far the roadworks would extend.

What Peter had not appreciated was that breakdown recovery crews have to establish their base of trucks and living units at the beginning of any section of roadworks. If called out, they can then move with the flow of traffic or on the hard shoulder to reach the stranded vehicle. Once their mission is accomplished, they need to get back to base by the quickest route, which means taking the next available exit and crossing over to the opposite carriageway to return to their station.

So after a further two miles of steady procession in the coned lane, Peter was much relieved when the truck turned off and headed up the slip road. The volume of traffic made it inevitable that vehicles were slowing down almost to a stop as they negotiated the intersection roundabout at the Hinckley turn-off, the two men in the truck being completely unaware that they had a passenger in the back. Their conversation was more keenly focussed on how they would spend the rest of Saturday night when their shift ended at ten o'clock. A hot curry with a dozen cans of lager would do, and if all went well, they could pick up a couple of birds at the local boozer for a fun evening back at their caravan. With such an absorbing prospect, they paid scant attention to what was going on behind them as they slowed down to cope with the roundabout traffic. When the speed had reduced to walking pace, Peter slipped quietly over the side of the truck and, to the amazement of the elderly couple in the car behind, dashed across the verge and disappeared into the night away from the huge amber beams of the motorway lighting, and, more importantly, away from the Mercedes and its angry occupants. Peter had escaped. The problem was what to do next.

Chapter 27

Italy - December 2003

In Old Masters' paintings of Genoa harbour in its heyday in the sixteenth and seventeenth centuries, square rigged sailing ships with jibs, top-gallants and mizzens crowd the quayside and anchorages. Handsome multi-masted vessels with sails furled and shrouded in spiders'-web rigging ride serene at their mooring buoys back from far-flung shores. A plethora of lighters and hand-rowed tenders beaver away between their ocean-going sisters, loading and offloading supplies and cargo. In the mellow evening light, captured in so many of these paintings, the scenes are of tranquillity, prosperity, and beauty. They have long continued to adorn art galleries and the drawing rooms of the wealthy, conveying a timeless message of confidence, affluence, and calm.

Of course they do not tell the full story of life in the city in those days. Genoa had its fair share of hardship and brutality suffered by the ships' crews, the stench of rotting food, the putrefaction, the rats and vermin and dead dogs, the diseases, the drunkenness, the open sewers, the filth, the vomit in doorways, the back-street brothels, the gambling dens and seedy taverns. Not much of this finds space on the canvases. Genoa was no different from any other energetic seaport. The well-to-do merchants and aristocrats enjoyed the benefits, while the poor and wretched provided the toil and labour. Masters and servants lived different lives, both dependent on each other, but the latter dispensible at a whim.

The city had changed dramatically in the last four centuries. Modern ships and mechanisation meant only a handful of seamen were needed now compared to former times. The vast quayside warehouses had all gone. In their place, unkempt tenement blocks around the port area accommodated the wretched, the unemployed, the drug dealers, the alcoholics, the seedy bars and young ladies - and not so young ladies - of the night. These were precincts best avoided by respectable people.

When the windowless Iveco transit van carrying Habib and his companions turned into these narrow cobbled streets in the downtown harbour area of Genoa on Tuesday the 2nd of December 2003, the morning sun was well up and traffic was thick and furious. It had been a chilly uncomfortable night. Not counting the two stops for toilet breaks and a stretch of legs in anonymous autostrada rest areas, the drive had taken eight tedious hours. The eleven passengers had huddled together, haphazardly bestrewn in the back of the van, using coats to keep warm and rucksacks as pillows to catch whatever catnap sleep they could. They were hugely relieved to have arrived, but where, and what next, they did not know.

One of the doors at the back of the van opened a few inches. Whispered instructions and hand gestures conveyed the message; they were to exit one at a time as inconspicuously as possible. When it came to Habib's turn, he was ushered rapidly through a battered door into a tall four-storey block, probably built in Genoa's heyday, but now showing palpable signs of decay, stucco plaster falling off the walls, the stairwell dirty and smelly, the hand-rail rickety, and graffiti everywhere as he climbed to the highest level. Inside the bare bleak room at the top, a ladder was poking up through a hatch in the stained ceiling. His escort made it clear that was where he had to go. Inside the loft space there was sufficient residual light coming through a few broken and dislodged tiles for Habib to make out his other fellow travellers sitting on ragged Dunlopillo mattresses placed on thin sheets of plywood spread across the rafters. The roof was too low to stand upright. It was cramped, dusty and draughty. When the last of the group were installed, an Italian they hadn't seen before climbed the ladder and poked his head into the loft. He seemed in charge, and had a few basic words of English.

"You stay here. No talk. No noise please. Police not friendly here. Good if you sleep. Food I bring later. Tonight you go. You understand I think?"

Despite the economy of words the message was clear. This was a temporary staging post. They had to keep their heads down in both senses. Best catch up on sleep after their awful night. They would move on again quickly. The head disappeared and the loft hatch was repositioned. There was nothing to do except wait, and try to keep warm. The sound of the city reverberated up from the narrow street, shouts and chatter and incessant hooting of vehicles.

This was Italy, but in their cell-like loft space they might as well have been anywhere.

It seemed safe enough, but that was its only merit. Habib assessed the pros and cons. It was cold, and they had no idea when any food would arrive. By sharing their coats and huddling together they could generate a modicum of warmth. Most had some residual scraps of food and half drunk bottles of water in their bags, so they could get by. Conversation had to be in whispers but as most were exhausted that was no great hardship. The worst problem was they had no access to washrooms. And two of their number were having trouble with their bowels. Habib looked back nostalgically at the facilities they had enjoyed at the farm near Naples only yesterday. Nothing to do now but grin and bear it. He curled into a ball and tried to sleep, the simplest way of passing time.

Two hours later, though it seemed much less, there was a frenzied commotion in the loft. A distressed Albanian voice was whispering urgently.

"I need the shithouse quick. Let me out!"

Half-asleep Habib was conscious of the man's clumsy crawl across their restricted space, a tug at the ceiling hatch and a flood of light upwards from the bare room below. Silhouetted in the shaft of light, the desperate figure lowered himself through the hole until hanging full length on his outstretched arms. There was a loud thump as he fell the last two feet; then hasty footsteps on the stairs. It was possible only to guess what was happening. The rest of the group were in no doubt that the hatch had to be repositioned immediately and deathly quiet maintained until they were sure their hiding place had not been betrayed. Nerves were taut. No-one was sleeping now. Habib could feel beads of sweat on his palms. Ears strained trying to decipher any noise that might give a clue as to what was happening.

Some floors below there was a sound of raised voices. A door slammed. A toilet flushed. More shouts. More doors banging. Voices in the road. Running, shouting, then nothing – just the usual street cacophony, strident, invasive but normal. They never saw the man again. It was a hard lesson, but this was a game where there were no second chances if you didn't play by their rules. And now their number was down to ten.

More time elapsed. Habib checked his watch. It was almost midday. The group were subdued, pensive, anxious, barely warm and increasingly hungry. The worst part was not knowing what would happen next or when. The dramatic disappearance of one of their number reinforced their sense of vulnerability. Their fate lay in other people's hands, people they neither knew nor trusted. But they had no other option.

The strained solitude was at last broken. Voices and movement in the room below, then the hatch pushed open by the ladder being thrust up into their roof space. Urgent shouts – "Down, everyone down, quick. Bring bags - everything".

Despite the evident stress in the commands, it was a relief to be doing something. Habib rapidly gathered his belongings. Shoes with their precious contents secure on his feet. His leather jacket zipped, rucksack laced up tightly and slung on his back. He was ready for whatever. They descended the ladder one by one. As soon as the last was out, one of the Italians climbed back into the loft and threw down the meagre mattresses, carefully replaced the hatch and urged them to get down the stairs quickly.

"Big problem. Very quiet please. Police take your friend. They come soon - search house. We find new place you stay. Much danger here. Go quick."

At the foot of the stairwell they were ushered unceremoniously through a rear exit into an enclosed yard strewn with rubbish, a rusting washing-machine, a cannibalised motorbike, piles of old bricks and split bags of solidified cement. The mattresses were jettisoned on top of the heap. The ladder was placed against an adjacent wall and, in quick succession, they climbed over and jumped down the other side into a similar yard of junk. Then into the rear door of the next-door property to find themselves in a basement boudoir, walls painted lurid pink, a once white, now much-stained, thick pile carpet covering the floor. In the middle of the room was a huge double bed overlaid with a garish purple bedspread laced with gold brocade, On the ceiling was a mirror and another on the large wardrobe doors. All natural light was excluded by red velvet curtains draped across the solitary window. Chintzy coloured lamps either side of the bed provided the subdued lighting. It was not difficult to imagine what went on here, but that was of minimal interest to their Italian guides who were making it abundantly clear what they wanted. Four people hid under the bed, three stood in the locked wardrobe, and three in the cupboard behind more junk and hanging clothes.

Habib found himself under the bed. There they waited, no one daring to speak although the Italians had left and all was now quiet. After fifteen long minutes of cramped inertia they heard a police car siren in the street. Simultaneously the door to their room opened. A woman and man came in and threw themselves on the bed. Habib could see discarded clothing falling to the floor while the bed springs began heaving. The cooing and grunting above him had lasted no more than a minute or so when the door was flung open again. Habib could just see the boots of two policeman engaged in animated conversation with one of the Italians. Interpreting their laughter and macho postures, Habib gathered they were amused at catching the two bedmates in flagrante delicto. More ribald conversation and then they left.

As soon as the police had gone, the couple on the bed aborted their performance and dressed. The distraction had been sufficient to deter the police from searching the room. They sat on the bed talking quietly till the Italian returned, presumably signalling the all-clear. He proceeded to extricate the group of illegals from their respective hiding places. Then it was a reverse run, out into the yard, over the wall, pick up the discarded mattresses, into the original house, up the stairs and back into the loft, all done with enhanced expertise. They seemed to have thrown off the police, but it had been very close and nerve-wracking. At least they had had a chance to visit the washroom en route and happily, though rather belatedly, their host appeared to have registered they were getting desperate for some food and drink. Half a dozen pizzas arrived with a carton of large bottles of sparkling water. $10 each, worth every cent. They sat wrapped in their coats and munched hungrily. Hopefully this wouldn't last much longer. The risks to the Italians themselves was incentive enough for them to want the group to move on as quickly as possible. Certainly Habib and his friends had no wish to prolong their stay here.

In the late afternoon they had even more reason to hope for an early getaway. The weather had broken. Steady rain was splattering the tiles just above their heads, and as it coursed down the runnels so it found the cracks and crevices where maintenance had been neglected. Four thin streams of water were dribbling into their hiding place. It took some careful manoeuvring to ensure that everyone could keep dry. Habib could understand now why the ceiling of the room below them was so stained.

The earlier psychological lift the food and drink had given them gradually dissipated as the afternoon darkened into evening and the thin December rain persisted unremittingly. They were reluctant to use torches lest their beams betray their position. It was now dank as well as dark and cold. But worst of all, was the interminable waiting, not knowing how long this uncomfortable vigil would last.

Traffic in the street below had quietened. Habib judged that most people would now be in their homes enjoying their evening meals, watching television or out in the cafes and bars. He envied them. He wondered how long it would be before his life returned to some sort of normality. How soon would he be able to go out with friends again, and when would he ever see his family again? It was hard not to feel homesick. Why had he ever taken on this mad adventure? In the dark tears welled silently in his eyes. But he had to be strong. There was no turning back – not yet at least. The Italians would want to move them tonight. Probably, they could expect to embark on their next stage around midnight. He checked his watch using his torch under his coat. Four hours to wait. Nothing for it but to be patient. But he guessed wrong.

It was about nine o'clock when they heard a vehicle pull up outside. Shortly afterwards, there was noise below and the ladder pitched up through the loft hatch again.

"OK. We go. Everyone down. Bring all your bags. Quiet and careful. No lights."

Climbing out of the loft and down the ladder was precarious in the dark but within a few minutes they were all safely downstairs. They assembled in a heavily curtained, sparsely furnished room on the ground floor.

"You all ready to go. Next we take you to France. No long journey. Maybe four hours. You give me $250 now."

The necessary financial transactions were completed. $2,500 for a four-hour ride, and the Italian drivers would be home again before breakfast. Habib wished he could make money so easily. One at a time they filtered back into the same van in which they had arrived earlier that morning. The prospect of another uncomfortable ride loomed, two nights on the trot, but at least this was supposed to be much shorter. Habib was happy with that. Better to be moving than cooped up like chickens in the roof space. The van drove off through the backstreets of Genoa and joined the autostrada heading west towards the border crossing into France at Ventimiglia. Like nocturnal animals – resting by day, travelling pell mell during the night – they had crossed from the south to the north of Italy in less than two days, and most of that time had been spent sitting in this van. So much for the charm and beauty of Italy thought Habib, as yet more kilometres of tarmac hurtled past unseen beneath the metallic floor on which they crouched.

Chapter 28

Moldova - Spring 2001

Her return to Chisinau was stocktaking time for Nina. She was not yet nineteen years old. She was now convinced beyond doubt that village life was not for her. On the plus side, she had made good friends in the capital, and had learned much about life and people that she never knew before. She was altogether more sophisticated and streetwise. She had acquired a modest but enviable wardrobe from the profits of her erstwhile "work" at the Dukro hotel. She had the ready availability of the flat with her friends, and there were usually casual jobs around so she could pay her way. Whatever the emotional or psychological consequences of the abortion, home-cooking and rest had quickly restored her health, and she could expect her periods to start again soon. She also had two warm spots in her heart, one for her German friend and now, more recently and unexpectedly, for the young doctor at the children's hospital.

The downside was she had no money, no regular employment, and no immediate prospects.

On balance, things could have been much worse. The first priority was to find a job. Next morning she set about the task. She revisited old haunts. No joy at the DHL offices. Delighted to see her again. Mr Voronin would keep her in mind whenever he had a vacancy – be sure of that. But nothing for the present. The restaurant where she worked before could offer a few hours waitress work at the weekend, Friday and Saturday nights – a dollar a session, plus tips. Nina found it hard to readjust to this level of remuneration. Three weeks ago she was earning fifty times more than that in an evening. But these wages were the norm for the population at large. She would have to settle for that.

After a day footslogging around coffee shops and bars and restaurants Nina had managed to assemble a portfolio of odd jobs which gave her something to do most days and should generate up to ten dollars a week if tips were good. That would pay the bills. But it wouldn't be an extravagant lifestyle.

She called her brother. "Hi Pavel, I'm back. Mum and Dad send their love. Want to know when you're going down to see them again. I had a good time and feel fine but I'm really glad to be back in Chisinau again – it's so boring in the village. They're all so dull. My God, I'd go mad if I had to stay there much longer. I've got some beetroot, leeks and potatoes for you from Dad's garden. Can we meet later today and I'll tell you all the rest?"

"That sounds great – tonight at the coffee bar opposite DHL. Is that OK? By the way, you might be interested to know Dr Sturza has been asking after you. I'll tell him you're back."

A frisson of excitement passed through her. "Well, well," she said to herself. "That's nice to hear – things are looking up!"

"What about asking him to come along tonight?" she asked. Pavel said he would see what he could do.

Viktor was more than pleased to have the chance to meet up again. The three of them sat in the smoke-ridden cafe bar and drank coffee after coffee. Their animated chatter washed around the narrow-mindedness of village life, gossip from the hospital, the latest pop scene, Moldova's future, Viktor's smuggling expeditions, shortage of money, favourite foods, stupid waiters, and anything else that cruised into their minds. What mattered was the warm convivial interaction rather than the content. They laughed and put the world to rights. Neither Nina nor Viktor needed second thoughts about arranging to see each other again. A focus for their lives over the next few months had crystallised.

Spring was burgeoning all around. The grip of winter, which had corralled people in the sanctuary of their homes, gave way to warmer days and lighter evenings when escaping into the open air from the claustrophobic tower blocks became the norm. Not much money in their pockets, but they partied, and they danced. On non-work days, with the use of Viktor's brother's car, they picnicked in the countryside. And, in due course, one balmy evening under the stars by the lakeside, more circumspectly than with her first boyfriend, they made love. But this time there would be no mistakes. Nina made sure she was equipped and properly protected against the prospect of another unwanted pregnancy.

Life felt good. Congenial friends, a new boyfriend and one to be proud of, a roof over her head, enough odd jobs to keep money in her pocket, the Chisinau nightlife to drown any boredom, and occasional trips home to see Mum and Dad, always delighted to see her, and to be able to boast to neighbours about how well their daughter was doing, not to mention her boyfriend. For the first time in her life Nina felt a deep emotional attachment to someone who could be, not just a lover, but a husband.

Nevertheless the aberration in her life encapsulated in her Hotel Dukro experiences, now seeming years rather than weeks ago, could not lie dormant for long.

"Hi Nina," – it was call from Larissa at the DHL office. "How are you? We're all fine. Very busy though, hardly time to breathe. It's murder in the office some days. Why on earth they don't take on more staff, I don't know? We must meet up sometime for a chat. Yes, my baby's doing well. Mum looks after him while I'm at work. Really must dash – but just wanted to say we've had an email through today addressed to you personally. I've printed it off. Perhaps you could drop in to pick it up. From some guy in Germany, an admirer I guess!"

Nina absorbed the information voraciously, but was careful to feign only slight interest. "OK, thanks – I'll pop in sometime when I'm passing and pick it up. Not important – some guy I met in the restaurant where I was waitress - keen on Moldovan wines. Very chatty. Persuaded me to give him my contact address, but at least I got a good tip out of him."

She still had compelling memories of her German friend. But it was like re-engaging with another life. Two months ago he had been a beacon of light in her troubled world. Now another light was burning. The dilemma was whether to revisit that adventure. One thing was certain. If she did, it would be in secret. No-one would know, certainly not Viktor, not even her brother. Her friends often talked enthusiastically about two-timing – get the best of both worlds, they said. Now that the opportunity was here, it was not easy to manage. She really would like to see Gerd again. He had been so kind and loving, but her relationship with Viktor was the more immediate and more likely to lead to something in the longterm. She dare not jeopardise that. For her that was of prime importance.

It did not take long to reach the DHL offices. She passed the time of day with her erstwhile colleagues there as politely as possible but ended the visit as quickly as she could. She was desperate to get away to read the email.

> "Hello Nina – I think you remember me. I come to Chisinau again next week, on 21st May. I stay one week at Hotel Dukro. I telephone you then. Good to see you again. Hope all is in order with you. Gerd."

The date fixed itself indelibly in her mind. Her feelings during the days till he arrived were a heady cocktail of guilty anticipation and excited anxiety. Spot on the day, her mobile rang in the early evening. She was on her way to the bar for an evening stint of washing up duties. There was no dissembling her emotions as she took the call.

"Yes, hello Nina here. Hello – yes I am good. You want we meet in hotel. I think that OK. You want tonight? Not possible – sorry - I work, sorry."

Gerd was not to be put off. "No problem. You come when you finish work. Room 412."

"I work long time. Not possible I think. Maybe different day?"

"No problem if you come late. I wait for you. You beautiful. I want you much, please, you come."

Nina could feel herself melting. The sound of his broken English revived all the emotions of their last encounters.

"OK, I try. I hope you have good day."

In her heart she had looked forward to his call. In secret anticipation, she had made sure she was wearing her best underwear. She shut out of her mind what Viktor might think. She was caught up in a vortex of desire and adrenalin. What she felt for Viktor and what she felt for Gerd could both be described as love, but in essence they were profoundly different. Nina had difficulty sorting it all out in her mind. But one thing was sure. She enjoyed being with both men a great deal, and she was going to try to preserve her relationship with both as long as she could.

It was with renewed enthusiasm she tackled her duties in the bar that evening. The clock dragged slowly forward, but by eleven o'clock, being a Monday, the majority of the clientele had begun to go home. Nina made her excuses, pocketed her one dollar for the evening's work to add to the few tips she had received, and to save time took a taxi to the Dukro Hotel.

It was a strange sensation. As she made her way through the dimly lit foyer again, she recalled the other encounters she had had here. Best not to dwell on them. They were different. Gerd was different. He seemed to love her. The others just wanted her body. That was past now. The money had been good, but she could get by without it. Life was harder but more straightforward. A kaleidoscope of thoughts were still churning through her mind as she knocked on the door of room 412. It was half past eleven. She could stay for an hour or so, and then maybe arrange to see him again later in the week at a more convenient time.

When he folded her in his arms, it was as though time had stood still. With barely a word they took up where they had left off so many weeks ago. It was carefree, self-absorbed, intense and fulfilling. Neither wanted it to end. Their bodies wrapped themselves around each other. Gerd took the necessary precautions. Even that anxiety could be excluded from her thoughts. Nina abandoned herself to his urgent masculinity, cocooned in a capsule of space and time that excluded all else.

It was past one o' clock when their pent-up energies were at last exhausted. They lay entwined on the narrow bed, bodies moist with their exertions, shameless in their intimacy.

"I think I go now," said Nina.

"Maybe you stay night?"

"No, no – my friends want me go home."

She unfolded herself from his arms, luxuriating in his kisses on her body as she levered herself away. In faltering broken English they arranged their next meeting. Nina really wanted to see him again before he flew back to Germany on Friday, but it was crucial to keep the rest of her life intact. Her miscellany of jobs and, not least, her commitments to Viktor circumscribed when she could be free. They arranged to meet for lunch on Thursday and keep the afternoon for each other. Nina, now dressed and glowing, bent to kiss him goodbye. As she did so he proffered five ten-dollar notes into her hand.

"No, no!! – for me this very good. No money. You nice man. Me happy we love. No money."

Gerd was insistent. He pressed the money into her pocket, folded her again in a powerful hug, kissed her on the forehead and led her to the door.

"Money no problem for me. You buy nice dress for you. Make me very happy."

The taxi ride home was as if in a dream. Rightly or wrongly, Nina was exhilarated, and had the unexpected bonus of a pocket full of money for the first time since that fateful last day in the hospital two months ago. All she had to do was to ensure the last two hours of her life were kept absolutely secure as her own little secret. She would make up some story to tell her flatmates why she was so late. Viktor need never know about it. Tomorrow normal service would be resumed – at least till Thursday lunchtime.

Life was on hold for the Tuesday and Wednesday between their two assignations. Nina judged it would be easier to postpone any further meetings with Viktor till Gerd was out of Moldova, even if not out of mind. Two-timing was less stressful if things were kept as simple as possible.

Thursday came quickly – another happy time of wining and dining and fragmented English conversation, and then a blissful, carefree afternoon engrossed in each other as though the rest of their lives were of no consequence.

"I think it good you come to Germany soon."

"For me very difficult. Need much money for airplane," replied Nina.

"I hope you try. I meet you Frankfurt Airport. You say time you come."

Even as she lay there in his arms, Nina realised the chance of her being able to afford a trip to Germany was pretty well zero. But the prospect of travel to the West was exciting and unimagined. So, to keep open the possibility, she told him she would try to find a way to take up his invitation. She closed her mind to what might happen if she went - where would she stay, what would his wife say, what would they do - and instead cradled in her thoughts a little fantasy of being whisked along through the sunny German countryside in an open-top car with her beau beside her.

It was hard to say goodbye. Without words they both knew that they passionately valued, even needed, what they each gave to each other. Gerd promised he would keep in touch and would be sure to ring her next time he came to Chisinau. Nina would store that precious secret in her heart and left him in no doubt she would look forward to seeing him. Again, he insisted on her taking his gift of another fifty dollars, which, this time, Nina had fewer qualms about accepting. It felt good to have more spending money again. She had not realised how much she missed the relative affluence of her lifestyle three months ago.

By the weekend Nina was back into the normal swing of Chisinau life again. Viktor's love and companionship was steady and trusting. He had no suspicions. They simply picked up where they had been the previous weekend. Nina's only residual anxiety was how to find more regular and permanent employment, instead of the ad hoc variety of part-time jobs she had at present.

The summer months rolled on happily and when Nina was ready to celebrate her nineteenth birthday in the early Autumn, she felt on top of the world. Gerd had visited once more. Their clandestine diversion was the secret icing on the cake. Apart from the excitement of being with him, her pocket money was immeasurably enhanced by what he insisted on giving her, almost doubling her year's income. The rest of the time she was able to enjoy the faithful attentions of Viktor and the young people's lifestyle of a big city. Her periods were now regular again and the traumas of February were now a distant, even if grimly unpleasant, memory.

It was tempting to become blase. That would have been a mistake. Things were about to change.

Chapter 29

France - November 2003

The South of France has long been a watering hole for the leisured classes of northern Europe. Unlike the tourist haunts of Spain and Portugal, France has managed to avoid the pitfalls of over-development and loss of national identity in pursuing visitors' purses. The coastline from Menton through to Marseilles hosts millions of sunseekers each year, but it has never ceased to be French. Those who believe that shouting English loudly is the best way to communicate with foreigners have gone off to the South of Spain and Thailand. Meanwhile the South of France preserves its unique appeal for those who appreciate its cuisine, its wines, its language, its beaches, its climate and its ambience.

But for the French from the north who flock to le Midi every August for their conge annuelle, the price of accommodation and the cost of living make it an expensive sojourn if, as they do, they wish to spend the whole month there basking on the beaches. A less expensive option is to buy a modest caravan, site it for the month on one of the many campsites near the beaches, and then store it in a farmer's nearby field until next year. A month's bill for a family staying in a conventional hotel pretty well covers the purchase price of the caravan, so after the first year it has paid for itself.

Miguel Leroy had inherited his small farm and its attendant plot of land from his parents. Situated just outside the hamlet of La Moutonne, on the back road midway between Hyeres and Toulon, it was within half an hour's drive of many idyllic beaches and coves along the south coast. Though it was too small to plant up with vines, his parents had laboured long and hard on it to keep their extended family self-sufficient in vegetables and fruit.

Miguel was a trained electrician and when his time came to inherit, he could make more than enough in his trade rather than breaking his back trying to grow his own produce - much easier to fence off the ground and let it to neighbours for grazing their donkeys and goats. That was until he saw the chance of using it for caravan storage. It was off the beaten track, close to the beaches, adjacent to the house so he could keep an eye on things, and could accommodate almost a hundred vans packed in neatly. Much more profitable than donkeys and goats.

The nature of the business was that each year one or two of the owners gave up the August migration to the south. Some would ask Miguel to sell on their caravan, others would just forget about it. Steadily the number of abandoned vans increased. When it was clear the owners were no longer interested, Miguel could make a few thousand francs by selling them or offering them for storage facilities on site. When Abdul Rahiz and his brother from Toulon approached him for such a facility, Miguel was more than happy to do a deal. They wanted to rent the keys to three vans, which they would use from time to time, mostly for storing goods, but occasionally for accommodating people for a few nights. As long as they paid good money, that was fine. Miguel was not interested in their business. That was their affair. The less he knew the better.

Abdul originated from Algeria. His forebears had fought against French colonial rule in the bitter war for Algerian independence. Soon after he was born in 1953, his father had been incarcerated by the French authorities, and had died in prison without seeing his family again. The rumour was he had succumbed to torture. More upsetting was when Abdul's mother was taken away for interrogation. He was only seven years old but had vivid memories of the distressed state in which she returned home after a few days. It was only in later life he learned of the abuse she had suffered at the hands of the Foreign Legion soldiers. He vowed he would avenge the sufferings of his parents. He was honour-bound so to do by his Muslim faith, though, to be frank, he seldom went near the mosque. Political freedom was of little interest to Abdul. He was more attracted to the glittering lights and freer lifestyle of Mediterranean France, and it was no surprise when he moved to Marseilles in his mid-twenties.

He had learned the trade of ceramic tiling, but regular work was hard to come by. Further down the coast, he had friends in the large Algerian community in Toulon who persuaded him of better prospects there. He joined them in 1982 and moved in to share a large apartment in the poorer quarter almost totally occupied by immigrants from North Africa. Although he had a steady income, most of his friends did not, and it was clear that the policies of the ultra-right-wing Town Council were not sympathetic towards anyone who was not self-supporting. The social exclusion felt by his community was contagious and he was soon locked into hard line Muslim groups seeking ways of redress. They had contacts along the North African coast, but more especially with the burgeoning Al Qaeda cells in the Middle East. Abdul was not driven by their fanatical religious ideology. But they were his friends and he valued their friendship greatly in a hostile community. More pertinently, he sensed they could provide an avenue for him to honour his deep-seated obligation to avenge his parents.

For the fundamentalist Muslim cells, the events in New York on the 11th September 2001 were something to celebrate, not mourn. At last they had found a way to strike a devastating blow at the heart of the infidel. So when the USA with its Allies launched the assault on Al Qaeda in Afghanistan and the controversial invasion of Iraq to depose Saddam Hussein, the network of Muslim cells began planning their reprisals with malevolent conviction that they would succeed again. This time the targets would be Spain and the United Kingdom whose leaders had so treacherously supported the American war machine.

Abdul was the kindly face of the Toulon cell; a mature man, self-employed, not dependent on state hand-outs, with a broad range of friends and contacts along the south coast of France and in North Africa. He it was who would make the arrangements for getting the necessary materials from Libya to the cells in Madrid and the UK for the next "spectaculars". The twenty wooden crates, half-metre cubes, each containing twenty-four one kilogram sealed packets of pure semtex explosive, were loaded secretly at night in Tripoli harbour onto a battered Libyan freighter, known affectionately as a rust bucket. First port of call was Algiers to take on general cargo bound for Marseilles before the two-day chug across the Mediterranean. Timing was crucial. So was the weather. The Spanish captain bided his time, hove to in Algiers harbour till the signal came. Calm conditions for the next three days. Winds light and westerly. Light cloud and thin crescent moon. The rendezvous was to be at sea, 50 kilometres due south of Cap

Benat, the promontory topped with a television transmitter located 40 kilometres east of Toulon. Departure from Algiers had to be timed so he would reach there early evening on Wednesday, the 19th November 2003.

That same afternoon, a small pug-nosed fishing boat eased out of Le Lavandou marina, in the lee of Cap Benat, its nets ostensibly hung up ready for a routine fishing sortie to supply restaurant tables along the coast. Direction due south past the Ile du Levant, famed nudist resort, and out into open sea in the fading afternoon light. Hard astern, the red glow of the aircraft warning light on the top of the TV transmitter gave the crew the fix on the course they needed to follow. At ten knots heading south at 180 degrees they would be at the rendezvous by 19:00 hours.

They had been circling anxiously for half an hour when at last the dull thud of the freighter's engine came within earshot. At about the same time they were able to make out the white steaming light on its mast-head and both its red and green navigation lights, confirming it was heading directly towards them. They swung their small craft on a convergent course and began flashing the prearranged lamp signals – three long, two short, one long. Pause – then repeat. When a similar response came back they knew the rendezvous had been made.

Now came the hard part. Both vessels' engines geared down to minimum revolutions, slow steam ahead until they were moving parallel alongside each other, bows butting into the slight swell coming from the west. Although not a large ship, the freighter towered over the fishing boat. They manoeuvred until just a few metres of water separated their bulwarks. As the larger ship heaved gently beside them in the swell, two of the fishing boat crew, one in the bows and one in the stern, positioned long quant poles with heavy-duty fenders lashed at the ends against the side of the freighter, to keep a steady distance between the two vessels.

"*Nous sommes prets. Vous aussi*?" The freighter's captain's voice crackled out from a loud hailer in broken French.

"*Oui, oui – bien sur! Allez vite!*" came the shout from the fishing boat captain, firmly gripping the ship's wheel to keep the boat steady alongside.

An unsilenced two-stroke engine clattered into life on the deck of the freighter, overwhelming the gentle tick-over of the boats' main engines in the calm of the evening. Just as well they were a long way off shore, not least when a spotlight beamed down on the smaller vessel from the deck above to illuminate proceedings. A rusty derrick cranked outwards from the freighter, swinging round a cargo net containing five wooden crates. Painstakingly it lowered its load into the small hold of the fishing boat. The fourth member of the crew stowed the boxes quickly and released the net for the next drop. It took twenty minutes for the four hauls, five crates at a time. The men holding the quant poles were not sorry it was over. Their arms ached with the strain. But the weather had been kind and the transfer had gone as well as could have been hoped. The spotlight was switched off. The two-stroke motor died as abruptly as it had started, the freighter's main engines accelerated to a higher frequency, and off into the anonymous night it ghosted away westwards to complete its run to Marseilles.

The fishing boat, now much lower in the water, began its return to shore, its precious cargo sheeted down under waterproof covers. This time the captain steered a course east and wide of Ile du Levant heading for La Fossette, a small enclosed cove, five kilometres east of Le Lavandou. Surrounded on all sides by steep granite hills, it has a gently shelving sandy beach much sought after in the summer months. But in the off-season, the holiday villas nestling on its hillsides are deserted, the beach restaurant closed up, and the pleasure launches all carted away to winter storage. The concrete service road to the beach from the main coastal road is about 200 metres long, passing between a small vineyard on the west side and high reed grasses on the other. Nightingales are said to sing there. Half way down there is a convenient bend, which ensures that the point where the causeway reaches the beach is not visible from the main road. There is a monument in the cove commemorating the night of 6th November 1942 when General Henri Giraud was evacuated from the beach on a Lavandou fishing boat, Milan II, for a rendez-vous at sea with the British submarine, Seraph, which took him to North Africa to help lead the Free French in preparation for the co-ordinated Allied landings on the Southern beaches of France in August 1944. What was ideal for clandestine wartime operations was equally well suited to a clandestine landing of twenty crates of explosives in late November 2003.

If all went to schedule, the fishing boat should arrive at La Fossette soon after midnight. Abdul and his brother had borrowed a friend's unmarked van, nondescript white as always, a Renault Trafic. From Toulon it was less than an hour's drive. The coast road was almost deserted at this time of night. His brother jumped down to swing open the red and white barrier to the access road. There was a lock and chain on it, but it was only cosmetic. No-one ever bothered to secure it. Abdul negotiated the narrow causeway. At the bend, with lights extinguished, he executed a three-point turn and reversed the remaining distance. Engine off, lights out, loading doors open, and the rear wheels to the edge of the beach. They sat on the floor of the van, legs hanging out, drawing anxiously on their cigarettes, watching out to sea. Lights on the distant Ile du Levant twinkled in the blackness. The waves lapped against the sand gently only ten metres from where they sat. There was a night owl hooting somewhere in the hills. From time to time a late-night car sped along the main road above them, oblivious to what was below.

In the tranquil night air the rhythmic throb of its engine signalled the fishing boat was not far off. The captain had doused the lights as a precaution. Its dark shape slowly emerged into focus against the lighter blackness of the sea, its engine now at minimum revs. Gently its bows eased onto the shallow sand. Two men wearing thigh-length waders jumped into the water. The captain kept the bows head up to shore while the fourth crew member handed the crates to the men standing in the water. They balanced them on their heads, steadied with their hands, and waded ashore. Abdul and his brother were at the water's edge to receive them. Hardly a word was spoken. This was not a time for pleasantries. Speed, silence and above all keeping the crates well away from the seawater were what mattered. The transfer took ten minutes. A muttered farewell and the brief encounter was over. Financial settlement for the service rendered had been done elsewhere. The captain set his course back to Le Lavandou harbour. He should be in bed by 2:00 a.m. A fruitless night of fishing, but a most remunerative outing. He had no idea what was in the crates. Nor did he care. He had made more in a few hours than he normally made in weeks.

Abdul and his brother would reach his rented caravans at La Moutonne quicker than the captain was in bed. They covered the 40 kilometres in less than an hour and carefully offloaded the twenty unmarked crates one by one into the dark interior, covered them with a mattress, locked the door, and set off for Toulon. Things had gone well. Now to wait for further instructions on how and when the crates would be moved to their murderous destinations. Abdul wouldn't be part of that. He was just a link in the chain. But it was a link solemnly dedicated to avenging his parents' suffering and shame at the hands of non-Muslim colonial powers so many years ago.

Chapter 30

Moldova - 2002

"I thought you'd be happy about it," said Viktor, surprised at Nina's reaction. What he had just told her had not been well received.

Nina was sitting opposite with the remnants of a cup of coffee in her hand, looking somewhat dismayed. They had just celebrated her nineteenth birthday with a modest meal at one of the Chisinau Pizza restaurants. Although she knew very little about the game of golf, she had been amused by his rude card, depicting a golfer getting into bed with his girlfriend saying "And now for the nineteenth hole, birthday girl!" He had also given her a thin silver necklace with a small pendant crucifix, which she would treasure. She listened attentively to what he was saying, twisting and untwisting the crucifix in her fingers.

"I applied through the hospital manager's office for a training placement in the West. The EU has a fund for encouraging cross-country exchanges with countries like Moldova. They're especially keen to support young doctors. I'd almost forgotten about it – it was months ago I put my name down, but then today the hospital director called me in and said I'd been successful. I could hardly believe it – he says I'm to go to a hospital in England, called Princess Alexandra hospital in a town called Allo, - I think that's how they say it – it's spelt H-A-R-L-O-W. I looked it up on the map – it's about 40 kilometres north of London. Should be great. I went on the internet and read about the place. It's a new town surrounded by green countryside with a theatre, a library, a cinema and dancehalls – good place to live and work.

"They've sent through some notes about the hospital. It's got a modern paediatric department, a special baby unit, two consultant paediatricians, a registrar, and half a dozen SHOs – they're junior doctors like me, and I shall be one of the team for a six months internship. They call it a locum. And there's a doctor's flat in the hospital grounds I can have while I'm there, so I don't even have to find somewhere to live. And, can you believe it, I shall get paid the same as they do! They say living costs are much higher, but junior doctors there get about $1,200 a month. That's forty times what I get here! I'll be able to send money home. Isn't that great news?"

Viktor had hardly paused for breath. At last he had been able to pour out to Nina his news, which he had deliberately kept secret till the end of their meal. She could understand his excitement. She was happy for him. Of course it was an opportunity too good to miss. But for her it meant separation from the one who was beginning to give her life some long-term focus. Not least her thoughts were filled with an irrational, perhaps even rational, fear that Viktor might get swept off his feet by some clever, beautiful, young western doctor or a nurse working in the same hospital. She felt a stab of jealousy mingled with anxiety as the fragile structure of her lifestyle in Chisinau was about to be put to the test.

"Well, of course I am happy for you, Viktor, I really am - but I shall miss you a lot. I hope you won't run off with someone else while you're there. You'll have to promise to be faithful."

In the context of her clandestine relationship with Gerd, Nina realised this request was somewhat ironic, but from her perspective, the assignations with her German lover were supernumery activities. She never saw them as a potential threat to Viktor. Those adventures were quite different. But she had real anxieties that Viktor might all too easily find a replacement for her while they were separated by so much time and distance

"Don't worry. It's only for six months. I'll be able to send lots of money home, and all that extra clinical experience should mean I'll be able to get a better post than the one I've got now. So it's a really good investment for our future."

Nina noted he had said "our future". They had never talked about marriage, but their relationship had developed over the last six months. Viktor was nearly thirty years old and sooner or later might want to think about putting their friendship onto a firmer footing. What Viktor had said reassured her that that was the way things were moving. That meant more to her than anything.

"When do you start there?" asked Nina.

"Beginning of January, so I guess I'll have to get a flight just before the New Year starts. I'll write to you and send you emails every day. I wish you could come with me. That would be great."

So that was that. In three months Viktor would be off. Best make the most of the time till then. Once Nina had digested the news, her anxieties began to recede, and vicariously she even started to enjoy the envy and admiration of their mutual friends at her boyfriend's good fortune to be going to the West.

On Thursday 27th December 2001 she was at Chisinau Airport early in the morning to bid Viktor a fond farewell. There was a light snow covering and the Moldovan Airline staff were spraying the aircraft wings with an evil-smelling orange de-icing fluid. Viktor's parents were there too, and a horde of other well-wishers. Nina wished it could have been a more private moment, but that was not to be. There was much hugging and many tears, interlaced with spasms of contrived hilarity. At 8:10 a.m. the flight for Frankfurt took off. Once there he would have a four hour wait before catching the connecting flight to Heathrow. Someone would meet him when he landed. Beyond that his itinerary and timetable were something of a blur. Nina couldn't really imagine Viktor in London, with its underground trains and double-decker buses and policemen without guns and the Queen and Big Ben – she had seen all these pictures in her school books, but it was still more fantasy than reality. Viktor was taking a step into a world unknown to her. As his plane climbed high out towards the west, Nina was already yearning to receive his first email to hear how he was getting on.

It was good that his departure was so quickly followed by the short holiday break for the Orthodox Christmas celebrations at home with her parents. There was no better antidote to take her mind off things. For once, she was really glad to be back in the heart of her roots, cloistered in the warmth of family reunion and laughter. Even so, it was impossible to forget that it was exactly a year ago she had first missed her period at this time. Then the dark early months of the last year had begun. It had been a roller-coaster year. In the end things had turned out well. Nina was a different woman. She had left Mihailovca as a schoolgirl. She returned now mature beyond her years, streetwise and sophisticated. Her parents were proud of her. Village friends respected her, and not a few envied her. It was good to be back, at least for a short while. Viktor seemed a long way off, but in the closet of her heart, he held pride of place.

The festal celebrations were over. The grinding routine of village life in winter was starting up again. This was Nina's last evening before the cold bumpy bus journey back to the capital next day. They sat by the roaring log fire. The warm comforting smell of wood smoke permeated everything.

"Nina, I have a little problem I need to tell you about," said her mother as she sat knitting a woollen cardigan by the fireside.

"It's not very good news. I'm afraid. I have to go to the hospital in Chisinau. I'm sorry to have to tell you I have a lump inside my left breast. I thought it was nothing, but I've seen the doctor who comes to Cismilia. He thinks it's a cancer and I need to get some treatment at the big hospital in the city. My appointment is next week. It would be good if you can meet me and show me where to go. Could I stay with you, perhaps, or with Pavel, do you think? I don't know if I shall have to stay in hospital or what. I really need you with me to have someone to talk to. Dad's not much use. He just keeps saying it's bound to be nothing and I'll be back right as rain in no time at all. I don't think he understands."

"Oh, Mum, I'm so sorry. Course I'll meet you. I'm sure we can find somewhere for you to stay. Oh, Mum – I'm so, so sorry. What can we do?" Tears welled up in Nina's eyes.

"Now don't get upset. These things happen. Doctors can cure breast cancers these days, you know. We just have to hope for the best, don't we? Anyway, whatever would Dad do without me? I just have to get better, don't I?" she said with a gentle laugh.

They hugged each other tightly. Their tears fell against each other's cheeks. Suddenly the trendy lifestyle of Chisinau seemed less compelling. The bonds of family and relationships were so much more important. The prospect of losing the most precious person in her life was too awful to contemplate. This was her mum. She was always there. She would not let her die. It wasn't fair. Mum was too young. She hadn't had any grandchildren yet. And then another stab of pain pierced through her as she remembered she alone had been responsible for terminating that possibility a few months ago. No, she would do whatever she had to and make sure her mum recovered.

It was an altogether more subdued Nina who took up the cudgels of her life back in Chisinau. Viktor had gone. Social life was slotting down a number of gears. Another more pressing matter now weighed heavily upon her.

She met her mother off the bus as arranged and they went to the hospital together. Nina treated her to a taxi, the least she could do. She sat with her through the doctor's examination. He told them it was a tumour. Regrettably it had advanced significantly. Her mother confessed she had noticed the lump some months earlier, but hoped against hope it would go away. She realised she should have come sooner. The doctor said it probably needed urgent treatment, but they would do blood and urine tests first, and some more x-rays. If she went on the State waiting list, it would take a few months before they could operate. The hospital was very short of money and equipment. But if she could afford to pay the full costs of treatment, they could speed things up.

"Thank you for being so clear, doctor," said Mrs Snegur. "I guess I'll have to wait my turn. I really can't afford to pay. Let's hope it won't be too long."

"Doctor, I'm sorry to butt in," interjected Nina, "but could you tell us please what the costs would be if Mum wanted to get things done quickly? I'm thinking maybe I could help?"

Doctor and mother were both taken aback at her question and her offer.

"Well, the initial diagnostic tests will be about \$100. Then if surgery is necessary, which I suspect will be the case, that will cost another \$200. After that there will be a need for some radiotherapy and drug treatment lasting a few months till we're sure everything's cleared. That will be \$50 each time. I'm afraid it's not cheap. But we have to pay for the drugs and equipment through the blackmarket. They're all imported. The State can't afford them. So if we want to use them we have to pay. It's not the way I would wish it, but it is the reality of how we practise medicine in Moldova today, at least for the foreseeable future."

The doctor was being as honest as he could be. Nina was concentrating on the arithmetic. The treatment programme was going to cost over \$500. There was no way her parents could afford that in a lifetime. But Nina was not going to stand by and watch her mother fade away because no-one had enough money to save her.

"Thank you, doctor," she replied. "I'm sure we can come up with something. Are you able to do the tests today so we can start what's necessary as soon as possible? Every day counts, doesn't it?"

Nina's mother was having difficulty in taking things in. It was hard enough to absorb what the doctor had been saying about her condition, and the urgent need for treatment. It was doubly difficult to comprehend what her daughter was now saying. Money didn't grow on trees. How could she possibly imply to the doctor that they might be able to afford these sort of fees?

"Well, if you can raise the money," the doctor replied, "I'm happy to start immediately. If you can assure me of that, I'll arrange for the tests and X-rays to be done today. Then next week I'll see your mother again. If you bring $100 to cover the cost of the tests, I'll set the rest in motion, but from then onwards it will be payment in advance. I'm sure you will understand that, because I personally don't have the money to buy in the drugs."

"OK, that's a promise," said Nina. "We'll be here next week with the money. My mum deserves the best treatment she can get, and she needs it as quick as possible. I'll make sure you've got all the money you need. Just please get my Mum well again. That's the only thing that matters."

They shook hands. The doctor asked Mrs Snegur to come through with him for the further tests and X-rays. She was back within an hour. The doctor gave them a bill for $100, to be paid next time. The results would be ready then. That's when he would tell them what treatment was needed and when. Further handshakes and thanks, and they were leaving the hospital barely two hours after they had arrived.

It was mid-January. Chisinau was bitterly cold and bleak. Her mother was in a daze. She wrapped herself tightly into her thick woollen coat and clung protectively to her daughter's arm. She had never seen such forthright resolve in her daughter before. She hardly dare ask how they would find the money. It was Nina who broke the silence.

"Don't worry, Mum. I know how to get some money together. I've got good friends here. They'll lend me what I need. No need for you to fret about that. Just you concentrate on getting well again. Take it easy. Eat properly. No drunken orgies! Get plenty of good nights' sleep. We'll get you through it."

It was late afternoon, and well time for a hot cup of tea in one of Nina's favourite coffee houses. They huddled round the table and let the steaming drinks and warm muggy atmosphere permeate through their chilled bones. For Nina it was homely enough, but all her mother could think of was being back in the village by her own home fire. That would have to wait till tomorrow. Tonight she would stay with her daughter. Nina insisted she should sleep in her bed. She would curl up on the sofa. No problem. Much better that Mum had a good night's sleep.

Next morning Mrs Snegur caught the early bus to Cismilia and was back at home with her husband to tell him the sad news by lunchtime. It was hard for him to take in. He still seemed to believe it couldn't be that serious. Surely she would be in pain if things were really bad?

"Chin up. Expect they'll sort you out in no time. How about some nice hot soup to cheer us up?"

There was not much point in pursuing the issue. He really didn't want to know. Best get on with life as though things were normal. Next week would take care of itself.

After the bus had left, Nina knew what she had to do. She searched the memory of her mobile and pressed in the number she wanted. Five short rings and a voice answered.

"Hello, Zvetlana here. Who's that?"

"Hi, remember me? I'm Nina Snegur. We met and worked together at the Hotel Dukro a few months ago?"

"Sure I remember you! Nice to hear from you. How are you? Long time no see. What you're doing with yourself these days?"

"Zvetlana, I'd like to talk. Can we meet up for coffee some place - later today, if possible?"

"Sure, sure, it would be great to see you gain. Shall we meet at Zoe's? What about lunchtime? Hey, don't tell me you're in the family way again. Oh, my God, you really should be more careful!"

"No, no – it's not that. I'm very careful these days. I can assure you. No, it's something different. I'll explain when we meet. See you later and thanks a lot. Bye for now."

If she could earn money when she needed it desperately for herself, she would certainly do no less for her mother now she was in such desperate need. The moral issues faded into insignificance in the face of the inescapable logic of their predicament. It was self-evidently a good thing to try to get her mother well again. Any delay in the treatment reduced her chances. The only way to advance her treatment was to pay for it. That was going to cost over

$500. None of them had that sort of money. But Nina could earn it as she had before. The end justified the means. This was not a moral debate. This was just plain common sense. Nina knew what she must do. There was no equivocation in her resolve.

Zvetlana was looking her usual elegant self, lightly bronzed, painted fingernails, exactly the right amount of make-up, fashionable hair-do, and tailor-made skirt and blouse under her full-length dark coat, which served only as partial cover for her glamorous black-stockinged legs. She drew lazily on her cigarette as Nina outlined her problem.

"My Mum's probably got breast cancer and we need money quick to pay the doctor for her treatment. I was wondering if I could join you again in working the Hotel? I've promised I would help Mum find the money, so I've got to do something."

"Stefan's still looking after the Dukro girls," replied Zvetlana, "but I think he's got all he needs there at the moment. And none of them would take kindly to letting you take their place. They're too addicted to the money – in fact two of them are hooked on heroin so they need every dollar they can get to keep paying their supplier."

"But there's the Hotel Jolty – Vladimir looks after that. He's a nice guy, and last I heard, one of his girls was suffering from acute cystitis. Pretty unpleasant, and she's not keen on working till it's cleared. I think Vladimir would be interested in taking you on pretty quickly, especially as you know the ropes. He'll look after you just like Stefan does. Shall I give him a ring?"

Nina was more than happy that she should. Because they were in a public place, the telephone conversation was somewhat coded. Nina could hear only Zvetlana's side of it.

"Hello, Vladimir – Zvetlana here – I'm fine. How are you? -- Business good? – yes, yes, I had heard you're a bit shorthanded in the shop. Listen, I have a friend who's used to serving customers, and knows all about the money side. She's looking for another job. I was wondering if she could help you out. She's able to start straight away. How does that grab you? I can vouch for her. Customers find her very obliging and she's very professional. What do you think?"

Apparently Vladimir was interested, but he needed to see her first. They arranged to meet later that day, in the foyer of the Hotel Jolty. Zvetlana accompanied her for the purposes of introduction. There were echoes of her first meeting with Stefan in the Dukro almost a year ago. But this time things were very different. Nina knew what was involved and knew what she wanted. She was surprised how different was Vladimir from Stefan. Instead of being tall, dark and handsome, Vladimir was short, rotund with a copious beer belly, a small dark moustache, ill-fitting jacket, and podgy hands. But his grip was like iron, and his welcoming smile immediately dispersed any anxieties his appearance might have provoked.

It was clear that he was more than happy to do business with Nina. She was, perhaps, even more attractive than a year ago, having filled out in all the right places, but still with her nubile figure and lovely complexion. It was agreed she could start the next day after Vladimir had had a chance to sort things with his other colleagues, whatever that might mean. He would pick her up from the Zoe coffee bar at nine o'clock. Everything would work like it did at the Dukro. If she was familiar with that, she would have no trouble working the Jolty.

Nina went home that evening feeling focussed and committed. She was also feeling very tired, and in need of a good night's sleep. Tomorrow she would sign off most of the various jobs she had accumulated to keep body and soul together. She was moving back into her former routine, late nights, lie-ins in the morning, chores in the afternoon, and then a rest early each evening before the nights' exertions. She would find some excuse to defuse the curiosity of her flatmates, and keep one or two small jobs going to explain how she came to have money in her pocket. If she could work five nights this week, by the time her mother came back to Chisinau next week for her appointment at the hospital, she calculated she would be about $200 in profit. That would pay the first bills. Then she would have to work only a couple of nights a week to make sure she had sufficient income to pay off the ongoing treatment bills. The doctor had said it would take a few months, so all being well there was an end in sight by about June. It was a happy coincidence that Viktor would be away for the whole of that time, so there would be no complication on that front. As Nina dozed off to sleep, she was comforted by the prospect that by the summer Viktor would be home, her mother would be cured and she could once again abandon her hotel working. It was not long to wait. And it was more than worth it.

Everything went according to plan. The Hotel Jolty proved as straightforward and remunerative as had the Dukro. Vladimir was great fun with a mischievous sense of humour. Nina was confident she could rely on him if ever things got difficult. The clientele were a mirror image of those she had met before, varying demands, different nationalities, but all appreciative of her services and generous in their payments. After Vladimir's cut, the first week realised a profit of $230, and Nina's list of customers had increased by fifteen with no problem guys so far.

She met her mother off the early bus the following week and together they listened to the doctor explaining that things were serious. Surgery was necessary. They could operate in ten days time. It was best done as soon as possible. The surgeon would try to excise the whole tumour. But it was not possible to be sure how far it had developed secondary infections. The doctor would try to combat those with radiotherapy and drugs after the operation. She would need to spend a few days in hospital recuperating before she was strong enough to go home.

It was bad news, but they were prepared for it. Nina paid the bills. Her mother was so preoccupied with coming to terms with what the doctor had said, she expressed no curiosity as to where the money had come from. Nina had said she could borrow it, so presumably that's what she had done. The appointment at the hospital immediately after lunch had lasted less than an hour, so they were in time for her mother to catch the afternoon bus back home the same day. They shed a few more tears together as they bid each other goodbye till she came back again for the operation. There was nothing else they could do except put their faith in the doctor's skills and expertise. Meantime, Nina refocussed herself on the task of ensuring they had enough money to pay his bills.

It had been a harrowing three weeks. Nina had expected her thoughts would have been preoccupied with her absent Viktor. She had expected to be pining every day to hear from him, counting the hours to his next email. But since he left so much else had catapulted into her life, she had hardly had any space or time to mope over his absence or to try to envisage what he might be doing. It was the arrival of his first email at long last via the DHL office the day after her mother had gone home that rekindled her interest and longing for him. At least this was something happier to contemplate.

He spoke enthusiastically of a different world. They had medicines, and bandages and equipment in quantities he had never dreamed of. Everyone had cars and loads of money to spend. Roads were all paved – no dirt tracks. At night there were streetlights everywhere. Shops were full of stuff. He had a two bedroom flat all to himself, just a short walk across the hospital campus. But everything had to be paid for – he had to pay rent for his flat and for heating, he had to pay for his food in the hospital, the taxis were so expensive, and things in the shops cost so much more than in Moldova. And he had to pay tax and insurance out of his salary. He wasn't going to be as rich as he had hoped. People had been very kind. He was feeling more settled. It was a terrific experience. The Special Baby Unit was brilliant. He was sorry he hadn't emailed earlier but there was so much to do, and he didn't have his own computer. He hoped all was well at home. He missed her a lot and sent all his love.

Nina read and re-read the print-out. Little did he know what had happened since he left. She would tell him about her mum, but how she was paying for it, he would never know. At least he was happy, and he still seemed committed to her. She would count down the weeks till he came back. Three, almost four gone; less than twenty-three to go.

By courtesy of her DHL friends and their office computer, she was able to email a reply to him and establish a regular weekly exchange of chatter. At week five of their separation, her mother came back to the Chisinau hospital for the mastectomy. She stayed a few days till she was strong enough to go home. Nina paid the bills. Then they moved onto the regular routine of coming back to the hospital for the follow-up treatment and radiotherapy. The operation and the invasive treatment were taking their toll. Her mother looked drawn and pale. She had lost pounds in weight. She put on a brave face joking she was glad to be slimming down. When the treatment was over she was determined to stay slender like she had been in her twenties, and bask in the admiring glances of the menfolk in the village.

Nina's nightly routine of servicing clients at the Hotel Jolty, a few hours' part-time work in the day to serve as a cover, exchanging emails with Viktor, and caring for her mother on her frequent trips back to the hospital was absorbing all her energy and emotion as she counted the weeks away. That is until her next visit to the DHL office to pick up her email, when there were two waiting for her. One was from Viktor – the other was from Gerd.

"Hello, Nina. How are you? I hope you remember your friend Gerd. I come to Chisinau next month. I phone you then. Have a good time. Gerd."

Nina had not forgotten him. How could she? But she was taken aback at the intensity of her reaction. Immediately she read his note, she was consumed with a deep-seated longing to see him again, to be enveloped in his arms and let all her worries and responsibilities evaporate in the enclave of their love-making. And intermingled with those emotions was the guilt, the guilt of unfaithfulness. But Viktor was a long way off. He would never know. This was her respite. This was something she needed as well as wanted. It was therapeutic. She was not short of sex, but she was desperate for love. She would not disappoint him.

As promised, Gerd came in April. It was an action replay of all their previous encounters, this time without having to fabricate excuses for not seeing Viktor. It was equally fulfilling. Nina drank deeply of his gentle passionate embraces. Again he pressed her to come to see him in Germany. Again she stalled. But she assured him she would gladly meet up whenever he could get to Moldova. Then he left, as he always did, leaving delicious memories, some extra money, and nothing else but to carry on as before trying to help her mum by paying her bills.

It was the middle of June when the doctor asked to see them for a further consultation. He was sorry to have to tell them the treatment was not working. Secondary cancers were proliferating. He regretted there was no more they could do. It was just a matter of time. They would be able to control and reduce the pain, but it would be better if Mrs Snegur could stay in the hospital so the painkillers could be administered as and when needed.

On Friday 21st June 2002 at 5:30 a.m., a bright sunny morning, Mrs Snegur gave up her struggle, and died peacefully in her sleep. She had not yet reached her fiftieth birthday. Nina and her brother, Pavel, had stayed by the bedside with their distraught father all that night, trying to console him.

At 9:43 a.m. the same morning Nina received a text message from her friends at the DHL office to say there was an email from Viktor waiting for her. Leaving her father with Pavel at the hospital, she plodded, weary and desolate, across the city to pick it up. At least that would bring a glimmer of uplift for her at this desperate time.

> "Hi Nina. Great, great news! The locum doctor who was coming here to replace me has pulled out, so they've asked me to stay on, probably for a whole year. So I'm not coming back after all. They say I can have two weeks leave in August. So I hope to see you then. Never dreamed I could be so lucky! Celebrated all last night – a bit hung-over today, but thought you'd be dying to know. Lots of love, Viktor XXX"

Nina Snegur's life was falling apart.

Chapter 31

France - December 2003

So much time had been spent dozing during their uncomfortable daytime sojourn in the loft space in Genoa, Habib and Bledar were more inclined to spend the journey time chatting quietly to each other in their native Albanian as their van sped on towards France.

"I thought they said we were going to split up when we reached Genoa?" asked Habib.

"God knows what they're doing," replied Bledar. "All I know is that five of us are supposed to be going to Germany. But if you think about it, they can't take us through Switzerland because there's border posts there and we'd need passports, so I guess we have to go round through France."

"I've no choice anyway. If I'm going to get to England, I've got to cross France to reach the English Channel. They seem to know how to get us across it. Trouble is I don't trust any of them. Just have to go with the flow and hope to God we don't get double-crossed," said Habib

"And it's all so bloody expensive, isn't it?" said Bledar. "I reckon I could find my own way from here without lining the pockets of these buggers."

"Bit risky," replied Habib. "If you forget about the money side, we couldn't have crossed Italy so quickly on our own. And I don't have a sodding clue how I could make it from here, so I guess I'll just stick with them – at least till my money runs out."

The van began slowing down. Habib checked his watch. Not yet midnight. They had been travelling for less than three hours. Surely they couldn't be there yet? A few more turns and the vehicle came to a stop. The engine died. It was eerily quiet though they could still hear the sound of motorway traffic not far off. No-one dared speak. The van driver's door opened, then banged shut. In the back of the van Habib and Bledar tensed, unsure what was going on as the rear door opened.

"OK, we in France now. This place good for piss. We stop ten minutes here."

Cautiously they climbed out one by one. The Italian minders seemed more relaxed now they had passed out of the jurisdiction of the Italian forces of law and order. They had stopped at a small motorway service station in a dark parking area, some distance away from the main restaurant building. Late at night, early December - not surprisingly custom was slack. A few long haul trucks were parked up for the night in their allocated bays, most of the drivers asleep in the curtained cabs of their vehicles. The panel outside the restaurant read "Aire de Canaver". It meant nothing to Habib, but he guessed it was in French. Inside four people were eating a late-night snack, each sitting at separate tables and minding their own business. The arrival of a dozen new faces, mostly heading for the toilets, raised barely an eyebrow. A plump, spotty-faced girl, with spiky hair and a small silver button through the side of her nose, was busying herself behind the counter, showing little enthusiasm to serve new customers.

"What about a coffee?" asked Bledar.

"Will she take dollars?" asked Habib.

"No problem. I've got Euros. I knew I would need them in Germany, so I changed some before I left. Come on – let's go for it!"

They chose a table well away from the other customers, and wrapped their cold hands round the cartons of steaming black coffee.

"Did you see what I saw when we came through the truck park?" said Bledar with a broad smile. "Answer to my prayers, I think!"

"What do you mean? So dark I could hardly see a bloody thing."

"Big yellow truck. *Willi Betz* marked on its side. From Germany. That company does all the Mercedes spare parts delivery across Europe. And where do Mercedes get made? At the huge factory at Boblingen. And where's that?"

Habib looked at him blankly. "How the fuck should I know? What the hell are you on about?"

"Boblingen is just south of Stuttgart. And that, my friend, is where I'm supposed to be heading. My contact address is in Stuttgart. Don't you see? If I get a lift on that truck, it'll take me where I need to be."

Habib did see. He also saw it might not be as easy as that to scrounge a lift, and in any case the truck might not be going back to Stuttgart. He had no wish to crush his friend's enthusiasm, but all the same he ought to try to help him be realistic. There was no point in having got so far and then throwing it all away on a rash impulse.

"Hell of gamble, isn't it? What if the driver won't take you? What if he asks too many questions?"

"For God's sake, this is too good a chance to miss. I'll talk my way through it. I'll offer him some money – bloody sight cheaper than paying this lot, and I could be there by tomorrow. When we go back to the van, I'll come with you and slip off round the back of the trucks. They'll not notice once we're all out of the cafe. Pity you can't come with me, but I guess it's the wrong destination for you."

Habib suddenly felt choked with emotion. He was alarmed that things might go wrong for Bledar, but more poignantly the prospect of losing his companionship so abruptly filled him with dismay. He hadn't realised how much he had grown to value his friendship.

"I'll miss you. But I guess if that's what you want to do, I just pray that Allah will give you blessings for your journey."

The ten-minute stop was over. The Italians rounded up the group from the bookstall and foyer and ushered them back to the van. A perfunctory count confirmed that they were all there. Bledar and Habib lingered till they were at the back of the group. When they reached the dark end of the parking lot, Bledar slipped away. The rear door of the van was opened. Habib mingled with the rest as they climbed in. Even if anyone was trying to count, it was so dark no-one could be certain who was where. The Italians were more concerned to get on the road again as quick as possible. The door closed and the van eased off back towards the motorway

Inside the van, Habib was in sombre mood. It was dark and no-one had noticed yet that Bledar was gone. Now there were nine. Habib judged the best thing to do was to get the maximum distance behind them before making any comment. He pretended to sleep. Good way to avoid any questions. What would happen when the Italians found Bledar had disappeared, he had no idea, but by then it would be too late to do anything about it. He would just have to play dumb. Pretend he thought he was on board. He'd tell them the last time he saw him was as they'd walked to the van. No idea what had happened to him. Perhaps he'd gone for a last minute piss and they'd left without him. Not his problem. At last he dozed off, but not for long.

The van had pulled off the motorway after another hour's driving and was now negotiating slower, less busy roads. Then it stopped. Outside someone was talking to the driver through the cab window, the engine still running. A sound like creaking hinges suggested a gate was being opened. The van moved forward jerkily for a hundred metres or so and stopped again. This time the engine was killed. Wherever it was, Habib guessed they had arrived at their next port of call. He checked the time. It was just after 1:00 a.m. He gathered his belongings and then realised that Bledar's rucksack was still in the van. He grabbed that too and pretended it was his. No need to leave any clues to alert others that they were one short.

Both rear doors were flung open. "OK. We here now. You stay in nice caravan."

They climbed out and tried to take in their surroundings. In the feeble moonlight, they could see they were in a field full of what looked like empty caravans packed in close to each other. About 100 metres away up the track along which they had just driven was the dark silhouette of a farmhouse. The other end of the field sloped down towards a railway. A night goods train was passing by. Someone had opened the doors of two of the caravans and they were ushered into two groups, one group into one caravan and one in the other. Still no-one had registered they were down to nine people. A large dark skinned man was talking with their Italian minders. They searched the van interior with a torch to check everyone was out, closed the doors quietly and then manoeuvred the van out of the field, its lights still doused till they reached the road proper. Then it set off into the night. Habib was not sorry to see it go.

The big man came across to each caravan. "My name is Abdul. You stay here maybe one, two days. You got big tank water outside. You shit, piss in field. No go walk about. We bring some food drink for you. I take money now. $500 each. Then I fix transport for you."

Habib thought of Bledar's remarks about the price they were having to pay for each stage. This latest demand meant half his original savings had already gone. But hopefully this should see him across France. He went to the end of the caravan, took off his shoe surreptitiously, retrieved the necessary cash and paid it over. After various fumblings in bags and pockets, the rest of the group delivered their respective payments.

Abdul counted it all carefully, his friend holding the torch. "Someone not pay - $500 short. Who not pay?"

"Oh, shit," thought Habib. "This is when they discover Bledar's not with us anymore."

Abdul became more and more agitated. There was confusion amongst the illegals. Everyone protested they had paid.

"Ten people. $500 each. I must get $5,000. Here only $4,500. Who not pay? Big trouble for you I tell you," said Abdul.

More distressing argument among the illegals. Tempers were fraying. Habib had tried to keep out of it all, but something had to be done if they were going to keep onside with Abdul and his mates. No choice but to break the news.

"You say ten people. We only nine people. So you get right money."

"No, no – must be ten people. Italians tell me ten people."

"Italians not count good. We only nine people. You count."

With undisguised irritation, Abdul did the necessary headcount. "OK, nine people. That not good. Fucking Italians trick me. But money not enough. Everyone he pay more. I take $50 each man. No pay, no transport. You understand, I think?"

More mutterings and dissent amongst the illegals, but at the dead of night in a deserted field, in a country whose language none of them could speak, miles from where they had to be, they quickly reconciled themselves to the fact that they had no option but to pay up. Habib deemed it prudent to say nothing, but ruminated philosophically that while Bledar's "escape" had probably saved him a load of money, now they were each having to pay to make up the deficit. Such was the price of friendship.

Coughing up the further $450 seemed to lower Abdul's blood pressure.

"OK. Sleep now. I come back in morning." With that, he and his companion walked across to a car parked near the field-gate and left. The two groups, five in one caravan and four in the other used their torches to sort out bedding and mattresses and settled down to another strange night of makeshift sleeping arrangements. At least it was dry, quiet, and reasonably comfortable.

Next morning, Habib took further stock of the surroundings. There was water, but it was in an open tub outside, and looked brackish – best used only for washing not drinking. The rest of the caravans were empty. In surrounding fields there were stretches of polythene tunnels and glasshouses, used no doubt for early propagation of market produce, but all looking rather forlorn at this time of year. There was modest activity at the farmhouse a hundred or so metres away, washing hanging on an outside line, smoke from the chimney, and a small white artisan's van in the drive. But, so far, no sign of any people. Another train trundled past on the track bordering the edge of their field. Across the valley there was a range of mountainous granite outcrops. The early morning sun was catching their tops. In the crisp daybreak air it was an agreeable vista. So this was France. "Could be a lot worse," thought Habib as he swilled cold water from the tub round his face and arms to freshen himself up for whatever the day had in store.

Abdul turned up again at about ten o'clock. He had half a dozen baguette rolls under his arm and some bottles of Evian water. That was breakfast. Not exactly four star service, but enough to get by on.

Habib had greeted him with "Salaam alaikum". Abdul responded warmly with "Alaikum salaam!" and from then on decided that Habib would be the spokesman for the group.

"You tell your friends. German bus go tonight. Everyone ready eight o'clock. OK?"

Habib communicated what he had said, although most had sufficient English to comprehend what he meant.

"Then tomorrow morning bus go Brussels. Seven o'clock." Habib registered that was his own deadline. He knew it was a long journey, maybe a thousand kilometres, probably twelve hours driving and that without stops. But at least they were going to move in the daytime. That should make it more interesting.

"OK, now we go find food for you. I think hamburgers good. Give me $20 each. I bring many food for all day."

Then pointing at Habib, he said, "You come with me."

Reluctantly the group of nine delved again into their pockets and produced the necessary cash. They had to eat and there was no other way but to rely on Abdul. He moved off to his car taking Habib with him. Their brief Arabic exchange had created an understanding between them. It felt good at last to be driving along ordinary roads in a normal car looking out of the windows at workaday France. They approached a huge retail shopping mall signposted "*La Valette*". On all sides there were huge stores selling shoes, furniture, lighting, televisions, DIY stuff, cars, everything. Habib had never seen anything so vast. They pulled into a Mcdonalds and ordered two dozen burgers, milkshakes, French fries and a carton of cans of Coca Cola. After leaving the mall they stopped at a roadside stall to buy fruit, carrots, lettuce, tomatoes and radishes – anything that could be eaten raw. Loaded with this feast they drove back to the caravans to be received with beams of relief and gratitude as the group tucked into their first decent meal for some time.

Abdul reminded them of the timetable for tonight and tomorrow. The afternoon was their own to do as they liked, the only proviso being they couldn't leave the field, which constrained them to resting in the caravans or sitting around outside in the milky December sun chatting and smoking.

The calmness didn't last long. One of the group launched a question direct to Habib.

"Where's your friend, then? Because of that bugger we've all had to fork out another $50."

"How do I know? Last time I saw him was in the cafe. Then he disappeared. What the hell can I do about it?"

"Maybe you knew all about it? Why didn't you tell us? Why should we have to pay for him? He's your friend. You're the one who should pay. What about it boys? This little tosser pays up or we make sure he's going no further! What do you think?"

Suddenly the atmosphere was tense and threatening.

"Fuck you! I hardly knew the guy. Only met him in Tirana before we got on the boat. You knew him as well as me. Why didn't you tell our Italian friends he'd done a bunk?" Habib tried to gauge the mood of the group. He was scared, but if the worst came to the worst, he could run as fast as any of them and the farmhouse at the end of the track was where he would make for. He had anticipated all sorts of dangers, but not this; direct threats from those in the same plight as he was.

"Anyway, whose friend nearly gave us all away in Genoa when he left the loft for a shit? At least Bledar's disappearance hasn't nearly buggered the whole of our trip." Habib played for time and tried to engage them in a more reasoned appraisal of their situation. Another member of the group chimed in.

"Leave it off! If we start anything, we could all be fucked up. This Arab guy's already got our money. We don't know where the hell he lives. If we do anything that frightens him off from coming back for us, we're all in dead trouble. Just forget it. What's another $50 when we're so close to getting through?"

The mood lightened. Habib relaxed a little, only too conscious of how much he wished Bledar were still with them. Just a few more hours and they'd be on their way. He still had a few packets of cigarettes in his rucksack. No better time than to hand some around. But from now on he would need to be especially vigilant about his belongings and his money. No-one could be trusted.

Habib was not sorry when the promised minibus arrived prompt at eight o'clock. Perfunctory farewells and four people climbed in – it looked more comfortable than their previous vehicles. The remainder watched as it lurched across the uneven grass out through the gate and then out of their lives. Four fewer people to worry about potentially double-crossing him. Habib huddled down under his blanket, made sure his shoes were tightly laced on his feet and his rucksack straps wrapped round his arms. For once he had the prospect of an undisturbed night. Within twenty-four hours he would be in Brussels, and then within striking distance of his goal, the dream he had formulated so many years ago. Five years to save the money he needed, and now, only six weeks since leaving home, it was all coming good.

Chapter 32

Moldova - Summer 2002

The good thing about life in villages where people have so little is that the community pools its resources and pulls together to face whatever difficulties come their way. Mihailovka was no exception. Everyone rallied round to help. The untimely death of Mrs Inga Snegur, Nina's mother, had stunned them all. She was popular and well known, not least because most of the village children had passed through her classes at their local school. Nina and Pavel had sorted out the transfer of her coffin from the hospital back home, and the Orthodox priest would conduct the funeral service.

It was unseasonable weather for late June, a cool blustery wind bringing unpredictable bursts of heavy rain. Umbrellas kept turning inside out. The assembly of mourners, bedraggled and bereft, moved dolefully from the church, still in a state of half-finished restoration, to the nearby cemetery to complete Mrs Snegur's last earthly journey. Son and daughter were doing their best to hold themselves together but her husband was stricken with grief and inconsolable. Friends and neighbours supported him on either side for fear he might collapse. Sombre and tearful, eyes mopped frequently with spotless white handkerchiefs contrasting with the obligatory blackness of their dresses and coats, the untidy procession wound its way round the waterlogged potholes in the street to the garden of rest. It was a scene played out a million times over in every land and every tribe, the lament for the dead, the unutterable sadness, the incomprehension, the emptiness, the pointlessness, the impotence to change things, the brief clutch at religion to anaesthetise the grief, and the loneliness.

Back at the house, when the necessary rituals had all been duly performed, the neighbours immersed themselves earnestly in the task of providing the traditional food and drinks after the burial. The mood lightened somewhat. The Snegurs' dearest friend, Ludmila, and her husband took responsibility for trying to cheer everyone up. They reminisced about Inga's wonderful contribution to the lives of all their children, and the happy times they had had when they were young and carefree. They would all rally round and help Vladimir. Ludmila would make sure he didn't go hungry. He had two fine children of whom he could be proud. They were doing so well working in Chisinau. Inga wouldn't want them to be so sad. She would want them to get on with life and keep smiling. In honour of her, that's what they should all do. "Let's drink a toast to her – our dearest Inga, and may God grant she rests in peace." Nina shared in the celebratory toast, but with deep-seated sadness in her heart, made more poignant because of her longstanding dislike of the woman, Ludmila, who was queening over the farewell rites.

A huge chapter in Nina's life had closed. It had all happened so quickly. She was still in an emotional daze as she and her brother bid farewell to their father to return to the capital. He had recouped some of his composure and was sure he'd be OK. "Ludmila and her husband will help me along. I'll get by. Not to worry. You go on and make the most of your lives. That's what Mum would want. I'll be all right. See you again soon." He put a brave face on it, but it was hard to leave him so alone. They had had so many happy family times together over the years - now that was all at an end.

Back in Chisinau, somewhat belatedly, Nina had to face up to dealing with the other bombshell in her life. Viktor was going to stay another year in the UK. She missed him more than ever now. A chasm of emptiness was opening up under her. There was no longer any need to earn money to pay the hospital bills, and so no longer any obligation to continue her services to clients at the Hotel. Vladimir, her minder had been very sympathetic about her mum, but she wasn't going back to that work unless she had to. Life had suddenly become rudderless and void.

But there was one small positive glimmer: the planned return of Viktor for two weeks holiday in August. That was something to look forward to, even though it was tinged with anxiety because at the end of the two weeks she had no idea how or when she would see him again.

After paying the hospital bills, Nina still had some money saved from her earnings. She could afford to go home more frequently to make sure her dad was coping. The village had rallied round and Ludmila was going in each day to make him a hot meal. He had lots to do in his garden. The weather was good and he seemed to be coming to terms with life on his own. He was always glad to see Nina. She was a treasure to him, but he knew her life was now elsewhere and he never pressed her to stay. In Chisinau she busied herself with her part-time jobs and socialised energetically with her friends. She counted down the days till Viktor would come.

When he did, he was a changed person, couldn't stop talking about England, and London, and the hospital, and the medical facilities, and the money everyone had, and all the food, and shops loaded with goods, and new cars everywhere, and everyone had computers, and the great discos and nightclubs – the list went on and on - his enthusiasm was exhausting. And in the end his audience either got bored or jealous or both - all except Nina. She hung on every word. He painted a glittering world, with so much to see and do, and so much opportunity. She longed to be able to share it with him.

Most important, Viktor still seemed to be deeply in love with her. No sign of any diminution in his ardour. But when they made love, she couldn't prevent herself being distracted into thinking about the inexorable approach of their separation. Even in their most passionate moments, there was always that shadow hanging over them. This whirlwind reunion was time-limited. Soon, too soon, he would be winging his way back to England and after that who knew what. Their bodies fused together, releasing into each other the pent-up energy of their adolescent fervour. It was so different from when she made love to Gerd, she mused to herself, and then guiltily, quickly she extinguished such thinking from her mind. Viktor, she hoped, would be her husband and the father of her children. Gerd was not part of that agenda. That conundrum was something she would sort out later.

Too rapidly the time passed. The days had been long and hot. There was no doubting they were both special to each other. They would be faithful, even though there had been no time to think, still less to talk about marriage. Viktor kept saying he wanted her to come to join him. But how could she ever get a visa, let alone the money? No, she would wait for him to come home. It would be a long wait, but she promised she would. He had to make the best of his chances. They would still write to each other. The time would pass and then they would think about the future. Viktor gave her a silver ring as a mark of his promise. She hugged him for the last time and then he was off through the departure gates with a final distant wave. He disappeared from sight. She mopped her tears and took a taxi back from the airport to get on with the rest of her life.

Her next weekend visit home to see her Dad was in September. These were mellow days. The autumn leaves were beginning to fall, and the last crops from the fields and gardens were being harvested before the winter set in. Winds were light and the orange sun hung low in the sky as the late afternoon bus delivered her to Cismilia. Then it was by cart to her village, hopefully in time for an evening meal and catch-up on the gossip before bed. It was dusk as she opened the living room door quietly to give her Dad a surprise. A small welcoming fire was burning in the hearth. There was an open bottle of red wine and two glasses on the table. It was a convivial scene. The muted noise from his bedroom told her he was at home. She knocked lightly on the door.

"Hi, Dad, surprise, surprise, it's me Nina, home again. How are you?"

When she opened his door things were not quite as she had expected. The scene that greeted her was difficult to take in. Her father was standing inelegantly with his trousers round his knees, his unseemly buttocks pounding enthusiastically against the rather ample naked buttocks of a middle-aged woman with her skirts round her waist bending over the bed. The woman was Ludmila.

Nina retreated in dismay banging the bedroom door closed behind her. She ran to her room, but it wasn't her room any more. The curtains had been changed. The furniture had been moved around. All her ornaments had disappeared from the dresser. Her posters on the walls had gone. She collapsed on the bed. She sobbed in despair. Her life was falling apart. This was her home, her only home, and now at a stroke she was a stranger there. How could her father be so unfaithful to her mother? It was only three months since the funeral. And with that Ludmila woman, the one person in the village that Nina hated.

Her thoughts raced back to that dreadful evening just after her fifteenth birthday. She had always been friendly at school with Ludmila's son, Mihai, who was in her class, although about four months younger than her. They had been to the village club. It was late October, and evenings were dark. Behind the old community centre not far from the village well, there was a secluded corner, which provided youngsters with privacy for surreptitious assignations. On the evening in question Nina and Mihai were locked in passionate embrace, oblivious to all else. His hand was groping under her skirt, inexpertly exploring between her legs. Her hand had unzipped his trousers and was stroking his erect penis. The elastic in her much washed knickers had given way and they had dropped to her ankles. They were so engrossed they had not heard the approaching footsteps, that is until they were caught in flagranti in the beam of a powerful torch.

"What in God's name is going on here? How dare you? Nina Snegur- you little bitch! Leading my Mihai astray! You little tart! Should be ashamed of yourself!"

The tirade poured out in the darkness. No doubt from whom it came. Mihai had run off into the night. Nina tried to do the same, but immediately tripped on her knickers and fell full length. Ludmila advanced on her and slapped her hard across the face. "Just remember to keep your hands off my lad in future, you dirty slag! He's worth twenty of you and your sort! What a family of shits you all are!"

Nina kicked herself free from her encumbering pants and made her escape. She brushed herself down, straightened her clothing, and flounced back home trying to pretend nothing untoward had happened and went to bed early in the hope she would have recovered her composure by tomorrow.

Next day was market day. She was with her mother buying some vegetables when Ludmila breezed up to them. Nina was petrified, but the conversation turned out to be as normal as ever. How could this be the same woman who had said all those horrid things last night? Her mother moved to another stall. Ludmila grasped Nina's arm and whispered into her ear quickly.

"You little whore. If you ever go near my lad again, your parents will hear about it. Do you understand? And if they want any proof, I've got your pants to prove it. So mark my words. You can shag about as much as you like with the rest of the boys in the village, but I'll not have you leading my lad astray. Now fuck off, you little bitch!"

The events of that evening had etched themselves in Nina's mind. She had never passed a civil word with Ludmila since. And now that same woman was usurping her mother's place in her own home and with her own father. It was a prospect too awful to believe. As she struggled to make sense of it, her father came into the room.

"Nina, I'm very sorry – I really didn't know you were coming home this weekend. Meant to tell you about it. Ludmila's been very good to me. She's a nice lady - not getting on too well with her husband. We thought we might make a go of it. She moved in last week. Been really good at sorting me out. Gone through the house like a dose of salts. Everything's nice and clean and tidy now. I just couldn't live on my own, you know. Can't cook very well. Need to have a woman around. I'd hoped you'd understand. I'm just so sorry you had to find out this way."

He prattled on. Nina buried her head in the bed sheets. Even they were different. She didn't want to talk. She just wanted to be on her own. She had some hard thinking to do. The one fixed parameter in that thinking was her hatred of that woman. She had been humiliated by her five years ago and now Ludmila was destroying her very roots. There would be no place for Ludmila in Nina's future plans. If father had so lightly and so quickly replaced her dear mother with this hypocritical bitch, then he would have to come to terms with the estrangement of his daughter. She would keep faith with her mother. She could not forget the spectre of this woman with her skirts around her waist, flesh and buttocks exposed. She was an arsehole. Nina would have nothing to do with her.

Next morning, soon after daybreak, with no fond farewells, she left the village and made her way back to Chisinau. She was nearly twenty. Her mother had gone. Her boyfiend was distant. Her father had betrayed her. Her home had been dismantled. Her village was a hive of spiteful gossip. Nina Snegur was on her own. In less than two years her life had turned inside out. But she would survive. She had learned her lessons. Now she was going to take control.

Chapter 33

France - December 2003

It had not been an easy night. Despite the blankets, the beds felt damp and the caravan cold. Once or twice someone went outside, presumably for a piss, and clattered back noisily. Habib was tired, but his adrenalin was still pumping. He couldn't stop thinking of all the things that could go wrong still. Having got so far, he dreaded not making it. Abdul might just disappear, then what could they do? The transport could break down. The police could pick them up. What about checkpoints? Were there such things in France? They were all over Kosovo. His companions could turn nasty again. What if he got sick? He fretted the night away and was glad when he heard the noise of a vehicle outside. It was still dark, but his watch said 6:30 a.m. Things were on schedule. They stumbled out of their bunks, gathered their modest possessions and made for the minibus, its idling engine the only noise in the still morning air.

Abdul spoke quietly. "Wait five minutes. We put some boxes inside. Then you go inside."

The minibus was big enough to take about twelve people although there were only five of them left. It was parked alongside what Habib had thought was an empty caravan. Two men from the minibus entered the unoccupied caravan and began carrying boxes from it. They loaded them into the rear doors of the minibus. Habib counted ten. When he and his colleagues clambered in, they saw the boxes had been covered in blankets, some at the back and some down the aisle. They stacked their own bags and rucksacks on top and sat in the accessible seats. Abdul gave the two drivers an armful of baguette loaves and some bottles of water. There were a few brief exchanges in a language Habib could not understand. Then the minibus jolted its way across the field, through the gate and out into dim early light to join the French autoroute system. Habib settled into a window seat for what he knew was going to be long drive. After his restless night it was good to be on the move again, and the steady rhythmic motion soon lulled him into comfortable semi-conscious dozing. First they drove through a large city. Then the autoroute arched through magnificent mountains, opening up panoramic vistas of the Mediterranean coastline.

Unfortunately Habib's appreciation of the immediate environment was tempered by nagging worries about the frequent stops at the motorway toll stations. Each time he was anxious lest police should be there doing spot checks. Only after they had negotiated four or five did his fears begin to recede when it became clear that little more transpired each time other than an automated ticket drawn from a machine or the payment of a few Euros to bored toll booth attendants, who showed not the slightest interest in passengers or baggage.

The bread and water were passed around and after two hours they stopped for their first comfort break at a parking rest area – no restaurant, but welcome toilets and washroom. Then on again, now travelling north. Alongside the autoroute ran a high-speed railway. At regular intervals a bullet-like train would speed past, sixteen gleaming coaches snaking furiously along the valley. In the distance on either side, there were mountains, some snow-capped, and beside the road from time to time, he caught glimpses of a mighty river, the biggest Habib had ever seen. The weather was deteriorating but it was a landscape to marvel at. This was the first time since leaving his family he had been able to savour at first hand "the West" that he had watched so enviously on television at home. Everything seemed to work. There were no potholes in the roads. The toilets were clean. The food and water were reliable. Traffic flowed like clockwork. Trains were frequent and fast. Hundreds of modern cars, trucks and coaches hammered along the motorway. Manicured fields and vineyards stretched out on each side. Beautiful houses and well tended villages nestled effortlessly everywhere. And there were no signs of poverty. The contrast with Kosovo couldn't have been more stark. Habib's resolve was strengthened. Somehow, somewhere he would find a niche for himself in all this.

His geography teacher in Mitrovice had taught them the names of foreign countries and their capitals. In class he would let his mind wander around the globe, the countries, the cities, the rivers. He had longed to travel to some of those exotic destinations. Now he was fulfilling his dream. He could read the name "Paris" on the blue road signs indicating how it far was. He counted down the kilometres as they progressed from junction to junction. The other frequent name was Lyon. Close to that city they had their second stop. Again no cafe or eating place, so the bread and water had to suffice. It was almost midday. Habib calculated they had covered about 400 kilometres. Not halfway yet, but no problems so far.

The day was grey and overcast. Intermittent rain splattered the windscreen as they negotiated the Lyon ring road. Conversation at the back of the minibus was minimal, each absorbed with their own private emotions. The two drivers talked with each other in hushed voices but paid no regard to their passengers, save contributing to the fug of cigarette smoke in the vehicle. The windows steamed up as the pitiless cold rain swept across the landscape. A periodic wiping of condensation from the window pane with the palm of his hand avoided complete encapsulation in the bubble of their own vehicle. Habib strained hard to absorb the changing vistas. Factory after factory slid past, all neat, clean and prosperous, a marked contrast to the dereliction that characterized Kosovo and Albania. He felt envious that his family had never had the privilege of being born into such an affluent society. The trucks fascinated him. From time to time he saw the yellow *Willi Betz* mark that his friend Bledar had hoped to hitch a ride with. But most frequent were bright red trucks with *Norbert Dentressangle* scrawled proudly across the length of their sides. Habib liked the way the firm's logo formed a wave made of the N and D. How could one man own so many trucks?

After two more hours, another toilet stop and change of drivers, the road signs no longer mentionned Paris. Now they were heading for Dijon and Metz. Habib tried to visualise the geography of Europe. To reach Brussels it was probably more direct to go through Luxembourg. So they had already made their swing to the north-east. He guessed they were about halfway. The monotony of the autoroute was tedious. The fug in the minibus became ever more oppressive, stale cigarettes, sweat, unwashed bodies, condensation, and always the palpable aroma of anxious souls.

Then it happened. There was no warning, just the sharp crack. Someone had fired at them. How could that be? No-one knew where they were or who they were. Habib dived between the seats, covering his head with his arms. Angry shouts came from the driver. The vehicle swerved to the right and braked hard. Seconds

- long seconds – elapsed. No more shots. Habib peered cautiously from the fragile sanctuary of the seats. The front windscreen was shattered, intact but almost opaque. Gradually it dawned on him. Not a bullet, but a stone thrown up from the road. His relief was bitter sweet. A shattered windscreen was a major complication, which might bring the police along. Then what would they do?

They had pulled onto the hard shoulder, and slowed to a crawling pace. The consolation was that the windscreen had not burst. Forward visibility was almost impossible, so the driver had wound down his door window with his head out to see the way ahead. Thin meagre rain still drizzled down. Even at such low speed, driving like this was wet, cold and windy. Habib huddled down in his anorak between the seats. A further uncomfortable five minutes with hazard-warning lights pulsing, and the inevitable happened. Two autoroute patrol motorcyclists hauled up in front of them with blue lights flashing and signalled them to stop. Six weeks Habib had been travelling and now, within half a day of reaching Brussels, a solitary chip of stone thrown up by a passing truck might destroy all he had been hoping for. Should he make a run for it? But even as he panicked about what was best, he realised that would be madness. Just sit tight. Act normal. Say nothing. Leave it to the drivers. They had as much to lose, if not more, than he did. They'd got to sort this out.

The policemen seemed cordial enough. Much gesturing and pointing, and then they were off again, this time escorted by the police patrol bikes, one in front and one behind. Habib wondered if they had been arrested, but the convivial exchanges with the drivers made it more likely that they were being helped on their way to a garage or somewhere safer. Five kilometres further on they pulled onto a slip road and into a large service station. With a cursory wave of their black-gloved hands, the two patrolmen peeled away. There was a huge easing of tension in the minibus. The driver was now on his mobile phone. The name Abdul punctuated the conversation. No doubt from his Toulon base he was advising how to deal with this setback. The five illegals sat tight. Best to lie low for the present. It was mid afternoon and the light was fading, but the service station was busy.

The phoning stopped. One of the drivers turned to the passengers. "We stop maybe one hour. Someone come fix glass.

You want money – you give me dollars, I give Euros. You go piss, take food."

Although it meant a delay, Habib welcomed the chance to change some money into Euros, to eat something more substantial and to stretch his legs. They mingled with the anonymous travellers in the self-service restaurant. Unkempt, unshaven, and unwashed for a few days, Habib felt that they stood out like sore thumbs, but no-one seemed even mildly interested in them. On a wet, grey, overcast December afternoon all that mattered to the transient community at the service station was moving on, not fraternising with fellow travellers. Habib's fretting was unnecesary.

By the time they returned to the minibus, two specialist glaziers had removed the shattered screen and were springing a new moulded glass into position. A perfunctory signing of forms in triplicate, appreciative handshakes, and the minibus was ratcheting through its gears back onto the autoroute. It was now dark so Habib's view of the route signs was dependent on the beam of their headlights. Ninety-eight kilometres to Metz. Probably one hour and then how far to Brussels? Habib guessed they had at least four hours driving yet. It was even more tedious now that all they could see was the endless autoroute stretching out ahead in the dipped beams, and the windscreen wipers working tirelessly to slough off the persistent mist of rain from the new glass. It would be late when they arrived. And then what? Habib tried to imagine what it would be like. Maybe they would be put into a roof space like in Genoa? How long would he have to stay there? Where were the others going? He felt like a postal package, identity-less, shuttled from one place to another at the whim of others, with no control over his own destiny. He longed to be with his family again, to be able to talk to someone he could trust, to share jokes with his friends, to taste his mother's cooking, to be in familiar surroundings. In the oppressive darkness and silence of the minibus, still forging on relentlessly through the inclement weather, Habib sank into depressive nostalgia. He buried his head against his rucksack, tears in his eyes. All he really wanted was to be home with his mum. When would he ever see her again? He turned his face away so the others would not observe his distress, wiped his cheeks on his sleeve and tried to sleep. He had no choice. The parcel was on its next stage of delivery.

The incessant glare of the ring road lighting around Brussels roused him. He checked his watch. It was almost midnight. The busyness of the city, the high-rise buildings, the kaleidoscope of neon advertising lights, the clanking trams, the gleaming Mercedes taxis, the wide brightly illuminated approach roads, all contrived to catapult him out of his depressive mood. There was a buzz and excitement about big cities that struck a cord with his intrinsic youthful enthusiasm. Habib waited and watched eagerly to see where he might end up in this vibrant metropolis.

The minibus turned off the arterial roads and navigated through quieter backstreets to the north of the city. They drew to a stop in a dimly lit road buttressed on both sides by four-storey-high terrace houses. It was well past midnight. The only sign of life was a mangy dog scavenging in a plastic sack of rubbish. It shot off furtively at the invasion of his privacy. They had stopped outside a house with a steep ramp down to a basement garage. The vehicle lights were doused and the engine silenced. Neither of the drivers made any move to leave the vehicle, but instead dialled a number on their mobile phone. Conversation was monosyllabic and brief. Then the inevitable cigarettes were lit up, and the door window lowered a few centimetres to allow the smoke an exit. Habib wondered what was to happen. Nothing to do except wait and try to be patient. It had been a long tedious day. He longed to stretch out for a proper sleep.

After ten minutes, a black Mercedes saloon cruised to a quiet halt behind them. Two men emerged and spoke to their driver in hushed voices. One man walked down the ramp and undid locks at either end of an iron girder positioned horizontally midway across the garage door. The rear doors of the minibus were opened and the ten boxes were carefully unloaded one by one and deposited in the garage before its door was re-secured behind the girder.

The driver of the Mercedes then climbed into the minibus and spoke to the five passengers in broken English.

"Two man who go England – you stay here. Three men stay Belgium. We take you different place sleep."

It was the first time Habib had discovered the ultimate destinations of his co-travellers. So one of them was planning to get to England as well. The two of them gathered their rucksacks and climbed out onto the pavement. More brief exchanges between drivers and the Mercedes men. The minibus pulled off. No farewells, just another functional conclusion to another stage in Habib's journey. The Mercedes man produced more keys and opened the house door at the top of a flight of steps, and gestured them inside. Conversation was minimal.

"My name Mitch. You stay here wait for ship to England. You pay 20 Euros each night. OK?"

Habib and his colleague nodded. "How long we stay for ship?"

"One month I think. I tell you when ship come. For ship you give me 2,000 Euros now, and 1000 Euros when you take ship. If you got dollars – $2200 now; $1100 later."

They stood in the hallway and paid what they had to. No point in arguing. Habib did some rapid calculations. He only had dollars, and a dollar was worth less than a euro. He had just about enough left to meet these demands, but little else to spare. In Tirana he had managed to find work to pay for his lodgings while there. Perhaps he could do the same here?

"OK, we stay one month. Maybe we find some work to pay for house?" he asked.

"Plenty work in Brussels – no problem. You sleep now. Tomorrow you find work."

They were taken downstairs to the basement and into small dark room measuring about two metres square. Habib judged it was immediately behind the garage where the boxes had been stored, probably separated by a temporary partition. There were two three-tier bunk beds on each wall with no more than a body width to walk between them. In the beam of light from Mitch's torch they could see three of the beds were already occupied. The occupants stirred momentarily to take in the new arrivals, then turned over burying their heads under their blankets.

"Good place you sleep here. Toilet outside." Mitch showed them another door under the stairs down which they had come. Inside was a toilet and washbasin.

"No food here. You go outside get food. Not good you go front door. You go outside from back house. OK – all understand?"

They nodded.

"I think you tired. I say good night." Then he was gone, together with his torch, plunging them into pitch darkness. Habib fumbled in his rucksack for his own torch with its weakening batteries.

"I guess we're together now. My name's Habib."

"Mine's Toci." They shook hands. Although they had travelled in each other's company since embarking on the boat from Albania, this was the first time they had had any meaningful exchange of conversation with each other.

"Toci! I knew a guy in Tirana called that. Maybe you knew him? Are you from there?"

"No, I come from Durres – don't know anyone called that in Tirana. Where're you from and where're you heading?"

"I'm from Kosovo - that's why I speak Albanian. Want to get to England. Guess that's where you're heading too. Do you have friends there?"

Before he could answer there was shout from the top bunk. "For fuck's sake, belt up. We're trying to sleep." Non-Albanian, but the message was unequivocal.

Habib and Toci clammed up, shook hands again, mouthed good night to each other and sunk wearily into the two bottom bunks. As welcome sleep suffused over him, Habib reflected on his next challenge – how could he earn the extra money he needed in a foreign city? Without that he couldn't pay his dues, and if he didn't pay, he had little doubt the tenuous thread gradually pulling him towards his goal would sever. At best he would have wasted all his money and be picked up as an illegal immigrant, or at worst be left as an anonymous corpse in a Brussels backstreet skip.

Chapter 34

Moldova - Autumn 2002

Living in an impoverished country, with no particular skills, no qualifications, no friends in high places, no family back-up and little or no money, taking control of one's future is no easy task. Nina had called Pavel as soon as she had returned to the capital and they were huddled in a private corner of their favourite coffee shop. She had to talk to someone, and her brother was the only one who would understand her feelings about what was happening at home.

"Did you know about Dad and Ludmila?" she asked.

"No – but I'm not surprised Dad would want to get his leg over again whenever he has a chance."

"Men, bloody men - you're so crude! It's barely three months since Mum died! How could he?"

"He's still only fifty – plenty of life in him yet. I don't think Mum would expect him not to look around, and they both always got on well with Ludmila."

"Well, as far as I'm concerned she's a bitch – shows no respect for Mum and I know she hates me. If Dad wants that turd, he can have her – but they can count me out. No-one's going to replace my Mum." Nina's feelings of loss welled up within her and she couldn't staunch her tears. Pavel clasped her hands across the table.

"Don't fret so – things aren't that bad. Dad's got a life to live – we need to let him get on with it. And we just have to get on with ours."

"But what sort of life is there for me?" she gasped. "You're OK – you're a qualified nurse. You've got a steady job and regular money. I'm still scrabbling around with part-time work. I can't go back home. I should die if I did. I can't see any way ahead. Viktor's miles away – says he will be home next year, but who knows? I'm shit-scared he'll find someone else and then what'll I do? If only I could join him in England. He keeps telling me that's what he wants. But how the hell can I do that?"

"Can't you go to visit him? Why not see if you can get a tourist visa? Plenty of people go abroad these days. Maybe you should go to the British Embassy and hear what they suggest."

It was a glimmer of hope. Perhaps if she could get to visit Viktor in England, or better still, stay with him, it would cement their commitment to each other. It would be something to look forward to. It would shorten their time apart and give her a chance to share in the experiences he talked about so enthusiastically.

The British Embassy is one of the more elegant buildings in Chisinau. The well-polished oak doors open into a quiet vestibule where a grandfather clock comfortably ticks away the seconds. The dark wooden floors are spotless, the rugs thick and refined. The place breathes an assured sense of poise, composure, and professionalism – even integrity. The contrast with the world outside was palpable. Nina felt reassured and less pessimistic as she explained her mission to the receptionist at the visa application counter.

"Yes, a temporary stay visa is possible, but you will need an address in the UK for the duration of your stay. And you will need a UK sponsor who must be able to vouch for you. You will also need to have sufficient funds to cover the whole of your stay and a return air ticket. And of course you need a valid Moldovan passport."

Nina could not have wished for a more courteous and sympathetic discussion. But the hurdles she needed to overcome were daunting. It was explained that Viktor could not be the sponsor, nor could his hospital flat be used as her address, unless the Health Authority in the UK had agreed in writing. Getting together the money was probably the least of her worries. She knew how to deal with that, but she still had to secure a passport. And that meant dealing with Moldovan bureaucracy.

The country had been independent of the USSR for a decade or more, but the vestigial attitudes and working practices of the former Soviet regime lingered on, deeply embedded in the culture of Government departments. The prime role of employees seemed to be to protect the interests of the State. Meeting the needs of its citizens was only a secondary consideration. The Ministry of the Interior, located in a grim five-storey concrete block in the government quarter of the city, was no exception. Nina approached the steep flight of stone steps at its entrance with trepidation. The cavernous foyer was milling with people. Rows of battered benches were anchored to the floor space in the centre. A hundred or more seats were occupied by expressionless individuals, who looked as though they had been there for days. Most clutched an assortment of papers in their hands. One or two babies were crying, their strident cries echoing across the vaulted ceiling. Despite the time of year, there was a dank chill in the air, and a pervading sense of resignation. Nina mingled with the motley array of supplicants, unsure what to do or where to go.

At the far end of the hall there was a barely legible sign above one of the cubicles saying "Passports". The small shelf in front of the cubicle was at chest height. The applicants were expected to stand at it to make their requests. Behind a protective shield of well-fingered glass sat an anonymous middle-aged woman, rosy cheeked, hands bedecked with rings. She looked down from her elevated position. Nina rested her hands on the shelf, and spoke up to her through a hole in the glass. There was no doubting who was the one in authority.

"I need a passport. Can I get one here?" Nina asked.

"*Niet*" – the most popular word on the lips of the bureaucrats of the Soviet Union was the inevitable response. Nina persisted.

"So where do I go to get one?"

"This is the office that controls passports," came the unhelpful reply.

"So how do I get one?"

"You need to fill in the forms – and you need your birth certificate, your marriage license, and a letter from your next of kin. You need to explain why you want a passport, where you intend to travel, and the passport fee. If you want a fast track application, you have to pay a higher fee."

With no more ceremony, Nina was directed to a further cubicle in another part of the hall to obtain the necessary form. She waited patiently in a line of longsuffering applicants, emerging out of the oppressiveness of the government building after almost two hours, clutching the important piece of paper – the passport application form.

Over the next few weeks she assembled the necessary supplementary documents. It meant another visit home to secure a note from her father. He was fawning and apologetic, told her time and again how much he cherished her, and would do everything he could to help her achieve whatever she wanted. Nina ensured it was a short visit. Any contact with Ludmila was kept to a perfunctory minimum.

The return visit to the Ministry followed its usual course – lengthy queues, monosyllabic clerks, nit-picking queries - but at last Nina succeeded in persuading them to accept her application, and handed over the $30 fee. She had said she wanted to visit the Ukraine. This was the least contentious destination and most popular with Moldovans because of its proximity and language affinity.

Six weeks later she returned to the first cubicle she had visited to collect the precious passport. She was greeted by the same bulbous lady, officiously guarding her domain.

"Fast-track fee please."

"But I've waited six weeks. I thought it was ready. I didn't ask for a fast tracking service."

"Your choice dear. Pay up or come back in a few months and it might be ready then."

Nina gave in. "So how much is it?"

"$50 for the fast-tracking service."

Nina still had some savings left over from the summer and paid over the money.

"Don't I get a receipt?"

"We don't issue receipts for fast-tracking – I'm sure you understand. Now would you like your passport or are you going to argue the toss?"

No need to ask into whose pocket the $50 was going. Nina meekly accepted the proffered document, thanked her with as much good grace as she could muster, and exited gleefully clutching her prize. For the first time in her life she could now think of herself beyond the borders of Moldova. It was a good feeling.

The passport was the first step. Now she had the other hurdles to tackle. She arranged to meet Larissa in their usual coffee bar. They often met up together. Her friends at DHL all knew her boyfriend was in England.

"I need to send an urgent email to Viktor," she said. "Is it OK if I use the office computer?"

"No problem," replied Larissa. "Vladimir is always pleased to see you. Why don't you come in tomorrow?"

Next morning Nina was there as soon as the office opened and sent off her email.

> "Hi, Viktor. Hope you're well. I've got my passport, but the British Embassy won't issue a visa for me to come to England unless I can give a UK permanent resident as my sponsor. I also need confirmation in writing from your hospital that I can stay with you there. Can you fax me something, please, to the DHL office? Really can't wait to see you again. All my love, Nina. XXX"

His reply took a few days and when it came it wasn't what she wanted to read.

> "Hi Nina. I've spoken to the hospital manager. He says he can't give written permission for you to stay in my flat at the hospital. Sorry, I don't know any English family well enough to ask if they would sponsor you, but there's a nurse called Janet Evans who works with me on the children's ward and she says she'll ask her parents if they'll do it. She reminds me of you. She lives in a hospital flat near mine and we often eat together when we've finished our work. Let's hope her parents agree. I'll let you know as soon as I hear. Love Viktor."

Nina's heart sank. She was pierced with dismay and jealousy. Her chances of getting a visa now looked slim, but her desire to visit Viktor had immeasurably increased since it appeared there might be a rival for his affections. Janet Evans loomed as a huge threat to all Nina had hoped for. She couldn't bear to think of Viktor spending so much time with this Janet while she eked out a dismal life in Chisinau alone. Everything around her was disintegrating. Her lovely mother was dead. Her home had been taken over by a woman she hated. She had no regular job and no prospects. She had little money in her pocket. And now her relationship with Viktor, which was the thing she treasured most, was in the balance. And to add to her wounds she noted he hadn't put a kiss at the end of his email.

The follow-up email confirmed the worst. Mr and Mrs Evans were not happy to sponsor someone they did not know personally.

So that was that. The normal route was blocked, but the desire to get there was even more desperately urgent. She shared her frustration with Larissa next time they met.

"I really, really must get to England to see Viktor again, but I can't get a visa. How does everyone else get out of Moldova so easily? Why can't I? My life's all fucked up. It's not fair. I'm so pissed off."

Larissa's experience of working in international package delivery at the DHL office had taught her a great deal about border controls across Europe.

"It's very hard to get into the UK," she said. "But if you can reach the Schengen area you can go anywhere without having to show your passport or a visa till you want to leave."

"Schengen? I've never heard of it. Where's that?"

"It includes Germany, France, Spain, Portugal, Belgium, Holland, and a few others, but not the UK. So if you're keen to reach Viktor in England, you'll have to find a way across the English Channel, which is tricky, unless you're a good swimmer! But lots of Moldovan girls do go there to earn some real money and get a better life."

Nina listened intently. An idea was crystallising in her mind. If she could get permission to visit Gerd in Germany, that would be her access to the Schengen countries. But first she needed to learn how the girls managed to get from there into England. If they could do it, so could she. If anyone knew the answer to that question it would be Svetlana. She searched out her number from the memory bank and pressed it into her mobile. It was answered quickly.

"Nina here – remember me? How are you, Svetlana? Still looking like a glamour model, I guess?"

"Hello again, how nice to hear you! How are you? Long time no see! Really sorry to hear about your mother. Such a shame, and so young. I hope you're coping OK. So, to what do I owe the pleasure of this call from you? Hope you're not in trouble again – but if you do want more work, I know Stefan would be happy if you joined us again. How about it?"

It was good to hear Svetlana's confident self-assured voice again.

"No, not in any trouble, and for once not too much in need of extra cash. Though I might be, if the rest of my plans drop into shape. I'd like to pick your brains about something. Best not on the phone. Can we meet for coffee?"

They agreed to meet next day in the late afternoon. The meagre Christmas lights strung haphazardly across the city centre streets rocked precariously in the biting wind and flecks of snow stung her face as she made her way to the snug smokey warmth of their usual haunt.

Without giving too much away, Nina explained the outline of her plan. She wanted to visit Viktor, but the prospects of getting a legitimate visa for England looked slim. She knew lots of Moldovan girls somehow did get in. She would like to do the same. Did Svetlana know how they did it?

"You're right - lots of our girls do make their way to the West, including the UK. They can earn much better money there for doing the same tricks. But many end up unhappy and lonely and life can be hard for them. Their marriage prospects here evaporate and sometimes their families don't want them back. I usually try to persuade them not to go."

"But how do they get there?"

"There are two routes – one overland through the Ukraine, into Poland then across the German border. Once inside Germany, no trouble with passports or visas till you reach the English Channel. Then it's more tricky. That's why many girls decide to stay in Holland or Belgium. Stefan has contacts with the guys who organise the trips – usually two or three girls in the car. They also fix up the false passports and visas – but it's not cheap, and then there's the little extras that the border guards expect. They all take bribes and usually insist on some free sex as a bonus.

"The other way is to fly – there are direct flights from Chisinau to Frankfurt. Once you get there you take your chances the same as if you'd travelled by road. But the border controls at airports are rigid. You will need a proper passport and visa and valid return tickets and a destination address."

"How do the girls who go to England get across the sea? No point in me going all that way unless I can do that."

"Stefan's friends have contacts in Belgium. They smuggle girls across in lorries. You have to pay, of course, and it's a bit risky."

"How much would it cost me, do you think?"

"You'd better ask Stefan – but to go by car overland, I think it's about $2000 for the car journey and another $2000 to get across the channel. If you fly, there's the return air ticket and the costs of reaching the coast from Germany, and then the cost of the channel crossing. But you need valid documents to do that. That's why most girls do the car journey."

Nina absorbed every word. No-one knew about Gerd, but he was the ace in her pack. He could give her the legitimate reason to reach Germany. Then it would be up to her. It was some months since she had heard from him. Should she sit tight and wait for him to contact her again or should she take the initiative and send him an email saying she was thinking about accepting his invitation to visit him in Germany? Perhaps a friendly Christmas email greeting might be the best way to re-establish contact. It was now nearly six months since she had last heard from him.

Nina need not have worried. She meant more to Gerd than she realised. He was delighted to hear from her. The precious times he had spent with her were a secret treasure that helped him cope with the barrenness of his marriage and the stresses of his work. He was doing all he could to keep the EU Moldovan wine consultancy scheme alive, mainly because it gave him good cause to keep returning to Moldova, even though, to be frank, the Moldovan viticulture programme was now in reasonable shape. When he received her greetings, it galvanised him into re-contacting the powers that be in Brussels making out the case to for a further trip to Moldova in the early spring to verify that the winter months had not set back the advances made the previous year. For politically correct projects such as helping emerging democracies develop and westernise their economies, the coffers of the EU were easily accessed.

Nina's plans began to take shape. When Gerd's reciprocal Christmas greetings arrived, it contained the news that he expected to be back in Chisinau in mid-February. The project he had been working on had been extended for another year into 2003. Nina had been planning to spend Christmas in the capital with her friends there rather than face the tensions and complications at home, but this news from Germany and the opportunities it opened up were so exciting she felt a new surge of confidence, so much so she was no longer daunted by the prospect of Christmas at home, and she knew her father would be so relieved if they could re-establish more amicable relations.

The New Year was dawning with promise. She had a gleaming new passport. Gerd would be here soon. With him came the chance of reaching Germany, probably in the spring and then, if Svetlana's contacts came good, she could spend Easter with Viktor in England, and see off any competition from Janet Evans. The one issue yet to be tackled was raising the funds. If the figures she had been given were right, she was going to need about $4,000. Nina knew what she had to do. She had done it when in distress because of her unwanted pregnancy. She had done it when in distress about her mother's health. Now, to save the prospects of her own marriage, she would do it for herself. A few nights a week at the Hotel Dukro and an average of three clients a night should accumulate the funds within a few months. She pressed the appropriate buttons on her mobile phone.

"Hi – is that Svetlana? Hi – it's me again, Nina. You remember what you said when we spoke a few weeks ago. Well, I'm thinking I might try to get to Germany and then use Stefan's contacts to get me into England. But I need to get the money together first. Do you think Stefan or Vladimir have room for me to work the hotels again?"

Their reply came before the day was out. Her experience, her good looks, her youth, and her ebullient good nature were the ingredients that most clients craved for. She could start that weekend. It was the second week of January. Chisinau was gripped in freezing temperatures. By the time the springtime blossom was on the trees again, Nina hoped her future plans would have crystallised. She emailed Viktor with her exciting news. She told him what she hoped to do and when. But she kept a close veil over how she would raise the funds and how she proposed to secure a visa into the EU. Those were her own secrets.

PART 5

BELGIAN WINTER

Chapter 35

Buitelaar - November 2003

Arjan van Buitelaar was not a particularly happy man. Life had not gone according to plan. Then again, he had never had a well-conceived set of goals or objectives. But if anyone had asked him twenty years before what he would be doing at the beginning of the New Year 2004, he would never have guessed in a thousand years. Nor would he have been particularly proud to relate it.

He had grown up in the suburbs of Haarlem in Holland, went to the local mixed comprehensive school, and left with no great academic distinctions nor any sporting achievements, except perhaps in scoring with the more promiscuous girls in his class. His first job, at the age of sixteen, was as office boy in a haulage firm. Never likely to admit it to his peer group friends, he had a child-like fascination for the huge, multi-wheeled trucks that moved seamlessly in and out of the depot day and night. They travelled to destinations outside his experience. Their drivers had an assurance and confidence he envied. The vehicles were proud, indomitable creatures, self-sufficient. They had deeply sprung cabs and living quarters, cavernous loading spaces, mammoth engines, enormous tyres, and raw power surging from their air-brakes. Freud would probably have summed it up disparagingly as infantile sexual envy – the worship of big, powerful, penetrating prowess. But for Arjan the haulage depot was just a really good place to work.

It was not long before this emotional attachment to the trucking scene translated itself into driving lessons on heavy-goods vehicles and his elevation to be a fully qualified long-distance haulage driver in his early twenties. At the same time, his variegated lovelife was crystallising around Margreet. They weren't into religion, so didn't bother with a formal wedding but set up home together as partners in a small apartment in Hemstede. The two children they quickly produced more than occupied Margreet's time and energy. Arjan's driving assignments took him further and further afield. Often he was away for most nights of the week. On the third time he arrived back from one of these trips suffering from a mild sexually transmitted disease, Margreet had moved into the spare room, and a year later she left him to share her life and body with another rather more homely soulmate.

Arjan buried himself in his truck driving and from a distance watched, with some dismay, his two children growing up with little respect for or interest in him, and then their moral disintegration, as his teenage son became addicted to the Amsterdam drug scene and his daughter opted for a punk lifestyle.

Arjan's only satisfaction derived from his trucking and, after ten years as an employee, he decided he would try his hand at being his own boss. The bankers were impressed with his knowledge of the trade, his networks and his single-minded commitment. His truck would be parked in the road when not working so there were few overheads. It was to be a one-man band and the only mouth to feed was Arjan's. He was prepared to plough all the profits back into the company and would live on the road in his truck working the maximum hours possible. The bank advanced the money without a qualm and Arjan was in business with his own privately owned articulated flat-bed Mercedes twelve-wheeler.

The world shipping-container market was his prime source of income. Thousands of containers from all over the globe were passing through the Dutch and Belgian ports on a daily basis. Arjan's truck hauled these ugly, soulless metal boxes to their final destinations across Europe, containing all manner of machines, equipment or commodities.

Antwerp is reputedly the world's largest container port. Its prodigious lengths of wharfs and docksides stretch miles along the water channels feeding into the massive estuary of the river Schelde, which drains off the Lowlands into the North Sea. Piled high like giant lego blocks, containers cover every square metre of space. Similar in shape, size and colours they tower gracelessly on every vista, hundreds upon hundreds, seemingly forgotten in some surreal landscape. Beavering away between them, in and out the tall metallic avenues, day and night, truckers like Arjan keep the logistics of transporting goods around the globe on schedule. There was a never-ending demand for his service. Within five years he had taken on two other owner-drivers, on a sub-contract basis, and acquired a small warehouse and storage yard on the outskirts of Aalst, adjacent to the high-speed dual carriageway linking Brussels to Ostend and its ferry terminal, Zeebrugge. The Buitelaar Haulage Company was in growth mode.

Being close to Antwerp and the channel ports was where the focus of his company's work and profit rested. Dutch was freely spoken in this part of Belgium, so he had no problem communicating. He had no reason to stay near Haarlem after the breakdown of his short-lived domestic arrangements. At the age of forty-two he had in effect relinquished family responsibilities. For physical relief there was a plentiful supply of available women wherever his trucking took him, none of whom made any long-term demand on him. His sedentary lifestyle and frequent recourse to instant foods and alcohol had contributed to a steady growth in his girth. When not in his small flat in Aalst, his truck cab was his home, with its microwave, mini TV, radio, CD player, heater, and bunk bed behind the cab seats. It was a way of life he was content with but it was the buoyant business that gave it all substance.

The introduction of the Euro in January 2002 made financial transactions within Europe so much easier for him, but it brought with it an unexpected upwards shift in prices when everyone cashed in, as they always did, on currency changes. This reduced his profit margins almost overnight by about 10%. On top of that, the effects of the fateful events in New York on 11th September 2001 were beginning to feed through the world's economy, resulting in a marked downturn in the volume of container shipping. The trucking business was beginning to feel the pinch. The more prudent commentators were predicting this would be no more than a blip in the steady growth of international trade, but small firms, such as Arjan's, had no financial cushion to withstand short-term decline in cashflow. Diversification of business interests would have helped, but Arjan's only interest was trucking and that was rather too concentrated on the single activity of container transportation. The year 2003 was a poor year. His income-expenditure account barely broke even, despite his having taken only minimum living expenses out of the company. The following year looked considerably gloomier unless trade improved, or unless he could find new sources of income.

So Arjan was mildly gratified when he received a telephone call in late November 2003 asking whether he would be interested in using his truck for another type of business. It might involve some risk but would pay a big bonus and one which avoided tax liability. It was agreed the caller would meet him privately to discuss things further at an insignificant cafe tabac near the Municipal Town Hall Square in Woluwe in the northern suburbs of Brussels later that evening.

Two men arrived for the meeting, one a tall well-dressed Belgian called Francois, fluent in both French and Dutch, and the other of oriental appearance, who said he was known as Mitch and who spoke a modicum of Dutch. No business cards were exchanged, but Arjan was given a mobile phone number for each, which was the only way they could be contacted. They were to be called only by their first names. Indeed Arjan was not told their surnames, nor for that matter any other information about them.

They were taking delivery of a full-sized sea container being shipped from Shanghai, due to arrive in Antwerp within the next few weeks. They had contact with the Hoogang International Logistics company who had confirmed the container was already at sea. Average shipping time was twenty-nine days so it should arrive in mid-December. It contained two major items of machinery, one for delivery in Holland and one for onward transport to a city in the UK called Leicester. The container would be opened under Customs surveillance in Antwerp. The machine in its wooden crate and packaging destined for the Dutch address would be unloaded and taken by separate transport to its destination. The other machinery would remain crated in the container, which would be resealed by Customs for road transit delivery to the UK. Francois and Mitch would like Arjan to use his truck to transport the resealed container and contents to the UK. The fee for this would be at the usual rates, but a very large bonus would be payable if he would agree to an additional commitment.

Arjan had listened intently. The container transportation was child's play. What he wanted to hear was what else was expected.

"We want you pick up resealed container from Antwerp dock," said Mitch in his broken Dutch. "You take it your depot in Aalst. You put truck inside warehouse. We meet you night-time. You not worry. We do everything. You stay in office. We put extra things in container. No problem we seal container like Custom man. You no worry you drive to England. We meet you and take our things quickly. You then take machine Leicester – all OK. No problem."

Oriental Mitch might have been of the view there would be no problems but Arjan was by no means convinced.

"So what's the cargo? Drugs? Booze? Cigarettes? Immigrants? Explosives? I need to know."

"Better you not know – you leave everything to us. We look after it. You know nothing about what inside container."

"Well," said Arjan, "you'd better look elsewhere. I don't put stuff on my truck unless I know what I'm carrying. So we don't have a deal. Sorry, but that's it: you'd better find someone else, mate."

"OK, OK ," intervened the Belgian called Francois, "but before you finally decide perhaps you need to know that if you do agree to the deal, we'll give you 5,000 Euros up front, another 10,000 when you deliver. And you get the normal container transport fee as well. Does that help?"

"No deal, unless I know what's on board. End of story, chum!" said Arjan.

The two visitors looked across to each other, and nodded.

"OK, mister Arjan, we tell you – we got some people who must go in England. You know cargo now. That OK but you get big trouble if you tell somebody. You understand I think."

Arjan looked on impassively trying hard not to betray any emotion. Inside he was churning. It seemed he was now party to an illegal immigrant deal whether he liked it or not. He needed the money desperately, that was sure. These people seemed to be taking all the responsibility. All he had to do was the driving – no problem in Belgium. Customs could be tricky. He would have to cross-examine Mitch and Francois how they proposed to deal with that - both sides of the Channel. But once in England, again no problem, and if he could unload at a secluded rendez-vous there, after that he was in the clear. The whole operation should be over in less than twenty-four hours and he would be 15,000 Euros better off tax-free. Pretty good rate of return. Moral issues didn't enter into it. These people wanted to be in England, just looking for a better life, who could blame them? It was just bloody bureaucracy that wouldn't allow it. Better they were in England than competing for scarce jobs in Belgium or Holland. What had he to lose, just as long he could be assured the Customs side of things was taken care of?

"So how do you think you can get through Customs with a living, breathing payload?" he asked, not at all convinced they could give a satisfactory answer.

"No problem mister Arjan. We do it many times before you know. We have special box we put inside container. We put proper customs seal on container. No-one look inside. Container stay on your truck. You not leave container. We make special breathing holes in side. You no worries. It work good all time before. You say you not know what inside if Customs ask. All documents from China for machine good. No worries, mister Arjan. Easy money for you!"

The tall Belgian then took up the conversation. "We do all the business. All you do is the driving. A normal scheduled run from your depot to the Zeebrugge terminal. Onto the ferry, and into Dover. Then the UK motorways M20, M25, and M1 to a drop-off in a secluded warehouse just before you reach Leicester. We do all the unloading and make sure there are no traces of your extra cargo left. You just carry on as normal with your container delivery. From your depot to the off-load point in the UK will take about ten hours. It's good money for you and you wash your hands of responsibility all along the line. Go away and think about it. We'll call you by phone in two days. If you don't want it, fine, but remember, whether you do it or not, if a word of this gets out to anyone else, you're a cripple for the rest of your life. I think we understand each other, don't we?"

Francois and Mitch took their leave, and walked off incognito into the evening mist shrouding the clean, neat streets of Woluwe. Arjan sat squarely in front of his half-empty glass of lager, pensive and solitary, staring fixedly at the smudged beer mats on the well-worn bar table around which the dramatic exchanges had taken place. He did not usually smoke, but this was one occasion when he needed a cigarette. He inhaled deeply of the comforting vapour and considered his options. This was not a time for hasty decisions. But it was a time for a decision.

Chapter 36

Moldova - 2003

Counting, counting – the next few weeks for Nina were going to involve a lot of counting. First there was the countdown of the few days spent at home for Christmas. In the end, things weren't as bad as she had feared. Pavel was there and he was a kindred spirit. Her father was his usual self, over talkative, often slightly worse for drink, embarrassingly full of bonhomie, all of which Nina found difficult to reconcile with her own emotions, the stark fact being that this was their first Christmas without her mother orchestrating the festivities. Ludmila tried hard to be an adequate substitute but Nina had no illusions. This was not a woman she was ever going to like. Civil courtesy was all she was prepared to muster. Her father's new paramour would have to like it or lump it.

More engaging was the countdown of the weeks and days before Gerd was due back to see her in mid-February. Until then there was the hard reality of earning sufficient money to fund her consuming need to go to see Viktor in the UK. She decided to keep a small notebook. Encrypted in it she noted the number of clients she dealt with each night and more especially the count-up of the accumulating total of dollars she was able to secrete away. To be on the safe side, she had opened a personal bank account and lodged her profits there. No-one asked too many questions these days. Many people were finding ways and means of making a little bit extra on the side.

The all-important countdown was how soon she would be able to put into place her journey plans to the UK. The key was reaching Germany. She detected a shift in her motives for seeing Gerd again. Before it had always been the desire to re-engage with his unaffected passion for her. Now she was conscious of another motive. She was going to use Gerd to effect her entry to Germany. But he was not to know her ulterior motive. That meant she would have to deceive him - not something she relished, bearing in mind how much pleasure he gave her; but needs must.

The confirmatory email came. Gerd would arrive on Monday 17th February. He would stay till the Saturday. He would be at the Hotel Dukro again. Nina recalculated her likely earnings. After paying her dues to Stefan each night, the six weeks till Gerd came should yield a net profit of about $250 per week. And she knew Gerd was always generous. She felt guiltily mercenary thinking of that, but hopefully he would reward her with an extra $100 or so. That would leave another $2,400 to earn before she could contemplate leaving. Two months more work if all went well. A potential departure date of early May began to crystallise as a reasonable target. The weather should be good then and Gerd had talked of how lovely the Rhine valley was in springtime.

By contrast, January in Moldova was seldom other than pitilessly raw and cold. It was always a relief to reach the warmth of a client's room in the hotel after the icy sprint across the forecourt from the muggy conspiratorial confines of Stefan's dark-windowed BMW hidden in the trees in the car park opposite. Nina's experience had honed her skills and expertise in meeting the range of demands her clients made. Her increasing confidence contrasted with the nervousness and apprehension of many of her customers, only thinly veiled by their brash macho posturing. Seldom did she have to call for Stefan's help. But once a self-important Ukrainian businessman had tried things on. Because of their more buoyant economy, Ukrainians always thought themselves a cut above Moldovans.

After their energetic encounter, he was lying back on the bed, one arm looped behind his head, the other holding a cigarette on which he was drawing contentedly, the crumpled sheet partially dragged across his mid-rift to obscure his nakedness. Nina had finished dressing and was taking her leave with her usual affectionate kiss to the client's forehead. It was then she discovered the door was locked - no sign of the key.

"Dear girl, surely you're not leaving already! I reckon I deserve a bit more for my money, don't you? God, I've paid you $50 and you've barely been here twenty minutes – you couldn't earn that in a normal job in Moldova in two months, could you?"

"Well sir, I think I made it clear at the beginning what the price included, didn't I?"

"Be buggered you did - but you don't think I'm settling for that, do you? You'll go when I've had my deserts, so you'd better get your kit off again and earn your money like a good little whore!"

Nina knew what she had to do.

"OK," she said coyly. "I just need some tissues from my bag to clean up a bit."

As she felt into her handbag she pressed the call button on her mobile. Now it was just a question of counting down the minutes. First a trip to the bathroom. Then let him finish his cigarette, before she pretended to start undressing again. She had timed things right. Only her coat had fallen to the floor when the knock on the door came.

"Room service!"

"I didn't ask for room service – what's going on?" shouted the Ukrainian.

Before he could finish, the door opened and Stefan entered holding a tray supporting two glasses of clear liquid.

"Two gin and tonics, sir, - $20 dollars for the drinks and $10 for the personal service."

"You must be joking! Sod off, we're busy. I don't want any fucking drinks. You've got the wrong room mate!"

In his state of undress and torpidity, he was ill prepared for the split second when the glass of white spirit was hurled unceremoniously into his face. He screamed as the stinging pain temporarily blinded him. Nina took her cue, picked up her coat and left speedily through the open door. Meanwhile Stefan located the man's wallet, as the Ukrainian charged inelegantly for the bathroom to bathe his eyes. By the time they were open again his evening visitors had long since gone, Stefan stopping only momentarily at the hotel reception to return the duplicate room key and pay the $20 "fee" for its loan, courtesy of the Ukrainian's emptied wallet.

Nina was surprised how easily the hotel work slipped into a routine. What gripped her most was the countdown of weeks till Gerd arrived. However great her eagerness to see him, she was careful to ensure their reunion betrayed nothing of her additional motive in seeing him again. The week passed pleasurably on a roller-coaster of anticipations and fulfilments – he was able to see her three times, including two lunchtime encounters that unwound into a carefree afternoon together. It was on the last of these that Nina took the opportunity she had been waiting for.

"Maybe I come see you to Germany?" she asked in her halting English.

"You think you can come?"

"Now I have passport. I think it easy I fly to Germany"

"I like very much you come. Flight cost much money you know."

"I get job now – I get plenty money."

Gerd was under no illusion how a girl like Nina could accrue enough money for such a trip. He himself had first met her as a client, and there was no reason to believe that she had abandoned her profession just because he had come along.

"I very happy show you my country. When weather good you come. I email you - find nice hotel for you."

A pang of disappointment pierced her for a moment. She had somehow assumed they would be staying together, but then quickly recognised that would be out of the question. He had a wife and two teenage boys at home. She kissed him tenderly on the lips and slid her hand to his groin.

"You make me very happy I come to your country. I want make you happy also."

Her head moved down towards her hand. She fastened her lips around him and relished the guttural sounds of pleasure she provoked while his hand gently caressed her hair in resonance with the movements of her mouth.

He left the next day. It was not such a tearful farewell. They would be seeing each other again soon. Nina would be busy till then. But the countdown had begun. Spring was just around the corner. All she had to do now was wait for his email to confirm the dates. Everything was going according to plan. A week in Germany at the beginning of May, then across the channel to join Viktor in England – maybe she could stay with him till he finished at the hospital in the summer, and make sure Janet Evans was no longer in the picture. Then home together when surely he would be ready to get married – and then maybe a baby. How proud her mum would have been! The traumas of last year would be behind her. She could already feel her spirits lifting.

But things did not go according to plan.

The email from Gerd did not come quickly. She consoled herself that it would take some time for him to get things organised – she would just have to be patient. But it was now many months since she had last seen Viktor and she fretted about their prolonged separation. More worrying was the conversation she had just had with her two flatmates.

"Well, who's a dark horse then?" they asked. "Tanya was out drinking last night with friends at the Hotel Dukro. Said they'd seen you in and out three or four times like a yo-yo. And you telling us you'd been out with a boyfriend! Guess we know now why you're not short of money – should have put two and two together really, shouldn't we?"

Nina had been caught off guard. Her immediate desperate fear was that Viktor or her family might find out. Should she try to bluff things away or come clean and seek their confidence in not spreading the information wider afield?

"I had to do it to get enough money for my mum's treatment – now I'm saving up to go and join Viktor in England. You won't tell anyone else, will you?" She tried to trade on their sympathy and understanding.

"What you do is up to you. Nothing to do with us. Just as long as you pay your rent. You never know - we might even consider joining you!"

"Just let me know when and I'll arrange some introductions," Nina replied with some relief. Even so she could feel life beginning to press in on her. In reality, in such a tight-knit community, sooner or later her nocturnal secrets would leak out. She just had to get through the next few weeks as quick as possible, earn the money she needed and then get away. Why didn't Gerd get in touch? He seemed such a good reliable man. Had something gone wrong?

At last the email came. She picked it up from the DHL office.

> "Sorry much work here till July. Better you come then. Tell me what flight you come to Frankfurt. I meet you there."

So that was it. Two months' delay. Understandable from Gerd's point of view, but when was Viktor coming home? He said he'd been given a year's extra work. That meant he would be about to come home in July. So what was the point in going? Suddenly

Nina was in turmoil. She used an Internet cafe to send her urgent pleas to him so her DHL friends were not able to read it.

> "Hi Viktor. Thanks for your last email. My plans have had to be changed. I can't come out now till July. When does your contract end? Maybe we could come back here together in August when your work is finished? Let me know soon so I can book my tickets. All my love and kisses everywhere. Nina."

His reply came four days later. He expected his contract would finish at the end of July. He would be returning in August, but might do some sightseeing before he left. If she could get there by then, they could do it together.

Happily no further mention of Janet Evans. Nina whooped with joy when she read it. In any case the delay was not altogether bad news. It gave her more time to get things organised. First she needed a visitor's visa for Germany. That depended on a formal invitation from Gerd. He sent her an email in German confirming it and undertaking to be her sponsor while staying there. Next she needed a return ticket. They had settled on the week the 7th to the 14th July, Moldovan Airlines flight leaving at 8:00 a.m. on the Monday morning. Armed with these, and her crisp new passport, she presented herself at the German Embassy. Two weeks later there it was – all in German, but the dates on the visa she could read. Her German trip was fixed. She danced down the steps. Now to tackle how to get from there to the UK as quickly as possible.

It was Stefan's friends who knew what was necessary. A meeting was arranged in the early evening before she began one of her working nights at the hotel - the venue a seedy bar, smoke filled, in one of the suburbs. Stefan agreed to give her a lift and introduce her to the two men. She was glad he stayed while they talked. He gave her some added security.

"You got plenty of money? No deal if you can't pay!" They were men of few words and even fewer preliminaries. They hunched over a stained wooden table in the half-light, wreathed in their own tobacco smoke. Neither had shaved for two or three days, which served only to emphasize their swarthy complexions. Their calloused artisan hands were wrapped round large glasses of vodka.

Nina noted their dirty broken fingernails. These were not people she liked to do business with, but what choice did she have. Without betraying her apprehension, she confirmed she could afford to pay.

"OK. When you planning to go?"

Nina told them the dates and that she would be starting from Germany.

"Right -you gotta get yourself from Frankfurt to Brussels in Belgium. We'll give you an address and contact there. They'll fix you up with a way to get into England. We need $100 now. Then we meet again the week before you leave, and give you the address – that's when you give us the rest of the cash - $200. And one last thing, sister – if any of this conversation gets to anyone else, you won't be a pretty girl any more. Lovely cheeks and sharp razors don't go well together. All understood?"

Nina nodded, trying not to flinch at their unashamed brutality.

"So we meet here again at the beginning of July?"

Stefan intervened. "Don't worry. I'll fix that up nearer the time. But they need the deposit now. Can you give to them?"

Nina handed it over. She had come prepared for that but the amount of extra money they were asking was more than she had bargained for. She felt sick and angry that the address she needed in Brussels was going to cost almost as much as she had spent paying the hospital bills in her vain efforts to save her mum's life. It wasn't fair. But unless she played by their rules she knew all too well she was stuck. Perfunctory nods signalled the end of the conversation. Stefan and Nina took their leave. That was one more piece of her jigsaw in place. There were still others to deal with.

Her DHL friends had taught her how to browse the internet. She logged on to Google and searched for Europe's rail networks. She was relieved to discover trains went direct between Frankfurt and Brussels. One-way tickets were about $100 and the journey took three hours and thirty-two minutes. There were three trains each day. She would need to catch the one around midday. She could buy her ticket at the Frankfurt Haupt-Bahnhof. Another piece of her jigsaw was falling into place.

The delay in going out to Germany meant that she had more time to earn the funds she needed. By mid-June she had settled all her debts, and paid for her return flight. She had also been able to send some money to her father each month, a sort of recompense for going home so infrequently. The last two weeks before she was due to leave, she gave up her hotel work and focussed on getting together the clothes and luggage she needed for her journeying. Each day she steadily withdrew money from her bank account and hid it under a floorboard in her flat. In due course that would be transferred to a waist money belt under her clothes. The final rendez-vous with the two guys who were going to give her the crucial Brussels address was arranged. She handed over the extra $200 and received from them the precious scrap of paper with the contact name, Mitch, and the Brussels address. She stowed it away in her money belt.

There was a wild last weekend of partying and goodbyes, but certainly no tears. She was excited, prepared and yearning to get away. Monday 7th July dawned clear and bright to match her mood. She had never flown before and arrived well on time. She checked and rechecked everything – passport, visa, money, tickets, handbag, make-up, wash-kit, and suitcase well locked. At last, through the ticket check-in and passport control and into the departure lounge. All the other passengers seemed calm, even blase - no doubt they had all done this before, but Nina had butterflies. Would she be sick on the plane? Would she be scared the plane was going to crash? Would Gerd be there to meet her? What would she do if he wasn't? What was going to happen in Brussels? Could it really be true she would be joining Viktor in England in about two weeks?

Then through the last checkpoint, a walk across the 100 metres of tarmac, up the steep metallic steps and into the snug seductive tube of closely packed seats. Seatbelts fastened, safety demonstration completed – more reasons to feel nervous – tables stowed away, and then the surge of raw power that pinned her back into her seat as the roofs of Chisinau gradually diminished and filtered away beneath them. What had she worried about? This was great!

It was nearing lunchtime as they touched down in Germany. So many planes, such a huge terminal, so many people - where should she go? The air-hostess explained in Moldovan, the last she would hear for some time, what she should do. First to passport control, then baggage reclaim and then head for customs. Best just to follow other people off her flight. So many long corridors, all so clean and modern, so many escalators, so many trendy shops, so many restaurants and bars, so many carousels, and so much baggage, but at last one that was marked for her flight and then, almost like magic, her suitcase popped up onto the conveyor. Nothing to declare at customs so onwards with the stream of impatient travellers to the exit.

And there he was, smiling, waving, holding up a big hand-written placard; "Nina – Welcome to Germany".

She surged to him, brimming with relief and excitement, dragging her suitcase behind her on its two small wheels. Her cabin luggage was strapped round her shoulders and with her free hand she held onto her coquettish black hat, matched by her short black bolero jacket and tight black jeans topped by her big buckled belt. She had wanted to look good for this special moment. Beyond the huge plate-glass walls of the Arrivals Hall and the queue of gleaming Mercedes taxis waiting outside like vultures for custom, the hot sun bathed the surrounding landscape in shades of green and yellow. This was Germany - the first time she had ever set foot outside her homeland. Nina had never felt so happy. She flung her arms out and buried herself against him. Their lips met hungrily as she felt herself lifted off her feet. It was as though she were acting her part in a glittering movie. Could all this be real?

"So you are here! Very good. You look very beautiful. I take your case. We go find my car."

She locked her arm into his and walked dizzily through to the vast short-term car-park, her case trundling behind them. It was no surprise that his car was a Mercedes, dark blue, with white leather seats. The boot lid opened automatically like a gull's wing to swallow up her case. She sank down luxuriously into the front seat as they glided effortlessly down the multi-levels and into the suburbs before picking up the autobahn heading west for Koblenz. Nina had arrived in the West. She was not disappointed. Moldova seemed very far away. The car was cruising at 140 kilometres an hour. The autobahn stretched out ahead like a glistening snake. Soon they were passing sun-soaked vineyards along the Rhine valley. Nina snuggled closer to Gerd as his strong hands directed where they were going. This was how things should be.

Chapter 37

Buitelaar - November 2003

In making choices there are pros and cons for either way forward. Sometimes these are finely balanced, but the consequences of getting it wrong can be devastating. The worry of deciding what to do can be debilitating. When the choice is to do something or not to do it, the maxim "When in doubt - don't!" is a safe enough guide.

As Arjan drove back the 30 kilometres to his flat in Aalst, he was not too stressed about his dilemma. It was not something he could share with anyone else, but he did have two days to think about it. If he told them he wasn't interested, and kept his mouth shut, that would be the end of it. On the other hand, if he agreed to do it, it would mean a day or so of tense anxiety, but the pay-off was very tempting. Not a bad dilemma - he would sleep on it.

If he had expected to have a fretful time deciding what to do, he had not taken into account that sometimes decisions make themselves for you. He arrived at his office next morning to a small pile of mail. One was a letter from the tax office reminding him that his annual tax payment was due before the year's end. The sum demanded would more than empty the company bank reserves, and thereafter he would be dependent on the goodwill of his bank manager to keep his business afloat while his account was in the red. How long they would be prepared to do that he wasn't sure. But it was a major headache. As he ruminated on this unwelcome prospect, his phone rang. The shipping broker was ringing to tell him because business was slack at Antwerp docks, the container terminal was going to scale down operations over the Christmas and New Year period, so his workload would be reduced for the next month or so. Arjan registered the information with a less than enthusiastic grunt and contemplated yet another blow to his cashflow difficulty.

The rain was slashing down as he finished the final delivery of the day, a short round trip from the docks to Eindhoven with a 70 cubic metres container of sophisticated electrical parts from Kobe in Japan. He picked up a meal from the local Chinese takeaway, opened a can of lager, and settled down in front of his TV to watch the European soccer match between Ajax and AC Milan. It was after 10:30 p.m. when he finally roused himself from the sofa to take the dirty plate back into the kitchen. Only then did he notice the flashing red light on his answer-phone.He pressed the play button as he walked past and continued into the kitchen to put down the tray.

> "You have one message, received today at eleven twenty-five this morning. Good morning. This is Police Inspector Lange from Haarlem Police Station. I have a personal message for Mr Arjan van Buitelaar. I understand you are the natural father of Emma van Buitelaar. I have to inform you that Miss van Buitelaar was admitted to the Haarlem hospital two days ago where she gave birth to a little girl. I regret to say the baby was addicted to heroine at birth and died within a few hours. Miss van Buitelaar discharged herself voluntarily from hospital the next day. The body of a young female was found floating in the canal near Amsterdam Central Station early this morning, and has been identified by her mother, Mrs Margreet Rikj, as that of your daughter. I have been asked to inform you that the funeral for both the baby and mother will be at Holy Trinity Church, Zuider Strasse, Haarlem, on Thursday 4th December at 2:00 pm, prior to cremation. End of message."

There are moments when, without the slightest premonition, bleakness and despair crash catastrophically into the mundane routine of life. Arjan stood transfixed at the sink, the stale odour of the remnants of the takeaway meal in his nostrils, the baleful commentator's voice from the television in the sitting room groaning on about Milan's winning goal being offside, the harsh November rain still pounding against the windows. He gripped the side of the kitchen work surface to steady himself as tears streamed uncontrollably down his cheeks. His nose ran – his head was in a daze. His body shook with sobs of anguish as he raged inside at the unfairness of life, and tried to cope with the surge of guilty despair that racked his mind. He had never felt more alone and desperate. What should he have done to save his own sweet little daughter, his pride and joy when she was first born, his own flesh and blood, from such a desperately sad and derelict end. All that she had hoped for and loved extinguished in the cold and lonely waters of a dark canal, unseen, unheard, unloved, unwanted.

He staggered from the kitchen to the drinks cabinet in the sitting room. He took the whisky straight from the bottle. He crashed down onto his bed and took more and more gulps of the fiery fluid. The saltiness of his tears mingled on his lips with the comforting taste of Scotland's most famous export. Gradually the bottle emptied and, equally gradually, his senses became more stupefied. Without knowing when, he fell into a deep comatosed sleep. He knew no other way to deal with such distress.

The next morning the storm-tossed night had given way to gentle sunshine and a pallid blue sky. The wind was quiet; the trees were still. The rain-washed pavements shone clean and fresh. As he emerged back to consciousness, Arjan's first awareness was that his head was very thick - not unexpected - but in sympathy with the clarity of the new dawn, his mind seemed strangely clear and focussed. Today he was to receive the crucial call from Francois or Mitch. The events of the intervening hours since he had first spoken to them had crystallised the issues. He needed money desperately. His truck was momentarily under-utilised. He had lost irretrievably one of the most precious things in his life, and he really didn't care now what else he might lose. The so-called illegal immigrants were all poor sods, desperate to escape from lives of hopeless poverty in their own countries, to try to do better for themselves in the West. He could almost convince himself it was altruistic to help them. He would do it.

He showered, shaved, took some paracetamol tablets with his coffee and croissants and headed to the depot. The call came through at ten o'clock. He was calm and measured. He had made his decision. What next?

"OK," said Francois, "I'll tell you what you need to know, nothing more, nothing less. The container is expected into Antwerp the third week of December. The shipping agents will clear it through Customs and off-load the crate destined for the Dutch company as soon as they can. This may take till after Christmas.

When Customs have resealed and cleared the container for leaving the docks, it should be ready for pick-up early January. You should plan to collect it from the docks on Thursday 8th January. The paperwork will be all sorted by then and will be given to you when you arrive. After loading the container on your truck you will drive back to your depot. You then garage your truck and the container inside your warehouse out of sight. You must ensure there are no other people in your depot for the whole evening except yourself. You must stay there the whole time. Do you follow me so far?"

"I have no problem with any of that. I've done that many a time," said Arjan.

"You need to know no more than that for the time being, except you must expect to leave your depot with the container later that evening to catch the 3:00 a.m. ferry from Zeebrugge. The shipping agent will make the booking arrangements. Just tell me now the details of your truck registration number, your full business name and address, email and fax number, and commercial licence details."

Arjan dictated these over the phone. Francois then rehearsed them back to him again to check their accuracy. Nothing in writing as far as Arjan was concerned.

"Now you do nothing and say nothing until we call you again. Just ensure your truck is available, fuelled and equipped and ready on 8th January for the pick-up from Antwerp docks, the overnight ferry to the Dover, a drive up to Leicester in the UK Midlands and return back to Aalst on Saturday 10th January. We'll call as soon as the container is here to confirm the schedule, and then again the day before you need to do the run. Your first payment will be delivered to you in cash when you arrive at your depot from the docks on 8th January. The second payment will be delivered to you at your depot on your return from the UK. Is that all understood?"

It all seemed carefully and precisely worked out. Arjan had no queries about what he had been told so far. As far as he was concerned the less he knew the better, and, for that matter, the quicker it was over, the better.

"One last thing, Mr van Buitelaar," said Francois. "We now have a deal. You will appreciate we have nothing in writing. That means we have to trust each other. We will honour our side by giving you a third of the money up front. If you do not honour your side, you will be responsible for the consequences. I need to make it doubly clear that if you breathe a word of this to anyone, my colleagues will show no mercy. I hope you fully accept that."

Arjan felt a cold chill run down his spine. He knew he was dealing with ruthless people. But he was no fool. He knew what he had to do. He knew how to do it. He did have their mobile phone numbers. If things did go pear-shaped, as a last resort, he could call in the police, admit his folly, and in these days of modern technology they should be able to trace these guys and their set-up. He was prepared to take the risk. He had cleared the logic in his own mind earlier that morning. No turning back now. He was a grown man. And the freedom and life fulfilment that some of his frightened passengers might discover would compensate fractionally for all that his darling daughter had never enjoyed.

"OK, all understood. You can count on me. I'll wait to hear from you."

The ephemeral Francois disappeared again into the ether. Arjan took some deep breaths and walked out into his depot yard. He had much to think about. But, for the present, his emotions would reconcentrate on his daughter and how he was going to make time to get over to Haarlem for the funeral, and how he would conduct himself with the relatives and acquaintances that he would meet up with again there. It would be a difficult time. But he had no doubts that the very least he could do now was to be with his daughter on her last lonely journey, and he would shed more desperate tears for her as she travelled on so alone, so cold, so frightened, and so sad.

Chapter 38

Germany - July 2003

If anyone had asked Nina before she left Moldova what her expectations were, she would have been hard pressed to articulate them. Her impressions of the West were derived from television and films, and from the sort of people she had met in the course of her hotel work. The massive Frankfurt Airport, the glitzy shops in the arrival lounges, the journey along the German autobahn, the streams of elegant cars and huge trucks, the smooth efficiency of everything – all this, though dreamlike, was not unexpected. But when they turned off the main thoroughfare into the Koblenz suburbs, something was different.

Nina had difficulty in putting her finger on it. Yes, she expected clean streets, well-tended gardens, smart houses, trees and parks – they slid past, all neat and tidy, as Gerd confidently navigated the route to her hotel. He had left the autobahn and was approaching the city from the south heading for the Moselweiss district sandwiched between the confluence of the river Moselle and the mighty Rhine. Suddenly she registered what was so unfamiliar. There were so few people. By Chisinau standards it was like a ghost town.

It was mid-afternoon, a lovely summer's day, but the pavements in these sprawling suburbs were almost deserted. Occasionally there was a lone young mother pushing her baby along in a pushchair, and then a solitary old man laboriously inching his way along the pavement behind a zimmer frame. Here and there a few people were waiting at bus stops, but all so different from Moldova. There, people were everywhere at all times of day, even in the villages and towns. People walking - walking from here to there and back again, women shopping at makeshift stalls along the streets, men congregated in groups at every street corner smoking, passing the time of day, pontificating on the world's problems, long queues at bus stops, children playing on patches of bare ground kicking battered footballs or riding homespun go-carts, teenagers lounging in groups at the base of the tenement blocks - in short, Koblenz seemed bereft of life compared with Chisinau.

"Where are the people?" she asked.

Gerd seemed surprised at her question. "People? What people? Everyone go work in day. Children in school." Nina absorbed the information wistfully. So this is what it's like when everyone has a job. It was something she had never expected.

Gerd turned the car into Gulser Strasse and slowed down to drive through a small archway into a hotel forecourt – Hotel Christina. There were two stars beside the name above the entrance. Three other cars were parked outside. The reception desk was small and neat. A middle-aged woman with dyed blond hair, its roots betraying its natural mousy grey colour, acknowledged their arrival. Her thick red lipstick had been too generously applied, and the tightness of her trousers and blouse betrayed her losing battle with weight control. The number of extravagant rings on her fingers suggested an unsettled matrimonial life. Nina absorbed all this while Gerd talked to her in rapid German. Then he spoke to Nina.

"Your room number is 34. You must give passport to lady, please."

Nina handed over her precious document. In exchange the lady gave her a plastic card, looking much like a credit card. She looked at it quizzically.

"Your room key," explained Gerd. Nina had never seen a key like that before. "Tomorrow, the lady give you passport again." There was more conversation in German.

"The lady say you eat breakfast on ground floor seven o' clock to nine o' clock in morning. Hotel not serve food at lunch or dinner."

He picked up her case and they took the compact silent lift to the third floor. There were six rooms leading off the corridor. Gerd showed her how to use the plastic card to unlock number 34. A green light blinked for a few seconds. Gerd turned the knob, and the door opened into a dark room, heavy curtains closing out the strong sunlight. Nina tried to switch on the light. It didn't work. Gerd put the plastic card in the security slot on the wall near the door. Then the lights came on. Another lesson learned. A large double bed filled most of the room, and on the desk a television set had suddenly burst into life with gentle music and a green screen displaying "*Wilkommen, Fraulein Snegur*". On her left was a gleaming bathroom of polished chrome and spotless white tiles. Gerd hoisted her suitcase onto the low table and gave her a big hug.

"I show you everything," he said. "Bathroom first, here is shampoo, and soap, this for dry your hair." He explained how the shower worked, and translated the words on the array of bottles in the wicker basket into English as best he could. From there into the main room again.

"Television, many programmes. You like films - OK, I pay. No problem." He demonstrated how to operate the remote control.

Then he opened the refrigerator, packed solid with all manner of drinks. "If you want drink, you take here. If you like tea or coffee, you make water hot here." He showed her where to plug in the electric kettle.

This was a modest hotel room compared with what Nina had seen in films, but by Chisinau standards it was sumptuous. For her it was perfect. She flung her arms around Gerd and kissed him passionately. "Everything very good. I very happy here."

They opened the curtains and the late-afternoon sun flooded into the room. Above the rooftops to the west, the river Moselle reflected like silver through the thin net drapes that protected their privacy. As she clung tightly to him, Nina registered the subtle change in roles. In Chisinau, she would visit him in his hotel room. Now he was a visitor in hers. It was a new sensation, and sufficient to justify her taking the initiative. She slid his jacket from his shoulders, undid his tie and pulled it through his collar. One by one she unloosed the buttons of his shirt as she felt his hands reciprocally uncoupling her belt and trouser zip. They lay on the bed and feverishly removed the last of their garments till their naked bodies were at last free to lock into each other unfettered. It had been some months since their last encounter and the urgency of Gerd's desire was contagious. He stroked and kissed her all over. His welcome fingers penetrated deep into her, while she caressed him. All too soon he was at his climax. He clung to her even more fiercely.

"*Schon, sehr schon* – beautiful, beautiful, thank you – thank you. So schon," he breathed adoringly into her ear.

Nina's previous experience was sufficient to be reassured that a man of his age and virility would soon be ready again and keen for more measured lovemaking. They had been in the room for barely fifteen minutes. He would surely want to stay for another hour or more. This was the moment they had both waited for for months. Nina had made love many times before. But in the Chisinau hotels it was for money. And with Viktor, her boyfriend, it was the natural expression of their love and friendship. But with Gerd it was for the unabashed joy of it. Her body yearned to engage with him, to feel him impaled deep inside her. She respected and trusted him. He was handsome and accomplished. She knew he cherished their time together. He had opened new experiences for her. She was prepared to give him whatever he wanted; she knew whatever she gave, she received reciprocally from him her own deep fulfilment.

As they lay together, she continued her caresses. When he had recovered his hardness, she knelt over him, slipped a contraceptive over the bulbous head of his penis, and guided it into her. Then she took control. Unashamed and abandoned she made love to her man– Nina Snegur was alive in every vein of her body and it was great.

In the distance a church clock sounded six times. Gerd looked at his watch.

"Sorry - I go now. Tonight I come back eight o'clock. We go dinner in town. OK?"

Nina watched him dress as she lay curled up in the rumpled bedclothes. In Chisinau, she had been the one who dressed while he watched – but today no money was involved, except, of course, he was paying for her hotel. He kissed her on the forehead and took his leave. Nina unpacked, ran a hot bath, brimming with foam from one of the bottles in the wicker basket, and sank luxuriously into its embrace with a beer from the fridge to complement her sense of indulgence. Life felt very good.

The evening went as planned. Nina wore her smartest clothes. They ate in candlelight in a private alcove at a fish restaurant near the centre of the city. The air was warm and balmy and afterwards they sauntered along the river quays on the Deutsches Eck, the point at which the two great rivers joined. It was past eleven when they returned to her hotel. It had been a long eventful day. It hardly seemed possible she had been in Chisinau that morning.

She had been awake now for almost twenty hours. Surges of tiredness were dragging over her. Would Gerd be wanting more lovemaking tonight? Would she be able to stay awake? And what of tomorrow? Nina felt so sleepy it was hard to get her mind round these questions.

"I think you tired now. I come see you tomorrow. Maybe six o'clock? OK?"

Nina was relieved he understood how she felt. He kissed her goodnight at the hotel door. "Have good dreams!" he said, waving from the car as it slid away effortlessly into the night. She remembered how to access her room with the card, momentarily forgot it had to be located in the security slot to activate the electrics, threw off her clothes and sank happily into the sheets with their delicious recent memories.

The curtains had been left open which meant that, despite her sound untroubled sleep, the early-morning light prodded her awake. In any case her biological clock was still a few hours ahead so rising in time for breakfast was no problem. As she showered and dressed for the day, she realised this was the first time in her life she had woken up other than in Moldova. It was strange she should feel so at ease.

The breakfast room was in the converted basement of the hotel. There were about a dozen small circular tables. Two middle-aged businesswomen shared one as they talked animatedly to each other, a cup of coffee in one hand and a cigarette in the other. Most of the rest were occupied by men sitting on their own, all in dark suits, all poring over newspapers, all drinking black coffee and all studiously minding their own business. Nina hesitated as to what to do. Along the wall was a long table laden with all sorts of bread, fruits, cakes, cereals, yoghurts, fruit juices, sliced cheeses and meat, and hot silver dishes steaming with sausages, eggs, bacon and hash browns.

A spotty faced, slight young girl dressed in waitress uniform was moving from table to table refilling cups with coffee or tea from two heavy jugs. She motioned to Nina to help herself and sit down. After her rich dinner last night, Nina was content to take two slices of bread with some cheese, an apple, a glass of orange juice, and some coffee. She chose one of the two remaining free tables.

Another guest came down for breakfast. She watched in some awe as he piled two plates high with food, one with the cold array and the other with the hot. Instead of taking the one remaining table he headed straight for Nina's. She understood not a word he said, but it was clear he wanted to join her. She beckoned him to sit down.

"Sorry – no speak German," she said in English, hoping he would comprehend. He did. In fact his English seemed better than Gerd's judging by the easy way he switched into it. She guessed he was about thirty years old. He had a young man's hairstyle, and unlike the other businessmen in the room, he wore no jacket, just a white open-necked shirt, and dark trousers. He introduced himself as Gunter and chatted on about this and that – where did she come from, what was she doing in Koblenz, how long was she staying, did she have her own car – most of which was incomprehensible to Nina, but when he slowed up and spelled things out more simply, she was able to hold a modicum of dialogue with him. It was fun, and made breakfast more agreeable than it might have been.

They were finishing their coffee when the crunch came. "Maybe you come to eat with me tonight?" he asked.

"Very sorry – thank you. I go with friend tonight."

"Then what do you do today? Maybe we meet in town for a drink sometime?"

Nina felt she was being cornered but knew all she had to do was to keep saying "no". Then the idea dawned on her. She raced through in her mind how she could use this young man. He was unknown to Gerd – a bonus. He could speak German and English. He knew Koblenz. He wanted to be friendly to her. Nina on the other hand did not know Koblenz, could not understand nor speak German, but needed someone to help her plan her exit route to Brussels, someone who could be trusted not to tell Gerd. It all added up. Here was her chance.

"Maybe we take lunch together in city?" she suggested. The young man beamed.

"OK, where do we meet?" he asked.

"Maybe at the big train station? You know it?"

"Sure I know it," he said. "But it's a big place. You have to go to the treffpunkt – it's in the middle. It's the place everyone meets. He wrote it carefully in big letters on one of the paper serviettes.

HAUPT BAHNHOF – TREFFPUNKT. 13:00UHR.

"How I find big station, please?" she asked. Gunter held up his hand and motioned her to wait a moment. He disappeared to the reception desk and returned quickly with a guide to Koblenz, which he spread between them.

"I give you this plan. You take bus outside hotel on Gulser Strasse. Go to Zentral Platz." He marked it in ink on the map. "Then take any bus to Haupt Bahnhof. Very easy." He wrote down the bus route numbers on the map and gave it to her. "You understand?" She said she did and thanked him for his help.

"Now I must go to work." He stood up, shook her hand, wished her a happy day and went off to do whatever he had to. "*Auf Wiedersehen*!"

Suddenly, she felt very alone. All the other breakfast guests had disappeared one by one while they had talked. Only the timid waitress remained and she was preoccupied with clearing the tables and taking away the leftover food to the kitchen. Most of the cars had filtered out of the carpark. The lipsticked lady still sat at the reception desk, but Nina merited not even a glance from her as she waited for the lift back to her room. What to do now till her lunchtime rendez-vous? While she was at breakfast the maid service had tidied the room. Everything was just so. She flopped on the newly-made bed and flicked on the television. Channel after channel of incomprehensible chatter. She wondered about watching a film, but how would she understand what was happening?

She looked out of the window at the barges in the distance, plying their trade up and down the wide river. How sure of themselves they seemed, heading somewhere with a purpose, confident of their direction and steady in their progress. It was in stark contrast to her mood. Since leaving home she had spoken to only two people, Gerd and Gunter. Somewhere they were out there, but she knew not where, nor what they were doing. Yesterday, her room seemed like paradise, now it seemed more like a prison. It was her only fixed point. Outside these walls she was a stranger. She sat on the bed, tears in her eyes, as she mulled over what she might have expected - not this perhaps, but if not, what? It was a question to which she had no answer except she knew only too well her predicament was entirely of her own making. She had arrived here of her own volition, and the option of flying back to Chisinau using her return ticket next week was still open to her, but that could not be contemplated. Best dry the tears, decide what she should wear for her trip to the city centre, check her money belt and take out what she might need for what she had to do there, and then look forward to her meeting with Gerd again that night. Like the barges on the river, she had set her course and she would stick to it.

She decided to go into the city early, which would give her plenty of time to make mistakes. The precious serviette on which Gunter had printed her instructions stood her in good stead. The buses were clean, comfortable and prompt. Most people seemed able to speak simple English, so her sense of isolation was relieved. She reached the meeting point an hour ahead of herself and sat nearby in a cafe drinking a cappuccino watching the world go by. So much better to be here than moping on her own in her room. Gunter arrived on time, but hot and bothered – such a hectic morning, so many frustrations, none of which she understood, except he was all smiles, and was there with her, and that was what mattered. They ate al fresco at a pizza place. In the vibrant city bathed in sunshine the beer tasted twice as good. Nina bided her time. Gunter had relaxed and was continuing his optimistic chat-up lines. Now was the moment to make her move.

"Please you help me. I go Brussels from Frankfurt on train next week. Maybe you help me get ticket, please?"

"No problem, let's go to the booking office." He paid the restaurant bill and off they went. She explained what she wanted - a single ticket and seat on the train to Brussels from Frankfurt on Monday 14th July 2003 leaving about midday. She remembered what she had gleaned from the internet.

"You want also take train from Koblenz to Frankfurt?" asked Gunter.

"No, my friend take me in car to Frankfurt."

The ticket clerk confirmed that was no problem, and Nina paid over the money for both the ticket and the seat reservation. Gunter showed her how to read the ticket, - the departure time, platform number, carriage number and seat number. It was all so easy. Most important, Gerd would be completely unaware of all this. Her new friend went off to his afternoon's business, wherever, and Nina returned to the hotel, buoyant in her achievement, to relax till Gerd came to her again.

Six o'clock came and went. Where was he? She had found a nature programme on one of the channels and with the sound muted, it helped pass the time, but each minute was dragging more and more as her sense of isolation and dependency bore down on her again. When the phone rang, it startled her. She picked up the receiver tentatively.

"Nina, Gerd here – sorry, big problem with my son. He go in hospital – play football he break his arm. My wife still work so I must stay. Very sorry – I come see you tomorrow. Maybe lunchtime – one o'clock. OK?"

Nina listened in stunned silence.

"Nina, Nina – you hear me? Gerd – so sorry. Very difficult – you understand, I think?"

She did – all too well. An avalanche of understanding swept over her. It was all very clear. She was the optional extra. Family first. Nina tucked away in a non-descript hotel, well out of the way of his real life, ready to be taken out at his whim. She crashed the phone back into its cradle and threw herself on the bed distraught. For ten, maybe fifteen minutes she sobbed uncontrollably into the pillow. Twenty-four hours ago she was on top of the world. Now she felt desolate. All the careful expectant preparations she had made for him – her prettiest underwear, her best perfumes, her trendiest clothes – all useless. Perhaps she should go back to Chisinau after all – at least she had masses of friends there. What good was all this if she was so dependent on one man's convenience? But one thing she was sure about. It made her even more determined to reach Viktor as quick as possible. With him alone lay the prospects of lasting happiness.

She needed a drink. It was already seven o'clock, but the setting sun was still blazing into her room. In the distance the barges were still forging ahead on their steady courses. So would she. First another luxurious bath and a large beer. Then what to do? Go into the city alone to eat – not a good idea. In any case she wasn't too hungry: she had eaten well enough at lunchtime. The crisps, biscuits and nuts supplied by room service would do. They would wash down well with a vodka and tomato juice. She wrapped herself in the white woollen bathrobe hanging in the cupboard, and lay on her bed, smelling deliciously of the bath oils, and flicked through the television channels. Maybe a film? – but she couldn't understand them. What about the adult movies? Not much dialogue there – easy to watch. The alcohol had relaxed her marvellously, but a third vodka would do no harm. Blearily semi-intoxicated she watched explicit erotic scenes she had never seen before. She could not believe these women allowed themselves to be filmed doing such private things. Even so it made her think again of Gerd, and their times together. Already she felt warmer towards him, and understood his dilemma. What could he have done except care for his son? Nina knew in her heart he had done the right thing. She respected him for that. He would be with her tomorrow and they could pick up where they had left off. It was nearly ten o'clock. She had drunk enough and seen enough. The alcohol would act as a sleeping draught. Time to curl up and dream. Tomorrow would take care of itself.

Then came the knock on her door. She half fell out of bed, only then realising how unsteady she was. Perhaps it was room service – even so, better put the chain on the door before opening it. Her lonesome evening was about to dissolve.

Chapter 39

Brussels - December 2003

There was loud hammering on the door. Habib woke startled and disorientated. He had slept soundly and momentarily had difficulty in fixing where he was. The banging stopped as abruptly as it had begun with a shout from outside.

"Time everyone go out!"

The men in the top bunks levered themselves down to the floor. One by one they used the ablution facilities opposite, the light from the corridor relieving the pitch-blackness of their sleeping quarters. Habib and Toci exchanged thoughts.

"Guess we just get up and do the same."

When the three others had finished, they too used the washroom, gathered up their belongings and headed up the rear stairs. At the top, an expressionless woman of Malaysian appearance gesticulated the way they should go down the corridor and out through the back door.

"How we go to city centre?" they asked.

"Take tram at end road. No come back till you sleep."

So that much was clear. They were vagrants in Brussels during the day, but at least they had a bolthole at night. It was 7:30 a.m. The rain had stopped but the weather was still grey and cold. First thing they had to do was fix in their minds the address they had to get back to that night. The tram was at subterranean level, and not difficult to find. They simply followed the tide of early-morning commuters. The few residual Euros in their pockets were sufficient for the fare and within half an hour they were strolling like backpackers in the Grand Place at the heart of the city.

"OK, I think we should get a bite of breakfast first. Then we can change some dollars into Euros," said Habib.

They chose a bustling little restaurant, Cafe Eloise, down one of the pedestrian walkways, and drank deeply of real coffee and sank into warm fresh croissants. The room was snug and smelt sweetly of newly baked bread and pastries. They stretched out their legs under the table and leaned back in their chairs. For the first time in many days they luxuriated with time to relax and enjoy some of life's simple pleasures. Although confident that no-one would understand their Albanian, they talked in hushed tones as they took stock of their situation.

"So we've no choice but to stay here for a few weeks. I've got to earn some money, and quick. I'm running out. We've got to pay Mitch for our beds, and buy food and pay for trams. And still have enough to pay him the final 1,000 Euros to get on the ship," said Habib.

"Too fucking right," replied Toci. "We can't mooch about the city all day with nothing to do. I guess we'd better go separately. See what we can find."

Reluctantly they finished the dregs of their coffee, and made for the nearest Exchange Bureau. They agreed to meet back at Cafe Eloise at midday and compare notes. Habib set off along one of the narrow pedestrianised streets leading off from the central square, lined with restaurants, bars and cafes, many not yet open. It was a relief to see a number were advertising for staff- waiters, waitresses, kitchen hands - on signs outside in three languages "Waiter wanted – apply inside" . Habib approached the first one that was open. He had taken the precaution of shaving that morning. He was wearing his least crumpled shirt and had combed his hair tidily.

"You want waiter. I work very good." He addressed a thin pallid-faced man wearing a waistcoat, pin-striped trousers, and a long white much-splattered apron. A cigarette hung limply from his lower lip. He was rearranging tables and chairs, and sweeping up the remnants of last night's business.

"Parlez-vous francais? Sprechen-sie Deutsch?" came the reply.

"I speak English good. I work hard."

"Waiter speak French and German and English. Maybe you work in kitchen?"

"I very good wash plates. Make all clean."

"Kitchen work 5 Euros an hour. You work lunch and night. Maybe you start today?"

"Yes, very happy start work today. My name is Habib."

"Call me Jan. Come back at 12 hours."

They shook hands and that was that. He retraced his steps back to the Cafe Eloise, bought himself a celebratory cappuccino, and waited for Toci's return. It was still only 10:30 a.m. He might have a long wait, and if Toci didn't get back well before noon, he wouldn't see him for their rendez-vous.

No sign of Toci. That was not his problem, but it was 11:45 a.m. and time to make tracks back to the restaurant. Jan was still there, another cigarette suspended from his lower lip. Habib was ushered through to the kitchen area. He hung his rucksack and anorak on a peg in the corridor, rolled up his sleeves and waited for orders. Steam boiled up from cooking pots. Frying pans sizzled, and the aroma of grilled steaks and fish assailed his nostrils. He had lived on a meagre diet for so long, he craved to sink into one of the heaped plates of food the waiters were delivering at speed to the diners in the restaurant. Dirty plates and cutlery started to pour back and Habib's task accelerated. The commercial dishwashers did most of the work, but loading, unloading and stacking was continuous. The waiters were scraping the leftovers into an evil-smelling garbage chute in the wall of the kitchen. Habib looked enviously at what diners had rejected. How could they leave so much - chips, rice, vegetables, half-eaten pastries? Habib was famished. He spoke to one of the waiters in his faltering English.

"Maybe you leave food on plate. I throw rubbish for you."

The waiter needed no second invitation. They were run off their feet taking orders, clearing and resetting tables, delivering the food to customers and dealing with their complaints, but above all making sure they pocketed the tips from their tables before anyone else might slide off with it. For Habib the extra time and effort of clearing the plates before loading them into the dishwasher was more than compensated by being able to pick up morsels from the leftovers, so much so that after an hour of surreptitious gleaning, his pangs of hunger had been satisfied. By mid-afternoon, the frantic pace was slackening. The stacks of cleaned plates began to mount. The cutlery drawers filled up and by four o'clock the last diners had left, the stoves were all off and a sense of calm after the storm settled over the kitchen. Jan, inseparable from the cigarette grafted onto his lip, came across.

"You work good. Come back seven o'clock. Much work then."

"When you pay me?" asked Habib.

"I pay next time. No come back, no money. You understand." Habib nodded. He had worked four hours. That was 20 Euros, enough to pay his lodgings that night. The rest of any earnings he made later that day were his. Should be at least another 20 Euros. That should pay his way till the ship came. But he really needed more to supplement his much depleted reserve, still secreted in the polythene envelop in his shoe. The immediate problem was how to while away three hours before his next shift began. The Grand Place was milling with people. There were stalls everywhere all decked out in Christmas bunting and glitter. There was a choir on a raised dais at the far end of the square singing seasonal carols. The aroma of roasted chestnuts filled the air. False frost on the Christmas trees glistened in the twinkling lights. It was a warm and exciting place to be, but all Habib wanted was to take the weight off his feet, somewhere to sit down and rest.

He meandered aimlessly, sat down for a few minutes on some stone steps but they were penetratingly cold, so he moved on again. Then past the open doors of a church. There was some sort of service going on inside, and people were coming and going. He mingled inconspicuously with the arrivals and found a secluded seat against a pillar near the back. It was warmer inside. The music and singing were soothing even if incomprehensible. He leaned back, put his legs on the chair in front and closed his eyes. Not ideal, but this was as good a place as any to while away the time.

Someone was shaking his shoulder. Blearily he tried to gather his thoughts. He must have fallen asleep. A man in long black robes and a white collar was addressing him in a language he didn't know. He looked at his watch. The church bell was sounding. It was seven o'clock. Panic – he must get back to the restaurant speedily. He smiled awkwardly at the one who had disturbed him, thankful that he had not been allowed to sleep longer. He raced back. Pale-face with the omnipresent cigarette was arranging serviettes in glasses on the tables. Early diners were already eating.

"You late – not good. Lose one hour pay. If you no come, you no good to me."

"Sorry, I work hard now. I not come late next time. Too many people in Brussels," replied Habib rather lamely. Then it was into the kitchen and non-stop action for four hours.

"OK, I give you pay for morning work now. Lose one hour. I give you 15 Euros. Tomorrow I pay tonight work. You come midday. OK?"

Habib had no choice. He nodded agreement. His priority now was to get the tram back to his lodging as quick as possible. He was exhausted, and it was no comfort that he had to be out again next morning as soon as dawn broke. The back door to his temporary home was locked. It was after midnight. He knocked gently, not wanting to wake everyone, but desperate that someone should let him in. No response. He knocked more firmly. "Please, please come!" he pleaded silently to himself. It was pitch-dark, cold and dank. Uncollected refuse bags lent a malodorous smell to the night air. His sense of alienation and aloneness bore down on him. "Please, please let me in!"

A dim light appeared above the frosted pane of glass at the top of the door. "Thank God," he whispered. The Malaysian lady opened the door, and shone a torch in his face.

"What you want?"

"I sleep here," said Habib desperately.

"What you name?" He told her.

"You no pay last night!"

So that was the problem. He hadn't realised it was pay as you go. He proffered her the 20 Euros. A day's hard work, and he was worse off that when he had started. But at least she took the money, and at last he was inside. He found their sleeping cell and shone his torch fleetingly to see if Toci was there. He was. That was a comfort. He slumped onto his bunk. Not the time to talk. They would catch up with each other in the morning. He tried to take stock. The next few weeks would be hard, but he had to keep going. He began calculating his money prospects.

Bang, bang – someone was thumping on the door in the middle of the night. He turned over and buried his head in the pillow to drown the intrusive noise. Then he heard the shout.

"Time you go out."

Surely not! He shone his torch on his watch. It was already seven o'clock. The sleepers on the top bunks lurched down and into the washroom. Habib leaned across to Toci.

"Toci, how are you? How did you get on? Did you get any work?"

"Where the hell did you get to? I came back to meet you - waited an hour until I got bored. Then went off to try to find some work. Bloody difficult. Don't know the language. Wish I could speak English like you. Spent all day farting about. Completely fed up. Came back here about six and just tried to sleep. What the fuck should I do? I need the money."

Habib had been keen to tell him about his success in finding a job, but that would have been no comfort to Toci.

"Maybe you should come with me today. I'll try to find some work for you. I'll speak English for you."

They retraced the previous day's routine - wash and brush up, out the backdoor, catch the tram, and into Cafe Eloise for their morning breakfast. Then a mooch in the city till midday. Habib made sure he wasn't late again. The cigarette man was there as usual doing his jobs.

"Hello Mr Jan. I have friend want some work."

"No more job here. Maybe you go other place."

Toci had registered the message without the need for Habib to translate.

"Look Toci. Meet me here at four o'clock, and we'll go off somewhere together to see if we can find something."

Toci took his disconsolate leave and Habib re-engaged with his, now familiar, kitchen duties. Jan was as good as his word and paid the 20 Euros owed from last night without any further quibble.

When Toci returned they trawled along the alleyways looking for somewhere for him to work. It didn't take long. Habib translated. Kitchen work. Same rate of pay. Same hours. Start tonight. They went off to celebrate at their place of good cheer, the Cafe Eloise.

Work, travel, sleep, washing themselves and their clothes, and searching out cheap ways to eat and drink filled up their days. Habib introduced Toci to the afternoon respite opportunity in the church. As Christmas neared, the excitement and bustle in the Grand Place became even more palpable. The beneficial spin-off for Habib was increasing demands on him to work longer hours. Mind-numbingly boring, but it was only for a few weeks and he knew he could tolerate that. The big bonus was that his average income each day left him about 30 Euros clear, which he stashed away miserly in the polythene envelopes in his shoes.

It was the weekend after Christmas when the Malaysian landlady unexpectedly accosted them in the early morning as they were about to leave for their Sunday chores.

"Mr Mitch want see you today five o'clock. You bring money."

"OK – no problem, we come back in afternoon." Habib replied on behalf of them both.

The day's work now had a new focus, and the hours dragged by more tediously than usual as Habib waited impatiently for their rendez-vous and contemplated what Mitch would have to say. There would be no time for resting mid-afternoon in the church today. They returned well in time. The landlady ushered them into a room on the top floor. The curtains were tightly closed. There was no carpet. A solitary unshaded light bulb lit the room contents. There were five upright chairs and a scratched wooden table at which Mitch was sitting, leafing through some documents.

"Very nice to see you again. Hope everything is happy for you. The ship is coming. You pay $1,000. Then I tell you what you do."

The early morning conversation with the landlady, even though minimal, had prepared them. They had the money ready and paid it over. Habib pondered again how vulnerable they were to being double-crossed, but they had no choice. This guy had kept his word so far, and that was some comfort.

"OK, you listen good. No write anything. Must remember. Thursday 8th January. Be here ready to go. 8:00 p.m. You take plenty warm clothes. One small bag. No come - no problem, but you not get money back. You tell no-one. This all secret. Big, big trouble for you if you talk. You understand?"

So that was it. Eleven days. Then the next crucial stage – crossing the sea to the UK. For five years Habib had dreamed of this. Now he was on the brink. That night he worked as though he was walking on air. This was the final countdown.

Chapter 40

Buitelaar - December 2003

The day of the funeral it was raining hard – sheeting mercilessly across Belgium and the Netherlands from the cold grey reaches of the North Sea. There was no relief in the downpour all morning as Arjan drove the 200 kilometres northwards to Haarlem. He located the crematorium, parked his car and hunched himself against the elements to walk to a nearby cafe for a tired slice of pizza, some strong coffee and a cigarette.

Funerals are never easy, especially for those not used to religious occasions. The clothes, the rituals, the smells, the location, the motley assembly of half-known faces, the incongruous black limousines, the wreaths with their cryptic sad farewells, the unfamiliar hymns to tunes half-remembered, all lend a sense of unreality to something that is intensely personal and poignant.

Arjan was seated in the chapel beside his ageing parents ten minutes before the ceremony began. His mother was weeping copiously into her handkerchief. His father, suffering from shortness of breath as a result of emphysema caused by years of chain-smoking, sat stoically upright, staring ahead, grey-faced and wordless. Across the aisle were Margreet and her partner, and beside her, his son, Kries, looking ill, pale, ear-ringed, and remote. There were nine other people sprinkled around the stark polished pews. Some nondescript taped church music was playing softly in the background. The two lonely wooden coffins, mother and baby - his daughter and grand-daughter -rested on the pedestal at the front. The fresh flowers in two vases either side supplied the only beauty around.

The pews were brown, the coffins were brown, the floor was brown, the walls were grey, the windows gave onto grey scudding clouds and rain, the cortege cars were black, their funeral suits and dresses were black. The minister matched the solemnity in his black cassock. The meagre congregation stood as he led the last rites – "dust to dust, ashes to ashes" – "a sure and certain hope of resurrection" – at least the religious intonations gave a certain dignity and conclusion to such tragic, hopeless lives.

The soft hum from the motor under the plinth activated the rollers and they watched impotently as the coffins slid gently and peaceably from their view, brocade curtains closing automatically as they passed out of view – no-one daring to visualise their final holocaust moments in the furnace only metres from where they stood. The strains of Beethoven's Ninth symphony filled the chapel from the high-level speakers. The mourners exited through the doors at the far end so as not to interfere with those arriving for the next cremation scheduled for half an hour later. They examined the wreaths with exaggerated interest, read and re-read the last messages, embarrassedly shook hands with each other, exchanged a few pleasantries, said how sad a day it was and shed more tears, and then filtered away in separate cars to pick up again the pieces of the other worlds in which they all lived.

It was all rather grotesque but there was no other option. The rituals were done and last respects paid. History could not be rewritten. Things were not meant to be like this, but they were, and no amount of ranting or raging would bring Emma back, still less transform her life into something lovely and rewarding.

Afternoon tea at his parents home allowed opportunity for Arjan to tell them his news. They seemed glad to hear of his business progress, hoped he could get over to see them more often, especially at Christmas. He promised he would try. Affectionately they remembered Emma as a little girl, but they drew an inarticulate veil over her later life. They could not conceive it and did not want to know. To try only made the pain of the loss of their granddaughter more difficult to bear.

They gave him a homemade cake as he left. The rain had slackened and the journey back to Aalst was easier and more tranquil. Arjan's thoughts steadily refocused on what lay ahead. The help he would give to desperate people seeking a new way of life would be a simple compensatory memorial to his lost daughter. There was no more he could offer her now.

Two weeks later the call came. It was the voice of oriental Mitch on the ansaphone.

"Message for Mr van Buitelaar. Mitch calling. I call you again six o'clock tonight."

Click. That was all. The call had come in at ten o'clock in the morning while Arjan was at the docks. He had picked up the message on his return. The phone was located in his portacabin office in the haulage yard he rented. Alongside was the warehouse that could accommodate two full-length trucks. A middle-aged lady from the town helped out with the paperwork three mornings a week, but on Thursdays she was not in the office.

It was three days before the shortest day of the year as Arjan sat alone waiting for the phone to ring. Outside it was dark and quiet, the stars bright in the early evening sky. It was like waiting for an exam result, a sense of nervous anticipation, steadied by long draws on a cigarette held in two fingers of one hand, gripped by the other, positioned directly in front of his face by means of his two elbows firmly planted on the desk. There was a distant drone of traffic on the night air. Apart from that the only sound came from the electric clock on the wall flicking the time forward second by second. Despite all his preparedness, the phone startled him when it rang. He could feel a clammy sweatiness in his palm as he held the receiver to his ear.

"Mr van Buitelaar? Ah, good! Mitch speaking. How are you? Hope everything good for you. I think you happy to know sea container now at Antwerp. No problem. Customs say ready for transit after New Year holiday. We get papers ready for you pick up at docks Thursday 8th January. I ring you again day before check everything OK."

Arjan listened and acknowledged what had been said. No problem as far as he was concerned.

"Mr van Buitelaar, we got one small change. No go Zeebrugge now. Instead you go to Calais. Better that way – less time on sea you know. Zeebrugge three and half hours – if sea rough, not good for passengers. Calais only one and half hours. Much quicker. I think you drive Calais easy from your garage. Calais ferry at 4:30 a.m."

Arjan did some quick mental calculations. Calais was another 100 kilometres or so further than Zeebrugge, but it was a later ferry than they had said before, so he would have no trouble getting there in time if he left his depot about midnight. Mitch confirmed that everything would be ready for him to leave at that time. There were no frontier customs in the Shengen area and there was so much trucking traffic passing through Calais, it was doubtful if they would have time to give his container more than a cursory glance. It was at the Dover end where examination might be more thorough, but that was the same whether he went via Zeebrugge or Calais.

"I think you still got my mobile number. Any problem, you phone me. If not, I speak again on Wednesday, 7th January. I wish you a merry Christmas, Mr van Buitelaar. Hope all your dreams come true!"

That was that. Mitch evaporated again into the atmosphere. Presumably, out there, he was beavering away with a phalanx of associates bringing the whole operation to a coordinated climax, but as far as Arjan was concerned, he had nothing more to do for two weeks except bide his time. He grabbed his coat, switched off the lights, set the burglar alarm, though there was precious little to steal, and headed off to the nearest bar. He already felt more relaxed but a few beers with some mates would help him wind down completely.

Notwithstanding Mitch's enthusiastic best wishes, it was going to be a bleak Christmas break for Arjan. He did spend some time at his parents, but conversation was stilted. The time not eating or sleeping was spent watching television. Christmas is really for families, but when families have disintegrated, the festivities take on a counterfeit facade, strained frivolity, false bonhomie, and contrived enthusiasm, while at bottom the residual participants are really more interested in getting it over quickly and returning to normality.

Arjan spent the New Year break with a few trucking mates back in Aalst in a mild but continuous alcoholic haze. Although it left him rather thick-headed, he had eaten well, spent a good deal of time in bed - not always on his own - and felt pretty rested. Over breakfast on the morning of Monday 5th January, as he listened to the news of outcome of the Georgian Election – the new president there had a Dutch wife, so he must be a good bloke - he focussed his thoughts on what was to be a watershed week. By this time next week he should be 15,000 richer and, assuming things worked smoothly, there were prospects of more to come. A venture such as this every three months would solve all his cash-flow problems and stabilise his business until the world economic situation got onto a more even keel. As all the New Year greeting cards enjoined, 2004 could well be a prosperous year. He viewed the prospects with a mixture of apprehension and optimism.

Chapter 41

Germany/Brussels - July 2003

"Gunter," Nina exclaimed. "Why you come?" It was of course a stupid question. Even in her befuddled state she didn't need two guesses why an eligible young man should call on an unattached young lady in her hotel room late at night.

"Maybe we take a drink together before you go to bed?" he asked cheerily.

"I think I drink too much," she replied as she took the chain off the door. He had his hands full of small bottles and cans from his fridge.

"You have good time with your friend tonight?" he asked.

"He no come. I no go for dinner."

"So you take no food! - you must be hungry. Perhaps I bring you a Chinese meal. Do you like that?" Nina nodded. The global Chinese takeaway revolution had reached even Chisinau, so she was familiar with that, and it might not be a bad thing to try to soak up some of the alcohol coursing round her veins.

"I come back in quick time."

Nina was still struggling to think straight. She ought to put some more clothes on before he returned. But inebriated logic told her that was unnecessary. If Gunter went back to his room as soon as they had eaten, she would have to take them off again to go to bed. On the other hand if he stayed and they made love, she would also have to take them off again. So why bother putting them on – the bathrobe covered her nakedness sufficient for the needs of the moment.

He was back in twenty minutes. They ate with plastic forks from the silver foil platters, and washed it down with more beer. Nina was hungrier than she'd realised. He gathered the remnants into a polythene bag, tied it tightly to mask any lingering smells and poured her another drink. He was solicitous, energetic, good-looking and forever smiling. Nina knew she was melting but she no longer cared. There was only one chair in the room and Gunter had occupied that while they ate. She lay on her bed. He kicked off his shoes and lay down beside her.

Next morning the church clock was striking ten as she surfaced at last. Her head throbbed. That was nothing new. She was alone in bed. She had only the vaguest recollections of the night's events. She just hoped he had used a contraceptive. She remembered he had put the light on at some stage and left in the early hours. Pulling herself together was now the most pressing priority: a glass of water and two aspirins first, then a shower as cool as she could bear it, then large cups of black coffee. Open the windows wide to remove any residual odours of the night before and more glasses of cold water. No sign of room service – she had slept through that - so tidy the room and make the bed herself. Gerd was due at one o'clock. All being well she should be recovered enough by then to avoid betraying last night's aberration. It had been fun while it lasted, but there was always the price to pay the morning after.

She needn't have worried. Gerd was too preoccupied with having let her down. He called her from reception. That was good. He wouldn't be coming up to the room, at least not yet. Somehow it seemed tainted with guilt and Nina was worried he would pick up those vibrations. He greeted her with a bouquet and abject apologies, which she comprehended without understanding his words.

"I fix everything. My son OK now. He rest at home. Play on his computer. I stay with you all afternoon. We take ride in my car. OK?"

That was fine for Nina. It gave her more time to recover and other things to talk about. After half an hour's drive the river Rhine appeared. They were at the ferry terminus called Boppard. They had a beer and snack lunch at one of the riverside restaurants and then spent two effortless hours cruising the river in an old fashioned Rhine steamer. They passed a castle on a towering rock in the middle of the river. It was like one she'd seen in a fairytale book. Gerd told her it was famous. Nina revelled in it all. By the time they had returned to the hotel, last night's adventure had faded enough for her to be able to abandon herself with Gerd in their own familiar ways. She was sure he suspected nothing.

The week unwound itself into an agreeable routine. Gerd visited each day, sometimes for lunch, sometimes for dinner. Gunter joined her for breakfast whenever she was up in time for it. He continued his happy chat-up lines, but Nina had decided where her priorities lay and studiously avoided any repeat performances. She spent the hours between Gerd's visits by taking buses in and out of the city and ambling round the city streets to soak in the atmosphere and marvel at all the shops. She had money so was able to treat herself to costume jewellery and clothes that would be the envy of her Chisinau friends, and hopefully Viktor too would approve. And all the time, she was counting down the days to when she would leave. Koblenz was a great adventure. It was great to be with Gerd. Gunter had been an unexpected bonus. But from Monday onwards she would be in uncharted territory. She looked forward to it with excitement and trepidation.

It came all too quickly. On Sunday evening Gerd had difficulty in making excuses to be away from his family, so their farewell meal together and amorous good-byes were attenuated. Nina didn't mind too much. She had to pack and be ready for an early start next morning. She was out of her room by 6:30 a.m. and managed a quick breakfast before Gerd arrived. He settled the bill while she stood aside in the foyer. Then off out of Koblenz in the early traffic heading for the Frankfurt autobahn.

Only then did she begin to focus hard on how she could orchestrate her final goodbye to Gerd pretending she would board the flight back to Chisinau, but actually giving him the slip, so she could get a bus back to the Haupt Bahnhof to catch her train to Brussels. She hoped he would just drop her off at the departures terminal. Then she would be on her own. The problem was going to be if he insisted on accompanying her to the check-in desk. Her suitcase would be checked through and then she would be committed to the flight. She had to avoid that, but her experience of airport terminals was limited. It was difficult to know what other way she could devise to prevent him from going with her to the check-in. Fingers crossed, he would just drop her off.

He didn't.

"I come with you to check-in – better if I carry your case," he said as he drove into the airport multi-storey short stay carpark. Nina had to think quickly.

"I want kiss you goodbye. Maybe better in car. Hard for me – I think I cry at check-in."

Gerd got the message and drove to the highest level where there were fewest cars. He parked nose-in so they were as private as possible, switched off the engine and took her in his arms for the last time. They had a last fifteen minutes together. Gerd was wearing a short-sleeved shirt and light coloured summer trousers. Nina was more heavily clad in jeans and leather jacket for her journey.

"Maybe I give you one more pleasure?" she said as her hands loosened his belt and slipped into his trousers. He needed no persuasion. He was already hard and regretting their week of unrestricted lovemaking was ending too soon. He pressed his lips fiercely against hers and hugged her tightly as she brought him to his climax. He was all but oblivious as Nina ensured his ejaculation spread itself profusely over the front of his trousers. He reclined his seat and lay back while Nina wiped her hands on a tissue and mopped him up. But her plan had worked. His linen trousers were extensively bespattered with the damp evidence of her ministrations.

"I so sorry," she said, "I think it dry soon." Gerd surveyed the damage. To be seen in public like this was going to be acutely embarrassing. It would dry in half an hour or so and he could always go home and change and take the trousers to the cleaners. But the prospect of standing in a queue at the check-in desk in a busy airport for the next half-hour in such telltale trousers was no longer on the agenda.

"I think it difficult for me to go to airport check-in now," he said, smiling at her and gesticulating towards the problem.

"No problem," said Nina, equally happy. "I think you have nice souvenir of me now!" She laughed and gave him another hug.

He stayed in the car while she fetched her case. Their last long lingering kiss was through the car window. "I wish you good journey. I hope I come Moldova again soon."

"That very good. I hope the same." They waved till she was out of sight, and then she was free.

To keep up appearances, she headed first for the departure terminal. She had about three hours to catch her train. Give Gerd enough time to clear the airport precincts. Then to the information desk. They spoke perfect English, of course. Yes, there were buses into the city centre every fifteen minutes. She could buy her bus ticket there. They all stopped at the main railway station. The efficiency of the German transport system ensured she arrived at the station an hour ahead of the scheduled departure to Brussels. Time for a bite to eat and then onto the train to find her reserved seat. There it was, a ticket attached to the headrest matching the ticket Gunter had fixed for her. She stacked her case and sank into the window seat with a huge sigh of relief. All had gone so well. Now she could relax and let the train whisk her northwards towards her goal. What would happen in Brussels she was not sure, but that could wait. Now she would sit back and enjoy the unfolding German landscape as the train hurtled her towards Belgium.

She must have dozed off. She had been far away in her dreams, back in her childhood in Moldova, playing with her school friends in the fields behind her father's garden plot. It was all happy. And then they had all run away and left her alone, and she couldn't find her house again and it was getting dark and the rain was pouring down, and she was crying for her mummy. She woke with a start.

It was indeed pouring with rain, beating hard against the carriage window, the landscape had now changed dramatically, windswept and dark, even though it was still mid-afternoon. Congruent with the weather, Nina's mood had also darkened. Her friends were far gone and it was now almost exactly a year since they had buried her mother. Unhappy plaintive cries to her, asleep or awake, could never again summon her consoling presence. It was only a week since she had left Moldova. It felt much more. It had all seemed so simple then. Now there was a fearful emptiness ahead. The only thing that gave her any bearing by which to steer was a scrappy piece of paper, given to her by Stefan's unsavoury contacts in Chisinau, with the precious address in Brussels. The vulnerability of her predicament closed in on her. Koblenz and its joys seemed not hours, but a lifetime away.

Crowds of people were milling in every direction as she stood forlornly in the forecourt of the Brussels Central station. No cheery Gerd to greet her here. Just hundreds of expressionless faces concentrating on their own intents. The information desk might help? Nina stood in the queue waiting her turn. A greasy haired man in the glass cubicle spoke rapidly to her in a language she couldn't understand.

"Maybe you speak English. I show you address I go." She proffered her scrap of paper.

"Information here is for trains. You want train?"

"Maybe train? How I go this place please?"

"That's in Brussels. You take bus or taxi. Sorry - only train information here." He motioned her away impatiently so he could deal with the rest of the queue.

Outside the station, rain was still lashing down. The skies were leaden and thunder rumbled in the distance. Nina waited disconsolately under the forecourt awning until the downpour eased a little. Dragging her case through the puddles of water everywhere, she approached the taxi rank. The driver opened his window a fraction. She showed him her piece of paper. Another incomprehensible response.

"Please I speak English little. You take me here?" she almost pleaded with him.

"No problem –long journey, big price."

Nina had no choice. She opened the door and struggled to get herself and her case out of the wet into the snug plush interior. She watched as the meter charges clicked up inexorably. It took twenty-five minutes to negotiate the inner-city traffic and arrive at the nondescript northern suburb. She paid the driver 55 Euros. The rain had eased but all around the buildings looked grey and unwelcoming under the overcast skies in the late afternoon. The streets were almost deserted. She tentatively rang the bell at the door of the address she had been given. No response. Her insipient feelings of panic began to burgeon. She was totally alone. She had no plan B. If this didn't work out, what could she do? No-one knew her. She couldn't speak the language. Her return ticket to Chisinau had expired. In any case she would have to get back to Frankfurt for that. Why had she embarked on this foolhardy adventure? At that moment there was nowhere she would rather be than at home. But it was the home of her memories she yearned for. And she knew there was no way back to that.

She kept pressing the doorbell. It was a four-storey house in a long terrace block. She could see a light in the top room. Apart from that, no sign of life at all. Maybe the house next door could help? She tried their doorbell. An elderly woman, tightly wrapped in a shawl despite the time of year, with lank grey hair falling either side of her crenulated face opened the door a fraction, Nina tried to explain her problem in faltering English. The response was a few incomprehensible words and the door banged shut in her face unceremoniously.

Maybe the other neighbour could help? This time an unshaven young man answered, clad in a stained T-shirt and tatty jeans with tattoos on his forearms. He was marginally more helpful, and had a modicum of English.

"Yeah – guys next door maybe sleep. You wait - they come and go. Come inside – you wait here. Have a drink! You look nice girl."

Nina dearly wanted to get off the street, but accepting this unknown young man's invitation was far too risky. She thanked him and made to go off and come back later. But there was nowhere to go. She walked to the end of the block, found as much shelter as she could from the swirling wind and intermittent showers, sat on her suitcase, put up her umbrella, made sure she could still see the front door of the address she had been given, and waited. She felt utterly desolate, like a street-corner vagrant, but what else could she do? Her tears fell untended onto the wet pavement. A harsh gust of wind turned her umbrella inside out and fractured the fragile frame. She no longer cared. Her leather jacket kept her top dry, but the drizzle gradually soaked her jeans as the minutes ticked by desperately slowly. Every so often a lone walker passed by, huddled against the elements, giving her no more than a curious fleeting glance.

After an hour and a half her uncomfortable vigil was at last rewarded. A woman laden with shopping had put a key in the door and entered the crucial address. Nina raced back down the road and quickly pressed the bell again. The woman reappeared.

"Please I look for Mitch. He live here I think?" she asked anxiously. The woman looked vaguely oriental, but at least she too had a smattering of English.

"Why you want Mr Mitch?"

She showed her the piece of paper. "I think he help me go to England."

"Why you say that? Mr Mitch - he respectable man. Who tell you come here?"

"Please, please, maybe I talk to Mr Mitch. Maybe he understand?"

"Why you think he want see you? He no want trouble with police."

Nina could contain her despair and frustration no longer. She began sobbing uncontrollably. The woman stood there unmoved. Inside a telephone rang. Would she terminate their conversation?

"You come wait inside – I answer phone"

A glimmer of hope. The door closed behind her. Nina stood at last, albeit bedraggled and forlorn, inside the address that had been her goal since leaving Chisinau. It was a small step forward, but at least it was forward. The telephone call was over – Nina had not understood a word, but the outcome seemed to be that she needed to answer more questions.

"What your name? Where you come from? Where you live in Belgium? You got some money? Why you go England?"

Nina answered circumspectly. Happy to tell the lady her name and where she came from, and that she had arrived in Belgium only today, but she was deliberately vague about how much money she had secreted away.

"OK, you wait. Mr Mitch he come see you in one hour." Another small advance. Nina sat in the lobby and took in her surroundings - sparse furnishings, a wall mirror, a Chinese wall hanging, a polished wooden staircase leading to the upper floors, and a smell of curry lingering from somewhere, and not much else. But she had at least escaped from the inclement weather and was beginning to dry out.

Mitch arrived. He too looked oriental, probably originating from Malaysia or somewhere she thought. He shook her hand.

"Me Mitch - I think you Nina from Moldova. Welcome. You want go to England, yes? That very difficult. Cost much money."

Nina told him she could get the money – she didn't tell him she had it already – but she wanted to know how soon she could go. Her whole plan depended on getting to England quickly so she could spend time with Viktor before they made their way back to Moldova together.

"Very difficult. Must wait for ship. You stay in Brussels. We send message when we get ship for you."

"How long you think - two days, three days, maybe one week?" she asked.

He shrugged his shoulders and raised his arms wide in a gesture of uncertainty.

"I not know how long, maybe one week, maybe one month, maybe three months. We must find special ship, special time."

Nina looked at him in disbelief. No-one had ever intimated to her there might be this sort of delay. Equally she had never thought to ask, because she had somehow thought it would be like catching a train or plane, just a matter of the next scheduled departure.

"That big problem for me," she said. "I must go England quickly."

"That your problem, Miss Nina, not mine. You got visa, then you take train to London. You no got visa, then Moldova girl need my ship. Where you stay in Brussels?"

For over six months Nina had worked and saved to reach this point. Now it was all dissolving into nothing. A country she didn't know. Languages she couldn't understand. No friends. Nowhere to stay. No idea how long she would be stranded here. The only thread she could cling to was this man Mitch. She had paid $300 to get his name and address. He had to help her. She tried to explain things to him.

"Maybe I give you money you help me go England quickly?" she pleaded.

"You give money. I try find ship. Give me $3,000. OK?"

Nina knew that dollars and Euros were almost on a par, but this would exhaust all the precious reserves she had in her money belt. Flashing through her mind were the hours and hours she had worked the Chisinau hotels for this huge sum of money. Now she was being asked to give it all up to a man she had met just five minutes ago. How could she possibly trust him? It would be madness to do that. But what other options did she have? It was hard to think straight, but the only other choice seemed to give up and use her money to get back home to Moldova, and then what? She couldn't bear to think of that. On the other hand, if a payment in advance to this man could secure her a passage to England in the next week or so, why not? That's why she had come. The risk was enormous, but that was always going to be the case. Sooner or later she was going to have to pay to get across the Channel. Whenever she paid over her money, she was always open to being double-crossed. So she may as well take the risk now. At least she wouldn't have the continuing worry of her money being stolen. Perhaps he might take less?

"I think that too much. Maybe I give $2,000 now and $1,000 when ship come?"

"Dollars OK. You got money now?" She turned away from him and opened her money belt as discreetly as she could. She counted twenty $100 bills and handed them to him.

"OK, that good. I give you small paper. You trust me. I good man." He gave her a scribbled receipt. "You come with me. I find nice place for you stay."

It was evening but still quite light when they pulled into rue d'Aerschot, near the Gare du Nord. On one side of the road there were the high-level railtracks in and out of the city. On the other there were sights that Nina had never seen before. In house after house scantily clad girls were desporting themselves in the front windows, garishly illuminated by coloured neon lights, beckoning to the passers by. Along the footpath walked a desultory stream of men of various ages, casting furtive guilty glances into each room, while pretending to be going about some other business.

"OK, we get nice room for you here. Maybe you find some girl friend from Moldova or Ukraine. Maybe they speak same language. Maybe help you get some good work, I think."

Nina was having great difficulty getting her head round all this. A room where she could stay with girls from Moldova was indeed a welcome prospect, but this was a street of brothels. Whatever she had done in Chisinau, it had always been discreet and professional. She had never descended to this tackiness. Was this the sort of work Mitch thought she might do? Never! She had enough of her own money to pay her way till Mitch told her a ship was available. She could steel herself to living here, but the rest was not her scene. It would only be for a short time.

How wrong could she be?

Chapter 42

Brussels - Autumn 2003

Two things signalled that Western materialism had arrived in Moldova. One was the opening of the first McDonald's in Chisinau, and the other, the proliferation of mobile phones amongst the young people. Regardless of the wherewithal to pay, mobiles were the new generation's "must-have". Nina and her boyfriend were no exception, but once he had gone abroad the cost of calls was prohibitive. Fortunately the other technological advance, the email revolution, provided a cheap and direct way of keeping in touch. That was so long as Nina could access her emails on the DHL office computer in Chisinau. In Germany and in Belgium that avenue was closed to her. She could use Internet cafes to send messages to Viktor, but without an email address of her own, he couldn't respond. Now she had arrived in Brussels it was critical to communicate with him again. Text messaging was the other option, but would her mobile work in a foreign country?

> "Hi Viktor, I'm in Brussels. Waiting for ship to UK. Hope it will be soon. How are you?"

She pressed in his mobile number and then "send" . The LCD flashed it had gone. Would it get to him?

Meanwhile there was the problem of adjusting to her new lodgings. A cramped room at the top of a four-storey building above one of the brothels. Three single beds with barely room to walk between them. Three battered lockers. A filthy roof-level window. A solitary electric light bulb. No carpet and everywhere bestrewn with discarded attire belonging to the other two residents. And for this she was expected to pay $200 a week. But there was a big bonus. One of the girls, Tanya, was from Moldova and the other, Irina, from the Ukraine. How good it was to be able to talk about things they had in common in a language she knew.

"So when are you going to start working with us?" they asked.

"No need. I'm going to England soon, probably next week."

"Who's a lucky girl then?" they retorted. "Believe that when it happens, don't you think?"

Nina had made sure she had a contact telephone number for Mitch and her intention was to phone him regularly to learn when the ship was ready. The conversation with her new friends was interrupted by her mobile's bleep. A message had arrived. So it was working. Great.

> "Hi Nina. Good to hear from you. Come quick. Can't wait to see you and show you everything. Finish work in two weeks. Then two weeks holiday in UK. Back to Moldova 18th August. Loads of love .Viktor X."

Suddenly new deadlines had loomed into view. It was already mid July. Nina had to get a ship soon or she would have little or no time with Viktor. It was only two days since she had last spoken to Mitch, but she must contact him again to see if he had any news.

"Nina. Nina who? Ah, yes. You - the new girl. Hope you happy in your house. No, no ship yet. Maybe two, three months I think. No problem - you stay in house. Very nice for you there I think. You get plenty work there. Plenty money to pay the bill. No worries."

He hung up leaving Nina confused and distraught. She had survived hard knocks before, but she had never felt so trapped. She kicked herself that she had already given most of her money over to this Mitch. If getting a ship was going to take so long, perhaps she should try to retrieve her money and go back to Moldova? She phoned him again.

"Sorry - money pay for ship. No can give back. I keep my promise. I find good way for you to England. No worry – just you wait. Everything OK."

"But I must go quick – not good I wait long time," she pleaded.

"Maybe next month, maybe two months. Very difficult find good ship. I call you when ship ready."

Nina hung up again in even more despair. She couldn't get her money back. She hadn't enough left in her money belt to buy a ticket home. Her visitor's visa to Germany had expired. She couldn't cross the Channel until Mitch fixed up a ship. She had no job. Her lodgings were awful. The rent was crippling. In a month the funds she had left would be exhausted. Her room-mates she hardly knew. How far they could be trusted she didn't know. They had their own worries anyway. The only thing she could think of doing was texting Viktor again.

> "Hi Viktor. Big problem. No ship to England. Maybe many weeks I must wait. Very unhappy. Everything's gone wrong. What can I do? All my love, N. XXX"

But what good was it asking Viktor questions like that? How could he visualise where she was or what she was doing? He only knew her in the context of Chisinau and their times together there. Nina had little sense of what his life was like in England, and she had to face up to the fact that he had little clue about hers. What could he really say to help her?

> "So sorry things are not good. Just hope something turns up. Let me know if you hear any better news. Love V. X"

It was good to have his response. At least he'd signed the texts with a kiss this time, but it did nothing at all to assuage her distress. If anything, it confirmed that their communication was becoming sterile, and that was cause for greater anguish. And no doubt nurse Janet Evans was still around. Nina felt out on a limb. Her predicament was of her own making and only she could sort it out.

"Sod it! Sod it!" she said under her breath. "I got through before. I'll get through again. Can't mooch about all day doing nothing just waiting to hear from Mitch. In any case I'll soon run out of money. Best try to get a job, at least for the time being."

Next morning, when her room-mates eventually emerged after their night's exertions, Nina confided in them her idea of getting a temporary job.

"No problem, darling! Just go downstairs and talk to madam. She'll fix you up in no time. Not enough girls – always room for more, and it would take some of the fucking pressure off us, if you get our meaning! At least it pays the bills!! But it does leave you a bit bow-legged and weary!" They fell about laughing. But Nina was working on a different agenda. She knew all too well what their work involved, but they weren't to know that.

"No, I want to try to get a job in a bar or a cafe like I used to in Chisinau. They must need help. Do you know where I could look?"

"You won't make much there my darling! You'll work all night in a bar to earn what you can earn on your back here in ten minutes! You must be mad – they pay slave wages out there for girls like us. They know we're over a barrel with no visa or work permits."

"Well, at least I can give it a try. Where should I go? You must know Brussels pretty well by now."

They suggested the pedestrianised walkways branching off from the Grand Place. Next lunchtime she took the tram into the centre and began trawling her services from restaurant to restaurant. It didn't take long. Lunch and evening work washing dishes and general dogsbody. By Moldovan standards the wages were a dream, but Irina and Tanya were right. In Brussels they were a pittance. Five Euros an hour cash, no questions asked, and working split shifts - a basic wage of 40 Euros a day plus the bonus of any tips and some free food. It was better than nothing and would pay the rent – just. If Nina wanted any extras it would have to come out of her own savings or from the tips. She could start that night.

A roof over her head, a bed to sleep in, some friends who could speak her language, a job and some money in her pocket. It wasn't a glittering lifestyle, but things could be worse and it was only temporary. Everything now depended on Mitch. She willed him to find a ship soon. She was tempted to phone every day, but she knew that would irritate him. Once a week should be OK. Probably Saturday mornings. She would count down the days till then.

Nothing the first Saturday. Nothing the second. Mitch was very clipped on the phone. Her emotions were concentrated each week into those precious few seconds hoping for good news. Then the despair of yet another blank week ahead till she could phone again. She was treading water, going nowhere, but in England things weren't standing still. Viktor was about to quit his job and start travelling. She tried desperately to keep in touch.

"Viktor. Sorry no ship yet. What are you doing? I don't know what to do. Maybe you can come to Brussels? All my love Nina XXX"

"Great news Nina! Big hospital in UK give me job for one year start September. So I come back from Moldova then. Love V. X"

Their lives were on different wavelengths. Nina was trapped and frustrated, living off her wits, and down in spirit. Viktor was free and buoyant, with a rewarding job and on top of the world. The contrast could not have been more stark. The content of the text messages began to betray this gulf. Nina had sacrificed everything to try to reach him – he was her goal. But Viktor was by no means so focussed on her. In short, she needed him more than he needed her. It was a sobering thought. But the news wasn't all bad. The new job meant Viktor would be going back to England. So even if Mitch's ship didn't materialise for a month or so, Viktor would be there when she eventually did make it. By then it would be nearly a year since they had last seen each other, but she was sure their affection for each other would quickly revive, and if that led on to marriage Nina could still see an enviable future beckoning - a well-paid doctor as husband, the prospect of continuing to live in the West and children not shackled by Moldova's desperate economic plight.

"Very happy to hear of your new job. No ship yet. I work and live in Brussels OK. I'll tell you when I come to England. Love you very much. Please wait for me. All my love Nina XXX"

"Start my holiday now. Visit London, Cambridge, Brighton. Then to Moldova August. Come back start new job Monday 1st September. Whipps Cross Hospital, near London. House doctor for children. Love V X"

Nina read and reread his message. What was a house doctor? He was in a different world. It was hard to comprehend. Her horizons were so constrained. But she had to hang on. Just count down the days. It didn't matter there was no ship yet. Viktor wouldn't be there until September. But then he would be there for the whole year. Best of all, he would be away from that Janet Evans. Mitch had promised a ship would come soon. So that should be OK. She resolved not to phone him again until September.

> "Sorry no ship yet. But my man in China, he say maybe one come soon. I not forget you."

The same prevarication. The same message week after week. Nina was numb each time she heard it. It was so predictable. She had ceased to expect good news. September dragged into October and then November. Nina clung on to the routine of her life. There was nothing else she could do – work five, sometimes six days a week in cafes and bars. That took up most lunchtime and evenings, and generated just enough money to pay her rent and food. Social life revolved around the girls from Moldova and the Ukraine with whom she shared her minimal lodgings, but it was severely limited by her unsocial work hours and shortage of money. Chisinau had been much more fun. And each week there was the steady exchange of text messages with Viktor, now back in the UK working hard and very long hours in his new hospital. He too seemed to have less social life than when he was at his first hospital. He often said he was tired and Nina was relieved to sense his increasing urgency to see her again. It was a glimmer of something to look forward to.

The beginning of December was grey and overcast as she cleaned table-tops in a small restaurant near the Grand Place at the end of another wearisome lunch serving wealthy customers their meals. Her mobile vibrated in her pocket. No doubt another bar calling her, desperate for some extra help that evening.

"Miss Snegur. This is Mitch. A ship is coming. I think it ready take you in four weeks. You still want ship?"

Nina spluttered an affirmative response. Could this be true? So long she had waited. Did this really mean she could be on her way at last?

"OK – I need rest of money. Then I tell you what you do. When ship come I ring you again tell you where we meet." And that was that. No more than a couple of dozen words and suddenly life had a new focus. Now it all seemed worth waiting for. Nina finished her shift with renewed zeal and quickly sent a text message to Viktor.

"Great news. I take ship to UK in one month. Not sure dates or where yet, but soon I'll know. Love you loads and loads. Nina XXX"

As the Christmas decorations burgeoned marvellously across the city, all at once Brussels seemed a good place to be. Nina kept her secret, but those near her could tell her mood had changed. There was a new enthusiasm in all she did. She smiled much more and bounced around like an adolescent. They assumed she must have a new lover and teased her. But Nina would not be drawn. She had planned and schemed for this for so long. She wasn't going to let idle banter throw up complications. Nina Snegur now had a clearly defined goal. Having got this far, no-one was going to get in her way.

The call came on Christmas Eve. Mitch evidently had no regard for conventional western festive occasions. "Everything in order. Ship ready soon. You come see me Monday 29th December. Same address before. 5:00 p.m – you bring $1000. I tell when you take ship. I think you happy now."

"Yes - thank you. What day I leave Brussels?" she asked.

"Maybe one week later. I tell everything when you come see me. OK?"

So that was that. Time to enjoy Christmas in Brussels at least a little, in between the huge demand on her to work as many hours as possible in the restaurants and bars bursting with custom at this busy time. Should she tell her friends? Should she give notice to Madam of leaving her lodgings soon? No, best to keep it all secret, and then just up and go. She owed nothing to them and didn't want any awkward questions.

Mitch was waiting at the prescribed time and place. He took her money and spelled out the instructions – nothing in writing. She must memorize it carefully.

"Thursday 8th January. You come here same time 8:00 p.m. Ready for journey. Better you have warm clothes. You carry one small bag. No come – no problem, but no money back. Last chance for ship for you. You tell no-one. This all secret. Big trouble for you if you talk other people. You understand?"

Nina absorbed every syllable. Ten days to get ready. She couldn't wait.

CHAPTER 43

BUITELAAR – JANUARY 2004

The expected call came early on the morning of Wednesday 7th January, but this time it was Francois on the line, the articulate Belgian. More disturbingly, the call came through, not to the office, but to Arjan's flat while he was eating his breakfast. They obviously knew more about him than he realised. Suddenly he felt more vulnerable, though when he tried to be more rational about it, he knew they must have done a lot of homework before contacting him in the first place. Locating where he lived and his home phone number was not a difficult job. Even so, a new sense of insecurity had disturbed his equanimity. If he put a foot wrong, he had no illusions that the consequences for him would be painful.

"Mr van Buitelaar – good morning. How are you? You will be pleased to know that all the arrangements are in hand. Can I take it that everything is still OK at your end?"

Arjan confirmed that it was.

"Fine. Now listen carefully. You may want to note a few things down. It's important you comply with these instructions carefully and promptly. Any mistake could be most unfortunate. I'm sure you understand.

"The bill of lading and customs papers you need will be delivered by courier to your depot in a confidential package this afternoon at 5:00 p.m. It's essential you are there to receive them personally. Then tomorrow morning you proceed to Antwerp docks, and load the container shipped by Hoogang International Logistics for onward transit to Polymer Plastics Limited, a company in Leicester, England. The papers are all in order and there will be no problem with this part of the operation. You then drive back to your depot and garage your truck and the container in your warehouse out of sight for the rest of the day. You may want to get some sleep in the afternoon as you will be travelling most of the following night. Above all you must be back at your depot no later than 6:00 p.m., and at that time there must be no other persons around for the rest of that evening – no-one in the office, the yard or the warehouse, except yourself. Is that all understood?"

Arjan listened intently. None of this posed any problem. He confirmed he was all set.

"OK. That's all you need to know for the present. You will be met at your depot soon after 6:00 p.m. tomorrow, when the next phase will be explained. All you have to do is the driving. You will of course make sure your truck is properly fuelled and ready for the return trip to the UK via Calais. You will leave the depot around midnight to catch the 4:30 a.m. ferry. Any questions?"

There were none and the conversation ended as abruptly as it had begun.

Arjan finished his breakfast, and checked his work schedule. He had arranged only local work that day. That had been completed by mid-afternoon. He returned to the depot and made sure the yard was clear. His office assistant had already left at her usual time of four o'clock to get home to cook her husband's evening meal. He drew some espresso coffee from the instant drink machine and sat down to wait.

Precisely at 5:00 p.m. a motorcycle courier clad in black leathers swung his high-powered BMW machine into the Buitelaar Haulage Company depot. Without removing his crash helmet, he deposited a set of papers onto Arjan's office desk. After rudimentary signatures he was off again into the darkening evening barely five minutes later, leaving Arjan to study the papers. Shipping notes, ferry bookings, customs declarations - everything seemed in order. No problem so far. No money yet, but the first payment should be tomorrow.

Arjan slept fitfully that night. He would keep well away from friends or social contacts for the next few days. As far as anyone else knew, he was engaged on a container delivery to the UK – a routine matter that would take him out of circulation for two or three days. No reason for anyone to be suspicious, but all the same he would keep his head down from now till it was over. By Saturday he should be back home, significantly better off, and able to relax. That's when he would meet up with his mates again.

The pick-up at Antwerp docks next morning went smoothly. The gatekeepers and security staff there knew him well. His papers were all in order and the resealed 70 cubic metre sea container, faded ochre colour with TRITEX in vertical lettering on its side, was manoeuvred onto his flatbed truck by the huge mobile gantry crane. The locking bolts were secured and he and his cargo were back at his depot by lunchtime. His assistant did not work on Thursdays and his two colleague drivers were on long distance deliveries, not expected back till the following week. There was no-one else in the depot and no-one expected until tomorrow. Arjan reversed the truck and container into the warehouse and closed the doors. Any neighbours who might have seen him arrive would regard it as normal routine. They had seen similar comings and goings on many previous occasions. Time now for a bite of lunch and short nap before the crucial evening's events began.

Arjan returned to the depot yard, dark and deserted, at 5:00 p.m. His truck was fuelled up and secure, out of sight in the locked unlit warehouse. He had spare food and drink in his cabin locker. His paperwork was all OK. He had showered and shaved. His log book was up to date. Within a few hours he should be on the road heading for the Calais ferry. Now it was all up to "them". Another cup of coffee, the evening paper and his feet up on the desk - all he had to do for the present was to wait.

The light in his office portacabin was the only sign of life when, at ten minutes past six, a dark Mercedes saloon car eased quietly through the yard's open gates and slid to a halt in front of the office. Arjan took the precaution of noting its registration plate, although he guessed it was probably false - a 190 C class four-door saloon with darkened windows. Its doors opened and closed discreetly. For the second time in his life, Arjan was joined by messrs Mitch and Francois. They were in relaxed but focussed mode.

"Hello Mr van Buitelaar! How good to see you again! Everything OK?"

No problems as far as Arjan was concerned.

"Fine – we're all set then. We just need access to the warehouse now," said Francois.

"You can join us if you want or you can stay here while we get on with things? Some of our colleagues will arrive shortly with equipment. When they've finished what they have to do, we will be joined by a group of twelve people brought here in another vehicle. They will be your passengers. Their future is in your hands. I'm sure you won't let them down!"

Arjan opened up the warehouse and took them in, closing the doors behind them before switching on the interior lights inside. The container loomed above them. Mitch went up to the rear doors. Within two minutes he had released the customs seals and manoeuvred the vertical retaining levers to open the container doors, so recently secured by Customs officers at the Antwerp docks for the final leg of the container's journey to Leicester.

Not often did Arjan have the chance to see the contents of his container deliveries. In the cavernous 70 cubic metres of space inside, at the far end, was a huge crate, firmly anchored at each corner to the floor of the container. The shipping labels on the wooden frame of the crate confirmed, in Chinese and English, it held a Plastic Injection Mould destined for a factory in Leicester in the UK. It occupied over half the floor space. In front of it, from where the shipment destined for Holland had been removed earlier, was about five metres length of vacant space.

"That good" said Mitch, gesticulating towards the vacated area. "We make small house for passengers here. Then we close doors. No-one know you got extra cargo."

There was the sound of a vehicle drawing to halt outside. Standing in front of the unsealed doors of the container, Arjan felt jumpy. Any unexpected visitors now would be a major problem. He was much relieved when his companions confirmed it was their support team arriving with the equipment they needed. He switched off the warehouse lights to be doubly careful, and the three of them exited through a side door to check the arrival. There was a long wheel-base white Mercedes Sprinter van parked back up to the warehouse double doors. They had obviously done their homework and were waiting to reverse into the vacant truck space inside the warehouse alongside Arjan's truck just as soon as he had opened up for them. The van reversed in and the warehouse doors were again closed. At Francois' suggestion, Arjan also closed the front gates to the depot yard and put out the lights in his office. Two men in working overalls climbed out of the van and joined the three of them in the warehouse. The warehouse interior lights were dimmed.

The Sprinter van doors were then opened. Out came an oxy-acetylene torch, welding gear with accompanying gas cylinders and a collapsible ladder. The two "engineers" took these to the front end of the container, and put on protective goggles. Standing on the ladder, they fired up the torch and proceeded to carve out two discs of metal from the leading side of the container, approximately 10 cms in diameter, a metre down from the top of the container, 30 cms in from the edge, one disc on either side. The fine-burn oxy-acetylene torch cut through the rigid metal leaving only minimum scorching around the perimeter of the cut.

Then onto the roof of the container where they cut two similar holes towards the rear end of the roof. When the metal edges of the two roof holes had cooled, using industrial superglue on the leading edge, they fixed a rectangular flap of heavy-duty rubber over each of the holes. To all intents and purposes the flaps would function as a valve to allow egress of air when necessary, but would prevent rain from entering the container.

Mitch then produced two thin rectangular magnetic metal plates measuring 20 cms by 12 cms. On each was printed some Chinese characters and the English words "Use No Hooks".

"OK, Mr van Buitelaar. You know we take good care of passengers -must have air to breathe, so we make this. When truck moves, air go inside through holes in front and go outside from holes on top. Before you go through Customs, you put metal plates on holes in front so no man see hole. Very simple. Plate is magnet so stick to container. I show you."

Mitch then demonstrated. It was simple and effective. The two metal plates clamped onto the container by magnetic attraction. Mitch then used a broom handle to push them upwards until they completely obscured the round holes. They were sufficiently high they could not be reached from the ground and looked an integral part of the container. To remove them, he reversed the broom handle. Attached on the other end was a horizontal piece of wood, which acted like a rake and when positioned above the top of the metal plate, allowed it to be pulled downwards to expose the holes.

"OK, when truck drive on road, you open holes. Before you reach Calais, you stop in lay-by and close holes. When you get through England Customs, you stop again on roadside and open holes till we meet near Leicester. You keep holes closed on ferry. Enough air inside for short crossing. No problem. I think you happy with this?"

Arjan had not expected all this. What was clear was that everything had been meticulously planned, and not only that, these guys had obviously done this routine before. They were very sure of themselves. Arjan was relieved they had worked out an effective means of ensuring adequate air supply to the interior of the container. The system looked effective and unobtrusive. Mitch gave him the adapted broom handle. He would stow it under his bunk bed at the rear of his cab until it was needed.

The engineers then unloaded from their van sixteen identical panels, in the form of large wooden pallets measuring two metres long by one metre wide. The outside of each was rough-hewn timber-like a pallet. Nailed on the inside was a flat piece of plywood of the same dimensions. Stuck against that, covering the whole side, was a sheet of metal foil similar to that used to keep athletes warm after completing marathon runs. Attached to that was a slab of polystyrene 3 cms thick, and finally another thin piece of plywood to protect the polystyrene. Each panel was like a giant sandwich 15 cms thick – rough-hewn timber frame on the outer side, then a sheet of plywood, then the metal foil, then the polystyrene, and finally another plywood sheet.

These were the mainframes of a cubicle to accommodate the "passengers". The engineers laid three of the panels on the floor of the container in the vacant space between the rear doors and the crate housing the plastic injection mould. These formed a base two metres wide, three metres long. They then erected three of the remaining panels vertically on each side of the base, and two at each end, bolting them together at the corners. Near the top of each of the vertical panels were a series of ventilation holes, pre-drilled right through the panel, about 5 cms in diameter spaced 20 cms apart. Finally, they levered into position the three remaining frames to form a roof. The whole operation had taken about 20 minutes. The result was a large rigid crate measuring three metres long, two metres wide, and two metres high, looking from the outside like any normal crate that might house a piece of machinery.

One of the vertical sections was hinged so that it could open outwards as a door with two interior bolts, which allowed it to be closed and secured from inside. Once closed, short of using a crowbar, there was no way of accessing the interior from outside.

Mitch then produced some pre-prepared shipping labels, in identical format to those on the Leicester-bound crate, and stapled them to the newly formed structure. The labels indicated that this crate was an integral part of the same shipment.

Arjan watched quietly, again reflecting how well these people seemed to have thought of every angle. Whatever their business, they could not be faulted on their professionalism and eye for detail. Francois turned to him and proceeded to explain more of what they had been doing and of how things were to work.

"Your passengers will stay inside the crate while going through Customs. At other times they will be free to open the hinged panel and move outside the box, but movement will be restricted. The metal foil and foam insulation prevents immigration officers' heat-detection equipment identifying internal container temperature changes caused by body heat. The air-holes in the container reduce the build-up of carbon dioxide, so if Customs use gas detection equipment this should present no problem. The polystyrene also reduces noise, and keeps the internal temperature at a moderate level to avoid hypothermia.

"There are some other basic matters you need to know about. You will have a mobile phone and so will the leader of the group of passengers. You will have each other's mobile number in your phone's memory and will be able to communicate with each other. You will phone to tell them whenever they must be inside the box and when they can be outside. The conversation will be in English, so keep it simple as the leader's English will be basic.

"They will embark later this evening, immediately before you start your journey. We shall issue them each with a baguette loaf of bread, a two litre bottle of water and an individual blanket. They have been told to wear warm clothes and to restrict personal possessions to one small suitcase each. They will also each be given half a dozen self-sealing thick plastic bags and a roll of toilet paper. There's a plastic stool with a hole in its seat to act as toilet facility. That will be outside the cubicle. We also provide a large black heavy-duty plastic bag. The passengers will use their plastic bags suspended from the hole in the chair for shitting or pissing, or if they are sick. They then seal the bag and deposit it in the heavy black bag. This keeps things as hygienic as possible and avoids the build up of smells, which can sometimes be a giveaway to Customs or immigration officers. The passengers know things will not be too private but that is their problem. They should be inside the container for no more than fifteen hours in total, most of which time they will be able to move outside the cubicle. Whenever they are going through Customs everyone and everything must be inside the cubicle with the door secured and bolted from inside."

By the time Francois had concluded this discourse the engineers had finished their tasks and were reloading the oxyacetylene gear and other tools into their van. The whole operation had taken less than two hours. The cubicle sat comfortably in the rear of the container looking just like any other shipping crate, secured to the floor with bracing chains. The hinged door opening towards the interior was ajar. The metal rear doors of the container were still wide open and fixed back against the sides. The rapidly assembled but professionally built accommodation module was ready to receive its guests.

As the white van drove away, Arjan realised he had exchanged not a word with the two engineers, still less did he know their names, from whence they came or where they were off to. But he did remember to make a mental note of the Belgian registration number of their vehicle, which he would commit to a secret notebook just as soon as he had a private moment. Events so far had been absorbing, so much so he was taken by surprise when Francois took out of his pocket a large brown envelop and handed it to him.

"What's this? I thought I already had all the necessary papers?"

"We just keep our side of the bargain, Mr van Buitelaar," smiled Francois. "You will find inside fifty one-hundred euro notes which we promised you at this stage. I think you should count them and then find somewhere to keep them safe."

Arjan felt rather stupid that he had temporarily forgotten about this little matter. It was after all the only reason he had agreed to do all this. He counted the money quickly, and then climbed up into his cab to open a small secure compartment governed by a combination lock underneath his bunk mattress in which he kept all his valuables while travelling. There he secreted his down payment. So far, so good.

Chapter 44

Belgium – Thursday, 8th January 2004

"Stuff happens!" Such was the infamous epithet used by the American Defence Secretary, Donald Rumsfeld, to describe the terrible and terrifying aftermath of sectarian killings proliferating day on day after the American led invasion of Iraq in 2003. Callous his words might have been, but what he meant of course was that most of life's endeavours generate unexpected and unpredictable consequences. No-one could argue with that.

Miles away from the events spiralling out of control in Iraq, contemporaneously in Belgium, on the morning of Thursday, the 8th of January 2004, three people's lives were unfolding in ways they had never foreseen when they had embarked on their respective endeavours. Unbeknown to each, their orbits were about to coalesce. Stuff was happening.

When Arjan van Buitelaar took up his truck-driving career, it was meant to be the basis of a steady income, a stable marriage, normal kids and respectable middle age. Now, with his marriage in tatters and the devastating loss of his only daughter and her stillborn baby, he was about to join the despised ranks of human traffickers. Stuff happens.

Five years earlier in Kosovo, in his resolve to escape the ethnic hatred and violence there, Habib had never envisaged a trek across the mountains, a sojourn in Tirana, a clandestine sea crossing and endless van journeys from the unknown to the unknown. Now in Brussels, his future was in the hands of individuals whom he hardly knew. They had taken almost all his residual money, and were ordering him about as though he owed them favours. Stuff happens.

When Nina Snegur's adolescent rebelliousness prevailed on her parents to allow her to leave the parochial confines of her native village and search out a new life in the bright lights of Moldova's capital city, Chisinau, never did she expect it would lead to an unplanned pregnancy, an abortion, prostitution, the heart-breaking death of her mother, an affair with a rich German, the prospect of marrying a doctor, and now four months' tedious slaving in restaurants in Brussels, but stuff happens.

On the Thursday morning, while Arjan van Buitelaar was picking up the TRITEX sea container from Antwerp docks, Habib had decided to try to make it as normal a day as possible. That is until the end of his afternoon work session. He had grown fond of Jan. Inseparable from his cigarette, Jan always looked slightly seedy and pale-faced, but he was always there, always keeping the restaurant running smoothly, and always paying Habib his dues. The dilemma for Habib was whether to tell him he would not be coming back that day and so probably forfeit the last payment of twenty Euros due to him, or should he simply just not turn up for the evening shift? Habib's family values had taught him to do the honourable thing. It was four o'clock, time to leave, time to be paid the Euros due for last night's work.

Inwardly compelled to be honest, Habib blurted out embarrassedly, "Mr Jan, sorry, I no come back tonight."

For once Jan seemed taken aback. He stopped wiping tables and put down the dishcloth. His hand rose shakily to search for the cigarette on his lips.

"That not good. Much work tonight. What I do? Too late find someone work now."

There was an awkward silence. Habib knew he was expected to respond, but he had no more to say, still less any way of mitigating the problem his departure created for Jan. For that he was genuinely sorry, but the harsh reality of the casual labour market was that nobody owed anyone any loyalty. It was hand-to-mouth on both sides. Even so, Habib felt guilty. He was letting someone down who had helped him.

"Mr Jan, so sorry, but I must travel tonight. No home in Brussels. Ship come take me."

He had said it. Too late he realised he should not have done. Mitch had put them on notice that everything had to be secret. Not a word to anyone. They would be in deep trouble if anyone said anything. Now he had let the cat out of the bag.

"What ship you take? Where you go?" asked Jan.

Habib's mind raced into damage-limitation mode. No choice now but to try to lie his way out.

"My sister very sick in England. I take ship see her. Parents too far in Kosovo."

"Why you go now? Better you work more days – then I find someone take your work."

Habib felt the clammy sweat of stress and fear. He could not compromise the prospects of getting away tonight. And he dreaded the consequences of betraying Mitch's clandestine operations. He had to find a way to mollify Jan, even at the expense of more lies.

"I think you remember my friend, Toci. He come for work with you before. Maybe I go find him and he come help you tonight?"

"OK – no come, I no pay you" Jan held back the twenty Euros he was about to give to Habib. So now he had lost last night's wages as well as not being paid for today's work. But on the back of the string of lies he had told Jan, hopefully he could exit without more questions or agro.

"OK, I think Toci good worker. I tell him to come. When I come back from England, maybe I come work for you next time?"

He held out his hand. Jan had the good grace to shake it. "Good luck. Hope your sister better."

Habib took his leave. He felt gutted that he was letting down such a good guy, shamed that he had lied so barefacedly, and shamed that there was no chance whatever of Toci being able to help Jan out, as he would be on the same ship as Habib. He walked off with heavy heart, thinking how badly his parents would think of him. But he had to survive, and maybe, just sometimes, honesty had to be the casualty.

He had four hours before he needed to be at the rendezvous. It was going to be a long night. Best to eat well now. Never know when the next meal might be. He called into MacDonalds and treated himself to a king-size hamburger and chips and large milkshake.

At exactly the same time, barely a hundred metres away, totally unknown to him, but following a similar course in another restaurant, Nina Snegur was taking her leave. She had given her notice of departure a week earlier. Work had slackened since the Christmas and New Year avalanche of customers, and after four months of conscientious service there, her employers were sorry to see her go, but no questions asked – that was the norm in such a transient labour market. They even gave her a little box of Neuhaus Belgian chocolates as a parting gift.

Nina felt in good spirits. She had said nothing to her flat mates. They were still "working" downstairs when she returned to her room in the late afternoon. She packed systematically. Essentials into the rucksack first. Then as many clothes and personal items as she could carry. What wouldn't go in she would leave behind. She wrote a short note in Russian for her companions.

> "Sorry couldn't stay to say good-bye. Have to leave urgently. Really enjoyed your company. Thanks for everything. Have fun, but don't overdo it!! Lots of love, NinaXX"

She put on her warmest clothes. Mitch had told her she needed to. She took a final affectionate glance round the room, still as basic as when she had first arrived, but it had been her refuge for a few desperate months and for that she was grateful. Then a quiet descent to the front door and inconspicuous exit. She had paid her rent in advance so had no conscience about leaving without notice. She slipped away into the dark evening, turned left, and walked purposefully down Rue d'Aerschot past all the garish brothel windows towards the Gare du Nord. There was a biting east wind. She was glad of her warm coat.

The next and crucial phase of her journey was about to begin. She had sent a text to Viktor telling him she was leaving that night and would contact him as soon as she was in the UK. As she thought of him and felt the fierce wind burning her cheeks, her mind went back to those harsh cold winters in Moldova. After the Soviet Union had collapsed, they suddenly found themselves desperate for winter fuel. Moldova had no natural resources. Coal was in short supply, electricity spasmodic. Both were prohibitively expensive as the Moldovan economy collapsed. In the villages the main preoccupation of children and adults in the lead-up to winter was to scavenge the countryside for wood to burn in their stoves till every living tree within miles had been cut to the ground, and even its roots hacked out. As conditions worsened, families would join together to share the heat of single rooms. And where the frail elderly became too feeble to cope, they would be found frozen in their beds. Winters were pitiless and for ordinary country folk without jobs there was no end to it. Each year was worse than the last.

Nina contrasted all that with the warmth of Brussels – the convivial restaurants, the heated public transport, the over-heated shops, and not least the comfortably snug temperatures in the brothels. Nina had no doubts where she preferred to be. One day Moldova might get its act together, but she wasn't prepared to wait. If she could find her niche in the West with Viktor as her husband, she wouldn't look back. She missed her friends and family, but maybe she could go back to visit them some day.

The kaleidoscope of thoughts coursed through her mind as she turned under the railway bridge and headed up the vast ramp to take her into the station concourse area. A long night ahead, so a good meal in the cafe, a last visit to the toilet and restroom to check out how she looked, and then a taxi from the forecourt. She had memorised Mitch's address but to be doubly sure she dug out the tattered slip of paper she had carried with her since she left Chisinau and showed it to the taxi driver so he knew the right place to go.

She arrived just before 7:30 p.m., well on time, and was ushered up to the attic room. There were five others already there, three men and two women. Her arrival was greeted with perfunctory nods. Most were smoking, drawing heavily on their cigarettes like babies sucking dummies. It was a comfort thing.

Nina felt in buoyant mood. "Hello, everyone! Nice to meet you! My name's Nina. I'm from Moldova. Does anyone speak Russian?"

Both girls and one man indicated they did. "So where are you from?" she asked.

The man, swarthy and with a hunted look, grunted that he was from Chechnya. It was some days since he had shaved. His rough clothes were shabby and stained. He wore a tight navy-blue woollen hat on his close-shaven head. Having declared where he was from, he sunk back into his own private world, arms tightly folded, leaning morosely on the wall, enveloped in the smoke from his cigarette. The two girls were more forthcoming.

"I'm Natasha from Belarus."

"I'm Tanya from Ukraine. Glad to meet you."

Nina went across and joined them sitting on the floor with their backs against the wall. She propped her rucksack between her knees, stuffed her gloves in her pockets, took off her hat and shook out her hair. "So what brings you here?" she asked in a low voice. Natasha was the first to respond.

"My home is a town called Loev, right on the Ukraine border. I was born just before the Chernobyl disaster. It's only 30 kilometres away from us, and the wind blew all the bad gas across the Belarus villages you know. Many women gave birth to children with problems. We couldn't eat stuff from the fields. Even now, nearly twenty years later, we can't pick mushrooms, we can't eat berries in the forest, and can't drink cow's milk. Many villages near my home are still deserted and it's forbidden to go there. They think the ground's still contaminated. There's nothing to do there. The old men get drunk all the time, and the young boys just watch porno movies – then they expect us girls to fuck around like the whores they've been watching on their videos. My father lives for his vodka, my mother's too fat, never goes anywhere, and thinks I should just settle down and marry a village boy. It's awful – I just had to get away. So I took a bus to Minsk, and then a train to Berlin and eventually got myself to Brussels. The only good thing that ever happened in Loev was my teacher who taught me English, so I thought England was the best place to go. So here I am!"

Nina shared her story, at least a highly censored version of it. She told them about the frustration of her village life, the bright lights of Chisinau, conveniently missed out the bad bits and went straight to her boyfriend in England and her hopes to join him soon. As she talked she wondered how far Natasha may also have edited her story. How had she financed her trip across Europe? Nina deemed it prudent not to pry too much, but chatted on excitably, realising that up till now she had never thought about the details of the sea crossing.

"Couldn't get a proper visa so had to do it this way. Wonder what the ship will be like? Haven't seen the sea before. People say you can get sick if it's stormy. Wonder how long it takes to get across to England?"

Tanya joined the conversation. "Shouldn't be too bad. Some of my friends have already done it. They say things are good in the UK, so I thought I'd join them. Ukraine's not so poor, but always it's arguments between the old folk who think the Soviet system was better and the young who want to be like the West. I think I'll make more money in London." She looked up at the ceiling wistfully and blew out two rings of smoke which circled sinuously in the thick air till vanishing. Neither Natasha nor Nina asked how she planned to make money.

Habib and Toci were the next to be ushered through the door. They had already been in this room before, but knew none of the people there this time. Perfunctory nods all round; then they too huddled up on the floor against the wall to wait. Despite the bleak surroundings, bare floorboards, dirty walls, and tatty furniture, there was a buzz of anticipation as the occupants talked quietly to each other in their own languages.

Just before eight o'clock four more men arrived. Now there were a dozen crammed into the small room. Habib recognised some speaking in Serbo-Croat. No love lost between Serbs and Kosovo Albanians, so they kept their distance. Then there was Russian, and Albanian and another language, which sounded like Italian, but could have been Rumanian.

After half an hour or so, the animated conversation began to flag as the motley assembly became progressively more absorbed with anxieties of what lay ahead in the next few hours. The arrival of Mitch with his colleague, Francois, was a welcome relief. He sat at the battered table in the middle of the smoke-filled room.

"OK – twelve people. That good. Everyone here." He spoke in his clipped English. "Many things I must tell you. I think everyone understand OK if I speak English?"

There were desultory nods of affirmation from various parts of the room.

"First very important. You all go England tonight on ship inside sea-container. Tomorrow you free in England. I think that good news for you? One thing not good – smoking. No smoke from now. Too much smoke make bad smell in container. Custom-man smell smoke and call police. So not good for you."

There was much muttering around the room as one by one cigarettes were stubbed out. Mitch opened the solitary window a few inches to allow in a penetrating cold draught of air, in turn allowing wreaths of smoke from the room to filter outwards into the dark Brussels night.

Mitch sat back at the table. He glanced over a sheet of paper and then swung his gaze around the room. He was not happy. Someone was still smoking. It was the man from Chechnya.

"I think you no understand? That not good. I am boss man here. I say no smoke – you no smoke," he said firmly.

The Chechnyan looked on impassively, still smoking, and unmoved by the steeliness in Mitch's voice. The rest of the group fell silent and looked anxiously from one to the other. Nina knew that Chechnyans had a reputation for being obstinate and self-willed. Some of their people were guilty of fearsome terrorist atrocities in Russia, but equally they had suffered appalling reprisals from the Russian army. Nina was worried the Chechnyan's attitude could compromise all their chances of a safe, undetected crossing to England. She decided to intervene to try to reduce the tension in the room.

"I think maybe the man not understand English. I explain him in Russian. OK?"

Mitch nodded. Nina proceeded to translate what had been said. The Chechnyan replied. He had no English, but was "fucking sure he wouldn't be taking orders from this little oriental shit about whether he could smoke or not". Nina was taken aback by the vehemence of his reply. She knew it would spell disaster for him if she translated accurately. She decided to be as diplomatic as possible.

"He say he no understand English good. He very worried – he need smoke to stay happy. He no smoke on ship."

Regardless of what Nina was saying, the Chechnyan's body language spoke for itself. Mitch was in no mood to compromise. "This trip very risky. I tell the rules. He no like that, he go home."

Nina translated again, trying to convince the Chechnyan that he could be in dire trouble if he wasn't more amenable. He dispatched his cigarette to the floor and extinguished it with a contemptuous stamp of his foot. The tension in the room eased a little, but clearly Mitch was irritated.

"So first I say again I speak English. I ask everyone if you understand good." He pointed one by one at each person. Only one man, other than the Chechnyan, indicated he had no English. He spoke Albanian so it was arranged that Habib, whose English seemed the best, would translate for him. At the same time Nina would translate for the Chechnyan.

Mitch spoke slowly giving time for everyone to understand.

"Everyone wear warm clothes. We take you to truck in one hour. You take one bag and we give you bread and water for journey. You stay inside container for maybe fifteen hours. We give you plastic bags if you sick or you want shit or piss. No noise inside container when truck stop on ship. And no smoking. Everyone understand?"

The quiet translations of Habib and Nina were the only distraction, until the hushed attentiveness was broken by a heavy Russian outburst from the Chechnyan. Nina explained tactfully. "He wants to know when he can smoke again?"

Mitch replied in ice cold terms. "Tell him he no smoke again till he leave container in England." Nina told him. His response was angry. "Tell the bastard I've paid for the trip. I'll not be dictated to by this little turd. I'll stuff the cigarettes up his arse if he keeps going on."

Nina cast about in her mind rapidly how best she could translate this without causing more agro. "He very sad he not smoke. He worried. He say cigarette help him. He try hard no smoke again," she lied.

Mitch and Francois acknowledged what she had said, transparently unconvinced, and took their leave. "We come back in half an hour. You all ready to go then."

As soon as they left the room the Chechnyan lit up another cigarette, and settled down in a corner on the floor. One of the other men spoke to Nina. "This guy is bad news for us. Tell him he make trouble for us all if he smokes."

Nina was reluctant to be cast in the role of go-between, but knew the group were on edge and this was not helping their stress level.

"The man said if you want to keep smoking, they won't take you on the ship," she said in her fluent Russian.

"I know what he said. But I've paid for this trip. The bastards can rot in hell as far as I'm concerned. Chechnyans know how to look after themselves."

"He says he do what he want. I think we just leave him to it. Not our problem." Nina was not going to get further involved.

When Mitch returned, wreaths of smoke surrounded the Chechnyan as he grudgingly extinguished the cigarette and made ready to depart. Mitch studiously ignored him, left the door open and signalled their exit to the vehicle waiting outside.

"OK, everyone quiet, no talk - we drive to truck. One hour we get there."

One by one, they climbed into the back of another white van with hardwood seats along both sides. For Habib and Toci there was a sense of deja vu when they observed the ten wooden crates, which had travelled up with them from Toulon, now stacked neatly in the centre space of this vehicle.

"Looks like this lot's going with us all the way," whispered Habib to Toci in Albanian.

"Wonder what's inside? Do you think it's drugs? Maybe we're not the most important cargo after all? I wonder if the other passengers know about it. Better keep quiet and see what happens."

Two burly drivers took their seats in the front and set off, with Mitch and Francois following behind in a black Mercedes. It was just after ten o'clock. The night was dry but cold, the strong easterly wind still blowing. Within a short time the vehicles picked up speed as they joined the autoroute north. Once more the Chechnyan chose to light up a cigarette and the back of the van soon filled with the smoke. No-one was prepared to remonstrate. Not their problem, as Nina had said.

After about thirty minutes the vehicles came to a stop. When the rear doors of the van were opened they found themselves in a secluded parking space at an autoroute rest area. There was a small toilet block and few weak overhead lights. Two large trucks were battened down for the night's rest, their drivers asleep in their curtained cabs. Otherwise the parking lot was deserted.

Mitch came across from the Mercedes. "OK, you tell Russian man he can smoke here for five minutes." Nina translated .

"Told you so," said the Chechnyan. "These shits just need firm handling. They know they can't fuck with me. They need the money too much and are shit scared we might let the police know who they are. You lot've got no balls!"

He stepped down from the van. The two drivers had come to the back and closed the van doors. The Chechnyan looked round as he heard them slam shut. That was the last he would remember. The blow on his neck was from a karati expert, precisely measured and deadly accurate. The drivers quickly rifled through his pockets to remove any sort of identity, then carried his limp body over to one of the travellers' picnic tables and slumped him on a seat with his head and arms on the table. As the drivers returned to the van in the darkness, Francois produced a small Russian made Baikal pistol from his pocket. From another pocket he took out the customised silencer and screwed it carefully onto the muzzle end. There was a dull thud as the bullet entered the Chechnyan's skull and ended the last moments of his life. The risk that he might betray the international network of human trafficking across Europe had been nullified. Mitch dialled a number on his mobile phone.

A sleepy policewoman on duty at the Aalst Police station, the nearest to the parking lot, received a call apparently from a concerned motorist on the northbound autoroute. He had just stopped for a toilet break and discovered a man on his own, either asleep or drunk, at one of the picnic tables. It was a cold night and maybe the police ought to have a look at him to make sure he was OK. No, he was in a hurry and couldn't wait for the police to arrive.

When the policewoman asked for the caller's identity and address, the phone had gone dead. She redialled the number but the phone was switched off. Mitch had already hung up and was back in the Mercedes, the little convoy on the move again, but with one less passenger. If the police did trace the number of the mobile phone, they would discover it had been stolen in Brussels some weeks ago.

The van occupants had heard the thud. Their belligerent Chechnyan colleague did not return. They could only surmise what might have happened to him. The final leg of their journey was completed in sombre, brooding silence.

PART 6

A WEEKEND IN ENGLAND

Chapter 45

The Channel - Thursday Night, 8th January 2004

Waiting is never easy, but doubly difficult when there's a deep-seated anxiety about the outcome. Arjan was on his own in his office. He was trying to read the evening paper, but it was hard to concentrate on events which weren't his immediate concern. The transistor radio in his friendly, familiar environment filled the vacuity of the night with energetic pop music, not much to his taste, but partially distracting. In the depot warehouse behind him, now dark and silent, his truck was all set to go, like a thoroughbred racehorse, eager, dependable and equally familiar, but now loaded with a sea container like none he had ever carried before, rear doors splayed open waiting to receive its guests.

Mitch and Francois had left some two hours ago. He smoked his third cigarette, anything to steady his nerves. He drank another cup of black coffee – must top up the caffeine level. Tonight would be long and taxing till he was through the Dover Customs. Must stay on the alert. Still hadn't been told where the rendez-vous was in England. Mitch and Francois would make sure he had that before he left. Their problem, not his. But it would be nice to know. If all went to plan, it would all be over in sixteen hours. Just had to keep cool and focused till then.

At precisely eleven o'clock the headlights of the black Mercedes and the white van he had seen earlier slewed through the gates into the yard. The Merc parked outside the office. The van reversed towards the doors of the depot's second vehicle access. The vehicles' lights were quickly doused. Arjan felt a strange measure of relief as he recognised the approaching silhouettes of Mitch and Francois. They always seemed to have everything under control. Why should he fret so much?

"Hallo again, Mr van Buitelaar. Everything OK?" Mitch was in buoyant mood. He didn't wait for an answer. "First I think we close yard gates, then we go inside"

Arjan needed no second bidding. The more private they were, the better he liked it.

"We put van inside depot, OK?"

Arjan opened the main doors and the van reversed in quietly. They delayed switching on the interior lights until the doors were secured again.

"Now I think it good you meet your passengers. We lose one man, so now you take eleven." Mitch elaborated no further. No concern of Arjan. His cut was the same, however many were on board.

The van driver opened up the rear doors and beckoned the group. They straggled out, bemusedly trying to take in the unfamiliar surroundings, each clutching their individual rucksacks like a child hugs its doll for comfort when facing the unknown. The truck and its container towered hugely alongside them.

"This is Mr van Buitelaar. He is your driver. He take you to England. He very good man. He got mobile phone so he speak to you inside truck. He tell everything when you make journey. Now I give someone mobile phone so you speak to him. I think this boy speak good English. He listen phone and tell all Mr van Buitelaar say when he call you."

He passed a mobile phone to Habib. "So you want me take phone?" he asked, taken by surprise.

"Yes, I think you know how phone work. You put Mr van Buitelaar number in memory box now. And Mr van Buitelaar put your number on his phone. OK?"

They exchanged numbers and logged them into their respective mobiles' memories.

"Now I show you room inside truck where you travel. When truck on road, OK for you outside box. When on boat and in Customs, you all stay lock inside box. Make no noise. No smoking. Understand?"

Mitch demonstrated the closing mechanism of the door on the accommodation module, and explained what they should do about toilet needs or if they were sick. He distributed a bread baguette and bottle of water to each, told them to wear their warmest clothes. Inside the module he indicated a pile of well-used blankets and a polythene pack of toilet rolls, and showed them the plastic chair to be used as a toilet facility.

While Mitch was briefing the would-be passengers, Francois went into the office with Arjan and produced the maps and detailed instructions for their English rendez-vous. Conversation in Dutch was clear and precise.

"You will be heading for Leicester for delivery of the machine parts to the plastic injection moulding factory - scheduled arrival time 4:00 p.m. tomorrow, Friday. You know the address – it's on the Troon industrial estate just off the Leicester ring road to the north of the city."

"Our meeting point is near Leicester on the west side. You need to be there not later than 3:00 p.m. That gives us thirty minutes to off-load the immigrants and the module, and then thirty minutes for you to reach the factory. It's about 15 kilometres, so that should be no problem." Francois produced a large-scale map of the Leicester area and some typed instructions which he went on to explain.

"You will cross over to Dover from Calais, arriving about 5:30 a.m. tomorrow morning, English time. You drive from Dover to the Dartford Tunnel, which I think you know well - then the M 25 north to the M1 junction. Head up the M1 to Leicester till you reach junction 21A. Take the A46 turn-off left on the slip road to the village of Kirby Muxloe on the B5380. It's well signed." He pointed it out on the map.

"At the roundabout in the centre of the village follow the sign for the next village of Ratby. When you reach the village centre, take the road to Botcheson, and then turn right along a narrow country lane signposted to Bury Camp. It comes to a dead end a few hundred metres further where you will see a derelict warehouse beside a small stream. There is a large area of concrete hardstanding alongside so you can turn your truck easily there. That's where we'll come to meet you. Half an hour later we'll all be gone and you just retrace your path to the A46 and deliver to the factory."

"Make sure you're at the warehouse no later than 3:00 p.m., but not earlier than 2:30 p.m. because we don't want to be hanging around unnecessarily. This is my mobile phone number. If there's any problem, ring as soon as you can. If all goes to plan, don't ring till you get to the meeting point. We'll be there within five minutes of your call. One last point. When we've finished, destroy these maps and rendez-vous instructions. Any questions?"

It was all set out meticulously, and Arjan could think of nothing that had been missed.

Meanwhile, during this crucial briefing, unbeknown to Arjan, Mitch and his van driver colleagues had carefully transferred into the container the ten boxes that had travelled up with Habib from Toulon. Mitch rationalised their inclusion to the passengers suggesting they should be used as seats for the voyage. When Arjan returned with Francois to check all was ready, he had no inkling the boxes were there, still less what they contained. The passengers were all on board, and the container doors already resealed, sufficiently expertly to pass Customs inspection.

Perfunctory handshakes concluded the evening's activity. It was almost midnight. The Mercedes and the white van eased quietly out of the yard. Arjan checked the depot and office. Lights out. Alarms on. Gates bolted. If any of the neighbours were awake, the truck they heard pulling out of the depot was Mr van Buitelaar leaving for one his routine long hauls overnight. "Rather him than me," they would say. "I'd much prefer to be in my own bed at this hour!"

The distance from Arjan's base at Aalst to Calais was almost exactly 160 kilometres. He knew every inch of the road, autoroute all the way, and it felt good to be behind the wheel of his truck at last, doing what he knew best and, for the next two hours at least, in charge of what was happening.

Just before reaching the ferry terminal, he pulled into the last lay-by. It was dark and secluded. A few other trucks were hauled up there for the night, their cabs in darkness and curtained off while their drivers slept. Arjan pressed in the mobile phone number to call Habib.

Inside the container module, the group had been sorting themselves out. Most had huddled up in their blankets sitting on the boxes with their backs to the module walls. Two had stretched out on the floor space. It was chilly but not cold. The road was smooth, the journey more comfortable than expected. Conversation had escalated, as their tension eased. Nina and the girls were chatting excitedly in Russian and, from time to time, had to be shushed. The men talked in more restrained tones. There was a mild euphoria amongst the group, like a team about to play a last crucial match. Each of them had planned and worked for months for this moment. They had come from all across Europe to converge together here in this surreal environment. Each had made the momentous decision to escape the desperate stresses of their lives back home – bleak economic futures, ethnic discrimination, physical threats, no jobs, no prospects, no hope. They all had a common goal. Like Israelites on the verge of crossing the river Jordan, they saw the English Channel as the watershed. Beyond that they hoped for better things – a land, metaphorically, flowing with milk and honey. This was the crucial night. Small wonder they were on a high.

The truck had slowed to a halt. The engine had stopped. Conversation aborted at an instant. Now what? Then the mobile rang. Habib pressed the receive button.

"Habib – you tell everybody. Go inside box now. No talk. No noise. We go Customs soon. Then we take ship. Then we go Customs England. Stay in box maybe 4, maybe 5 hours. I phone you when all good in England. I think you try sleep."

Habib acknowledged what he'd said and passed it on to his fellow travellers. Nina translated into Russian for the man who couldn't understand Habib's simple English. One or two took a last chance to relieve themselves. Nina sent a quick text message to Viktor in their native Moldovan.

> "We'll be in England in a few hours. Can't wait to see you.
> Love Nina XXX"

She switched the mobile off quickly. The battery was almost out.

Two of the men secured the module door from the inside. The next few hours were critical. A more subdued mood settled over the group. It was 2:00 a.m. Best to try to sleep as Arjan advised. They were virtual prisoners now until he called them again. From time to time someone used a torch to check the time. Otherwise it was total blackness, not very comfortable, and feeling colder. The consolation was that the construction of the module retained their body heat so they were unlikely to suffer hypothermia. They had food and water and adequate ventilation. And they were nearly there. They just had to be patient for a few more hours.

Arjan had climbed out of the cab. Using the adapted broom handle he pushed up the two small magnetic plates to cover the apertures drilled into the leading face of the container. "Use No Hooks" plates now covered up the holes. All set now. He fired the motor, pulled back onto the autoroute and ten minutes later joined the long crocodile of European hauliers waiting to board the ferries.

The exit formalities from Calais weren't too searching. His papers were all in order; his boarding ticket correct for the next ferry. With over 5,000 trucks passing across the Channel each day, there had to be something especially unusual if the French Customs were going to stir themselves unduly at this hour of the morning other than cursorily waving trucks through. Arjan knew the ropes. Calm as you like. Take it easy. Everything normal. Smile. Empathise with the Custom-man's lot at this god-forsaken hour. Have all the papers, ticket and passport ready. Wish him a good night and accelerate slowly as he waves you on your way. Straightforward as you like. Onto the ramp – into the cavernous hold on the P & O Pride of Dover – park close to the truck in front – shut down the motor – grab coat and wallet – lock the cab - and up to the drivers' deck canteen for coffee and a ham roll. Phase one completed without a hitch. Time to slump down on a recliner seat and doze for the next hour or so.

Inside the module, Nina and Habib and their fellow-travellers were conscious of the stop-start of the truck as it negotiated its way through customs and onto the ferry. The echoing change in the engine noise in the cathedral-like space on the ferry and then its close down signalled their arrival on board. Nothing happened for a half an hour or so. Then they felt the ship's engines throb into life. There was no more than a small perceptible sway as the ship eased out of Calais harbour, but as soon as it had passed the breakwater the swell churned up by the strong and persistent easterly wind began to make its presence felt. Habib at once remembered the nauseous crossing he had endured on the boat to Italy. He didn't relish more seasickness. He wasn't the only one. Most of the group had never been at sea before, and the cramped airless confines of their present predicament were not conducive to maintaining a calm stomach. One by one they used their torches to search for polythene bags. The stench of others retching just added to their discomfort, the only consolation being that once someone had been sick, they felt so exhausted they slumped quickly into sleep. Habib again was one of those to suffer. Why should it be some and not others? Odd that, but he knew the voyage would last only about ninety minutes so he just had to endure it till they reached Dover. He felt wretched. He vowed he would avoid sea crossings forever.

There was considerable relief inside the container when at last the ferry moved inside the harbour mouth at Dover. The sea motion reduced noticeably and they knew they would soon be on dry land. The ship's engines closed down and they sensed they were docked. They waited expectantly. Another fifteen minutes and the truck's motor started. They were on the move again. They could only guess what was going on outside. But so far there didn't seem to have been any hitches. They checked out their watches. Nina seemed to think English time was different. Others said it was an hour earlier. They eventually agreed to put back their watches by that amount. They spoke in muted tones. They still had to get through English Customs. That was the hard part.

Arjan manoeuvred his truck into the queue waiting to process through the Customs hall. It was 5:30 a.m. and still dark. The line of trucks inched forward. Because of the sheer volume going through, Arjan knew that Customs had time to make only random checks. About one in every ten trucks was pulled aside for more questions and examinations. He had a 90% chance of getting through without fuss. Fingers crossed. He could be on the road and away in ten minutes.

"Sod it, sod it, sod it!" he said under his breath as despairingly he registered that the Customs man was waving him into an examination bay. "Just stay cool."

He presented all his paperwork. Should be no problem with that. So what else will they do? Gas testing inside the container? But they'd have to open up the sealed doors for that – would they go as far as that? If so, would the accommodation module disguised as a crate be sufficiently convincing? Maybe they'd use heat-seeking gauges from the outside? Arjan wondered if the metal foil carefully constructed into the module would be an adequate baffle. And what about smells inside? God, there was so much that could give the game away. His heart was pounding.

"Welcome to England, sir. Just a few routine questions. I'm sure you appreciate we have to be careful these days." The Customs man was polite and friendly, and thoroughly professional.

"Don't get many sea containers through Dover. They usually go up to Folkestone. Any particular reason you're coming through here, sir?"

"English not good, sir, sorry. But I take container from Antwerp. I go to Leicester factory. I think papers good?" Arjan was economical in what he said. Tell the truth, but no need for the whole truth.

"So when did you pick up at Antwerp?"

"Yesterday morning."

"But you didn't catch the ferry till this morning? Why was that? Where were you and the container all that time?"

"I take truck my yard. Stay there while I go sleep. Then I go to ferry."

"So where is your yard, sir?" Arjan told him.

"What I need to know is whether anyone can have interfered with the container while it was in your yard? Were you there all the time?"

"No problem. I stay with truck all time. No-one touch container." Arjan lied as convincingly as he could.

"Seems a bit unusual to me, sir, that a Chinese container should go to Antwerp first when it's supposed to heading for the UK. Do you mind if we take a look inside? Let our dog have a sniff around a bit. Won't take long."

This was what he had dreaded. The only thing to do was to plead ignorance. Tell them he had no idea what was inside the container. He had just picked it up to deliver it. He was just a driver. He didn't prepare the papers. His mind raced as he stepped down from the cab to accompany the Customs man to the rear of his truck.

In the adjacent bay another Customs official was examining a dark green truck from Rumania. It had no markings on it, and was in poor condition by comparison with the other gleaming European trucks streaming through the terminal. No surprise that this vehicle had been called in for a closer look. The Customs man allocated to it had spotted something odd. He called across to his colleague.

"Eric, I need a second opinion here. This truck's got two fuel tanks, one well used and accessible, but the other looks much newer, even through all the muck on it. It's got an unusually large aperture for a fuel tank and the cap is locked, and the gentleman from Rumania whose driving it says he's lost the key to the cap. That's a bit peculiar? What's the use of a fuel tank that can't be opened? I think we need a closer look. Tell me what you think."

"OK, I'll let this guy go. His paperwork's all OK. I guess it's up to the shippers if they choose to route machinery through Antwerp to Dover."

He turned to Arjan. "Sorry, sir, - I think we've got more important business to attend to. So I'll not detain you any longer. Have a good trip."

And that was that. Arjan climbed back into the cab, heaved a huge sigh of relief, and throttled up to ease out of the customs shed. His tension slipped away fast. Mercifully he was through. Never had he so relished ratcheting down his gears to take the long climb up the north cliff past Dover Castle. He pulled into the first lay-by and called up Habib on the mobile.

"Hallo, you hear me? Good. We finish Customs. All OK. Soon I go for breakfast. I think no noise while truck is stop."

"How long we stay inside?" asked Habib.

"Long journey first. We meet people 15:00 hours. They open door. Then you go out in England."

Arjan opened up the vents. It was still dark, so his antics with the broom handle were not obvious to other truckers parked up in the lay-by. Then it was the short half-hour drive to Farthing Corner, the A2 service area. He preferred this route, rather than the M20, because it was the nearest and quickest place for a good breakfast. That replenished him for what lay ahead. At eight o'clock he was back on the road for the long drive north. The wind was still fresh, but the sky was clear. Things looked good. Very soon his worries would be over.

Inside the container there was relief all round when Habib explained they were through Customs and could open up the module to move around. The fresh blasts of air venting in through the forward holes were quickly dispersing the foul odours that had built up in the module during the crossing. At last the passengers could relieve themselves more easily and dispose of their various used bags in the large black bin liner. Now for the first time, they could see daylight through the vents as dawn broke. And they could begin to talk more freely again while the truck hammered along the motorway. They ate what bread was left, and drank deeply to eradicate the last vestiges of bad taste in their mouths. Some had brought extra rations of fruit and chocolate in their rucksacks. In a spirit of bonhomie this was shared around. The worst was over. They could relax. The only problem was trying to keep warm in the face of the relentless cold blast of fresh air surging in through the vents. Most retreated back into the module, curled up in their blankets and dozed off to make up for the disturbed night.

The drive took them through the Dartford Tunnel, round the M25 and then onto the M1. Conditions were good. The rush hour was over and Arjan made speedy progress. Inside the container, the steady measured pace made it easy to relax. The problem of the cold air blasting in was resolved by keeping the module door closed as much as possible. The increasingly more pressing matter was the need for a decent meal. None of them had eaten properly since yesterday. Arjan had had the benefit of meals on board ship and at service stations. The passengers, still de facto prisoners in the container, would have no chance for further sustenance till they were released. By the time Arjan was pulling into the Watford Gap Service station, just twenty miles south of Leicester it was midday and pangs of hunger were, for the men at least, their overriding concern. Nina's friend Natasha had another problem. Her period had started.

Arjan called Habib again. "We close now. I go take lunch. We stop here one hour. Many trucks here. You no make noise. I talk later."

While the truck was moving, psychologically it felt as if progress was being made. When the truck was stopped, patience was strained. At least the cold air blast had temporarily ceased. Now they were close to the end of their journey, anxieties began to escalate. Most were unclear what would happen when the container was opened. Food was their first priority. Some had addresses or contacts, but how would they reach them from the drop-off point? Not something they had given much thought to till now. They just had to hope that Mitch and his collaborators would do something for them. The winter sunshine shot two parallel beams of light through the container. They could hear the noises outside of people going about their business, and vehicles and trucks periodically hauling in and out. They needed no reminding to keep their noise level down. This was a very public place. No option but to grind out the next hour or two in their prison quietly and patiently.

No need for torches now. They observed on their watches it was just after 1:30 p.m. English time, as Arjan fired up the truck motor for the short last leg. A few minutes later Habib took Arjan's call.

"We meet people maybe one hour. Then you go out. I phone you when we there. Understand?" Habib transmitted the message. Inside the container tension began to give way to anticipation, even a measure of mild excitement. They had worked hard for this. They had each paid out a small fortune. They had waited a long time. This was it - at long last.

Another half-hour driving up the M1; then the slip road to Kirby Muxloe. Arjan had studied the map and instructions for the rendez-vous point during his lunch stop. They were imprinted in his mind. He proceeded cautiously through the village. Then took the Ratby road. Slower here because there were traffic calming humps right through the main street. It was a sleepy place at this hour. Even so one or two locals raised a fleeting eyebrow at the unusual sight of a foreign juggernaut easing its way through. When it turned left in the village centre, they assumed the driver had taken a wrong turn earlier on his way to the Timken Metal Works, and was now turning to get back on track. They gave it no second thought. A quarter of a mile further on, Arjan spotted the by-road on his right signposted to Bury Camp and swung round into the narrow wooded lane. It was almost 2:30 p.m. The abandoned warehouse should be three hundred metres down here. He would be there in less than a minute.

But he was wrong. Very wrong. As he eased forward slowly in low gear, the truck filling the width of the lane, what suddenly came into view ahead was not good news. A small British Panda police car was approaching. They were meeting head-on and there was nowhere to hide, nothing he could do. He braked to a standstill and waited. The police car had stopped a few yards from him. A young policeman, with a broad grin on his face, walked towards the truck.

"Shit," murmured Arjan to himself. "What the fuck do I do now?"

Chapter 46

Rendez-Vous - Friday 9th January 2004

Most people would have described Sheila Fletcher's upbringing as sheltered. Her parents were the sort of people that kept themselves to themselves. That is not to say they were dull or boring. Indeed her father had a degree in Politics, Philosophy and Economics from Oxford and had risen to a senior position in the Civil Service. He was based in Whitehall and commuted there each day from their home by the river at Putney. Her mother's archaeological degree and interest stayed with her all her life, and Sheila's early years were full of books, travel, and intelligent adult company.

But she was not much attracted to pop music or dancing, and boys generally she found rather wearisome. At Putney High School for Girls she devoured her academic studies with single-mindedness. Often she felt she moved on a different plain from her classmates as she lived vicariously in a world populated by the heroes and legends of the classics and the stirring emotions of Shakespeare's plays.

Her excellent A-level examination results in Latin, Greek and English secured her an Exhibition to read Classics at Girton College, Cambridge, which had long been her ambition. Her love of classical history and languages, the archaeological interest inherited from her mother, and her altruistic ambition to enthuse others with the same affection inevitably led to a decision to become a teacher.

Teaching posts in Classics were becoming increasingly confined to the fee-paying school sector, so, unsurprisingly, her career was channelled towards schools where pupils had both a desire to learn and an aptitude for more traditional scholarship. In due course Sheila was appointed Head of the Classics Department at Loughborough High School, where she spent the last ten years of her professional full-time employment.

Sheila had never bothered to marry – too much of a distraction really - there were so many other interesting things to do, her alpine flower collection, her two cats, her garden, her reading and research, to say nothing of the mountains of work at home preparing lessons and marking pupils' work. By most standards her lifestyle was simple, but for her it was full to overflowing with an abundance of experience in literature, travel, art and music - so much so she bubbled with enthusiasm for her subjects, which was contagious with her pupils and colleagues.

Her predilection for warm cardigans and consequent demands for classroom windows to be flung open – "Don't you find it rather stifling in here?" – earned her the nickname among pupils of "Hot Sheila", supposedly ironic in that the youngsters were of the unanimous view that Miss Fletcher's amorous interests must have been sub-zero. They were not to know - and never would - about the Summer School in Rome in 1962, where Sheila spent ten weeks of her long vacation, and at the hands of her thirty-two year old Italian tutor, literally and metaphorically, enjoyed the most torrid time of her life. On the embankment of the Circus Maximus, echoing with the blood lust of the Roman chariot races of old, they made love under the stars at night. In the holy portals of the arcade round St Peter's Square they did things she had never dreamed of. After wining and dining al fresco near the Spanish Steps, in a delicious state of mild inebriation she had plunged fully clothed into the Trevi Fountain, and then meandered back to their lodgings in the warm balm of the Italian night feeling deliciously decadent and liberated. Rather than "hot", if her pupils had known, they would have dubbed her "Incandescent Sheila". The memories were etched indelibly in her mind and she often mused affectionately on them, but that was then, and now was now.

On moving to Loughborough in 1992, her search for a property was based on a number of criteria. Not too close to school - or shopping at weekends and evening social activities might mean bumping into too many pupils out of school. She preferred to keep a distance between her professional work and her private life. But also it had to be not too far from school, so as to avoid a long tedious commute to work each day. Such a waste of time that. Most important she wanted a quiet secluded cottage with a garden and some character - a minimum of two bedrooms, so guests could stay, and sufficient distance from main roads to avoid the drone of traffic.

After too many fruitless viewings with young estate agents who thought character was about modern bathroom fittings and double-glazed windows with mock stained glass, eventually she identified what she was looking for. It was just outside the village of Ratby immediately to the west of Leicester, about twenty minutes' drive from school. The cottage was probably a hundred years old, modernised but not ostentatiously, set in half an acre of rambling garden, with a small orchard, located along a narrow country lane that went nowhere, except to an old derelict warehouse adjacent to the stream that ran close by the lane. The only traffic to pass were the occasional cars of late-night courting couples seeking some privacy for the conclusion to their evening out. At the far end of the lane over the stream was the old Bury Camp and the Ivanhoe Trail, which provided agreeable walking opportunities within easy reach of the cottage.

Sheila made the decision that this would be her home, and, by the time of her retirement from full-time teaching in 2002, the house had been furnished in her own style, comfortable and traditional, and the garden redesigned to her wishes. There was excellent shopping nearby in Leicester. She continued to attend occasional school functions by invitation and so kept up with the gossip there. Ease of access to the M1 meant she could travel conveniently whenever she wished to visit friends and erstwhile colleagues. In short, Sheila Fletcher was content in her retirement.

During the very hot summer of 2003, a new housing development was started in the nearby village of Ratby. Jarmans Construction were building lots of little boxes on a field that had just been given planning consent. The farmer had made a heap of money on the deal, and now Jarmans were going to make their little profit out of it. The building programme was behind schedule and the showhouse, which should have been open well before Christmas, was still not ready for viewings. A last minute rush immediately after New Year's Day, 2004, finished the interior. Furnishings were moved in en masse from John Lewis' store, but the plot of ground around the showhouse was still a builder's tip. The site manager contacted two local garden contractors from the Yellow Pages and asked for quotes to do a quick clear-up and establish an instant garden. "Instant New Gardens" was the firm that put in the lowest bid and were duly commissioned. Gerry and Pete, the two co-owners were not averse to cutting corners on one-off jobs like this. Never mind the means, it's the end that matters – an instant garden in a couple of days.

"No problem. Leave it to us, guv."

On the night of Thursday 8th January, while Arjan van Buitelaar and his truck with its precious cargo were being ferried sedately across the English Channel, Gerry and Pete set out to locate some instant shrubs and trees for Mr Jarman's showhouse. Their pick-up truck turned into the lane just outside Ratby heading for a little cottage where it was well-known a retired schoolteacher had established a delightful English country garden over recent years. Gerry was familiar with the place having spent a number of steamy late-night sessions parked in his car beside the old warehouse at the bottom of the lane. Their pick-up coasted to a gentle halt outside the gate leading to the garage at the rear of the house.

It was two o'clock in the morning, a cold chilly night with an owl hooting in the distance, as Pete and Gerry began digging up the five newest planted shrubs in the centre of the back lawn. They levered each out of its hole, placed the root systems on sheets of polythene, and bound each tree into a package, which they then ferried on a small sack barrow to their vehicle. It was hard labour, but pushed on by their adrenalin surge they had the job finished in less than an hour. They eased out the clutch gently and glided away with their prizes reflecting in self-congratulatory mood that the profit on the showhouse job was now going to be nicely enhanced by the value of five mature shrubs and small trees nestling in the back of their pick-up, for which they would charge Mr Jarman £500 plus expenses, but which had cost them no more than a few hours' sleep. "Bloody good business, this!" said Pete. "Yer gotta grab a good deal when yer sees it, y' know!"

As Mr van Buitelaar's truck was making its way up country from Dover, Sheila Fletcher had finished her breakfast and fed the cats and was hanging out a few smalls on the washing line when it gradually began to dawn on her that some very big moles had been at work in her garden overnight. More to the point it appeared that someone had stolen some of her shrubs. Her reaction was twofold

- first distress at the loss of the shrubs, and second indignation that her privacy had been so invaded.

Detective Constable Boyd and Community Policing Officer Stringer received the call from Headquarters at 10:00 a.m. that morning. A Miss Fletcher living in the lane just west of Ratby village had reported the theft of some garden trees. Could they get out to see what it was all about? Not an urgent job, but ought to be dealt with before the end of their shift today. Boyd and Stringer were on their way to a crime prevention meeting organised by the Neighbourhood Watch Committee at Glenfield Community Hall, due to start in half an hour. A quick call to Miss Fletcher on their mobile confirmed that she would be happy to receive them immediately after lunch.

In fact, both policemen would have preferred to have gone straight out to see her, but attendance at the meeting they were heading for was all but compulsory. Like many policemen, Boyd and Stringer regarded all this joint-participation stuff as a long way off why they had joined the police force. But if someone was prepared to pay them good money for wasting time at meetings like this, why should they worry?

They duly escaped at midday, took a half-hour lunch-break in the police canteen at headquarters, and arrived promptly at Miss Fletcher's cottage at 1:30 p.m., just as Arjan van Buitelaar was firing up the motor of his truck at Watford Gap Service Station on the M1 to begin the last leg of his journey to the rendez-vous point. He was well on time and had the detailed instructions and maps close by him. All had gone more smoothly than he dared hope. In one hour he should be at the warehouse and soon after that, relieved of his illegal cargo, he would be on his way to the Polymer Plastics factory to make the delivery of the main container load on schedule at 4:00 p.m. Thereafter he would be considerably richer and all for less than twenty-four hours of clandestine endeavour. A good deal at half the price.

Sheila was not at all sure whether it was proper to offer tea or coffee to policemen while on duty, but their friendly and helpful manner soon put her at ease. They were very happy with a cup of tea, even though they had not expected there would be no sugar in the house. Not something Miss Fletcher normally used. They inspected the scene of the crime. The five large holes surrounded by mounds of newly turned earth were eloquent testimony to the night's events. For insurance purposes what had happened needed formal reporting. They could then issue a crime number for it. Apparently this was essential to the bureaucrats in the household insurance office, though it was doubtful if Miss Fletcher could expect any recompense for her loss because of the voluntary excess clauses in her policy. The written statement was duly made out and signed and the courteous Detective Constable and Community Policing Officer took their leave. Their small Panda police car turned out of her drive to head back to Leicester at 2:25 p.m. It was Friday afternoon and very soon they would be clocking off shift for the weekend.

Sheila busied herself with the jobs she would normally have done straight after lunch, feeding the cats, watering the plants on the kitchen windowsill, and washing up the teacups. On reflection she was rather worried that her statement had not been as accurately worded as it should have been. In it she had said "I planted the shrubs last autumn". It occurred to her now rather belatedly that she ought not to have used the active voice. Much better to have used the passive voice "The shrubs were planted last autumn". Although she had supervised the work, it was her gardener who had actually done the planting. Oh, dear – she would have to give the policeman a ring on Monday to see if this needed to be altered. Such a silly mistake to have made when the beautiful structure and form of language affords proper precision.

While Sheila was musing on this theme, Boyd and Stringer were rather more preoccupied with ten tons of heavy metal in the shape of a Dutch container truck bearing down on them in the narrow lane barely one hundred yards from Miss Fletcher's cottage. With the truck brushing the vegetation both sides of the lane, there was no option but to stop. Passing was out of the question. The airbrakes hissed loudly as the twelve wheels of the truck were brought to a towering halt ten yards in front of the diminutive Panda car.

"Some geezer's lost his way! Better sort out where he should be," said Stringer as he got out of the passenger seat to talk to the truck driver.

Inside the truck cab, Arjan van Buitelaar was having to think quickly. He left his engine idling and climbed down from the warm security of his cab.

"Now, mate – I think you're on the wrong road. Nothing down here except trees and birds and a broken old warehouse," said Stringer.

"I speak small English. Sorry. I take wrong road I think."

"So where are you supposed to be going?"

Arjan was not going to tell him that he was actually on track for exactly where he wanted to be. But apart from the Plastics factory, he knew of no other convincing address in the area. He had no option but to tell them he was scheduled to deliver there. He showed them his paperwork. Boyd had joined Stringer by this stage and together they looked at the mystifying shipping documents in Chinese, Dutch and English relating to the sea container's official content and destination. At least the factory delivery address was printed in English.

"Polymer Plastics –Valley Road, on the Troon industrial estate. You're not far off, mate. About eight miles from here. You must've taken the wrong exit from the motorway junction. We're going back that way. Just follow us. It'll take fifteen minutes at most and we'll make sure you deliver this lot to the right place. We'll back up and turn round. Follow us to the end of this lane– about 300 yards. There's hard standing outside the old warehouse. You can swing round there. Then just follow us. You'll be there in no time."

Arjan van Buitelaar's English was limited, but like most Dutch people he spent a lot of time watching English TV programmes, so was able to follow the gist of what Boyd was saying. He didn't like it, but he saw no alternative but to go along with their suggestion. What would happen when he reached the factory he had no idea, but he would think of something. His overriding objective now was to offload the container and get back on the road to the coast before anyone opened it up.

Sheila was rather bemused to see the Panda car reverse back into her drive some five minutes after the policemen had taken leave of her, and then drive towards the end of the lane followed by a huge articulated truck such as she had never seen in the lane before. Then no more than two minutes later the same procession motored back past her cottage going in the opposite direction towards Ratby. How strange! She continued the more absorbing task of watering her plants.

In the cemetery car park opposite the church at Kirby Muxloe, one mile away, a black Mercedes was parked, its two occupants waiting patiently with their mobile phone switched on. Nearby, two unmarked white vans were also parked inconspicuously, one in Ratby village centre behind the Railway Inn, and one in the large layby outside the Timken Metal Works at Newtown Unthank, both within less than five minutes drive of the warehouse at the end of Miss Fletcher's lane. Both drivers had their mobile phones at the ready. It was 2:40 p.m. and the call from Arjan van Buitelaar was expected anytime – they all knew the rendezvous had been set for not later than 3:00 p.m.

When the phone in the Mercedes rang, the portly gentleman who answered it speedily was somewhat relieved, although he would never admit his anxiety to anyone. His clammy hands and quickened pulse rate bore testimony to the stress and risk involved. He could read on the LCD printout it was the Dutchman calling. He must have reached the rendez-vous. Once van Buitelaar had confirmed he was there, he would phone the two waiting vans and they would all converge on the warehouse to be with him in five minutes. One van would take off the immigrants, the other the dismantled accommodation module and the ten precious boxes. They would then go their separate ways into the darkening Friday evening. The container would be resealed and the Dutchman could make his normal delivery on schedule with the prospect of a relaxed weekend back across the channel.

Unfortunately, the message received from the Dutchman did nothing to reduce the stress levels in the Mercedes. Instead of being at the rendez-vous, Mr van Buitelaar's truck was heading at a steady 40 miles an hour along the Leicester ring road behind an obliging police escort car on its way to the Plastics factory where he would expect to arrive in about ten minutes. Unless they had any other suggestions, Mr van Buitelaar would be delivering the container and contents there and leaving as quickly as he could. He would wait for their call back, but it had better be within ten minutes or it would be too late.

Chapter 47

Leicester - Friday Afternoon, 9th January 2004

Gertrude Cameron's husband had died nine months ago. He was buried in the cemetery opposite the church in Kirby Muxloe village, where they had lived all their married life in the same cottage. She missed him terribly. He had been such a dutiful husband. Only now he was no longer with her did she realise how much she had depended on him. She too was in her late seventies. Her heart was frail and she suffered badly with arthritis. Life was so much more of a struggle now he had gone. It was the prostate thing; he just wasted away so quickly by the time the hospital told them how advanced it was. The problem was, you see, he went to the doctor too late, obdurate till the end, maintaining there wasn't much wrong with him.

At the time of the funeral she made her private promise to the one whose life had been meshed with hers for so long. Never would a weekend go by except that he had some fresh flowers by his headstone to remind him of the garden he had cared for so lovingly. So it was, on a chill windswept Friday afternoon at the beginning of January, 2004, clutching her posy of anemones, Mrs Cameron found herself in the cemetery at the same time as this car parked incongruously by the compost heap and water tap. If she had been asked to describe it, she might have remembered it was big and black, probably a funeral car, but she couldn't recollect seeing anyone in it - the windows were so dark. Strange that it should be parked there though.

In the far corner of the graveyard, she went about her business. Many of the other graves had had fleeting visits over the Christmas holidays from relatives whose token offerings of flowers were now wilted, forlorn and neglected. Gertrude looked at them disapprovingly as she arranged her anemones to replace last week's flowers. She put fresh water in the vase, straitened up stiffly, said a simple prayer for the soul of her loved one, and then retraced her steps, stopping briefly at the compost heap to throw away the dead flowers. It was tiring climbing the gentle incline back to the cemetery gate leaning on her walking stick. She gave the car no second look. No energy for that. Not her business anyway.

It was 2:45 p.m. Inside the car, through their one-way windows, Mitch was idly watching the old lady doing her duty when the call came through from Arjan. The portly gentleman answered the mobile, then swore and blasphemed violently. Mitch didn't need telling something had gone wrong.

"We're in deep shit!" The portly man rehearsed what Arjan had said. "Get the fucking map out quick. Where the hell is that sodding truck going?"

They knew the address of the factory in Valley Road on the Troon Industrial Estate. That was on the shipping documents. They knew it was to the north of the city, but they had never bothered to identify exactly where, because their interest in the truck should have terminated well before it headed off there. They pored over the map trying to find a Valley Road. The names of the industrial estates weren't marked. If they found a Valley Road, how could they be sure it was the right one? They needed to move fast but couldn't afford to race off to the wrong address.

"Give me those bloody shipping documents. Thank God there's a phone number for the factory on them. I'll phone them to find where it is." The portly man pressed the number into his mobile.

"Good afternoon. Polymer Plastic Limited. How can I help you?" simpered the receptionist.

"Good afternoon. Sorry to trouble you, madam. DHL delivery here. Got a package for you. Can you confirm where to deliver it please?"

"No problem, sir. Just bring it here we're open till five this afternoon."

"Not sure how to get to you. We're in Kirby Muxloe."

"Oh, Kirby Muxloe - what a lovely little village. My husband and I go for walks round there. Do you know the Ivanhoe Trail? Such pretty countryside, don't you think? Well now –let me think. I'm so bad at directions. My husband says I'm the worst navigator in the world! Can you believe it? Can't help getting all my lefts and rights muddled. You know how it is. Let me ask Sonia to see if she knows. Just put you on hold a moment."

While the sounds of synthetic music transmitted themselves down the phone line, the frustration inside the Mercedes was escalating. Every minute this conversation lasted was a minute less time to catch up with the truck. Van Buitelaar already had a big start on them and was likely to be at the factory any time now. After what seemed an interminable wait, the receptionist cut short the canned music.

"Hi there – still there. Oh good. Sonia says it's simple. Now let's see if I've got it right. First you cross over the M1 and take the inner ring road till you go over a big railway bridge. Then at the next roundabout take Waterside Road. Valley Road is at the top. We'll expect you in about half an hour, though the Friday traffic might slow you down. It really is terrible these days, don't you think? All this traffic. Don't know what's to become of it all. Anyway, see you soon - bye-ee!"

"OK, let's go. And fast." The Mercedes screeched out of the cemetery. "Second thoughts - for God's sake don't break the speed limits. We can't afford to be hauled up." They swept past Mrs Cameron trudging home, too preoccupied to register it was the car she had seen at the cemetery. Mitch used the mobile to call up their two vans parked up in Ratby village and Newtown Unthank impatiently waiting for the signal to race to the rendez-vous.

"Big problem. The truck's not going to the drop-off point. You stay where you are. Keep your phones on. We'll tell you what to do as soon as we locate it."

The portly man leaned forward from the back seat, urgent and anxious, scanning the road signs and marrying them up with the map. They were on the ring road. Traffic was heavy but moving steadily. If they didn't get lost, they should be there in fifteen minutes. But it was now already fifteen minutes or more since they'd had Arjan's call. He ought to be at the factory by now. They would just have to play it by ear when they got there. But things could get heavy. There was too much at stake. The ten boxes of explosives were needed by ruthless people and they wouldn't take kindly to their non-delivery. The illegal immigrants didn't matter. They'd already paid their passage. They were of no consequence now. If they got caught, that was their problem. But the boxes of explosives had to be got out of the container, and no-one was going to stand in their way.

★★★

The friendly policemen escorting the Dutch truck had done their good deed for the day. They stopped short of entering the factory gates but beckoned Arjan's truck through, waved a cheery farewell, and were off. The car-park in front of the factory office block was evidently mainly for cars. No sign of any trucks. Arjan pulled up pointing towards what looked like an access road to the factory premises behind the offices. He called Habib on the mobile.

"We got problem. Everyone very quiet. Good you go inside box. No talk. I call you later."

Inside the container there had been increasing frustration. When the truck had stopped in the lane, they had no idea what was happening outside but presumed they had arrived at the drop-off point. Then there had been other manoeuvrings and another twenty-minute drive. They hoped this was where they would be let out. Now Arjan was telling them things had gone wrong. Morosely, they huddled together in the crate that had been their home for fifteen hours. They were tired, and hungry, in need of a good wash and brush up, and deeply worried. And they could do nothing about it, except sit tight.

The office receptionist at PPL looked up from her desk console and watched the truck swinging to a halt on their forecourt. She phoned the Managing Director on his direct line.

"Hello, Mr Burton. Sorry to disturb you, but there's a big foreign truck just arrived outside. I guess it's the shipment from China you've been waiting for."

Michael Burton cut short his session with one of his sales reps. and together they hurried out. The driver was still in his cab, finishing a phone call and sorting through his papers. His electric window slid down silently. He reached out and handed down his delivery papers. Michael scanned them. Yes, this was the China shipment. Great. It had taken almost a year since he had first formulated the idea of doing business with a Chinese manufacturer. This was the start of what he expected to be a significant long-term cost reduction on the purchase price of moulds. That should give his company a huge selling edge over his rivals. Excellent. He shouted up to Arjan.

"Welcome. Glad you made it. I've been expecting you. Slight problem. This delivery is for our other factory site. We've no lifting gear here to offload the container. So we've got to go there. It's only five minutes away. Follow me. I'll lead you. Then we can get the container off and you can be on your way."

"Sorry, my English not good. I think this address OK on papers?" Arjan had not understood what he was saying.

Michael Burton painstakingly tried to explain things in simplified English. "Sorry – we go different factory. I show you. Five minutes. No problem." He waved five fingers and pointed to his wristwatch. "I go blue car. You come follow me."

He dashed back into the office to tell his PA, Judy Makepeace, what he was doing, while Arjan swung his truck round to face the entry gate, and then set off to tail the blue BMW. They retraced his route to the ring road, then beyond deep into another extensive industrial estate. Arjan tried to remember the road names, but they came fast and furiously at him as he concentrated on not losing the BMW – Barkby Road, Fairfax Way, Wyvern Road, Roseneath Drive - all meaningless to him, and in the end he had difficulty in remembering any of them. As predicted, they turned into the gates of the second Polymer Plastics factory five minutes later.

Michael stopped his car just inside and directed Arjan to park in a vacant hard-standing area to the side of the main factory. He came across to the truck.

"OK, just wait here. I'll go inside and get them to bring round the mobile hoist to lift off the container. Shan't be long."

Arjan got the gist of that and waited. Time to phone Mitch again. This could be difficult.

"Hello, Arjan here," he spoke in Dutch. The call came through as the Mercedes was nearing the Valley Road factory. The portly man passed the phone to Mitch. "Are you at the factory?" he asked.

"Yes, but not the one at Valley Road. I've been directed to their second site. It's not far away."

"So where's that for fuck's sake?" asked Mitch.

"Not sure. Had to follow the boss's car to get here. Another industrial estate."

"So what's the address? Tell us and we'll get to you."

"I don't know what the fucking street's called. It was all I could do to keep up with my guide."

Mitch rehearsed what he had said to his colleagues. The portly man was distraught.

"Tell that cunt we need to know where he is, or he'll not get the rest of his money."

By the time this was relayed to Arjan he was rapidly becoming less concerned about the pay-off than being caught red-handed smuggling in illegal immigrants. His one preoccupation now was to offload this incriminating container and get the hell out of it before anyone opened it up.

"OK, I try to find address, but the lifting hoist's coming so I can't speak any more now."

He clicked off, leaving a cauldron of seething frustration in the Mercedes, which had now reached the Valley Road factory and was parked discreetly a hundred metres away. Somewhere, within a mile radius of where they were parked, was their quarry. But it might as well have been a hundred miles until they knew where exactly. The portly man grabbed the phone. He couldn't speak Dutch but he would make sure this bastard driver delivered the goods.

"Mr van Buitelaar. You speak some English I think?" Arjan had answered the phone while watching the lifting hoist manoeuvre the container from his truck taking it along the service road towards the rear of the factory.

"We need to know where you are. We're not sympathetic to people who let us down. I'm sure you understand. Just find out which road you're in and let us know quick. Otherwise you might not get home again. Is that clear?"

Arjan had only partially understood the words, but the menace in his tone was unmistakeable. "OK, I try find address when I go," he replied placatingly.

The hoist had deposited the container in a deserted area behind the warehouses. The factory itself was just closing down for the weekend and the employees were streaming home. Michael Burton came back to the truck and signed the delivery notes.

"Thanks very much. That's all fine. We'll open it up on Monday to take out the equipment. Can't do that now. Everyone's gone home. It'll be safe here and undisturbed behind locked gates till then. Any problem I'll get in touch with the shippers. I guess your job's done. Have a good trip home." He tipped Arjan a £20 note.

"Follow me and I'll get you back to the ring road. I'm going back to my office anyway."

Arjan renegotiated the compact roads on the industrial estate trying desperately to remember the relevant names. The factory was located in Bassingthwaite Av., off Roseneath Drive. But how to pronounce those in English he had no idea. Nor could he accurately remember their spelling. There was no chance to stop and write them down.

From the window of the BMW Michael Burton's hand waved when they had reached the ringroad and pointed him to the route back towards the M1. Then he turned off heading for his office again, leaving Arjan with two consuming worries. First he had to get back to Mitch to try to tell him the address where the container now rested, isolated at the rear of a deserted factory, deep in the heart of a nondescript industrial estate. That was going to be difficult. Second he had to phone to tell Habib and his travellers what had happened. That too would be difficult. He was increasingly distressed at leaving them in the lurch, but for the present he didn't know what was best. He just hoped Mitch would have solution.

It was now 4:30 p.m. on a Friday afternoon. Traffic was heaving everywhere on the ring road as Leicester's working masses surged home like lemmings for their weekend's leisure. Arjan had expected to be equally relaxed and looking forward to his weekend by this time, but things had gone badly wrong. It took another fifteen minutes' driving until he could find a lay-by to make his calls. First to Mitch.

"The factory's the same name as the one in Valley Road." He tried to pronounce the address as far as he could remember it. But in Dutch it came over incomprehensibly. He then tried to spell it out.

"B-A-S–ING- like the Dutch Bank –T–W–H–A–T-A-V." Painstakingly he tried to revisualise the street name, but he couldn't remember all the letters or their proper sequence. "That's the best I can do," he said, "Definitely began B-A-S. Haven't you got a map? It's only five minutes' drive from the first factory".

The portly man in the Mercedes was furiously cursing his fingers all over his map, searching for something comparable, but could make no sense out of what Arjan was dictating on the phone.

"You useless load of shit! How can you lose a bloody freight container? You can say fucking goodbye to your payment." He slammed the end-of-call button on the mobile.

"Only one thing to do! We've got to go inside this place and find the address of their other factory. Leave the talking to me."

The Mercedes eased its way through the Valley Road factory gates and parked in a visitor's slot. The car-park was now virtually empty. As always, the admin staff were away early for the weekend. It was almost dark as the portly man and Mitch approached reception. The lady behind the desk was tidying away papers and reaching for her coat in the cupboard as the unexpected visitors walked in.

"Sorry sir, we're just closing. But if you leave a message, I'll see someone gets onto it on Monday."

"We need to see the manager urgently. Is he about?"

"Oh, is he expecting you? He's been very busy this afternoon taking delivery of new machinery. Not sure if he's come back yet. Maybe he'll be going straight home afterwards. Sometimes he has a game of squash on Friday night and that's always a priority for him. I'll try his office. Who shall I say is here to see him?"

"Tell him we're from the shipping company. We've come to verify delivery of the sea container."

"Ah, yes, well I can tell you it arrived this afternoon. So you needn't worry Mr Burton." She finished putting on her coat, closed down her computer and swung a black leather bag over her shoulder. Time for her to be away. It was already two minutes after five.

"We need to check the documents, and get an official signature. That's the way they do things in China, you know. Perhaps you could tell us where the container is and we'll go across and sort things out there?"

"Oh, I think Mr Burton took it across to our other factory. I never go there you know. It's all lorries and factories on that estate. Can't stand the place!"

"Just tell us the address and we'll find it ourselves?"

"No good going now, sir. That factory closed at four o'clock and it'll all be locked up. Perhaps if Mr Burton's here, he can sign your documents? I'll try to call him."

"Oh, Mr Burton. Elspeth here at reception. Really sorry to disturb you. Hope you don't mind but I've got two gentlemen here who want some papers signed about the delivery of the container that arrived this afternoon. Do you think you could spare them a minute? – That's good. I'm sure they'll appreciate that. Have a good weekend!"

"Mr Burton says he'll come through in a couple of minutes. Would you like to take a seat? He won't be long. He'll sort things out. 'Fraid I must dash. Lots of shopping to do. Bye-ee."

The portly man and Mitch did as they were bidden. They were resolute and focussed. Mr Burton would be unsuspecting. The offices were all but empty. They would be able to deal with him on their own terms. The initiative was with them. He was the vital link to reach their goal. If he was cooperative, no problem. If not, Mr Burton was in for a hard time. They owed him no favours.

★★★

Inside the container, uncertainty was slowly giving way to distress. Habib had transmitted the last message from Arjan to the others. They were all huddled inside the accommodation module, keeping deathly quiet. They had been conscious of more manoeuvrings of the truck, then a short drive, and then sounds of clanging metal against the sides of the container before sensing the container being swung upwards, causing some of them to fall off their makeshift seats on the boxes. Finally a jerky scraping bump, more metal clanging, the sound of a retreating vehicle and then silence. Nothing, except the claustrophobic blackness, the pervasive smell of unwashed bodies, the lingering odours of bodily functions, the dank invasive cold, and the gnawing pangs of hunger and thirst. Nothing, until, slowly, their whisperings began to articulate their subliminal anxiety that they might have been abandoned, and were trapped in this metal prison. But they had one lifeline - Habib's mobile phone. The driver had seemed helpful. Surely he wouldn't let them down. If he didn't phone them soon, they could always phone him. "Thank God I printed his mobile number into my phone's memory," said Habib. It was their only slender contact with the outside. Nina's battery was now dead and none of the others had workable mobiles.

After the abortive attenuated call to Mitch from the lay-by, Arjan pressed in Habib's number. When the phone rang inside the container there was a mini cheer. Habib grabbed it hungrily.

"Arjan, here – how are you?"

"We OK, but we want go out. Very hungry. The man come open door soon?" Habib's staccato English conveyed their fermenting anxiety.

"Small problem. I think you wait maybe one hour. Then everything OK." Arjan tried to be reassuring. He hadn't a clue what would happen or when, but he had a burden of concern for Habib and his friends sealed in the container. When he'd first agreed to do this, it was because of his sympathy for the underdog. Now things had gone pear-shaped. The image of his daughter floated through his mind. He had let her down. She had died alone, unloved and defeated. He had wanted to give this lot a chance. Now they were holed up God knew where. They'd spent a fortune to get here. What the hell could he do to get them out? Should he just head back for Dover and abandon them to their fate? He ruminated alone in the soulless lay-by, with Leicester's rush-hour traffic roaring past. He knew he couldn't walk away. He'd failed his daughter. For her sake, he wouldn't fail these poor beggars.

Chapter 48

Leicester – Late Afternoon, Friday 9th January

Judy Makepeace had worked at Polymer Plastics Limited for five years, initially as a secretary. Two years ago she had been upgraded to PA to the Managing Director. She liked her job and felt confident in it. Although not particularly well paid – PPL was not a big company – it provided her with congenial work colleagues and a pleasant, easygoing boss. In many ways it compensated for a less than satisfactory home-life, though she would have been reluctant to admit it.

She had been married for ten years. The first few years were agreeable enough, but when it came to starting a family all their efforts ended in failure. The more they tried, the more mechanistic became their lovemaking. Each month the arrival of her period with monotonous regularity sank them into deeper despair. Their intimacy gradually lost any degree of passion and with it any desire for sexual interaction unless it was yet another fruitless effort to conceive. If forced, Judy would have probably described her marriage as sexless rather than loveless. They got along happily as friends. Her husband was a senior administrative officer in the Inland Revenue regional office. He collected stamps, played chess and was a DIY enthusiast. So everything in their modest home worked properly. Two salaries and no dependents meant they were not short of money. Life could be a lot worse she often told herself.

It was probably inevitable that sooner or later this insubstantial relationship would begin to unravel. It was not premeditated. Just a few chance events and suddenly the ordered status quo collapses. The critical occasion was the farewell office party for one of her colleagues just before Christmas 2003 – on a Friday evening in a local hostelry, 7-00 to 9-00 p.m., light snacks, drinks and a farewell speech and leaving present. Judy enjoyed these occasions and took special effort to look her best, to wear her prettiest underwear and an attractive dress. She ate a few delicacies, chatted happily to everyone, and made sure her glass was continuously refilled. The fruit punch was delicious and she was on her sixth glass by the end of the party, unaware that it had been laced heavily with vodka. But when she visited the ladies room to collect her coat, it needed no-one to tell her she was in a pleasurably mild state of inebriation, perhaps not yet quite drunk. Everything and everyone seemed relaxed, happy, and touchy-feely. One thing for sure, she couldn't drive herself home like this. She picked up the phone in the hotel lobby and dialled her husband.

"Hello, it's me. Probably had a drink too much to drive. I think I'd better leave my car here for the night. Could you come and pick me up, please?"

"Oh, silly woman. I'm in the middle of watching a wildlife programme - all settled down for the evening. Can't you get a taxi instead?"

Judy's sense of euphoria evaporated a little. Why was her husband so unforthcoming? Just another of the many minor disappointments in her marriage. Never mind. A taxi it would be. She dialled one of the taxi firm's numbers displayed on the wall above the phone. No reply. She tried another. Same result. "Bother," she said under her breath. "Stupid taxis are never there when you want them."

Michael Burton, her boss, was just leaving the men's room, and overheard her. "Any problem? Can I help?" he asked.

"Oh, it's just I need a taxi to get home and none of them seem to be available at this time on a Friday evening. Typical!"

"I can run you home. No trouble. Forget about the taxi. Tell me when you're ready to go."

"That's really kind. You don't have to. I was just about to leave now, but I can wait longer if it's more convenient to you."

"OK, let's go – I was just about to leave too."

The drive to her home took about twenty minutes. The car was snug and warm. She still felt deliciously intoxicated. Sinking back into the leather upholstery, she luxuriated in being chauffeur driven home. Her semi-detached house was half way down a poorly lit cul-de-sac, lined by mature trees now with bare winter branches. The streetlight outside their home had not been working for two weeks. The Council didn't seem to care. It had been a good evening, one she was happy to prolong. Michael continued chatting. She knew he'd separated from his wife a few months previously, so maybe he too was in no hurry. When he touched the side of her cheek with his finger – just a light gossamer stroke – she knew she was melting.

"You're an attractive woman. It's good to have you working for me. I guess we ought to keep things professional, but I thought you should know that I don't take you for granted."

She leaned her head gently on his shoulder. "You're very nice. You know I do like you."

He stretched his arm round the back of her seat. She moved closer to him. It was dark in the car and the avenue was deserted. He kissed her softly on her forehead. She raised her head upwards and moved close enough for him to kiss her on the lips if he was prepared to take the initiative. He bent his head down and they sealed their intent with a long open-mouthed kiss. His hand moved cautiously across her breasts. She made no effort to restrain him. She arched back in the seat as she felt his hand begin caressing her knee. When she parted her legs wider, the signal was clear that he could go on. His hand moved higher. She was glad she was wearing her best underwear, and particularly hold-ups rather than tights, as he expertly eased her pants aside and caressed her. She reached across to unzip him. He was hard and erect but she couldn't find a way in. He momentarily moved his hand away from her to free his penis from the constraints of his underpants. She clasped it hungrily and began to massage him enthusiastically. His fingers were pumping into her with equal vigour, their lips still glued together. Not a word was spoken, nor was one necessary. A well of unfulfilled passion had been released and for two or three minutes nothing in the world was of any consequence except this intense cathartic coupling with each other. They reached their respective climaxes almost together. Then they were still, holding each other tightly, her hand clasped round his wilting penis, and his hand still clamped against the moist succulence between her legs.

Judy had no recollection of when she had enjoyed such abandoned bliss. Whether it was the alcohol or not, she had no regrets. Tides of well-being suffused through her. She wished time could stand still. Slowly he withdrew his hand and fumbled in his pocket for his handkerchief, which he gave her to wipe her hand, all without a word. Then he kissed her again lightly on the forehead.

"That was really good," he said softly. "Maybe we should do it again sometime?"

Judy needed no time to think for her response. "Yes," she said, "yes please."

"I guess we both know it's got to be discreet, but we'll work something out."

They adjusted their clothes, kissed for a last time and he drove off. Judy opened the front door. "Hi, I'm home," she called through to her husband. Her legs felt like jelly, but she was trying to appear as normal as usual. "How's everything?"

He was still glued to the television. "All OK. Don't forget to put the milk bottles out before you lock up."

True to his nature he showed not the slightest interest in her evening out, but Judy was still on cloud nine and for once that bothered her not one jot. She looked at herself in the hall mirror before going through to the sitting room. There were some telltale white stains on her skirt. For her they were treasured souvenirs, but she wondered if her husband would notice. If so, she would say she had spilt some cream on herself when taking her coffee. She went in. His eyes remained fixed on whatever he was watching. Her emotions were still racing. She was surprised at her own reaction to his indifference. Part of her wanted him to notice the stains to see if he would say anything. She let her coat hang open and stood close beside him so that if he turned his head he would be staring straight at the level of her skirt with it's compelling evidence. He gave her not a glance.

"Well, I think I'll have a bath and go straight to bed," she said.

"Fine, I'll join you later. This goes on for another hour or so," he replied, without faltering in his attention to the television. She'd given him a chance. He had not shown a flicker of interest. She climbed the stairs. His behaviour convinced her she should have no regrets. She would happily repeat tonight's events. She could still smell the lingering aroma of lovemaking on her left hand as she slipped into the bath. Some things were already different. Her bar of soap was now needed only for its proper purpose of washing herself. Over the Christmas period there were further secret assignations, culminating in the plan to spend a night together on Friday, 9th January, the same day the factory was expecting delivery of the freight container from China. Judy's husband was going up to Preston for the weekend to stay with his elderly parents to help his father fix a leaking garage roof. Michael had arranged a squash match in the early evening. Then they would meet up for dinner before moving on to his flat for the rest of the evening. Both were highly charged with anticipation throughout the day. Judy did not know whether Michael had had other lady-friends since his marriage had collapsed but that didn't matter. She was enjoying herself whether or not this adventure led onto something more permanent. It had highlighted the emptiness of her own marriage. Now it was only a matter of time before she would decide to end it. If the punch had not been so strong; if her husband had been prepared to fetch her; if the taxi firm had answered the phone; if Michael Burton had not gone to the men's room; if the Council had repaired the street-light; if their neighbour had been walking his dog – on such thin threads of chance a whole new life would be woven.

★★★

The portly man and Mitch had not the slightest idea about Michael Burton's domestic circumstances, still less his plans for spending the night with his lover. Indeed, they couldn't care less. While they sat impatiently in his factory foyer waiting for him to appear, their only interest was to extract from him the whereabouts of the container. If that could be achieved swiftly and without raising suspicion, all well and good. If not, he might be in for a hard time. Regrettably Mr Burton's evening plans were going to impose severe constraints on their objective.

"Ah, Mr Burton. Glad to meet you. Hope all's well. We're from the shipping importers handling container freight inbound from China. Your young lady at reception told us your container had arrived safely. That's good. Just need to tidy up our paperwork. Always lots of unnecessary signing and checking when we ship stuff in from China. Guess it's their inscrutable style. Never trust anyone, do they?"

The portly man feigned a chuckle and prattled on light-heartedly trying to engage Burton's confidence. "Shouldn't take too long. The bother is they insist we carry out visual checks on the container to confirm it's suffered no damage or interference in transit. Can we take a quick look?"

"'Fraid that's not so convenient right now," replied Burton. "It's at our main manufacturing plant and that's all secured for the weekend. Maybe you could come back on Monday? I did sign all the dockets the driver gave me. Everything seemed in order and he left quite happy. The container seemed in good shape. We'll open up on Monday. Much better we see each other then when we've had a chance to check the contents, don't you think?"

"Trouble is we've come up from London. Can't really hang around till then. Maybe just tell us the address where it's stored and we can go across and do a quick visual external check. Just a formality. No need to bother you unnecessarily."

"Not so easy to do that. It's in a compound behind the factory warehouse. Someone would need to go with you to let you in."

The conversation had started amicably enough. But now Michael Burton detected a degree of edginess in their persistence. Polymer Plastics Ltd had used freight containers before, but never had they received a personal visitation from the shippers. Perhaps China imports were different? The problem was his squash match was at 6:20 p.m. and he had to go home first to pick up his kit. There was patently no time for him to take them across to the other factory. Nor was there anyone else around who could do it, and some sixth sense made him wary of giving them the address to go there unaccompanied.

"Look, I'd like to be there when you check it out, but I really can't do it tonight. Can you come back tomorrow morning and we'll do it then – say about 9:30 a.m.? I've arranged to meet a guy here at 10:30 a.m. to talk about squash sponsorship at the Hinkley Road club where I play, so that should fit in nicely."

The portly man was doing all the talking. He was still relying on sweet talk to achieve his goal. Much better to do things diplomatically so no-one suspected anything untoward. But Burton was proving awkward. The dilemma was at what point friendly talk should be abandoned in favour of more compelling pressure on him to reveal the information they needed. He was their only link. Whatever it required, he was going to have to comply. But for the present Burton had no idea how high were the stakes.

The new question posed was whether they could wait till the morning. The immigrants could lump it. They didn't matter. But the ten boxes of explosives were vital. They couldn't be unloaded in broad daylight, but if they could just establish where the bloody container was, they could come back the next night, on the Saturday, to open it up, let out the illegals and repossess the boxes. The portly man weighed up the options. Unfortunately, not only was Mr Burton being rather obtuse, but he had now had the benefit of face-to-face visual contact with both him and Mitch. If things went completely pear-shaped he would be able to recognise them both, and identify them to the police. The logic was fatally clear. Once Mr Burton had divulged the whereabouts of the container, he was dispensable. But they needed some hold on him till then. And now there was the additional problem of a mate of his arriving to talk about squash next morning when they had hoped to have Burton to themselves. The portly man was thinking fast.

"Well maybe we could do it tomorrow. We'll stop over in a hotel for the night. Charge it up to our Chinese friends! So we'll meet you again here tomorrow morning. Shouldn't take too long to do the necessary. Just wonder though if it might be a good idea to postpone your appointment with your squash mate tomorrow – might give us more time to check things out. What do you think?"

"It's not going to take more than an hour surely? Don't see any need to put him off. Peter Clayton's a nice chap. He'd be happy to wait a few minutes if we take a bit longer, I'm sure."

"Just as you please, Mr Burton. Only trying to be helpful. Don't like to cause inconvenience."

"OK then, I'll meet you here at 9:30 am." Michael began gathering his papers, increasingly anxious to close down this exchange so he could get off to his evening commitments, but completely oblivious to how much information he was inadvertently conveying to his visitors, which they in turn were memorising meticulously for future use.

"Oh, just one more small thing," persisted the portly man. "Our documents need proof of identity for the signature. And a passport is the only thing our Chinese friends recognise. If we could just borrow your passport overnight we'll fax the details over to Shanghai for them to do their silly verification, so we won't be held up by that piece of bureaucratic nonsense tomorrow. Only then can we release the combination number to unlock the container doors. Is that OK?"

Michael had never heard of combination locks on containers. Was that another Chinese idiosyncrasy? Or was there something fishy about all this? Stupidly he had not thought to ask for some form of identity authorisation from them at the start. Perhaps this was the moment to ask? The portly man pre-empted him.

"Seems an unusual request I know, but to put your mind at rest, I'll give you my passport as security till you get yours back tomorrow."

"All rather odd this," thought Michael, "but if he's giving me his passport, that's a sufficient bond of goodwill I'd have thought, and if they do need proof of my identity before I'm able to access the container, then I guess I might as well go along with what they're asking."

"Problem is I don't have my passport here, and I haven't time to fetch it before my game of squash," he explained.

"No problem," said the portly man rather too peremptorily. "We can follow you home and pick it up there – save you the bother."

This was all moving too fast, but Michael had other things on his mind - not only the squash match, but the clandestine evening with his secretary as well. He really wanted these guys out of his hair quickly – too much else to fit in this evening, and no way could he afford his private life to be compromised. It would look bad at the factory if his assignation became public knowledge, and his wife would have even more ammunition against him in the divorce proceedings. The least complicated way forward seemed to be to acquiesce to their proposal, and get them off his back.

"OK," he replied. "Just follow me. It'll take about twenty minutes. If you get lost, no problem, I'll meet you here again tomorrow at 9:30 a.m., and we can sort things out then. We'll have to move fast else I'll be late for my match."

He rang the security office to say he was leaving, cleared his desk and told them to follow his BMW. They tailed him without difficulty, and waited outside his flat till he reappeared with his passport. Then he was off.

"Right," said the portly man, smiling tightly, "we've got him hooked. Better tell our boys what's happening."

They rang the mobiles of the two vans still waiting near Ratby village for instructions, the occupants by now thoroughly bored out of their minds. The last they'd heard any news was three hours ago.

"Listen, we can't do the container till tomorrow night. Knock off for tonight. Find somewhere to stay. Keep your phone switched on. Stay close to North Leicester. Not sure where the bloody thing is, but it's somewhere in that area. We'll talk again tomorrow afternoon. Don't give anything away, and stay sober. We've a lot to do tomorrow night." He clicked off.

"Now we find somewhere to doss down for the night, before it's too late." They moved off into the suburbs looking for an inconspicuous hotel that wouldn't ask too many questions.

★★★

Meanwhile, back in the lay-by on the Ring Road, Arjan van Buitelaar was considering his options. To decide his best course of action he needed more information. First he phoned Habib. It was an hour since he had last called him

Inside the container, whisperings had given way to more heated discussion. Nothing was happening, and there was no sound nor sign of movement, which might herald their release. Their predicament was becoming more desperate by the minute. They had to do something. They opened the door of their accommodation module and, using the light of one of their weak torches, moved further into the container where the huge crate housing the machinery from China was chained to the floor. Habib was hoisted up to the top so he could lean over to look out through the two circular apertures, which had been their air vents for most of the journey. The driver had slid down the metal covers after leaving Dover and they were still open. Outside it was dark but a good deal lighter than inside. There were street lamps at various intervals, which allowed Habib to make out other factory units and parking areas in the close vicinity. One or two offices had solitary lights on, but, in the main, it was deserted. He could see the container had been off-loaded and was now on the ground. No sign of the truck, nor Arjan, nor anyone else. Other than the continuous distant hum of traffic, it was ghostly quiet. The sky was clear and he could see stars. He called down to the rest to tell them what he could see.

A number clambered up to look for themselves. It was reassuring that they could at least glimpse the outside world. If things became critical, sooner or later during the daytime, people would pass by and they could shout to them to get someone to let them out. That would have to be a last resort, because then they would no doubt be handed over to the police and that would be the collapse of their dreams. They argued among themselves what was best. In the end they decided not much could be done until daylight so they had better keep quiet till then no matter how hungry and thirsty they were. They just had to hope that the driver would come up with something.

When the phone rang, there was relief all round. They were sure this must be the call telling them they were about to be freed.

"Habib, what happens now for you?" asked Arjan.

"I no understand," replied Habib.

"You stay inside container or you go outside?" asked Arjan.

"We stay inside. We want go outside. Quick, you come open for us please? We very hungry, cold. One girl, one man sick." Natasha had been curled up with periodic stomach pains for the last two hours, though she had not explained why to Habib, and the Serbo-Croat was also feeling ill.

"OK. Listen. I try help you. I call you back later."

Habib's remarks had confirmed in Arjan's mind that he had to do something, but first he had to find out what Mitch and his friends were doing. It was almost two hours since his last acrimonious exchange with them. He pressed in their number.

"Arjan here. Just checking whether you've managed to locate the container yet?" he enquired as friendlily as possible, speaking in Dutch to Mitch. "I'm still not far away and could go back now the coast is clear to see if I can give you better instructions."

"Wait," said Mitch, "I'll talk with my colleague."

The portly man gave him short shrift. "Tell him we don't need his useless help. We'll find the fucking thing our own way".

Arjan persisted. "So what about the people inside? Don't they want some food soon?"

Mitch translated his queries into English. The portly man grabbed the phone angrily. "Look, you arsehole," he screamed down the phone. "You lost the sodding container. Don't start getting all luvvy-duvvy about the bloody passengers. They'll like it or lump it. No fucking business of yours, is it? Just fuck off, and leave it to us to sort out the stupid mess. If they have to stay inside for a few days, their problem, not yours. And say goodbye to your last payment! Don't waste any more of my time!"

He passed back the mobile to Mitch and told him to make sure Arjan had got the message. Mitch explained the gist of the tirade in Dutch in rather more measured terms. Arjan had already comprehended how things were. It was clear they had not yet located the container. Equally clear, they had no concern about the plight of Habib and his friends. Nor were they in any direct communication with them. Arjan was their only lifeline. He knew what he had to do.

Chapter 49

Leicester - Early Evening, Friday 9th January 2004

Mr Patel's corner shop sold everything - baked beans, mousetraps, newspapers, string, stamps, fresh - or reasonably fresh – fruit, sliced bread, matches, batteries, rice, potatoes, tinned sardines, camera film, pens, sink plugs, writing paper, video cassettes, frozen peas, steak and kidney pie in tins (just warm and eat), paperback novels, torches, oven ready curry packs, ice cream, as well as a cornucopia of sweets and chocolates for the after-school invasion of kids. And the big bonus was his shop was open all hours, each evening and at weekends. Mr and Mrs Patel didn't mind the long days. They provided a service to the community when other supermarkets and high street shops were closed. They lived above the shop. It was their life. Their respective parents had immigrated to England from Nagpur after Indian Independence. They settled in Leicester where there was already an established Indian community and job opportunities in the dress-making factories. Mrs Patel senior was an accomplished seamstress and her skills at fashioning saris were much sought after by the burgeoning Indian population in the city.

Their children were Leicester born and bred, growing up more British than the locals. Entrepreneurial by nature, their eldest son identified the growing niche in the market for out-of-normal hours shopping. Leicester's indigenous shop owners were retreating grudgingly in the face of intensifying competition from Sainsburys' and Tesco's. Reluctant to work the unsocial hours necessary to compete, they were grateful to be able to sell on their ailing businesses to whomsoever was prepared to take it on. Mr Patel Junior borrowed money from his father and was in business, a microcosm of the nationwide cultural shift that saw traditional English corner shops transformed into prosperous multi-purpose stores staffed by ever obliging Indian families.

Friday evenings were always busy, but it was unusual for a large twelve wheeler foreign truck to pull up outside, its hazard warning lights flashing. Mr Patel presumed the driver was lost. He would soon put him right. He knew Leicester like the back of his hand.

"Can I be of assistance to you, sir?" he asked in elegant English, unconsciously suffused with the Midlands accent. "I have very good knowledge of Leicester and its suburbs. Do you want directions?"

Arjan van Buitelaar looked round the Aladdin's cave deciding what he needed. He was curt and to the point. "I buy food and water."

"No problem, sir. Would you like some ready-made sandwiches – very tasty – some Tuna perhaps, or maybe you like Coronation Chicken?"

Arjan had already decided what to buy. Wholesome food, easy to carry, easy to eat, no need for cutlery or plates, and all of it should be capable of being passed through an aperture about four inches wide. "I want twelve bottles water. Twenty-four tomatoes. Twenty-four bread. Twenty-four bananas."

Somewhat surprised, Mr Patel smiled benignly. "No problem, sir." He quickly assembled the order. "Maybe I can help you carry them to your vehicle?"

To pay Arjan used the £20 tip he had been given by Michael Burton only an hour earlier, and drove off to rejoin the ring road to relocate where he had off-loaded the container. It was dark and difficult to get his bearings. He decided first to head for the Valley Road factory. From there he would try to retrace the route that Burton had taken to the second site. The industrial estates were much less busy now and traffic had eased considerably. After crossing the ring road from the first factory he recognised Fairfax Road. He was on track. But where next? Hard to remember. There was a night security guard at the premises he was passing. He should know. He stopped and went across to the gatehouse. The night guard was dividing his time between scanning CCTV monitors, watching a TV programme on his portable, eating a greasy hamburger and reading the evening paper. But always glad to talk to someone.

"Polymer Plastics – you're not far off, mate. Take the second on the right, then first left. Can't miss it. But they're all closed up for the night now. Doubt if they'll open till Monday. You've a bloody long wait!"

Arjan was used to taking directions in English. That much he understood.

"I go find factory tonight. Then come back when open next time," Arjan replied disingenuously.

Two minutes later he was there. He drove past the main gates, now firmly closed and locked. The factory premises were surrounded by an eight-foot perimeter fence – green plasticised wire mesh stretched between sturdy metal posts at ten foot intervals, each sunk into a twelve-inch concrete plinth at the base. He took note of the CCTV camera monitoring the front gate and three or four others mounted at strategic points on the factory walls trained parallel to the walls and doors, but not across the space between the fence and the buildings. This was deserted except for two large skips at the rear, half-filled with rubbish, a pile of discarded wooden palettes nearby, and most importantly, the freight container, looking forlorn and abandoned, set down near the rear access into the factory on the hard-standing between the buildings and the fence. Low-power electric lights on each wall of the factory gave dim illumination to the surrounds.

Alongside the southern fencing, further down the road adjacent to the PPL enclosure, there was a clutch of purpose built industrial units. Each had its own vehicle access doors and spacious parking in front. They, too, were closed all up for the night. Arjan reversed his truck so that he was parked in the bay immediately adjacent to the PPL fence. He dowsed his lights, switched off the engine, and sat silently in his cab to take stock. The container was no more than fifty yards away. Hard to visualize, but Habib and his ten companions were still trapped inside there. It was just after 6:30 p.m. on a Friday evening. The place was quiet, a few lights in offices here and there, but not an environment for people to be walking around of an evening. A chill wind blew disconsolately round the featureless buildings. From time to time, a car went by taking a late worker home. None gave Arjan's vehicle a second glance. Perfectly normal for trucks like this to be parked up overnight on an industrial estate waiting for early-morning starts.

Arjan worked out what he had to do. First, a length of rope from his tool kit. He tied one end securely round the carton containing the twelve water bottles, opened the cab window which was at the same height as the top of the fence, swung the carton across and gently lowered it to the ground inside the perimeter fence. Then he placed the tomatoes, bread and bananas in a large black binbag - he always carried a few with him for rubbish - and using the other end of the rope, repeated the drop over the fence. The main length of the rope he left dangling across the fence.

He closed the cab window. Sitting in darkness he phoned Habib again on the mobile. No mistaking the desperate eagerness with which the call was answered.

"Habib – I bring food. I put inside hole in container. I come maybe five minutes. Everyone quiet. You understand I think?"

"Yes, that good. Thank you. I go hole take food. Very happy. We very hungry."

No need for further conversation. Arjan clicked off. The next bit would be more tricky. He took up the heavy-duty rubber matting from the footwell of the passenger seat in his cab. Leaning out from the cab window he laid this across the top of one of the metal posts supporting the wire mesh fencing. Then he took the duvet off his bed and spread that across the top of the matting. After a last check that all was unobserved, he locked his cab and levered himself from his truck so his stomach was lying across the duvet, then grasping the wire mesh inside the fence with his hands, he swung his legs over and dropped down quietly to the ground inside the perimeter. He paused again to check. Apart from the distant yapping of a dog, all was still undisturbed. He unfastened the rope from the carton of bottles and the bag of food. Hugging the perimeter fence, keeping well out of the splay focus of the CCTV cameras, he humped the lifesaving food and water towards the container. Leaving the food and water there, he moved over to the pile of discarded palettes, chose a sturdy one and brought it back to the front of the container, placing it vertically against the side. He knocked gently on the metal side and climbed up on the palette so he could reach the ventilation holes.

"Habib," he whispered as loudly as he dared. "Are you there?"

There was a faint response and a hand appeared rather incongruously from one of the holes. Arjan placed a bottle of water in it, only to watch disbelievingly that the hand couldn't retract through the hole while holding the bottle.

"Let go, let go!" whispered Arjan urgently. "Keep hand inside. I put bottle inside." Painstakingly he fed one bottle at a time through the hole, followed by the bread, tomatoes and bananas. Inside Habib grasped each as it came through and passed them on down to a chain of grateful recipients.

"OK," said Arjan. "That finish food. You eat. Keep quiet. I go find how open door. I call again."

Arjan climbed down, and made his way round the container to the rear doors. He examined the locking mechanisms. They were familiar to him. They shouldn't pose a problem. He carried the palette back to the fence where he had climbed over. It acted as a makeshift ladder so he could climb half way up and then swing himself back over to the outside. He retrieved his rope, the rubber mat and his duvet, and put the empty bottle carton and black bag back into his cab. Apart from the anonymous palette sitting against the fence, there was no evidence of what he had done. He sat back and heaved a sigh of relief. That had all gone as well as he could have hoped. Time now for a cigarette and a cold beer from the cab cool box. He needed some personal space to work out what to do next.

Inside the container, the arrival of food and water was welcomed enthusiastically. The bottles, bread rolls, tomatoes and bananas were shared out. Natasha was interested only in the water. Her stomach cramps were persistent. She had some aspirin tablets to deal with her period pains, and glugged down two to try to relieve her discomfort. Next she had to tackle her personal hygiene problems as discreetly as possible. She squeezed behind the large crate with the bottle of water and her weak torch to do the best she could. Nina and Tanya provided some rudimentary privacy for her.

The man who spoke Serbo-Croat was also in difficulty. He had suffered badly from seasickness on the sea crossing and hadn't eaten since. Despite the invasive cold in the container, he was sweating profusely. He had curled up in a ball in the corner of the module and showed no interest in the mini feast the rest were devouring. Just wanted people to leave him alone. Despite the ethnic animosity between them, Habib was the only one who had any knowledge of his language. Reluctantly he tried to encourage him to take some water. It was no good. He was waved away unceremoniously.

Among the rest of the group there was a burgeoning sense of optimism. They had been inside now for twenty hours or more. Conditions were uncomfortable and malodorous, but at least the cold wind was no longer shafting in through the ventilation holes, and they had been able to eat and drink enough to keep them going for another few hours. Most important, the driver had promised to do something to get them out. The critical question was when.

And then what? This was the increasingly pressing matter. Once the doors opened, what did they do next? Where were they? How were they to find the way to their contact addresses in the UK? What were the distances involved? What transport would there be? How would they pay? Most of them hadn't had a chance to change Euros into English currency. However unpleasant it was inside the container, outside it was a dark, cold and hostile environment. Till now they had kept quiet about their eventual destinations. No-one could be trusted, so no-one was giving away more than they needed to. All they knew about each other was they were all headed for the UK. But now on the brink of so many unknowns, there was more inclination to open up to each other in the hope of gleaning straws of information which might help one or other in what to do once they were out.

★★★

Meanwhile, two miles away, Mitch and the portly man had booked into a twin bedded room in the Meridien Deluxe Hotel, buried in Leicester's anonymous backstreets – two-star, bed and full English breakfast including black pudding, en suite shower room, cable TV and telephone in every room, off-street parking, and personal massage available on request. Mitch registered as Mr Chan, the portly man as Charlie Smith. Both gave untraceable addresses. No, they didn't want an evening meal. The platinum-blond receptionist noted they had little luggage. "No doubt they'll be interested in the massage services," she reflected to herself as she handed them their room key. "Better alert Veronica to be prepared to earn a few easy quid later on."

Once in the room, the portly man locked the door, closed the curtains and checked the phone. He spoke to his colleague in low measured tones.

"Now Mitch, we've got some bloody sorting out to do. First we need to deal with this bugger, Burton. When we've got out of him where the bloody container is, he's dead meat. Because of the fuck-up over the rendez-vous, he's seen our faces. Can't chance him identifying us to the police. They'd throw the key away if they caught us. We need to lay a false trail to buy us more time. One of our boys will use Burton's passport to travel abroad tomorrow. Just leave messages around so everyone thinks he's away for a week or so. That'll give us time to sort things out, get rid of the illegals and deliver the Semtex boxes. Then we disappear."

"Let's get on the Internet and see what flights we can get him on."

Despite his size and shambling appearance, the portly man - alias Charlie Smith - was a shrewd operator. He logged onto the RyanAir website on his laptop. There was a flight to Rome tomorrow from Stansted at 7:00 a.m. That should do. He booked online using Burton's passport details and registered a return flight coming back in a week's time. Then he copied out the details and reference number. To pay he used the number on a Switch card stolen from an unsuspecting soul a few days ago. The security code was on the reverse side. No problem. That was easy.

Next he phoned one of his local contacts. "Freddie, a little job came up, mate. Sorry 'bout the short notice. Meet me in Leicester tonight, Meridien Deluxe Hotel, then get your arse over to the Stansted Airport transit hotel so you can catch the Rome flight out tomorrow at seven. You're travelling as Michael Burton – but I need your photo in his passport tonight. So get your skates on. We'll make it worth your while." He told him the hotel address. He would expect him in an hour.

A soon as he had finished that call, he was on the phone again, this time to the mobile number of a Pakistani man who ran a small printing business in Loughborough.

"Ahmed, - that you? Good – look - urgent piece of work's come up. All in a good cause to help the Muslim brotherhood - you know what I mean. I'm sending a guy round later tonight. You need to fix his photo on a passport – silly really. The Foreign Office just got the wrong picture – you know what I mean? £50– no questions asked? No paperwork – that all OK?"

Mitch didn't hear the reply, but judging by the satisfactory grunts coming from his friend, the deal seemed to have been sealed.

"Right," said his portly colleague. "Now we've got to cancel Burton's stupid appointment with this other jerk he's due to see tomorrow morning. Don't want anyone else interfering while we're sorting our friend out, do we?"

He dialled Directory Enquiries. "I need the telephone number for Hinckley Road Squash Club, Leicester." It took only a few seconds before he had it. Next a call to the Squash Club.

"Good evening – just trying to fix a game with Peter Clayton, but seem to have lost his telephone number. Sorry to trouble you. Any chance of looking it up on your database for me please?"

"No problem," said the receptionist. "Let's have a look at the screen. Have you got his address? We might have one or two Mr Claytons."

"'Fraid not. But his first name's Peter."

"Ah, yes – here we are." The receptionist gave him two numbers, one his landline at home and one his mobile. The portly man terminated the conversation abruptly. He had what he wanted. Next a call to a woman he knew.

"Hello, Mary. Your old friend Charlie here. How are you, my little blossom? Long time no see. Been getting into any mischief I ought to know about? Well now my darling, just a little favour. I want you to phone this mobile number. Speak to Peter Clayton. If he's not there, leave a message. Tell him you're Michael Burton's PA. Message from Mr Burton. He's got a last minute opportunity to be in Rome this weekend and is flying out from Stansted early tomorrow morning, so will have to cancel his appointment with Mr Clayton tomorrow and rearrange it for some other time. Do you think you've got all that? Maybe you should write it down. Don't go into any more details. Just make sure he gets the message his appointment to meet Burton tomorrow is cancelled. OK?"

"Don't you worry Charlie. I've got all that. Anything to help an old friend. Don't get so many cuddles these days. When are you next down here? Got a few cold beers waiting for you. I'm sure we could test out the old bed-springs again. What d'ya think?"

"Ah, Mary, how can I resist? Just you do this little job for me and I'll make sure you're all right. Take care my little darling. See you soon."

"My God," said Charlie to Mitch, a broad smile on his face for once, as he clicked the phone off. "Fucking slag! Still hankering after it she is, and nigh on sixty! You'd need to be pretty desperate to plough into her, I tell yer! But she's a reliable lass and she'll do the necessary for us."

"Right – so that's all fixed. Freddie'll shoot off to Rome tomorrow morning posing as Burton. Mr Clayton won't be keeping his appointment, so we'll have Mr Burton all to ourselves in his office on his own at 9:30 tomorrow. Now we just go downstairs to wait for Freddie - should be here soon. Not much we can do after that tonight except go somewhere for a beer and curry."

★★★

Not far away, Michael Burton had finished his squash match, showered, changed and was picking up Judy Makepeace. They'd arranged to rendez-vous in an anonymous car-park behind a pub at eight o'clock sharp. No sense in his distinctive car being seen outside her house while her husband was away. Neighbours might put two and two together. Judy had bought a new set of underwear for the evening and was looking her best. It was a long time since she had felt so excited, so alive and so reckless. When she saw his car cruise into the car-park, she slipped out of hers and locked the door. It would be tomorrow before she came back to it. The thought of what would happen before she saw it again sent a frisson of eager anticipation through her. Michael gave her a quick peck on the cheek as she nestled into the passenger seat.

"So where shall we go to eat? What do you fancy? Indian, Chinese, Italian, French, English?" he asked.

"Oh, I'm happy whatever – but maybe we should avoid the curries. Might linger rather on my clothes! What about Italian?"

"Fine. Probably best if we get out of Leicester. Never know who we might bump into. I know a nice little place, Carmillio's, in Loughborough. How about that?"

"Sounds great. Can't wait!" she said.

Michael headed his car northwards up the A6. They would be there in twenty minutes or so.

Chapter 50

Leicester - Mid-Evening, Friday 9th January 2004

Two miles in the other direction, Arjan van Buitelaar, still sitting quietly in his cab, had finished his beer and cigarette. He'd worked out what he had to do. Habib and his friends should have made short work of the food by now. There should be no great problem in letting them out of the container, nor in helping them climb out of the factory compound. What happened then was the crunch issue. They would have no idea where they were and would stand out like sore thumbs wandering aimlessly around an industrial estate on a dark winter's evening with little or no English. Without a doubt someone would soon tip off the police and that would be that.

Arjan reckoned their best bet was to get to a railway station. There they should find washrooms and toilets, which he guessed they would be glad to see. And they might be able to change money at a station if they had no English currency. They could buy hot food and drink, and they could get trains or buses or taxis to wherever they wanted to go. Arjan had studied the map of Leicester city centre. In evening traffic it would take him no more than twenty minutes to reach there from where they were. He would unhitch the trailer and just use his cab tractor. Four passengers could squeeze into the cab. If they all wanted to go to the station, it would take him three trips at most. Assuming there were no snags, it should be all over before ten o'clock. He would then head off for Dover, and be well away from everything by the time Mitch and his friends had discovered what had happened. And there would be no evidence to link Arjan to their escape. After sleeping up in a service station on the M1 overnight he would be on the ferry again by lunchtime on the Saturday and home that night, firmly resolved never to get embroiled in this sort of business again.

He dialled Habib's number. "Hello, Arjan here. You finish food I think? Now I come open doors. Then I take you train station. Everyone very quiet. Understand?"

Habib transmitted what he'd said to his colleagues. There was feverish activity inside while each of them assembled their meagre possessions in the dark and made sure they were all set to go. The Serbo-Croat was still in trouble. He needed some medicine or a doctor, but staying inside the container was no option. He forced himself to his feet and struggled to get ready. Each time he had tried to drink, even a modicum of water, he had begun retching again. He would just have to survive without it.

Meanwhile Arjan had spread the rubber mat and duvet over the top of the fencing as before. From the wide selection of implements in the truck toolbox, he chose a set of pliers, heavy-duty bolt cutters, some screwdrivers and a compact torch. Then round to the rear of the cab to disconnect the trailer. After locking the cab door again, he swung himself gently over the wire fence and into the compound for the second time. The palette, still where he had left it, made it simpler than before. Circumspectly he made his way round the perimeter fence, keeping well outside the range of the CCTV splays. The doors of the container were secured with the usual custom seals. His bolt cutters made short work of the connecting wires. After that, manoeuvring the long vertical levers to release the two large doors was easy. The hinges creaked, but not loudly, as he eased them open. At once he was assailed by a waft of stagnant air, an unpleasant mix of odours, sweat, vomit, urine and human waste.

"Rather them than me," he thought. He used his torch sparingly. This was the first time he had actually seen the interior since the accommodation module had been built inside the container in his warehouse just twenty-four hours ago. It looked like a normal transit crate, filling the bulk of the rear opening, but had been offset to one side leaving a narrow passage into the heart of the container. Arjan shone his torch along it. Figures were already moving towards him.

"Habib, is that you?" he whispered.

"Mr Arjan. We ready we come out now I think?" came the response in hushed tones from within.

"Everyone very quiet – go slow," Arjan replied.

The motley group began to emerge one by one, heaving intakes of the fresh air as they did. Arjan ushered them towards the fence. The Serbo-Croat was being supported by Habib. Even outside Arjan could still smell the unpleasant odours lingering on their clothes.

"Stay still," said Arjan. "I close doors first. No-one see open."

He re-secured the doors with their levers, and threaded the Customs wire back through the lock holes. To all intents and purposes, from a distance, the container still looked intact. Until somebody went up to it and observed the seals had been severed, no-one would know it had been opened. That wouldn't be till tomorrow, at the earliest, and by then they would be well away. With hand gestures and waves of his extinguished torch Arjan herded them towards the palette by the fence. No-one spoke. When they reached the crossing point they crouched down on the ground while Arjan showed how they should climb over. He could have cut the wire mesh fence but that would have left more evidence. With the exception of the Serbo-Coat, they were all agile enough to negotiate an unfortified eight-foot fence using the palette as a ladder. One by one, they dropped over. Two of the men helped the Serbo-Croat. Then they all huddled together on the outside in the shadows between the truck and the fence. Arjan retrieved his duvet and rubber mat for the last time.

They were out. Now he had to explain in his fractured English what he next proposed. He addressed the group sotto voce. "I take you station. Four people one time. Understand? I come back. I take next people. Understand? You take train – maybe bus. OK?"

Nina translated into Russian what Arjan was proposing so everyone comprehended. During their discussions inside the container, they had established that each had contact names and addresses in England to which they would be heading. They were all in the London area. The prospect of being dropped at a railway station was good news, and arriving there in small groups would be so much less conspicuous. Arjan's plan was well received. Next question - who would go first?

The four men who had been the last to arrive at the safe house in Brussels seemed to want to stay together. It was agreed they would go first. They climbed up into the cab. Two squeezed into the passenger seat and two lay alongside each other on the cab bed. Each clutched their rucksacks like lost refugees. Arjan spoke to the seven who would stay behind.

"I come back maybe half-hour. You stay under trailer – man not see you there."

He fired the motor and eased the cab unit out of the industrial parking lot. The city centre was bustling with traffic and Friday night revellers. He followed the inner ring road signs to the station. When he reached the main entrance he drove past, and took the first left into Conduit Road. After about a hundred yards he pulled up on the roadside.

"Two man go first time. You go station. Then wait small time – then next two man go. Meet in station I think."

The two men sitting in the passenger seat opened the cab door, stepped down gingerly to the pavement, and set off towards the station, mingling as inconspicuously as they could with the other pedestrians. In any case, Leicester's Friday night citizens were far too absorbed in their own plans for the evening than to give a second thought to these two furtive-looking individuals. Two minutes later the other two dropped down and set off to meet up with the others in the station concourse. Arjan was glad to see them go. He opened the windows of the cab to dispel some of the residual odour of their presence. Now back to fetch the next load. So far so good.

While Arjan was away, Nina had taken the opportunity to use Habib's mobile to phone Viktor. It was so long since they had last spoken and so much longer since she had last seen him. She was nervous and apprehensive while she listened to the phone tones.

"Hello, Dr Sturza here. Can I help?"

"Viktor , Viktor – it's me, Nina. I'm here in England. I'm so excited." She could hardly contain herself. It was his voice. They were in the same country, probably only a hundred miles apart. "We're in a city called Leicester," she explained in their native Moldovan, pronouncing the name all wrong. "We're going to the station to get a train. You must tell me where I can come to meet you."

Viktor had been expecting her. He had read her text message sent just before she left Belgium the previous day. Even so it was strange trying to marry up his present lifestyle and responsibilities with the arrival of Nina who enshrined his Moldovan past. The two worlds meshed uncomfortably together. Viktor tried quickly to gather his thoughts. He was on late duty at the Whipps Cross hospital where he worked. That was in east London. It was Friday evening and Nina was miles away.

"I'm not sure the best way to get here," he said lamely. "Leicester's a long way. I guess you need to get the train to London. Then you have to get another train out to here. It's a bit complicated."

"Maybe I just get to London, then I take a taxi to you," replied Nina enthusiastically.

"No, no," said Viktor. "That will cost the earth! We're a long way from central London and it's a big city - much bigger than Chisinau and taxis are really expensive here. Give me some time to think about it. Can I ring you back in half an hour or so?"

Nina could only but agree. She felt deflated and anxious. She could hardly bear to think about what it had cost her to reach here, but now she was within hours of him, Viktor's enthusiasm to meet again seemed strangely subdued. Her eyes filled with tears as she passed the communal mobile back to Habib. At least the darkness hid her distress. All she could do was hope when he called again, things would be OK.

It was just over half an hour since he had left when Arjan turned his truck back into the parking lot again where his trailer was parked beside the PPL compound. The others had done as he had suggested. They were sitting bunched together on the ground behind the rear axles of the trailer, obscured from view by the fence on one side and the trailer wheels on the other. Arjan dowsed his lights and went to join them.

"Who go next?" he asked. There had been quiet but animated discussion while he had been away. Everyone was worried about the Serbo-Croat. His condition made him a liability. While everyone else would be striving to be as nondescript as possible, he was bound to be noticed. He was weak and feverish and hadn't eaten since they had left Belgium. The consensus was he should be dropped at a hospital, but the Serbo-Croat himself was desperate to avoid that. If he went to a public building, his illegal status would almost certainly be discovered. He wanted to find a place where he could just rest up for another day or so until he felt better again. But how they could find somewhere like that, none of them knew. In fractured English they tried to explain the problem to Arjan.

"Maybe we go shop buy medicine," said Arjan. He reckoned he could find his way back to Mr Patel's shop. Perhaps they would find something there to help him. "First I think it good I take next people station. Who come?" said Arjan.

The Serbo-Croat didn't want to go. Habib had the communal phone and could converse with him, as well as with Arjan by phone, so it was better if he stayed with him. Nina was waiting for a call back from Viktor so she wanted to stay near the phone. It was agreed those three would stay by the trailer, while Arjan transported the other four, including Toci, Natasha and Tanya, on his second trip to the station. He followed the same routine. Traffic was lighter now and he was more familiar with the route second time round. What his passengers did once inside the station complex was their problem, not his. Things had worked out well so far. The only remaining difficulty was what to do with the Serbo-Croat.

The mobile rang in Habib's pocket just as Arjan was returning from the second trip.

"Dr Struza here – may I speak to Nina please?" Having spent the last year working in English hospitals, his English was good. Habib passed to phone to Nina.

"Viktor – Viktor, I'm so happy you phoned back. I was so worried." Nina spoke in their native Moldovan.

"OK, Nina, I've checked trains and times. You can get a train from Leicester direct to St Pancras. That's a big London station. There's a train every half-hour or so. The last one tonight's at ten o'clock. How soon can you get to the station?"

"Maybe in half-an-hour. I don't know. But how do I pay? I've no English money? I've only got Euros. Will you meet me in London?"

"I'm pretty sure you'll be able to change your money at the station or they'll take Euros at the ticket office. I can't meet you at St Pancras. I'm working in the hospital tonight. I'll tell you what to do.

"Take the train to St Pancras. Then get on the London Underground train called the Victoria line. Take the tube train going north. Stay on the train till its reaches the last station. It's called Walthamstow Central." Although he was speaking Moldovan, the names were confusing.

"Wait," said Nina. "These names are difficult for me to remember. Let me write them down." She asked Habib for a pencil and while he held a torch she wrote in the back page of her small diary. Viktor spelled them out – St Pancras - Victoria line north - Walthamstow Central - taxi to Whipps Cross hospital - ask for Dr Sturza at reception. She repeated the instructions back to him to make sure she had them right.

"I hope we can catch the train in time. Maybe it will be very late when I arrive?"

"No problem," said Viktor. "The Underground trains run till late and there are always taxis on a Friday night. It's about 3 kilometres to the hospital from Walthamstow station. That'll take only five to ten minutes. Reception will call me on my pager and I'll meet you there. Then you can go to my flat on the hospital campus to sleep till I finish my shift. It'll be great to see you again."

"Oh, that sounds marvellous! We'll be together in a few hours. I'm so excited. I've waited so long for this. Lots of hugs and kisses. Bye for now."

Sitting on the cold ground, in the shadow of the soulless wheels of a large trailer, late at night on a featureless industrial estate was not the most likely environment for Nina to feel as elated as she now did. She didn't care. At last her ambition was within touching distance. Her tiredness and anxiety evaporated. Viktor was waiting for her and evidently looking forward to it. She couldn't be more happy.

In contrast their Serbo-Croat companion was in continued distress, feverish and sweating profusely despite the outside temperature. Arjan had decided his only hope was to get back to Mr Patel and see what he could suggest. Habib helped him to his feet and with Arjan lifted him into the cab so he could lie on the bunk. Nina and Habib climbed into the passenger seat beside each other.

It was just after nine o'clock when they pulled up again outside the Indian corner shop. Mr Patel finished serving the other customers.

"Hello, sir. Very good to see you again. Can I supply you with more sustenance?"

Arjan response was brief and to the point. "One man sick in truck. You got good medicine?" For once Mr Patel was temporarily lost for words. But it was his nature always to try to help.

"Oh, very, very sorry to hear that, sir – maybe it is a good idea if he goes to hospital. Leicester has very fine hospital, you know, and British National Health Service is free if you have serious illness."

"He no want hospital. What you give him?"

Mr Patel was unsure what to make of all this. He only had basic drugs for headaches and indigestion remedies. He needed to know what was wrong before he felt confident in supplying any medication. "Maybe he can come inside so we can see what his requirements are, don't you think?"

Arjan was not inclined to argue. In fact he was quite keen to get him out the cab. He didn't owe any favours to the Serbo-Croat. As long as they were lumbered with him, the sick man was a liability. It might seem ruthless, but there was always the possibility of leaving him at the shop. Habib and Nina helped him down from the cab. He slumped onto the chair in the shop. Mr Patel felt his forehead in a show of amateur medical competence.

"Oh dear me. He has a very high temperature. I think analgesics are what he needs and he must drink much fluid." He called to his wife. "Bring a bottle of water. We'll give him some paracetamol. And bring a blanket to put round him."

Arjan seized his chance. "I go move my truck - find better parking."

Mr and Mrs Patel concerned themselves with the patient, trying to persuade him to take some water without success. "Perhaps we should call a doctor? He seems very poorly."

"I no want doctor," was the pained response. The Patels looked at each other in mild bewilderment. Outside they could hear the truck motor start and move off. They conversed quietly together. "We'll talk to the driver when he comes back. Perhaps we should put him to bed till he feels better? But what if he gets worse? Who is he anyway? Where does he come from? Perhaps we should call the police? The driver will be able to advise us."

Regrettably for Mr and Mrs Patel, no such advice was forthcoming. The Patels would have to cope as best they could. Arjan had decided he needed to be out of all this as quickly as possible. Just one last visit to the station to drop off Nina and Habib and then he would be leaving Leicester in haste. He'd done his duty in getting the immigrants out of the container. Now they would have to make the best of it. Their problem, not his. It had been a long, harrowing twenty-four hours. He'd hardly had any sleep and had already exceeded his permitted driving hours. The little problem with his driving log he would have to solve when he got back to Belgium. With huge relief he bid farewell and good luck to his last two passengers and set off to collect his trailer to start his journey south. There was just one thing more he would do before he left England, but that could wait till tomorrow.

Habib and Nina had ascertained that they both needed to get to London, so they could travel together on the same train. It was due to leave in ten minutes, just enough time to buy tickets. The ticket office accepted their Euros in payment, but the cafe and food kiosks were all closed. Hopes of a hot drink and food were dashed. They still had some water left and in ninety minutes they would be in London where they should be able to get something. So far, so good. They felt dirty and dishevelled but at least they had each other for company. They talked in halting English from time to time. Habib was heading for Finsbury Park, and Nina for Walthamstow. They would ask how to get there when they reached St Pancras. The quiet confident motion of the train soon lulled them asleep. How good it was to relax in a warm, upholstered seat after the previous night of stress and discomfort.

They were both sleeping deeply when the train eased into the terminus. The rush of fellow passengers moving to the exits and the strident sound of station announcements over the loudspeakers shook them into befuddled consciousness. They grabbed their rucksacks and joined the throng moving to the exits. But where to go? There was a profusion of noise, milling people, lights, signs, cafes, and ticket machines. They approached a coloured man in uniform who looked official.

"Please, sorry – you help us? I go this station," said Nina, showing him the name Walthamstow Central written in the back of her diary.

"Victoria line, darling, – just follow the signs," came the reply. He pointed them towards the London Underground entrance.

"Please," said Habib, "I go Finsbury Park – maybe you tell which train please?"

"No problem - same Tube. The Victoria line goes to Finsbury Park as well. Need to get a ticket first though."

This time the ticket office wouldn't accept their proffered Euros, but a nearby Bureau de Change was still open which solved their problem. The mouth-watering aroma of hot coffee and cooked food was too much to resist. They sat at a round plastic table in the station foyer and devoured a hamburger and chips, followed by a cup of steaming black coffee. Much revived by it, they felt ready to tackle the last leg of their journey.

"That very good," said Habib. "We must go quick, I think."

It was just on midnight as they boarded one of the late-night Victoria line trains going north. They looked carefully at the station plan on the carriage wall and noted where each had to get off. Around them rowdy, boisterous, inebriated passengers laughed and joked, sinking their teeth into smelly take-away concoctions or talking noisily on their mobiles. Habib and Nina stayed quiet and close together. The atmosphere felt hostile and threatening. All too soon they would be on their own. It was not something they looked forward to.

Chapter 51

East London – Late evening, Friday 9th January 2004

While Nina and Habib were subsiding into deep sleep on the train to St Pancras, Arjan had located his trailer and made his way to the M1. He too was desperately tired now. It was thirty minutes drive to the first service station. He opened the cab window so the cold night air helped keep him awake and at the same time dispersed the residual odours of his erstwhile passengers. When he reached the Watford Gap service area, he found a distant parking bay, closed down his vehicle for the night, and slumped into his bunk bed. It was only then he discovered the Serbo-Croat had left his rucksack behind. Too late now. Tomorrow he would check its contents, - probably best to dump it into an anonymous waste bin somewhere. Now it was time to relax for the first time in twenty-four hours. He crashed out as soon as his head hit the pillow.

In Loughborough, Michael Burton and Judy Makepeace had wined and dined well. Michael had been the more restrained because he had to drive, but Judy had followed her gin and tonic before their meal with four glasses of Chianti to finish the bottle that had helped wash down their antipasto and spaghetti bolognese. She was marvellously inebriated and meltingly ready for what she expected would follow when they were able to spend their first full night together. Her only fleeting anxiety was how she would explain to her husband that she was not at home if he should phone her from Preston later that night. But if he was true to form, he would hardly give her a second thought while he was away, so a phone call was unlikely. Now all she cared about was what she and Michael would do in the next few hours.

She was not disappointed - just one small regret – he'd had to wear a condom. She had never been able to conceive with her husband, but with another man there was always that possibility. As their bodies lay entwined after their first urgent lovemaking of the night, she heard a distant clock strike midnight and reflected to herself that tomorrow she would start taking the contraceptive pill. In future there would be no rubber membrane to diminish her full enjoyment.

At the Meridien Deluxe Hotel, Mitch and the portly man, alias Mr Chan and Charlie Smith, had met up with Freddie and briefed him to get over to Ahmed in Loughborough to replace Burton's photo in his passport with his own and then drive to the Airport Hotel at Stansted, ready to catch the early morning flight out to Rome, posing as Burton. That done, they drifted out to find an Indian restaurant and some beer before turning in for the night. Predictably Veronica phoned their room at 11:00 p.m. "What about a nice full body massage, sir? I'm sure it will help you sleep. I can be with you in five minutes. I'll bring a friend if you like?" To her surprise and irritation, they were not interested. Tomorrow morning they had Burton to deal with. They wanted no distraction. By midnight they too were sound asleep, and Veronica was so much the poorer.

Not far away, Mr and Mrs Patel were in a troubled dilemma. What were they to do with this stranger who had been dumped on them? By 10:30 p.m. the driver had still not returned. This was the time they usually closed up shop for the night to avoid the inebriated late-nighters as they spilled out of local pubs at closing time. Their uninvited guest was fast asleep in the shop corner wrapped in their blanket. They could turn him out into the street. But he was clearly unwell and had nowhere else to go, so that would be inhuman, especially at this time of year. Should they call a doctor? But the man had been adamant he didn't want to see one. Should they put him up for the night? But they had no way of knowing how trustworthy he was. After much soul-searching, they decided. They must call the police.

The two constables, male and female, arrived quickly in their Panda car. Mr Patel outlined the evening's saga. The policeman took notes –

> "truck driver, foreign, probably Dutch, off-loaded sick man for help at the Patels' shop - about 9:00 p.m., Friday 9th January, 2004. Man speaks little English, has no baggage- cannot stay here overnight. Mr and Mrs Patel know nothing else about him."

They agreed to take him down to the police station for questioning to try to determine who he was and where he came from. Tomorrow they would return for a signed statement from Mr Patel, but the first thing was to get him seen by the police doctor as quickly as possible.

"OK, boyo – time to wake up and move on," said the policeman as he gently prodded the man awake. The Serbo-Croat was panic-stricken as he opened his eyes and saw two uniformed officers in front of him.

"No worry, chum. Just come along with us and we'll try to sort things out," said the policewoman, trying to reassure him with a sympathetic smile.

They took him to the local police station. The duty doctor was often called out on Friday nights, usually to examine rowdy drunken yobs who'd been involved in fights. This was different. He diagnosed a case of acute gastro-enteritis, gave him a small tablet to suck between his gum and his lip to combat the nausea, advised that he should be left to sleep for the night, and in the morning be given dry toast, a banana, and soft drink. When he had absorbed some nourishment, he should be more amenable to being questioned. Still covered in the Patels' blanket, he slumped down onto the bunk of the police cell, feeling weak and sick and defeated. He would be arrested as an illegal immigrant. His dreams had fallen apart. He wept silently to himself until sleep graciously soothed his distress.

A hundred miles further south, the Victoria line train from St Pancras stopped only once before reaching Finsbury Park. Habib and Nina were surprised how quickly they reached there, but time enough for Habib to dig out from his rucksack the precious slip of paper he had been given by Osman Ibrahimi in Mitrovice ten weeks ago. That seemed a lifetime since. It was the contact address in London he had carefully guarded through all his travels. Now its significance loomed more important than ever. He was totally dependent on it. As the train slowed he shook hands with Nina. He would have liked to have hugged her but their friendship had always been pragmatic rather than personal, so he held back. He wished her God's blessing and hoped all would be well for her. He felt bad at leaving her although they both knew all along their ways had to part. And after all, they had only met each other for the first time the night before in the Brussels safehouse.

He mingled with the other passengers jostling out towards the exit. Just time for a furtive last wave to Nina through the window as the train sped away into the tunnel. Outside, despite it being after midnight, there were throngs of young people milling around, shops, cafes, pizza bars, kebab stalls, hamburger take-aways, all open and doing business. Immediately adjacent to the station exit was a stretch of illuminated shop windows displaying Arsenal souvenirs and memorabilia. Habib, like most of his contemporaries, knew all about the English football scene – Michael Owen, Wayne Rooney, David Beckham, Manchester United, Chelsea, Liverpool, and Arsenal. He felt a fleeting but reassuring stab of familiarity as he approached the taxi rank.

"I go 56b, Blackstock Road. You take me please?"

"Cor blimey, mate – you can walk there quicker than I can take you! It's only just across the road."

"Sorry, I no understand. You take me?"

"Look laddie. Just cross the road. Fifty yards to your left. First right – that's Blackstock Road." The taxi driver leaned out of his cab window and waved his arm to indicate what he was saying. Habib got the message. He thanked the driver and set off. It felt strangely unreal that this was the destination he had been heading towards for over two months. He strode out resolutely with a brave face, his rucksack slung nonchalantly over his shoulder. But inside he was in a turmoil of anxiety and apprehension. What if the address didn't exist? What if they refused to admit him? What if they turned him over to the police?

Within two minutes, he was walking down the road he'd been directed to. Compared to the glowing pictures of England he'd seen on television back home – Blackstock Road was not quite what he'd expected. The pavements were strewn with litter, discarded plastic bottles, beer cans, polythene bags and takeaway cartons. Strung out on each side were stretches of slightly seedy-looking shops, most in need of some loving care and a fresh coat of paint. All sorts of ethnic tastes seemed to be catered for – Indian, Chinese, Lebanese and Ethiopian restaurants, a barber offering haircuts priced in Euros, launderettes open all night, DIY shops, food-stores and, of special note to Habib, two butchers selling Halal meat. He knew his Muslim relatives would approve of that. He located 56b. It was a tiny shop with a dirty front window.

Blazoned across it in large black print were the words, "Taxi and Private Hire – Anytime. Anywhere. Cheap rates." There was a telephone number to ring, but the entry door was closed. Above it was a small amber flashing light. Through the window in the lighted office he could see a man leaning on the desk reading a magazine, and smoking a cigarette. He had thick black hair and a swarthy complexion, made more intimidating by a few days growth of beard. Habib tried the door. It was locked.

The man looked up, slightly startled. "You want a cab, mate?" he shouted through the glass of the window.

Habib's worst fears began to materialize. He needed to explain who he was, why he had come, where he had come from, who had sent him. But he didn't want to broadcast all this in the open street. And in any case, the man behind the window looked less than interested. Habib had to try to keep talking to him somehow.

"Yes, – no, – I no want taxi, I want speak with man in this house, please."The telephone on the man's desk rang. He answered it, ignoring Habib, still standing outside impotently, helplessly peripheral to events inside. During his travels he had often felt alone and alien in his surroundings, but then he had always been moving onwards, so it didn't matter. This was different. Now he was at the buffers. This was his terminus. He had nowhere else to go. He was nothing here. He had no friends, no home, no identity. This was his ground zero. It was imperative to establish some dialogue with this man, if only to convince himself that this was in fact a dead end.

As soon as the man put the phone down, he shouted back through the window. "Please, let me come in - I explain everything to you. Then maybe you help me?"

"Not likely, matey," came the hostile reply. "Don't know who the fuck you are. But if you want a cab, I'll get you one in five minutes. Double rate after midnight, mind you, and payment up front. Where do you want to go?"

Habib could contain his despair no longer. Even if the whole street heard it, he had to say something. It was his only chance.

"No, I no want cab. I come from Kosovo. Mr Osman Ibrahimi give me this address. He say you help me." It sounded pathetic. Habib knew that. A shouted monologue, in a dark street, late at night, addressing an unknown, unsavoury looking man through a glass window. But there was no other choice. He had no alternative plan B.

The man looked up from his magazine, balanced his smouldering cigarette carefully on the side of the desk, and advanced to the window.

"You say you're from Kosovo. Where's your home town?" he asked.

In less time than it takes to blink, Habib's despair transformed to joy.The man was speaking in Kosovan Albanian. Habib had not heard his native Kosovan spoken since he walked over the mountains. His eyes filled with tears. His thoughts cascaded through a plethora of images of his home, his family, his school and his friends. Language embraced them all. He wanted to jump and shout with relief. The two ends of the circuit had been joined. Now all his trials and tribulations had come to his longed-for conclusion. He poured out his response in his childhood language. At last he could express himself fluently. He had not felt happier for a long time.

"Yes, yes, - I come from Mitrovice. I've been travelling across Europe for ten weeks. My name is Habib Peci."

The man moved round the desk to the door and unlocked it. "Come in," he said. "Salaam alaikum. You are very welcome my friend."

★★★

At almost the same moment, the Victoria line train was drawing into its terminus at Walthamstow Central. The few residual passengers shambled towards the doors. Nina had used the St Pancras ladies' toilets to revive herself – a prolonged brush of her hair to remedy the night's sojourn in the freight container, a change of underwear, a marvellous wash of face and hands with soap and hot water, and some fresh make-up. Now, with her peaked cap re-poised coquettishly on her head, her tight jeans smoothed down, her scarf retied insouciantly round her neck, her leather jacket buttoned tight, she felt presentable enough for her long-awaited reunion with Viktor.

There were two exits, one marked towards buses, the other to taxis and minicabs. She took the latter. Emerging from the tunnel, she found herself in a poorly lit, almost deserted parking area. A short distance further away on her left there was a small office with lights on. Outside was a large sign saying "Taxis". She headed towards it. Viktor had said it was only three kilometres from here to the hospital. A taxi should get her there in under ten minutes.

Nearby a small car was parked. A large man, presumably the driver, was leaning against it, smoking a cigarette. He spoke to Nina as she passed towards the office.

"You looking for a taxi, darling?"

"Yes, I look for taxi to Whipps Cross Hospital," she replied, over-eagerly showing the man the note in her diary where she had written the name at Viktor's dictation a few hours before.

"No problem, my lovely," said the man. "My mini-cab's here. Jump in. I'll get you there in no time."

"That very good. Please tell how much money to go?"

"Don't worry about that till we get there. We'll just see what the meter says."

Nina wasn't sure she understood his response, but couldn't wait to complete this last leg of her journey quickly enough. He opened the passenger door and she climbed into the back seat with her rucksack beside her. First they drove through well-lit streets and then joined a wider road. Traffic was light at this time of night. Nina's eyes scanned every new turn for her first glimpse of the hospital. The man tried to engage her in conversation.

"Don't sound English – where're y' from, luv?"

"I come from Moldova. I go visit my boyfriend. He doctor in hospital," Nina replied guilelessly, leaning forward.

"Been to England before, then?"

"No, my first time – I come today."

"So you got lots of friends here then?"

"No, I one friend here. He my boyfriend in hospital."

"Is that so! My, you're a pretty girl to be out so late at night. Need to be careful, you know - lots of odd blokes about these days."

The conversation petered out. Nina was only half interested in their exchange and not quite sure she understood what he meant, but she knew they must be getting close to her destination, and that's all that concerned her.

After about ten minutes the car slowed and turned off the main road into a side road. The headlights momentarily picked out the name – Oak Hill. A little way ahead on the right, Nina saw they were approaching a large well-lit building, which she guessed would be the hospital. But the cab continued on past. She read the floodlit sign outside - "County Hotel – Epping Forest". A hundred yards further on they turned right into a narrower road, and there on the left she saw a large block, about eight storeys high, with numerous rooms illuminated all over it. If this wasn't the main hospital, it was probably a staff residential complex. Her chauffeur drove past slowly. No sign yet of him stopping. "Surely we must be close by now," she thought to herself.

Then suddenly the tarmac road gave way to an unmade track. Nina was familiar with these in Moldova, but not in England. The track quickly weaved to the right into a dark wooded area, now out of sight of the lights and buildings, which had looked so promising a few moments ago. Nina sensed this was all wrong.

"Please, I think this different place. I want hospital."

There was no reply. A hundred yards further on the car stopped. The driver opened his door to get out. There was no time for indecision. Nina knew she had to get away. She could run back to the block of flats, and should be able to outrun him with a start. She grabbed the handle of the door furthest from him to make her get away. It was locked. She battered it to no avail. The man was now standing adjacent to it.

"Don't worry, darling – child-proof locks, you know. Work a treat, don't they? Now let me do the courtesy of letting you out."

As he did so, she heaved the door at him, but he was ready for that. He grabbed her hair with one hand and her arm with the other. Her hat flew off into the undergrowth. Struggling to escape she fought fiercely to unleash his grip, but she was no match for his strength. She screamed and screamed. Without loosening his grasp on her hair, he slapped her forcibly across the face. She tasted blood in her mouth. An owl took off overhead buffeting the crisp night air with its wings, but otherwise her cries dissipated ineffectually among the bushes and trees.

"Now, you little bitch," he sneered. "Better behave yourself or it'll be the worse for you. Understand? We said we'd talk about the fare later. Now's the time to pay up. Got it?"

Nina didn't understand his words but his message was clear. He wanted sex. She had little choice. To resist was futile. He was far too strong for her. But one thing was in her favour. She had all her

Moldovan experience behind her. She knew about men and their sexual appetites. Now was the time to draw on all that experience. She was so close to her destination. If she was able to satisfy this brute, she could still make it. If she tried to fight him, she was terrified what might happen. Here she had no Stefan to protect her. She had only her own wits to get her out of this.

"OK, you like make love. Then we go hospital," she said as agreeably as she could.

"That's more like it," he said, half dragging her into a clearing beside a fallen tree. There were no artificial lights to be seen, only the dim comforting silver illumination of the half moon, filtering sheepishly through the bare branches of the forest. There was a distant hum of traffic noise, but all else was silent. He still held her hair in a fierce grip. Her mouth was bleeding slightly, but otherwise she was unharmed.

"Get those fucking jeans down, or I'll rip them off you."

His words were still difficult to understand, but there was no doubting what he wanted. Nina unzipped herself and in one motion pushed them and her pants down to her ankles. Countless times she had done this in the Hotel Dukro. She reconciled herself with the thought that once more was a small price to pay to get this ordeal over with.

"I think I kneel down. You like make love from behind?"

"Now you're talking, darling. Just be a good girl and do what Daddy wants!"

She knelt on all fours, the rough bracken scratching her knees, and offered her naked buttocks to him, opening her legs as far as she could, her feet still hobbled together by the jeans round her ankles. She knew how to accommodate aggressive men, rampant with lust. Best to relax and be as open as possible. Then when they'd reached their climax, they became more malleable and reasonable.

He was still clutching her hair with one hand as she felt his rough entry into her. There was another lesson she had learned in Chisinau - Zvetlana's advice, "Always humour the man. It makes him feel good and he'll appreciate you all the more."

As his aggressive thrusting began, she voiced her well-rehearsed lines. "Oh, that's very good...you're so big ... best I've ever had... lovely big prick ...like a horse...oh, that's lovely..."

She could sense he was about to climax. Soon it would be over.

Her period was due in a few days. She prayed she wouldn't get pregnant, but even if she did,Viktor would know how to get rid of it. She'd done it before. No reason not to do it again. Just grin and bear what was happening now and then she would have her future with Viktor. As his final thrusts reached the point of no return, his grunts and obscenities became louder. She had heard them all before "…little cow,… fucking slag,... foreign bitch,.. cunt-face." They washed over her.They were easily tolerated. In a few minutes it would all be finished.

Then, suddenly, he grabbed the scarf round her neck, and jerked it backwards fiercely. Her hands were lifted off the ground and she could hardly breath. His other hand released her hair and in an instant she could feel the scarf tightening inexorably round her neck. She tried to scream, but her airways were too constricted. She grabbed the scarf convulsively with both hands to try to relieve the pressure, but he was standing behind her, legs planted akimbo, totally in control while she was still on her knees, unable to stand, her arms thrashing wildly in front, unable to hit him or take any protective action.

Her eyes were bulging in their sockets. Tears were streaming down her cheeks. Mucous was running out of her nostrils. Her lungs were bursting for breath. She was trying so desperately to scream, but nothing came out of her constricted vocal chords. Her hands were tearing hysterically at the scarf to try to loosen it. She could feel herself beginning to lose consciousness. As she did, her vision was taken over by a phosphorescence of bright coloured lights, cascading in every direction. It reminded her fleetingly of the firework display she had seen on her last Christmas in Chisinau. Then it all went dark.

Chapter 52

Leicester - Early Morning, Saturday 10th January 2004

It was 7:00 a.m. on Saturday morning, 10th January, 2004. Those already awake had much on their mind. Arjan roused himself from the bunk in his cab. It was still dark, but he'd slept like a log. Today he had important things to do, not least a score to settle. First a good wash and shave in the service area restroom, a trucker's English breakfast, then back on the M1 heading south as dawn broke. His brain felt as crisp as the early morning air. "Timing," he said to himself. "I must get the timing right."

The best time to call Mitch again, he decided, would be about nine o'clock. He was sure they wouldn't have located the container yet, but by then they should be up and about, still trying desperately to identify its whereabouts. They wouldn't yet know the illegals had already flown the nest. That was one of Arjan's trump cards. The other was that he knew where the container was, but they didn't. He would play those two cards with finesse.

He pulled into Toddington services truck-park and dialled Mitch's mobile number.

In the Meridien Hotel Mitch had also slept well, but the portly man had fretted most of the night, tossing and turning in his bed. The illegal immigrants could stew in their own juice. That was their problem. He didn't care. What mattered were the ten boxes of Semtex. He was being paid handsomely by the Luton-based Al Qaeda cell of the Islamic Brotherhood to use the immigrant route to get the explosives into the UK; half the money in advance, the rest on delivery. He had no illusions about the men he was dealing with. They were merciless, fanatical, blinkered, and committed, not a shred of human kindness in their souls. If the boxes weren't delivered, the portly man knew he was in deep trouble. Delivery had been promised for the Friday evening. He was already twelve hours behind schedule. Worse still, he still didn't know the whereabouts of the container. He had phoned the Brotherhood and left a feeble message about the boat being delayed, but he knew they weren't interested in excuses. Fear hung around his attempts to sleep like a coarse blanket. It was a relief when at last he could get up and get on with things. Mr Burton was in his sights. That jerk wasn't going to stand in his way. "Now or never, Mr fucking Burton. When we meet this morning you'll tell us where the bloody container is. No question about it."

He phoned the two white-van drivers. "Be at the PPL factory admin block by nine. Come in one van. Park round the back. Keep your mobiles on. We may need some muscle."

Freddie, posing as Mr Burton and travelling on his passport, would be en route to Rome by now, courtesy of RyanAir. The false trail had been laid.

Back in Michael Burton's temporary flat, a night of delicious decadence was gradually transposing itself into the cool light of day. Judy Makepeace lay naked in the rumpled bedclothes. Her lover was brewing morning tea in the kitchen. She savoured the residual odours of their night together lingering on the sheets. It was already eight o'clock and she knew Michael had an appointment with some guys about the sea container. She wished she could prolong their time with each other. Better not be greedy. There would be other opportunities. She sat up in bed drinking her tea, affecting some teasing modesty by keeping herself wrapped in a sheet. Michael drank his sitting on the mattress beside her wearing a pair of boxer shorts. It had been a really good night, but now he had to face the agents from the shipping company. They had been a pain in the arse yesterday, and they still had his passport. The weak early morning sun filtering through the drawn curtains did nothing to assuage his gut feeling that there was something fishy about those guys. He dearly wanted to snuggle back into bed with Judy, but time was pressing, and his emotions were now preoccupied with how to deal with the portly man and his oriental sidekick.

Any erotic fantasies that Judy might have harboured about intimate soapy showers together were quickly dispelled when she saw the mouldy, tatty state of the cubicle in Michael's rented apartment. They took it in turns. After a bachelor's breakfast of toast and freshly brewed coffee, they hugged and kissed passionately one last time in the confines of the flat. Then out to face the world, back into their respective public roles of boss and secretary. Judy was dropped off in the pub car-park where she had left her car. A final peck on the cheek and he was off, already late for his rendez-vous. Judy scraped the frost off her windscreen and sat quietly in her car with the engine running waiting for the heat to come through. A brief moment to take stock. It had been a memorable night. Life was changing – had changed. It was unclear where it was all heading, but she knew her marriage was doomed. The sky seemed a clearer blue, the co-ordinates of her life more precisely defined. She had tapped into unknown wells of need in herself. Whether Michael Burton was the answer she wasn't sure, but somewhere out there a more fulfilling life was beckoning. She was determined to embrace it before it was too late.

While Judy mused to herself, two miles away Mitch's mobile rang. The portly man was driving them to the PPL factory for their meeting with Burton. The phone conversation was in Dutch.

"Hi - van Buitelaar here. How y' doing? Did you manage to track down the container?" asked Arjan.

"Good morning, Mr van Buitelaar. How are you today?" Mitch was always inscrutably courteous. "We're just off to meet Mr Burton so he can tell us where to go. No problem"

"What about the people inside?" asked Arjan giving the impression he assumed they were still there. "It's been a cold night, and they'll be short of food and water, don't you think?" He had played his first finesse, trying to tease out whether Mitch or the portly man had discovered they had already escaped from the container.

"Mr van Buitelaar, I don't think that is your concern. As soon as Burton takes us to the site, we'll arrange for their exit tonight when it's dark. No problem."

"So you think they'll be out by tonight?" replied van Buitelaar disingenuously. "That's a relief. Wouldn't want them to die in there. The police would be bound to track back and identify it was me who delivered the container."

"No worries. Everything's under control. You forget about it all."

"And what about my final payment then? Your buddy told me to forget about that too. Not my fault everything went pear-shaped. I put myself on the line for you lot."

"Not my decision. Let me ask my colleague."

The portly man had comprehended none of the Dutch conversation. Mitch translated the query about van Buitelaar's final pay-off.

"Get lost! We wouldn't be in this fucking mess if he hadn't lost the container. He can screw his money. Tell him to get stuffed!"

Mitch passed on the ugly response in more measured terms, suggesting that Francois would be in touch back in Belgium. He terminated the call. There were more pressing things on their agenda. They had just arrived at the factory. It was twenty past nine. They parked outside the admin block, killed the engine and waited for their quarry in the silent morning sunshine.

A few miles away in the cell at the local police station, the Serbo-Croat man was awake. His nausea had receded and he had held down his breakfast of toast, banana and tea. The duty officer had established he was from the Balkans. A call was out for an interpreter so that they could question him properly. Another policeman had been despatched to get a signed statement from Mr and Mrs Patel about last night's events.

Arjan's truck was now back on the M1 on the last leg of his journey via the M25 to Dover. In spite of everything he was still on schedule to make his early afternoon ferry back to Calais. He had one more important call to make. He would time that just before he boarded - his second finesse.

Judy Makepeace had decided to do some shopping so, when she returned home with a few Tesco bags, any neighbours who saw her wouldn't think twice about where she might have been. Her husband wouldn't be home till tomorrow. She had ample time to gather her thoughts and feelings and catch up on sleep. Lazily in her mind she caressed over last night's experiences. She wondered whether Michael would be sharing the same thoughts.

Regrettably he wasn't. Instead, he was heavily focussed on conversation with the portly man and Mitch in his office at the deserted factory. He had tried to be polite, but they had declined his offer of coffee. He proffered the passport he had been given in exchange for his and asked for his back. They prevaricated.

"First things first, Mr Burton," said the portly man. "You promised to take us to the container so we could do our statutory checks. Let's do that, shall we?"

Burton was increasingly discomforted. Who were these guys? Why were they so obtuse? Where was his passport? What was all this nonsense about statutory checks? He wasn't going to be messed about. He would try to gain the initiative.

"Look, Mr – I'm sorry I didn't catch your name. What did you say it was?" he asked.

"Smith – Charles Smith - it's on the passport. Now shall we get on?" was the reply.

"Mr Smith, I think first I need to check your credentials before we take things further. Can I see your authority cards please?"

"Mr Burton, we really haven't time to beat about the bush. I'm sorry you seem reluctant to help us conduct our business. I think it's time you understood how serious we are."

He slipped his hand into his pocket and produced a small silver revolver, which he cradled in both hands just out of Burton's reach but pointing straight at him.

"Call the boys," he said to Mitch who proceeded to dial up the two van drivers.

"So, Mr Burton, forget about your passport. Forget about identity cards. This is our authority." He waved the gun menacingly. "Let's get straight to the point. Where's the fucking container?"

Two burly men appeared in the office. An hour earlier Michael Burton had some ill-formed suspicions about these people but never had he dreamed he would be facing this level of aggression and intimidation. He was no match for them physically but he did have the information they desperately wanted. If they killed him they would be none the wiser. He was not a particularly brave man, but he would try to stall as long as possible. His one fragile hope was that Peter Clayton was due to meet him at the office at 10:30 a.m. If he could hold out till then, he might be OK. He tried hard to remember whether he had mentioned this to them yesterday.

"What's so important about the container? It's just got machinery in it from China. How can that be so important?" He tried to play for time. It was no use.

The portly man produced a length of heavy-duty wire from his briefcase with a three pin plug on one end. At the same time the two heavies moved round the desk and pinned Burton to his chair in an armlock round his neck. Mitch put the plug into a socket in the wall and taped the two wire ends, one red and one black, round Burton's wrists.

"Now, Mr Burton," said the portly man idly waving the gun at him. "Do you want us to switch on the plug – or will you be telling us where the container is? We really don't have time to bugger about any more."

Although terrified, Burton felt a surge of belligerence against his aggressors. "Get stuffed," he said, almost without thinking. "You tell me why you need to find it and I'll tell you where it is." The two heavies momentarily released their grip as Mitch switched on the current for three seconds. Burton's body contorted in pain. His teeth clenched. Sweat poured out of every pore.

"Mr Burton. Let's be serious. We don't want to harm you. But we do have ways of finding what we want. Let's switch on your computer, shall we?"

They watched it boot up in silence till it needed the password for entry. "OK, what's the password? Or would you rather have another bolt of electricity?"

Burton was both frightened and intrigued. Where was this going? He couldn't see any reason to withhold the password. Mitch typed it in.

"Now Mr Burton, I'm sure you're familiar with pornographic websites. How would you like to be registered on the paedophile network? We can arrange that for you quite simply. Of course, if we tip off the police and they do a search of the site, your name will be there for all to see, won't it? So what do you think? Shall we go ahead and register you or would you rather tell us where the container is?"

The image on the screen was lurid and explicit, but so far not from a paedophile domain. Burton said nothing. The portly man nodded and Mitch sent another pulse of electricity coursing through his body. Burton arched involuntarily across the back of his chair. He was foaming at the mouth. Urine leaked in his pants. His shirt was soaked in sweat. His heart was palpitating viciously. He was struggling to breathe. Was it worth it? Just for the sake of protecting the container's location. The prospect of being labelled a paedophile was too gross to contemplate.

He told them the address of the second factory.

Then he felt a terrible pain shoot across his chest. He slumped into unconsciousness, and fell to the floor as his chair tipped sideways.

"What the fuck's going on?" said the portly man. "This shouldn't happen."

"Probably a heart attack," said one of the van drivers. "Couldn't stand the shocks."

Then they heard it - a car driving into the factory car park.

"Shit. Leave everything. Out through the back quick. Let's see who this is. Then decide how to deal with it. Maybe that joker who was due to see him today didn't get the message from Mary. I'll fuck her rigid if she didn't do what she promised."

They exited through the rear door of the Managing Director's office into the factory behind and waited to hear what transpired. Burton's body, lying contorted across the floor, was still wired to the wall socket. It was not a pretty sight.

CHAPTER 53

LEICESTER - MID-MORNING, SATURDAY 10TH JANUARY 2004

The portly man, alias Charles Smith, was endowed with all the innate skills of an East End barrow boy - little formal education, but a mind as sharp as a needle, never short of an answer, never missed a trick, always up to speed with events, and unerringly focussed and resourceful when in a crisis. He and Mitch and the two van drivers crouched in dead silence behind the door as Peter Clayton entered Burton's office. They heard his gasps, his attempt to use the office phone, then his retreat into the foyer. They listened as he painstakingly dictated to the police on his mobile who he was, where he was, and what he had encountered. The portly man made a mental note of his name and address. It was convenient he should have spelled it out so eloquently. When they were sure Clayton had moved out of the office, the four men slid back in quietly to do what they had to do.

Mitch pulled the plug from the wall and ripped the wires from Burton's wrists. The two van drivers picked up the body and carried him into the factory. Mitch killed the computer, while the portly man righted the chair and waste bin. A quick check to ensure all looked normal. On the floor were a bunch of keys – VW's. Must belong to the Clayton guy. "That's good," thought the portly man, his mind in overdrive. "We can make use of those." He pocketed them. Then he took the office door key from the inside and locked it from the factory side. Inside the factory, he rifled through Burton's coat pockets till he found his BMW keys.

The four men then hurried through the factory, Burton's body slung over their shoulders. Then out through the rear fire exit. Mitch checked the coast was clear, before a quick dash across to the Sulo industrial waste bins. Unceremoniously they dumped the body into one of them, taking care to ensure it was obscured from immediate view by plastic bags of rubbish and other factory debris already in there. The four then jumped into their white van parked at the rear.

While the van drove slowly round to the front car-park, the portly man addressed his colleagues in crisp urgent tones.

"Right. This is what we do. Mitch you take these VW keys and drive Clayton's car back to his home address and leave it there." He recited the address and gave him the street map of Leicester he had bought at the newsagent's earlier that morning when buying his newspaper.

"Barry," he addressed one of the van drivers. "You take Burton's BMW and follow Mitch." He gave him the BMW keys. "When he's delivered Clayton's car, you bring Mitch back to meet up with us again at the Meridien Hotel."

"Nick," he spoke to the other driver. "You bring this van back to the Meridien while I bring back the Merc. Is that understood? No fucking balls-up – we should all be back at the hotel within half an hour. Let's get to it!"

The fleet of vehicles with their respective drivers moved speedily out of the factory car-park to their respective destinations, while Peter Clayton, locked in concentration on his phone call to the police, was still in the factory foyer, oblivious to the various manoeuvres outside just out of his line of sight.

Half an hour later the rendez-vous back at the Meridien had gone without a hitch.

"Now," said the portly man, "let's take stock. To finalize Burton's false trail we need to get his car to Stansted Airport long-stay car-park quick. Barry, you've got the keys. Get going. When you've parked it up there, take the bus to the airport, then the Stansted Express to London, and catch the first train back from St Pancras to Leicester, then taxi here. Here's fifty quid to cover your expenses. You should be back late this afternoon. We need you here tonight. So get your skates on. Any hitches, give us a call." It was just after 11:00 a.m. He should be at Stansted in ninety minutes. Speed limits didn't matter. It wasn't his car.

The portly man then spoke to Mitch and Nick. "What we do now is recce the site. We know where the bloody container is, thanks to our dear departed friend. We just need to work out how we get at it and when. So let's go visiting, shall we?"

They climbed into the Mercedes. Guided by Mitch using the

street map, they located PPL's second factory site in under twenty minutes.

"Well there you are my beauty!" said the portly man as they parked alongside the factory fence almost at the same spot van Buitelaar had used the previous evening.

"There she is, looking just as she did when she left Belgium on Thursday night. My God – we should celebrate!" The portly man was in buoyant mood.

"So we do what we normally do, except it will have to be in the dark tonight. I guess we better say about midnight. We'll need both vans – one for the module panels and the boxes of Semtex, and the other for the eleven wankers inside. Looks like they've got security cameras. We'll have to fix them before we start. The gates shouldn't be a problem. Bolt cutters will sort them out. In and out in half an hour I should think. Then get the bloody boxes down to Luton before that lunatic Al Qaeda mob get impatient for their delivery. Now - time for a spot of lunch, I think. Then we can rest up this afternoon. Might even see if Veronica's available for some massage!" he chuckled.

"So, off duty till eleven tonight. But phones on and ready for a long night. Better keep off the booze."

Chapter 54

Leicester – Saturday Afternoon, 10th January 2004

It was a relatively quiet afternoon at the city police's Operations Department. The Leicester City football team was playing away, so that avoided a huge strain on police resources and manpower. The excesses of Christmas and the New Year had passed, and the general public were now consumed with making the most of the January sales in the shops. The weather was clear and bright, though cold, so no undue traffic problems. The Saturday night binge drinkers were not yet on the streets. The duty officers had more time than usual to filter and absorb the content of police reports of incidents across the city as they flowed in intermittently through the afternoon.

One was Peter Clayton's statement. Another was a report from the police support officers who had picked up an illegal immigrant from Serbia. The translator's statement dictated by the poor guy was pretty clear. He had travelled across Europe to Belgium, came across the Channel on Thursday night in a freight container. That had been dumped somewhere nearby – the Serb had no idea where – and because he was sick, he had been offloaded by the truck driver at a shop run by some Indians. That's who had called the police. He was now on his way to an asylum centre. The statement from Mr and Mrs Patel corroborated his story. They thought the truck driver was probably German or Dutch.

None of the reports required any further action for the moment at least.

At two o'clock that afternoon the Kent Police received a 999 call. Arjan van Buitelaar was playing his second finesse.

"Hallo, sorry I no speak good English. I want tell police some bad men do bad thing."

"Good afternoon Sir. What language would you prefer to speak to us in?"

"Me, Dutch – but I speak more good German than English."

"No problem sir. Hold on till I transfer you to someone who speaks your language."

Arjan listened to music being played. He was at Dover docks expecting to board the ferry in half-an-hour or so. He had prepared what he wanted to say in simple English, but if they could find a Dutch or German speaker, all the better.

"*Guten Tag, was mochten sie?*" came the response after a minute or so. OK – it was to be German. Arjan explained what he wanted to convey - the truth, but not the whole truth.

"My name is Mijnheer Boer. I am Dutch and live in Harleem." Arjan had decided to use a false name and address. He saw no reason to identify himself.

"I'm a truck driver. Yesterday I delivered a freight container to a factory in Leicester." He gave the address of the PPL factory, which he had been careful to remember from his repeat visits as he had ferried the three groups of immigrants to and from the station. But he made no mention of the immigrants. He knew they had flown the nest anyway.

"I have information that some thieves are planning to break into the container tonight and steal the contents. I thought I must tell the Police about that so they can take action to catch them. I do not know what time but it will be when it is dark."

"That's very helpful, sir. Can you let me have a contact telephone number, please?"

Arjan spelt it out, but took care to invert two of the digits. If they checked it against the digital read-out at the Police HQ, more than likely they wouldn't notice the small difference.

"*Danke schon. Viel Gluck.*" The conversation terminated. Arjan hoped he had sprung the trap. The portly man and his henchmen had shown no sympathy for him or the immigrants. They had denied him his second payment though it was no fault of his that the planned drop at the old warehouse in the country lane had gone tits-up.

Now they would get their come-uppance. If all went well, as a result of his call, there would be a police reception party waiting for them when they revisited the container tonight. He could complete his journey home this afternoon with that consolation, as well as the knowledge that he had enabled the poor beggars inside to get away.

That had been the prime reason he had originally got involved - and the money of course. But he was under no illusion. This was the first and last time. There were less stressful ways to earn a living.

The German report, translated into English, was faxed across to Leicester. It arrived mid-afternoon and didn't take long for the duty officers there to absorb. It was short and concise, even if rather odd. Had the Operations Department been busier, it might not have received much attention. But suddenly there were resonances with other reports that had come in that afternoon.

The Kent report mentioned the PPL factory – so did that bizarre statement from Peter Clayton about an unsubstantiated murder at the same factory. The Kent report also mentioned a freight container – so did the report from the Serbo-Croat illegal immigrant. Things seemed to be marrying up. Certainly worth a check-up visit to the factory to see if a container was there. Perhaps a talk with the boss there might clarify what had been going on? But there was this other anomaly. The Clayton report suggested he was discovered dead in the factory that morning, whereas RyanAir had confirmed he had flown out to Rome last night. When things don't add up, there's usually something fishy afoot.

The Operations Tactical Unit despatched a squad car to check things out. First a call to the PPL caretaker who had helped them secure the admin offices at the first factory after the police visit there that morning. The caretaker travelled with them to the second site. He opened the gates and the police offices went across to examine the container.

"Well, well, looks as though someone's been here before us!" They had noticed the severed customs seal. "Perhaps we'd better look inside?"

The swung open the rear doors. Residual odours of human occupation assailed their nostrils. "Police here – anyone inside?" they shouted. There was no reply. They climbed through the narrow passage beside the accommodation module. The access panel was open. They swept the inside with the beam of their torch. On the floor were a few discarded apple cores, a banana skin, some crusts of bread, empty plastic water bottles, and ten small wooden crates. A large black plastic bag lay outside in the body of the container. When opened it emitted a nauseating smell of human waste and vomit. It was quickly resealed.

"Pretty clear that a group of people, no doubt illegal immigrants, have travelled in here – and the Serb guy was one of them. But they've all scarpered. So what's this Dutch trucker telling us about a raid on this container tonight? He's probably got it all wrong and thinks the immigrants are still in here. If the Serb guy is right, they all left last night, so not much chance of tracking them down now. They'll have evaporated across the country. But surely the truck driver knew that – so why's he's told us to come here tonight?" The police officers were trying to piece things together.

"Perhaps we should check out these boxes?" They took a wrench out of the squad car's tool kit and levered open one of the boxes, then sliced carefully into the thick polythene cover protecting the contents. Inside were a number of smaller polythene packets, each weighing about a kilogram and containing an off-white powder.

"My, my - so what have we here then? Drugs or explosive I guess. We'll take one of these little jobs and get it analysed back at HQ. But either way there's twenty-odd packets in each crate and that's one hell of a lot of drugs or powder. Someone's going to come looking for this. Guess we'd better fix a little welcome party for them. This should be an interesting evening."

The caretaker was enjoying all this unexpected Saturday afternoon excitement. He was sworn to secrecy, and then showed the officers the layout of the factory, inside and out. He handed over to the officers a set of keys to the factory and the gates. "Best keep well away tonight. Things might get tricky," he was advised.

"Now – what about your boss? Michael Burton he's called, isn't he? How can we contact him about all this?" The caretaker had a list of telephone contact numbers for the senior staff.

There was no reply to Michael's mobile, so they tried his home number. They got short shrift from his estranged wife. "Michael Burton moved out of here some months ago – he lives in a flat above some shops. I don't know his address and I don't want to know it. Perhaps you could instruct the factory to change his contact telephone number on their list. I'm hacked off receiving calls for him on this number." She slammed down the phone.

The caretaker was rather nonplussed. He was not aware of Burton's domestic problems. But maybe Burton's PA, Judy Makepeace would have his present address? They could ring her. Her number was on the list.

"Good afternoon, Mrs Makepeace. Leicester City Police calling. Nothing to worry about. Just a routine enquiry you might be able to help us with. Could we call round to have a word or are you happy to speak on the phone?"

Judy had been snoozing in the chair catching up on the sleep she had missed last night. "No problem – how can I help?"

"We're trying to contact Michael Burton, Managing Director of Polymer Plastics Limited about an incident at one of his factories. We understand you are his PA. We're having difficulty in reaching him by phone and don't have his present address. We understand he might have travelled to Rome early this morning, and we just wondered if you have any contact address for him there?"

Judy Makepeace was suddenly wide awake. What on earth were they on about?

"Well, Officer I can tell you Michael Burton was very much in Leicester this morning. I saw him about 9:30 a.m. He was just about to go to his office for an appointment with the shippers about the freight container that arrived yesterday from China with new equipment for the factory. No chance he was off to Rome, I can tell you."

"Thank you, Mrs Makepeace. That's very helpful. Could you just verify where you saw him and what he was doing?"

Judy was beginning to feel hesitant. She had no wish to disclose their clandestine time together but she wanted to be as helpful as possible. How could she explain their presence together in a pub car-park at that hour of the day?

"Oh, we just happened to bump into each other. I was on my way to do some shopping. He pulled up and had a brief chat, that's all. That's when he told me he was on the way to the factory." She hoped she sounded convincing.

"Our main concern is to try to contact him. Do you know how best we can do that?"

"Well, I think he recently moved to live away from his wife - if he's not answering his mobile, you could always pop round to his new address." She dictated it to them.

"Thank you very much, madam. That's very helpful. Sorry to have troubled you. Good afternoon."

The visit to his flat was abortive. No-one in the adjacent flats knew much about him, but they thought he had been there last night because his lights had been on. Mr Burton was proving very elusive at a time when the police would dearly like to talk to him. Best to return to HQ and plan tonight's stake-out. The labs had confirmed the crates contained Semtex – enough to cause mayhem. This looked like a serious terrorist import. Leicester tactical squads were put on high alert. The armed police unit was mobilized. The PPL site was marked out and put under covert surveillance from all sides. The container was the epicentre. It was left intact as the bait.

Not far away at the Meridien Hotel, the portly man and Mitch had taken a siesta and were having a late afternoon cup of tea in the communal lounge area.

"I've been thinking," said the portly man. "We ought to sort out that little shit who disturbed things this morning. We know where he lives. He's the only witness who's seen Burton's body. But a dead witness isn't much help is he? I think he needs writing off. Let's pay him a visit. Plenty of time before we need to go back to the container tonight. It'll give us something useful to do in the meantime!"

They arrived at Peter Clayton's home in the dark of the early evening. The portly man had his story prepared. He rang the doorbell.

Chapter 55

Leicester – Saturday Evening, 10th January 2004

It had been a bad decision in the first place, though the portly man would not have admitted that to anyone, even himself. His automatic response was always self-justification. If it had been a game of chess, what they had done would have been seen as an unnecessary move, which had probably weakened their position. It was a stupid thing to have done. So why did they do it? Probably because they had had so much spare time on their hands on the Saturday afternoon before they could get at the container. It was always hard to remain inactive while the adrenalin was pumping.

But the efforts to write Peter Clayton out of the picture had failed. Somehow the bastard had got away. Now he posed more of a risk than before. Up to the moment they had rung his doorbell, Clayton had no idea who they were, still less had he made any connection between them and Burton's body. Now he had had face-to-face contact with them and could link the Mercedes he had seen parked outside the factory with the vehicle from which he had just escaped. That was bad news. But not something the portly man was going to be apologetic about, however much he sat cursing and blaspheming in the passenger seat while Mitch tried to navigate their vehicle out of the traffic.

"Follow that bloody break-down truck! I bet those sods gave him a lift somehow."

Mitch did his bidding and retraced the route behind the flashing amber light of the truck back to the lay-by which acted as its base for recovery operations.

The portly man jumped out and harangued the breakdown crew. "What the fuck did you do with the passenger in our car? He's a nutcase. We need to get him into hospital!"

"Who the hell do you think you are? No-one talks to us like that mate! Get lost!" The burly man in the truck cab waved him away dismissively.

The portly man tried again, in more conciliatory tones. "Look, we had a passenger when we stopped. He was helping change the wheel. He's disappeared since you left us. Did you see anything of him?"

"We do break-downs mate! We're not the bloody Salvation Army. Missing persons is sod-all to do with us. End of story! Bugger off – you're spoiling our Saturday night!"

The portly man gave up. He scrambled back into the Mercedes, even more furious.

"OK – let's get back to the Meridien. Even if Clayton's picked up, he's not going to know where we are, nor anything about the container. We just forget him. We've got more important things to do."

In the meantime Peter Clayton, huddled on the grass verge in the dark beside the dual carriageway, had watched the Mercedes drive by, in hot pursuit of the breakdown truck, oblivious to his presence. Walking back to Leicester from here was out of the question. No chance of any passing taxis, and no prospects of hitching lifts on a dark busy road at night. But he had his mobile. He would make two calls. First to Jenny.

"Hello, Peter here. How are you?"

"We're fine. Still at Margaret's. Leaving soon – should be home in half an hour or so. To what do we owe the pleasure of this phone call, may I ask?" His wife seemed in good spirits.

"A little problem. Listen carefully – don't show any emotion. Just keep it between us for the time being, but I think there's been an attempt to kidnap me. I'll go into the details when I see you again, but suffice it say I've escaped, and am at present sitting on a road verge in the dark just south of Leicester. I'm unharmed – but I think it must be the same guys that were involved at the factory business this morning. One of them looked the "kung-fu" type that Robert talked about this afternoon. Anyway, they've gone. I'm on my own and am going to ring the police to get me out of here. I think they'll begin to take my story more seriously after this."

Jenny struggled hard to keep her thoughts and emotions under control. She did her best.

"OK – Peter, thanks for calling. Thanks for letting me know. Hope to see you soon. Give me a ring if you have any more news. Take care. Bye for now." Her hand was shaking perceptibly as she hung up. She hoped Margaret hadn't noticed. The energetic activities of four small children should be a sufficient distraction.

"Peter getting bored without you, is he? Men really are like little kids when it comes down to it. Always wanting attention. Can't stand their own company for long, can they?" Auntie Margaret prattled on. Jenny was content to go along with the drift, but all she wanted now was to get home as quick as possible to see what on earth had been happening to Peter over the last two hours.

"OK boys – time to go home. Get your clobber together."

"Aw, mum – can't we stay longer? We're not tired. It's not time for bed yet," they pleaded - to no avail.

They returned home to an empty house. It was 7:30 p.m. Where was Peter?

Peter followed his call to Jenny with another 999 call. He explained to the emergency call operator what had happened and asked the police to marry up what he was now saying to the incidents in which he had been involved that morning which should be on their records. He stressed he was pretty sure the Mercedes he had seen parked outside the factory that morning was the same vehicle that had been used to abduct him this evening. The call operator took down the details, asked for his phone number and assured him someone would get back to him shortly. Peter pressed her to act quickly. He wanted a police car to come to rescue him.

He needn't have worried. The operations department at police HQ were now fully focussed on the events at the PPL factories. Peter Clayton was a significant player in what was unfolding. He had the benefit of face-to-face contacts with some of those who might be behind the Semtex imports. That would be crucial identification evidence. When his mobile rang a few minutes later, their urgency was unmistakeable. He explained where he was stranded. A police car would be with him in half an hour. "Stay where you are till then. Don't respond to any other overtures of help. Just wait for the marked police vehicle."

For the second time that day Peter found himself dictating a police statement. Then another police car journey to his home and another emotional reunion with his wife. It was 8:00 p.m. "OK – I'm OK. No worries. Let's get the kids to bed – then we'll talk over a drink. I'll tell you what's happened. It's been quite a day!"

A few miles away, the portly man and Mitch and the two van drivers were sitting down to some beers and a fish-and-chip supper. Barry had done the necessary. Burton's car was parked in the long-stay car-park at Stansted Airport. He had made it back on time. The portly man elected not to tell the drivers the abortive attempt to deal with Clayton. Not their business anyway. What mattered was tonight's operations. They would need both vans, bolt cutters to open the factory gates, tools to dismantle the accommodation module, and plastic bags to cover the security cameras. They would leave the security lighting on so any casual passer-by would think it was a bona fide unloading of the container, even though late at night. If it were in darkness, it might raise suspicion. One van would take the immigrants down to London overnight and drop them in Hackney. The other van with the boxes of Semtex would head for Luton to deliver the crates. They were a day or so behind schedule, but that should be OK as long as they were delivered intact. Then on to Finchley to store the dismantled accommodation module in a lock-up garage there till they were taken back to Belgium for the next trip.

"Tomorrow you can take a well-earned rest!" concluded the portly man as he checked each one knew exactly what he had to do. "And we'll all be a bloody sight richer! These Luton sods are not short of a bob or two. All fucking Arab oil money I guess. Better in our pockets than theirs, don't you think?" He was in happier mood as he contemplated the prospect.

The small convoy, two white vans and the Mercedes, slid out of the hotel car-park just after eleven. The blond receptionists had noted their departure, "Off into town boys for some action, are you? You don't need to go all that way, you know! We can arrange things here for you just as easily – cheaper and cleaner too. What ya think?"

They studiously ignored her. Twenty minutes later they were at the factory. The bolt cutters made short work of the gate locks. Mitch opened them wide and ensured they were chocked back to allow for a speedy exit. Barry drove his van under the first security camera, climbed on the roof and reached up to drop a black plastic bag over it. Further along he draped the second camera in similar fashion. The vans reversed up to the container. The portly man took out a pair of smaller bolt cutters to open the customs security seals. Only then did he discover they had already been severed.

"Bugger – someone's been here before us. We're in deep shit if the boxes have gone." He wrenched open the container doors. No sign of movement within.

"The birds have flown. That's their problem, not ours. Saves us a lot of trouble." He raced inside and shone his torch into the module.

"Thank God – the crates are here. Let's get to it. We can put the crates in one van and the module sections in the other. That'll make it easier. Barry and Nick dismantle – Mitch and me, we'll carry out he crates." They set to feverishly. The whole job was finished in less than half-an-hour. They closed the container doors so they looked as before.

"That's good. OK, let's get the hell out of here. We'll shut the gates after the vans are out. All being well, nobody's going to notice any problems till Monday. We'll be drinking our champagne by then!"

The drivers started their engines and began moving to the exit.

Suddenly the whole area was flooded by two huge spotlights mounted on the factory roof and another on the adjacent factory roof. Doors at the back of the factory sprang open and six armed police wearing bullet-proof vests and helmets ran towards the rear of the departing vehicles. Ahead of them two police vans with protective windscreen grills in place and flashing blue lights screeched to a halt, blocking the gates. Out of them another dozen armed police raced out carrying bullet-proof shields. A loud hailer cut through the silence.

"Armed police! You are surrounded. Switch off your engines. Get out of the vehicles. Lie flat on the ground face down. I repeat." The same message re-echoed through the night air. There was no escape. The portly man lay on the ground, prostrate. "Sod it, sod it, sod it," was all he could say. His companions were silent. They were already preparing their desperate defences for when they appeared in court. There would be no champagne tomorrow. The game was over. The home team had won.

Chapter 56

Epilogue

Habib Peci quickly became absorbed into the north London Kosovan community. His reasonable English stood him in good stead. He had no trouble picking up work, but it was all without formal immigrant status, so the pay was poor and conditions were often questionable. He used his spare time to improve his language skills. The Hackney Council night classes asked no awkward questions about legal status. His London compatriots had two prime preoccupations. One was acting as a conduit for feeding Balkan girls into prostitution rackets in the UK, and the other, political agitation in favour of Kosovo's formal independence from the wider Serbia. Habib had no interest in the former - his family values ruled that out, but he was increasingly caught up in the struggle for a free Kosovo.

He re-established communication with his family and as the months spun out he became more and more nostalgic. Life in the north London suburbs was not easy, not least because of his illegal status. Seldom had he much money left over when he'd paid all his weekly dues. He missed his family and friends, and he was becoming convinced the best way he could serve the aspirations of Kosovo's independence would be back home, rather than from the London backstreets.

He began saving up for a flight back to Kosovo, notwithstanding the irony that for the previous five years of his life, he had spent his time slaving to earn enough money to get him away from there. He had no passport, but if he had enough to pay his way, he hoped he would be able to give himself up to the authorities, ask to be repatriated, and offer to fund the return flight.

He arrived back in Mitrovice eighteen months after he had bid farewell on that momentous morning. He was overwhelmed by the reception from family and friends. Now, more mature, more worldly-wise, and proficient in English, he quickly secured a job as a translator for one of the plethora of non-government organisations working in Kosovo, and subsequently moved on to be a policy adviser. Eventually, he relocated to Pristina to work for the Office of Democratic Institutions and Human Rights, where in his spare time he took a leading role in the constitutional preparations for Kosovo's ultimate unilateral declaration of independence in January 2008. It had been a roller-coaster journey. Habib felt he'd played his part. He had no regrets. When he'd left Kosovo originally, he could see no future there. Now there was hope.

★★★

Dr Viktor Sturza was at a complete loss as to what to do when his girlfriend failed to turn up at the Whipps Cross Hospital reception desk in the early hours of Saturday, 10th January, 2004. He had spoken to her twice on the phone only a few hours earlier. She had seemed excited that they would soon be together. She was so close, but now she had disappeared without trace. He had tried the mobile phone number again - disconnected. Should he tell the police? But Nina was an illegal immigrant. What could he say? He didn't know what she was wearing. She could be anywhere between Leicester and London. And wouldn't it compromise his job in England if the police learned he was involved with an illegal immigrant? Reluctantly he decided to sit tight and wait, hoping against hope she would soon re-establish contact and all would be well. She didn't.

Days rolled into weeks. Viktor's life in and outside the hospital continued as before – busy and exhausting. Nina had never been part of that – so there was no difference there. Indeed they hadn't seen each other for over a year, and, as the days passed, it was almost as if their planned reunion had been more a dream than reality.

Towards the end of his year's contract at the hospital, he managed to secure an internship at the Johns Hopkins teaching hospital in Baltimore. There he quickly meshed into the American lifestyle, met and married a Filipino nurse, had two children and never returned to Moldova because his wife showed not the slightest interest in visiting impoverished ex-Soviet states. But on some days, when she had gone off with the children to visit her extended family, leaving him on his own, he would look back nostalgically to those harsh, happy days in Chisinau and grieve the loss of the early love of his life. There had been no proper closure. No-one would ever understand why a grown man should shed gentle tears. Where had she gone? Where was she now?

★★★★★★★★★★★★★

Nina Snegur's partially clothed body was discovered early on the Saturday morning by a retired man while walking his dog in the southern part of Epping Forest. It was a ghastly discovery. He had nightmares about it afterwards. The police established that the body was that of a white female, aged approximately twenty-three years. She had died as a result of an assault culminating in asphyxiation in the early hours of the morning. She had recently had sexual intercourse, and had probably been raped. She carried no papers but her clothes and skin colouring suggested she might be East European in origin. There had been no reports of a missing woman which fitted her description. The police were unable to make any positive identification, but they were successful in taking significant DNA samples from her body. The cold had helped to preserve their integrity. In due course she was buried at public expense by the Local Authority in an anonymous cemetery in Wanstead.

Three months later, during a community clean-up campaign organised by the local Rotary Club, a waterlogged rucksack full of personal effects was recovered from the Hollow Pond boating lake, just across the road from Whipps Cross hospital. It was handed in to the police. The clothes now ruined by long immersion in the water seemed to be those of a young woman. The writing in the diary and notebook was no longer legible, but some of the printed matter could still be read. Some was in Russian script. No one had reported the loss of a rucksack. The police kept it for a few months, then consigned it to the evidence archives.

Somewhile later a mini-cab driver was involved in a brawl outside Walthamstow Tube station. He was questioned at length and a routine DNA sample was taken. Within a few hours the laboratory had matched it in every detail with that taken from the corpse of the young woman found in the woods in January 2004. The man was subsequently charged and found guilty of the assault, rape and murder of an unidentified female, and sentenced to life imprisonment.

★★★

Peter Clayton's statements and evidence were of invaluable help to the police in unravelling the sequence of events and securing charges and convictions. He was able to confirm the identity of the portly man and Mitch as the two people who had kidnapped him and who knew, at the time of his kidnap, that Michael Burton was dead - they had pretended they were taking him to the mortuary to identify the body - whereas the police at that time had not yet accepted Peter's story of the morning events. That was the give-away. These were the same men subsequently arrested at the PPL factory on the Saturday evening following the police stake-out. Their link with both the murder and the illegal stash of explosives was incontrovertible. Inevitably it took some months for the matter to come to trial. Meantime the Clayton family re-engaged with their lives, comfortable and suburban. But those traumatic hours on Saturday 10th January, 2004, were etched in their memory for the rest of time.

★★★

The arrests of the portly man, Mitch and the van drivers and the content of Peter Clayton's statements immediately activated a search for the body of Michael Burton. It didn't take long to discover. The autopsy confirmed the cause of death was consistent with the statements made. The factory caretaker at the two PPL sites had wasted no time in spreading the news of the weekend's events to colleagues, but it was a confused and disbelieving workforce who turned up on Monday morning to learn the grim details. None was more distressed than Mr Burton's PA.

Judy Makepeace was inconsolable. "Quite understandable," said her colleagues. "She worked so closely with him, you know." Little did they know. Nor would they. And they saw no link whatever, when a few months later Judy Makepeace left her husband to live on her own. But they thought they understood when she handed in her notice and left the company. Who would want to work with the ghost of a murdered boss haunting you each working day?

Within a year, without Michael Burton's drive, the PPL business was faltering. The soul had gone out of the company. It was duly sold off and absorbed into a larger conglomerate of plastic injection moulding companies, now all contracting with Chinese factories for the manufacture of moulds and tools. Michael Burton had left behind at least one legacy.

★★★

Arjan van Buitelaar caught the Saturday afternoon cross-channel ferry from Dover. On board, he devoured the trucker's lunch ravenously. At long last things seemed calmer. His internal tensions were slowly subsiding – even the sea had quietened. Then the final leg of the journey, making speedy progress along the autoroutes of Northern France into Belgium on a fine crisp winter evening, and home. He would spend the night in, alone, contentedly slumped in front of the television with half a dozen cans of Stella Artois. He had much to think through.

The illegal immigrants had all got away – he was well pleased about that. The police had probably apprehended the trafficking gang – they deserved whatever they got. Despite the cock-ups, he'd returned unscathed, and was €5,000 better off by virtue of his advance payment. If the portly man had anything to do with it, he probably wouldn't get the final pay-off but that wasn't the end of the world. He wondered if ever he might be approached again to do a similar job. That Francois guy had seemed a shrewd operator. He would understand it hadn't been van Buitelaar's fault that things had gone wrong.

But he'd be mad to get involved again, he mused. Too risky, not as young as he was, - whatever his money problems, it wasn't worth it. Too much could go wrong. He'd been lucky this time - best not to chance his arm again. Much more sensible to get on running his trucks legally and hope the banks would be sympathetic to his overdraft problem till there was an upturn in the global economy and container traffic picked up the pace. Tomorrow was another day. Tonight he would sleep like a trooper.

It was exactly four weeks later, in the early hours of a Sunday morning, when he was woken by a call from the police. There was trouble at his haulage depot. The fire brigade were dealing with a fire there. He reached the scene in less than thirty minutes. A couple of fire engines were hosing jets of water onto the smouldering remains of his depot. The place was gutted. His two trucks were shells of blackened metal. The office was a charred skeleton. Arjan van Buitelaar was a ruined man. Without an ounce of sympathy, Francois had delivered the second payment with interest.

Abdul Rahiz in Toulon had done what he had to do. The ten crates of explosives destined for the UK had gone with the illegal immigrants to the safe house in Brussels. He knew from his drivers they had arrived there intact. What happened to them thereafter was not his problem.

The other ten crates of Semtex offloaded from the Libyan freighter had been taken by the same driver by road across Southern France, through the unsupervised border crossing just south of Perpignan into Spain, and thence on to Madrid. There they were received by an Al Qaeda cell. The members of that cell had but one brutal focus: to plan a "spectacular" to avenge Spain's participation in the American-led invasion of Iraq.

A few weeks later, in March 2004, the contents of the ten boxes were distributed amongst a variety of rucksacks and carried onto early morning commuter trains bound for the capital. The time clocks on each of the detonators were synchronised. One hour later Madrid's main rail stations were in chaos. Over two hundred people were dead and countless others injured. Spain had paid the price of going into Iraq.

Abdul did not know these were the explosives he had delivered. Nor did he know that the ten Semtex boxes he had sent north to Brussels, had gone on to England and been intercepted in Leicester. Nor did he realise the colossal consequences of that interception. The "spectacular" to wreak similar vengeance on the UK for participation in the Iraq invasion, planned for the same time as the one in Madrid, had been thwarted.

The UK had been lucky. But it was only a temporary reprieve. Al Qaeda were not to be diverted from their fanatical intent. Vengeance would just take a little longer- to be precise - till the London bombings on the 7th July 2005.